THE REVIVED

SECOND AGE OF RETHA BOOK 3

A. M. SOHMA

THE REVIVED

Copyright © 2018 by A. M. Sohma

Cover design by Myrrhlynn

Cover art by Nibelart

Edited by Jeri Larsen

www.amsohma.com

ISBN-13: 978-0-578-42026-4

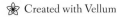 Created with Vellum

For my guild,
Who adopted me when I was just a trigger-happy hunter.

And special thanks to Melanie, Hannah, Alvin G, Cherie S,
Elizabeth D, Glowrius, Dawn, Ravi, Lydia, Zeke, Jake, and
Aidan, who lent me their amazing name ideas for some of the
characters in this book.

PRESS "A" TO RESTART

"WELCOME TO RETHA. YOUR ADVENTURE AWAITS!"

Kit rolled her neck as she watched the in-game greeting fade away. Her stomach and brain were still caught in that weird stage between reality and the game, causing a brief burst of nausea that faded almost as quickly as it arrived.

She was back in Retha, the full submersion video game she had given everything to escape.

Kit closed her eyes again and pressed a hand to her stomach. *It's almost...stupid...that I've returned of my own free will, imprisoning myself AGAIN. But it will be different. This time I'm not alone...and we're going after a much bigger target.*

Chronicles of Retha was in an uproar. The server Kit had (unwillingly) been playing on had gone down in a power surge. The game was forced to switch to backup servers...which contained corrupt files. Until Eternal Chase—the gaming company that created and maintained Retha—fixed whatever corrupt code was keeping them in the game, they would be forced to remain online.

But using a loophole in the game's coding, Kit had managed to log off. Her cousin, Bryce—who was an EC employee and used to play with her—managed to get a message to her that said defeating Malignus, the land's ultimate baddie, would force a log off as the computer code would need to double check she hadn't cheated or used a bot program. She had gathered a group of players just as desperate as she was to get off and attacked the necromancer. Surprisingly—*shockingly*—they had won.

Kit closed her eyes again and pressed a hand to her stomach. *First I need to confirm my reputation change. Once Riko and Prowl pop in, we can form a party—oohh, and I should check to see what kind of drops I got from our Malignus raid!*

A harp and choir sounded somewhere off to Kit's left. She cracked an eye open to see Pax Castus: a celestial being non-player character that was also her pet. The fanciness of his chain mail hauberk and white surcoat weren't enough to cancel out the crabby slant of his four wings and his pinched expression.

Kit tilted her head. "Where have you been?"

Pax dusted ash off his flashy clothes. "Chasing *you*."

"Huh?"

"Warping Malignus to the White Veil Nunnery was inspired—particularly given *your* cranial capabilities—but did you really have to warp out *here*? To this no-name village?" He pointed to the starter village just down the hill.

I forgot—last time I had Pax with me was back in the Weeping Wastelands before I used Triumphant Echo on Malignus. My Safe Haven skill must not include Pax—or he just didn't have enough time to get there before the nuns handed Malignus his arse.

Snickering at the way Pax meticulously groomed his white wings, Kit couldn't help cooing. "My poor ruffled chicken."

The light in Pax's eyes turned murderous. "*What* did you call me?"

Kit hurriedly scrunched her eyes shut. "Nothing!" She

flexed her fingers to test her coordination and returned to her mental to-do list. *Riko should get started contacting the more elite guilds... Maybe I should break into Milk Crown's guildzone then?*

The fizzy crackle of energy, accented by muffled murmuring, tugged on her ear.

Slightly worried that her pet might seek revenge for the chicken comment, Kit popped her eyes open.

A glowing portal whirled before her, spitting out the occasional spark as the murmuring continued.

She leaped to her feet. "Pax, what are you doing?"

"Nothing."

"Then shut off the portal!"

The celestial being raised an eyebrow. "I didn't create it."

Kit peered from her pet to the portal and was silent for a few moments. "Demon portal!" She sprinted away as fast as she could. "Just my luck. Someone probably broke a Cuckoo Toadstool in the area and summoned a high-level monster. Sadists!" Kit yelped when, against her will, she was dragged backwards. Some unseen force took hold of her arm and hauled her back to the portal.

"No, no, no! I just logged in—I can't die in under a minute. That is a record I don't want to break!" Kit tried to plant her heels, but whatever magic pulled her along yanked with such strength she nearly faceplanted.

She glanced at Pax—who once again wore a crabby expression—and braced herself for pain, but instead her arm was dragged through the portal, disappearing into the white light. She jumped when she felt something clasp her hand, then staggered through.

Her elf grace popped her upright before she mentally recovered. Fearing the worst, she sucked her head into her shoulders and peeked at her hand—which was clasped by a hand encased in a black gauntlet. Following the foreign arm up, she blinked in surprise at the black-haired and gray-eyed royal knight attached to the gauntlet.

"Miles?" she asked.

Solus Miles, the top player of the server, inspected her from head to foot. "Are you really Kitten Lovemuch?"

Kit squinted at him. "Of course I am. No one else would be stupid enough to put a wizard tattoo on an elf *and* be a dancer."

Solus shook his head impatiently. "No, I mean...Kit?"

Oh...Kit tucked a strand of her hair behind her ear and smiled. "Yep. It's me. Ta daaa..." Her cheer faded awkwardly as Solus, his eyes bright with intensity, took a step closer to her.

He placed a hand under her chin and tilted her face, as if admiring it. "You won the raid against Malignus. There was a server-wide announcement."

She cleared her throat. "Yes."

"You logged off. I received the notification." His dark eyebrows furrowed as he continued to study her face.

"I came back." She squirmed a little under his concentrated attention.

"I can see that," he said dryly. "But didn't you successfully get out?"

Kit shrugged a little. "Yeah, but EC shared an in-game method to force everybody off."

"And you volunteered to deliver instructions to the server?"

She tugged on the hem of her skirt self-consciously. "Sort of?" She was almost shocked into releasing a squawk when Solus let go of her face only long enough to slip his arms around her shoulders and draw her into an embrace. *I forgot he is a hugger,* she thought as her cheek pressed against the black metal of his chestplate.

"Thank you," he said. "I should have believed in you when you set out to fight Malignus."

Kit let her arms link loosely around his waist and snorted. "No, you shouldn't have. It was a crazy, insane attempt that worked only because of a last-minute idea."

"No," Solus said firmly. "I underestimated you once, Kit. I won't do it again."

Kit was glad her face was pressed against his chest—it meant he couldn't see her embarrassed blush.

"I'll help you this time. Whatever strength and power I have is yours," Solus said.

"Are you sure? I will unapologetically use you." Kit glanced up at the knight, but as she was sandwiched against his shoulder, she could only see his strong jawline. "I'm going to have to unite the guilds for this one. And I don't mean a few; I mean *all* of them. Or at least as many as possible."

Solus shrugged, making his armor creak. "Then use me." He paused. "What happened while you were out of the game? You were gone for days."

Kit winced. Time in Retha passed much faster than it did in reality. She had forgotten that the hours she spent mentally prepping for this new stage would be days for those still trapped in Retha. "I was studying up—memorizing, mostly," Kit said. Before she could continue, a screen popped up abruptly.

You have a private message from: Riko
Accept message?

"Umm," she said eloquently as Solus released her. "I need a second. Riko and Prowl agreed to come back in with me, and they must have just gotten on. Riko PMed me..."

Solus rested a hand on the hilt of his sword. "You will explain everything," he stated more than asked.

"Yeah, as soon as I chat with Riko," Kit promised as she brushed the button to accept the message.

"*Hey there, Fearless Leader!*"

Kit smiled at the druid's cheerful tone. "Hi, Riko."

"*I just wanted to let you know Prowl and I are both online. Prowl dropped out of La-Lune and is ready for an invite to the Heroes of Retha guild EC gave you, but I'm going to hang out for a bit longer.*"

"Sounds good—we might need the recognition of La-Lune." While the guild wasn't large, it was well respected and known— mostly because the founder had been a player back when Kit used to play *Chronicles of Retha* with her old guild, Milk Crown.

"*That's what I was thinking. Are you ready to get going?*"

Kit coughed—a wet noise that came from deep in her chest —and scowled when she realized the *Curse of Sickness* she had gotten when fighting Malignus was still on her character. "Not quite."

"*Oh? Are you getting clobbered by PMs, too? They haven't stopped ringing since I logged in.*"

"Uhh, no. I'm bringing Solus Miles up to speed."

"*Solus Miles already contacted you? In that case, tell him I say a very respectful hello and that you should take all the time you need.*"

"He's not going to give me money, Riko."

"*I never said he should!*"

Kit shook her head. "When we're done here, I'll meet you in Luminos."

"*Sure thing. Remember to send Prowl that guild invite soon.*"

"I will. I'll form a party and invite you, too."

"*Perfect. Have fun!*"

Kit rolled her eyes. "Goodbye, Riko." She ended the PM and turned to face Solus Miles again—though she let her curious gaze roam her surroundings.

They were clearly in the corridor of some sort of castle or

fortification. The vaulted ceiling was supported with wooden beams, though the walls were made of stone. One wall sported arched glass windows wrought with some kind of dark iron and decorated with mosaics of colored glass around the edge. Besides the windows, though, the corridor was pretty bare. Lanterns hung from the ceiling, and Kit could spy out one tapestry farther down the wall, but otherwise it was empty.

She didn't recognize the area or architecture—though that didn't mean much. It could have been from a recent expansion, or from a location she had never visited before. *This is clearly human made—and looks faintly like the old empire. Perhaps we're in Elba?*

"Are you ready to explain?" Solus asked.

"Sure," Kit said. She paused when he strode down the hallway then trotted after him. "Where are we?" she asked, her voice and footsteps echoing in the emptiness.

Solus passed the lone tapestry and paused outside a wooden door. "My home."

That explains the lack of interior decorating. Miles never struck me as the sort to clutter his space up. "And where is your home?" Kit asked as he opened the door for her. She glanced in and was hardly surprised to find the walls were covered with glinting weapons—broadswords, lances, daggers, spears, short-swords, and more—even though the rest of the room was relatively bare, sporting only a large pile of pillows and an unlit fireplace.

"North of Chosaint." Solus gestured for Kit to sit on the pillows as he approached the fireplace. He must have messed with the room settings, as a fire roared to life shortly after.

Kit swiped a giant cushion from the pile and plopped down on it. "Chosaint, hmm? It suits you."

Chosaint was home to a second group of elves—the far more war-minded kinsmen of the elves that populated Fione Forest.

The city was hidden in the mountain range that extended down Retha's south-eastern border. The elves of Chosaint were supposedly said to guard Retha from the lands beyond the mountains.

Rather than join her on the cushions, Solus remained standing and folded his arms across his chest. "Stop beating around the bush, Kit. What happened after you logged out?"

Kit played with her single glove. "Bryce—my cousin and my Eternal Chase contact—was right. Due to pre-existing code in the game, we were booted off after defeating Malignus so the system could confirm we really won and didn't cheat."

"How did you do it?" Solus asked.

Kit blinked. "Hmm?"

"How did you defeat Malignus? Given that everyone in your party was booted off after your win, no one was able to explain how you did it."

"I exploited his affinity for darkness. Between using a Mon-Mon Draught—which will let you force any skill on an enemy, including skills that don't usually work on them—a dancer skill that makes an enemy copy my exact movements, and the Safe Haven teleport skill, I transported him to the White Veil Nunnery."

Wrinkles spread across Solus' forehead. "You teleported a *boss* monster?"

"Yeah, I was surprised it worked," Kit admitted. "We never did anything like that in a raid when I was in Milk Crown."

"You never had any reason to," Solus pointed out. "We players always knew the other raid bosses were possible to defeat. Everyone assumed Malignus was an end-game boss that wouldn't be available to actually slay for many more years. Until you insisted otherwise." He paused. "I assume the White Veil Nunnery canceled out many of the debuffs and curses his presence casted?"

"Yeah. Being in the nunnery also put some pretty hefty holy debuffs on him. But that wasn't what took him out."

Solus jutted a thick black eyebrow up—a nonverbal command to continue.

"The NPCs at the nunnery wailed on him. The nuns, priests, crusaders, acolytes, bishops, all of them. They tore through him like tissue paper." Kit shook her head, still stunned over the memory. "In the end, I don't deserve any credit. My raid had taken off less than 2% of his health. The NPCs did everything else."

"It was you who thought to transport Malignus to the nunnery?" Solus asked.

"Only because I've visited there so often I remembered one of the novice nuns telling me it was the most holy place in Retha. Given that the Weeping Wastelands and Castle Dolor have to be the darkest bits of the land, I thought the difference would work to our advantage. I just never imagined it would be quite so...powerful."

Solus slowly nodded. "Retha has changed."

Kit perked up. "What? How?"

"Lord Valdis Moarte has returned. New quests, raids, and game content have appeared. Already there have been several raids who have tried to explore Castle Dolor now that it's officially unlocked. They've wiped every time—slain by skeleton soldiers and goblins."

"That's depressing to hear," Kit grumbled. *I knew Lord Valdis was going to enter the game, but I didn't think it would have such far-reaching consequences. I should have known as much. Retha lore always said Malignus was just Valdis' servant who was trying to restore him.*

"You defeated Malignus and logged out?" Solus prodded.

"Sorry, I was lost in thought. But yes, we were all logged out. Bryce kept a virtual eye on me because he knew I would try to make a break for it eventually with Malignus, so EC was aware of our fight and was standing by when we popped out of it. They gathered up my party—"

"Party or raid?" Solus interrupted.

"Party—the crew I was running around with when you helped us level," Kit said.

Solus nodded.

"They had us meet via video conference, and then explained to all of us their new plan. They said that because we offed Malignus, Lord Valdis would return...and if we can get players to unite and manage to slay him, the *entire* server will be logged off."

"The whole server? Why?" Solus again rested his hand on the hilt of his sword and slightly adjusted his stance.

Kit winced. "For the same reasons my raid was kicked off after defeating Malignus. It's going to be such a difficult task, the game will have to verify it was a legitimate defeat."

"But they force everyone off—regardless of whether they were a part of the raid or not?" Solus asked.

Kit nodded.

He sighed and briefly closed his eyes. "I assume, then, that means this fight is going to be next to impossible, and a thousand times worse than Malignus?"

"Yep."

"EC has several other servers and iterations of *Chronicles of Retha*. Have any of them managed it?"

Kit slowly shook her head. "No. Not even the Asian or European servers."

The corners of Solus' mouth tugged down in a slight frown. "This impossible fight is what they have pinned their hopes on? And they sent you back into this potential deathtrap when you aren't even an employee?"

Kit shrugged. "I'm here for tactical help. They felt between my experience with my raid guild and with slaying Malignus, I will be able to do something."

Solus shifted slightly. "Did you at least let Riko negotiate with them? They should be paying dearly for the risks you are taking."

Kit laughed. "Yes, Riko and Prowl made the negotiations. I'm not sure exactly what they set up, though."

"Let me guess. You agreed to come back because you couldn't leave everyone in-game to die?" Up went the eyebrows again.

Kit narrowed her eyes. "I didn't know I was that predictable."

"Predictably noble," Solus corrected. He crouched down in front of Kit, his eyes thoughtful as he studied her.

Unused to the close scrutiny, Kit sank deeper into her pillow.

"I am grateful for your bleeding heart, Kit. You could have stayed safe, but you came back for us. Thank you." The barest hint of a smile curled Solus' lips upwards and made his gray eyes start to crinkle. He opened his mouth, but there was the trill of a harp and a choir.

Pax stepped through a portal, his wings flattened and his mouth warped in a sneer. "If you teleport again," he said through gritted teeth as he stalked up to Kit, "next time we are on the battlefield, I will make *certain* every enemy on the map knows where you are."

"Hey there, Pax." Kit waved to her "celestial being" pet. "I was wondering when you would catch up."

Pax scoffed and tugged on his ornate silver chestplate. When he glanced at Solus Miles, he straightened fractionally and nodded.

Kit sighed. "It still rankles me that my own pet respects my pledged more than me."

"It wouldn't be a problem if you leveled," Solus said.

Kit rolled her eyes. "You're obsessed with leveling."

"Only because you are terribly deficient in levels." He nodded at the nameplate that hovered over Kit's head. "Though I see you have leveled from your fight with Malignus...and that you have a guild?"

Kit glanced up at her name and health bar and was pleasantly surprised to see she was now level 50. "Yeah, EC gave it to me. They thought it might convince everyone I know what I'm talking about. But I hadn't noticed I leveled. That's nifty! I should also have some neat drops and gear from Malignus. Unless they give me gear for a different class. That would be awful, but very likely on Kitten Lovemuch, given my perpetual bad luck on this character." She started to laugh hollowly but broke off into a hacking cough that ate away at her health bar and made her spit up blood. It took a minute for the coughing jag to fade, and Kit scrunched up her nose, grossed out by the metallic taste of the blood that coated her mouth. "I also caught this great cough from my encounter with Malignus. Really, he was super pleasant," she said, sarcasm dripping from her words.

"So EC sent you to organize a raid against Lord Valdis. I assume that means you have a plan?" Solus asked.

Kit considered wiping her slightly bloodied palm off on Pax's pristine surcoat. Her pet seemed to sense her thoughts and pointedly stepped away from her. "Sort of. I don't have any solid plans to actually fight Lord Valdis yet—that's more of our long-term goal. In the moment, though, I need to go to Luminos to talk with the more elite guilds and work on recruiting NPCs."

"The NPCs will fight with us?" Solus asked.

"The game developer I spoke with promised they would. We have to talk to them and win them over, though." Kit tapped her lower lip. "I don't know which is going to be more difficult: convincing the NPCs or trying to unite all the guilds."

"Uniting the guilds for certain," Solus said. "There are too many egos and proud players involved for it to be an easy task."

"But by now people must realize how desperate the situation is," Kit pointed out. "Wouldn't that make them eager to work together?"

"Perhaps if we were under a direct assault, but we're not," Solus said. "Defeating Lord Valdis will require time and preparation—which will give everyone the chance to convince themselves how much more superior their plans would be."

Kit squinted up at her accidental-pledged. "I think I'm starting to understand why you are such a lone wolf."

He blinked. "What do you mean?"

"I always assumed you were doing it on purpose because you knew it made you look cooler," Kit started.

"What?" Solus' tone was both flat and offended.

"But now I think it's just because you are really, perhaps majorly, a total downer."

"*What?*" Solus repeated in a slightly edgier tone.

Kit waved a hand through the air. "I mean, I get the realism of your words, and you have a point, but did you seriously have to remind me of that when I haven't even been in Retha for an hour yet?"

"I said I was grateful for *your* personality quirks." Though he scoffed, his stance was relaxed, and he smirked slightly.

"Yeah, but I didn't rain on your parade," Kit pointed out.

"Untrue. You have refused to level," Solus said.

Kit laughed. "You have me there."

Solus waited for her amusement to fade. "I just want to make certain you are prepared. You're going to be our leader. I don't want you to be...*hurt* by the stupidity of others."

"What, you mean you don't want to lead?" Kit asked.

Solus' left eyebrow twitched. "I would rather risk the dangers that would come from EC disconnecting us."

"You don't like leading?" Kit asked.

"*No.*"

"Well. Can't say I would have guessed that—though I don't like it very much either." Kit cleared her throat, then had to briefly hold her breath to keep from coughing again.

"So your focus is recruiting NPCs and uniting the guilds?" Solus asked.

"Yeah. My short-term plan is to go to Luminos first and get the guild talks underway. I'm betting that will take the most time to achieve, so I want the leaders to start considering it now," Kit said.

"I assume your future plans include dropping by the White Veil Nunnery to remove your curse?" Solus asked.

"Yes, I should drop by...oh! But I have good news! EC reset my reputation level. Instead of being hated by everyone due to Bryce's meddling, it's now neutral, so I can stroll through Luminos without getting arrested by Imperial guards or stabbed in the back by a member of the Court of the Rogue!" Kit beamed, ignoring Pax when he made a judgmental "tisk" somewhere behind her.

"Good," Solus said. "That will make your task to recruit NPCs possible, and it will make it much easier when you no longer have to return to the White Veil Nunnery whenever you are cursed."

"True, but I'm still going to stop there before I drop in on the guilds. I want to see if anything has changed," she said. "I should actually head out soon."

"I'll summon Sinistre." He headed for the door with a sure step.

"You don't have to come." Kit easily popped to her feet with her elven elegance. "I'm just going to zip over to the nunnery using my Safe Haven skill."

Solus flattened his lips. "I'll fly you."

"Teleporting would be faster," Kit pointed out as she joined him at the doorway.

"No," Solus said.

Kit raised an eyebrow. "No?"

"I just—" Solus paused and furrowed his brow in thought. "You left," he said, enunciating carefully. "As your pledged, I received the notification that you logged off."

Kit waited, but he seemed unwilling to say more. "That's not going to happen again. It *can't* happen again." She slowly reached out and set a hand on his forearm. "We're stuck together until we beat Valdis. I'm not going anywhere."

Solus stared mutely at the ground.

Kit stifled the desire to shake him. *Why does he have to be so hard to read? I can't tell if he's just an unemotional potato, or if me logging off really bothered him. I mean, he's the top player, and I'm some random girl he's known for only a little while! It seems awfully stuck up to presume he doesn't want me to leave him.* She grimaced slightly. *I hope I don't feel like a narcissistic idiot for this...* "So where is Sinistre?"

Solus strode off immediately. "This way."

Kit shrugged at his back and ambled after him. "Come on, Pax!"

"I am not a dog you must call to heel," Pax sneered as he joined her.

"Why so grouchy? I thought you would be happy since we're flying, not teleporting." Together they followed Solus down the corridor. "Do you want to go back into your egg?"

"It's a *pearl!*"

"Right, right." Kit paused to cough for a few seconds, then staggered after Solus—who waited for her at the end of the hall-way. "This curse is the pits. I can't wait to get it off me. It makes me wish I traveled with a priest or a healing class that can purify curses."

"You need to travel with a priest not because of your propensity to be cursed, but because you barge into areas above your level and die with record-breaking swiftness," Solus called back to her.

"I am okay with that because I have achieved inner peace and enlightenment." Kit trotted up to him with a grin. "When you have reached that stage, you realize what's *really* important."

Solus tilted his head. "Positive reputation?"

"So you aren't shot on sight—yes! Very good, Miles—whoa," Kit trailed off when they left Solus' home and ventured outside.

The view was spectacular. His home was positioned so it looked down into a green valley with small waterfalls spilling down the mountainside around it. Mountains stretched on to the south, and Kit could faintly see the glimmer that was the elven city of Chosaint.

"Sinistre, come," Solus beckoned.

Kit was so taken with the view, she barely noticed when the giant black dragon landed in the gardens directly in front of them, his black scales gleaming in the sunlight as he fixed his coppery eyes on them.

Solus strode up to the dragon, stopping at the beast's shoulder when he realized Kit hadn't followed. "Are you coming?"

"How can you be so indifferent to this beautiful view?" Kit pointed to the vibrant valley and ribbon-like rivers.

Solus shrugged. "I purchased this plot for its remoteness."

"Why am I not surprised?" Using her elven athleticism, Kit bounded up Sinistre's leg, settling into place behind Solus, who sat directly behind the dragon's shoulder blades. "Hello to you, Sinistre, by the way." She fondly patted a scale, then almost coughed up a lung due to her curse.

Though she doubted the dragon even felt her greeting, he rumbled pleasantly in return.

"Hold on," Solus instructed. "Sinistre, to the White Veil Nunnery."

The dragon stood—a swift but rocking motion—then leaped into the air. Pumping his wings, the dragon climbed higher—using air currents to gain altitude.

Pax kept up with ease. Using two of his four wings, he settled into a glide and took up a position to the dragon's right.

Curious, Kit wriggled around to peer past the dragon's rear, watching for a glimpse of Solus' house as they left it behind. She choked a little when she saw it, nestled into the mountain so it was sheltered from the whistling winds.

His "home" could have been described as nothing less than a castle—and a masterpiece at that. The castle was split in level, and was built to look as though a stone dragon was intertwined with it. The dragon's neck twined around the single tower located at the back of the castle; its wings folded around the outer walls, while its carved tail splayed across the gate. With her elf eyes, Kit could see the dragon had been so meticulously carved that there were individual scales—and some of them were plated with jade and sparkled green in the sunlight.

The castle was smaller—it was nothing comparable to the giant palace in Elba—but the unique architecture rendered it gorgeous.

Kit leaned into Solus so she could speak into his ear. "You really bought it for the *remoteness*, huh?"

Solus shrugged. "I would have preferred if it had black scales."

Kit choked at his audacity but then had to consolidate all her concentration to keep from coughing. *If I get into a coughing jag here, with my luck I'll fall off Sinistre and plummet to my death!*

Just as the ticklish itch faded from her lungs, a screen popped up—splaying over Solus' back.

You have a private message from: Prowl
Accept message?

Kit flicked the yes button and switched over to the private conversation. "Hey Prowl."

"*Hey yourself,*" Prowl drawled. "*Are you going to invite me to Heroes of Retha anytime this century?*"

"Sorry, I was explaining things to Solus and got distracted." Kit hurriedly flipped open the all-new—for Kitten Lovemuch anyway—guild panel. It took her a moment to get her bearings—not only because it had been a while since she had used one, but also because it looked different. There were more options and settings available.

That's right...I'm the guildmistress of Heroes of Retha, so I have extra permissions. Kit shook her head and flipped through the panel, pausing when she found the invite section. She quickly transcribed Prowl's name and sent off a message. "You should get an invite shortly."

She blinked when large golden letters flickered around her.

Prowl has joined Heroes of Retha!

"*Finally!*" Prowl boomed over the guild chat, his voice echoing oddly. While the party chat channel was almost like talking on a phone (as everyone always sounded like they were sitting next to you), the guild chat channel echoed slightly, as if Prowl was standing on the far side of an empty building.

"*So what kind of drops did you get from Malignus?*"

"I'm just about to check, actually." Kit adjusted herself so she had one arm twined around Solus—if she fell off the side, she was taking him with her to increase the odds of Sinistre diving for them—and opened up her item storage with her free hand. "What did you get?" she asked as she scrolled through her storage.

"*A new dagger, some boots, and a new chest armor piece.*"

"No more endless buckles?"

"*My buckle shirt was cool!*"

"Yeah, if you have a fetish for buckles. What did Riko get?"

"*New robes and a staff, so we were thinking you might have gotten an armor set that finally covers your stomach as you have so dearly—and loudly—wanted.*"

Kit studied her storage and sighed in disappointment. "Nope, no armor. I got a really nice anklet though—it has big dexterity buff—and a fantastic belt."

"*That's all?*"

"A few really high-leveled healing potions and—wait, what's this?" Kit perked with hope as she came to the final item in her storage. "Oh. Oh my."

"*What? What is it?*" Prowl demanded.

Kit smiled so widely she almost split her own face in half as she sang, "I got two named scimitars: Caolan's Sorrow and Caolan's Agony!"

"*Who is Caolan?*"

Kit selected the weapons, bringing their information boxes up. "Caolan was the legendary dancer who fell in the battle against Lord Valdis. He slayed her beloved, and she gave up her life energy to the Imperial wizards to help power their spell to lock him away."

"*Sounds unnecessarily dramatic...but very dancer-like. But, scimitars? You mean...swords?*"

"Yes! They're much smaller than the average scimitar, but it looks like I can wield both of them at once. They have amazing stats with huge dexterity bonuses. They're going to majorly upgrade the buffs my dances give!"

"*Wow, that is surprisingly butt-kicking considering your class.*"

Kit brought up the swords' information panel. "Looks like I can upgrade them, too! This is *awesome!*"

"*Congrats.*"

Though Kit wanted to preen over her swords a bit longer, she made herself flick the screen away and concentrate on her friend. "Thanks! So have the PMs finally stopped coming?"

"*Sort of. Everyone is just talking with Riko, now, since I snapped at a twerp who asked me for the fifth time if I had really logged off. Riko has been talking with White Lady from the Silver Army. I think she's trying to get the big guilds caught up so we don't have to spend five days telling them how we defeated Malignus and came back. We're both already in Luminos. Are you on your way here?*"

"Not yet," Kit responded as she started a new party. She paused before naming it *Exit Plan*. "Solus and I are swinging past the White Veil Nunnery first. I have a curse I need to have removed, and I want to talk to some of the NPCs."

"*Even though you could get your curse removed at the cathedral here in Luminos?*"

"I want to see if the nunnery NPCs have changed at all, and I'm wondering if they could give me some sort of proof that we were the ones who defeated Malignus. The rest of the NPCs might be easier to convince to join us if we have the nunnery backing our claim."

"*I suppose it's smart to do some homework before the elite guilds rip us apart.*"

"You think it's going to go that well, huh?"

"*Some of them will be on board, but others are led by a bunch of thick-headed fighter types. It might take crushing a boulder on*" *their head to get through to them. Unless you can trot Solus Miles out like a good trick pony?"*

Kit squirmed on Sinistre's back. "He said he would help, but I'll ask him if that means I can use his name in our talks."

"Mmhmm. Oh, yeah. You'll probably be interested to hear this: as a perk for being the raid to defeat Malignus, the first NPC you talk to will give you a pretty dang elite recipe for your highest-leveled craft."

"Really?"

"Yep. Riko and I already got ours. Your most-leveled craft is... candy making, right?"

"Yeah. I can't imagine what sort of elite recipe they can give me given that candy is used solely for reputation, but I'm glad for any new recipe! Did some EC employees tell you about it?"

"Yeah, I got a bit of a run down while they had you memorizing all that housing info from Milk Crown. We also get a special title—whoopee."

"Ugh, thanks for reminding me about the housing info." Kit opened her character panel, flicking through screens that displayed her character and armor so she could open up the memo application. An opalescent screen popped up in front of Kit, settling on Solus Miles' back.

Kit reluctantly let the royal knight go and started tapping housing information in as fast as she could recall it. *I need to record this all as swiftly as possible, or I'm going to forget it all.*

Prowl continued, *"I gotta say I am looking forward to ransacking your old guildmates' places."*

"They'll have a lot of great stuff," Kit admitted as she hurriedly typed away. "But I don't want to get the elite guilds' hopes up that we'll have tons of amazing gear. Everything is going to be old and underleveled. The level cap has gone up since we played, and the legendary classes had just been introduced."

"*Sometimes it's better to have underleveled armor if it's elite.*"

"I guess. Either way it will still be dead useful for all of us players who aren't at level cap."

Solus brushed Kit's thigh, drawing her attention. "We are almost there." He pointed over Sinistre's shoulders to the White Veil Nunnery—a beautiful spot of white on an island that jutted out of a deep blue river.

Kit finished typing in another line of housing information. "Prowl, I'll have to go for a minute. We're almost to the nunnery. Here's a party invite—Riko should have one too." She stopped recording information long enough to send the saboteur a party invite.

"*'Kay. I'll tell her what you're up to when she comes up for air.*"

"Thanks, I appreciate it." Kit glanced up at her health bar, nodding in satisfaction when Riko's and Prowl's information were added as they accepted the party invite. She slid an arm around Solus' waist again but doggedly kept typing with one hand. She switched out of the guild chat so she could speak to the royal knight. "Where are we going to land?"

"Near the bridge," he said, referring to the immense white bridge that spanned the river and stretched all the way to the nunnery. "If Sinistre tried to land in the nunnery itself, it would cause an uproar."

"I'll bet." Kit bit her lip as she tried to remember the password Black Mage—an old guildmate of hers—had used for his secret house. It came to her after a moment, and she moved on to the next house. "I have a party started with Riko and Prowl. Do you want to join?"

"Send the invite."

Kit flicked him the party invitation, and after a moment, his status and health bar information joined Riko's and Prowl's.

"Hello, Solus Miles!" Riko greeted in a sunny and welcoming tone. "I'm so glad you are joining in our merry group."

"What are you, a grandmother? No one uses the word merry," Prowl scoffed.

"I don't want to hear that from a snot-nosed delinquent who insists on wearing goggles," Riko snarled.

"They have a great stats boost!"

The druid snorted. "Yeah, ten levels ago! You can't tell me you've been unable to find anything better since our massive leveling party with the honorable Solus Miles."

Kit grinned with delight as Sinistre twined through the air in a rippling movement similar to curling ribbon as he circled the nunnery. "If you want to leave the party, Miles, I'll understand," she said in the party chat channel.

"It's fine," Solus said. "But we're landing now. Hold on."

"Talk to you later, guys," Kit said before switching out of the party chat channel.

"Yeah, bye," Prowl said. "Riko, did you get a message to that overly aggressive werewolf guildmaster yet?"

"Half-Fang? Yes. Pretty sure I nearly grew a beard just from talking to the guy. He oozes an unnecessary amount of testosterone and bloodlust." Riko trailed off as she and Prowl copied Kit and Solus and took their conversation outside the party chat.

2

THE WHITE VEIL NUNNERY

KIT SQUEEZED SOLUS' waist as Sinistre landed elegantly, lowering his belly to the ground and extending a leg for them to climb down.

Kit waited for the royal knight to rise before she clambered up. "This feels a bit like deja-vu."

"In what way?" Solus started down Sinistre's leg and jumped off when he reached the dragon's claws.

Kit hopped after him, smiling when her elf elegance made her landing graceful. "I mean the last time I saw you, Sinistre flew us from the White Veil Nunnery to Luminos, and I was going to talk to some medium-sized guilds in the hopes of rallying them." She pointed herself in the direction of the white bridge and started for it, grimacing in pain when she squeezed out another wet, rattling cough, and her health bar briefly dipped.

"While the circumstances might sound similar, it's a vastly different situation." Solus fell in step with her, easily keeping pace. "You will be talking to larger, more elite guilds; you've managed to successfully beat Malignus, and you've proven it's possible to log out of the game."

"We'll see, I guess. Anyway, I think with my stupid reputation issue taken care of, I'm going to like this character a lot more." Kit squinted up at the cloudless sky. Pax hadn't landed with Sinistre and was still hovering in the air. As she watched, he landed on one of the bridge's massive support pillars and ruffled his wings, much like a pigeon.

"This is the first time you are returning to the nunnery since Malignus' defeat, yes?"

"Yep. I was booted off before I got the chance to talk to any of the NPCs, and they dropped me just outside the starter town I had started in when I logged on before the servers went down." Kit rubbed at her chest, frowning slightly at the pain in her lungs. "That reminds me, what did you do while I was off? Some more questing?"

Solus shrugged.

"I have no idea what a shrug means."

"I stayed in my castle," Solus said.

"I was off for several hours—which means several game days. You stayed at your home that whole time?" Kit asked.

"I was contemplating my stupidity of underestimating you," Solus said dryly.

Smiling sadly, Kit reached out with her palm that wasn't bloody from her coughing and rested it on his arm. "It was a long shot, Miles. We shouldn't have made it."

"It doesn't matter," Solus said as they approached the magnificent cathedral gates. "This time, I will stand with you."

Kit squeezed his arm—though she wasn't sure he could feel it through his black armor—and opened her mouth to speak when they were loudly interrupted.

"Kitten Lovemuch? It is you! Kitten, how the heavens smile upon us!" Sister Miriam—the NPC nun Kit usually asked to remove whatever curse she had gotten herself entangled with—flew down the steps, the black fabric of her habit streaming behind her. At her side ran the novice who carried a small wooden chest that rattled with coins.

Kit smiled as the duo approached her, but she straightened in alarm when they didn't slow, and instead barreled straight into her, throwing their arms around her in an enthusiastic hug.

Solus watched the display with a tilted head. "Are they usually this...eager in their greetings?"

"No," Kit said, the curse burning her lungs even as the tight embrace limited her air supply.

"Child of the light, I am so glad you have returned," Sister Miriam said, stepping back—though she kept her hands on Kit's shoulders. "Since the defeat of the necromancer, Malignus, many of us have so wished to speak to you."

Please don't let it be they want to hold me accountable for any damage dealt by Malignus on the cathedral grounds! With her luck, the thought wasn't completely out of the question. "Did you?" Kit asked weakly.

"Indeed, we did," said a paladin with a deep voice as he joined the nun and novice. His golden armor glinted in the sunlight, and his white cape was so bright Kit had a difficult time looking at him.

"We wish to thank you." A white mage dressed in cream-colored robes edged around the hulking paladin, a bright smile stretching across his face.

A choir arranged on the steps of the cathedral sang a sweet hymn, and Kit blinked rapidly and questioned her supposedly perfect elf hearing. "I'm sorry...did you say *thank* me?"

The mage nodded eagerly. "Exactly so!"

Pax, who had abandoned his pillar on the bridge for one of the cathedral's lower flying buttresses, scoffed.

"You delivered the enemy straight into these hallowed grounds!" The paladin released a booming laugh and slapped the poor white mage in his glee. "You gave us a chance to seek vengeance on behalf of all that is right in this world. You gave us the chance to *fight!*"

"Ah...I see." Kit finally put on a smile, still slightly confused. *I don't get it...they seemed delighted when I brought Malignus to them, but he caused a lot of damage...why are they so grateful?*

"You also showed us the error in our ways." Sister Miriam's beaming smile turned soft as she gently squeezed Kit's shoulders.

"Error?" Kit asked.

"Yes," Sister Miriam said. "For too long we have hidden in this haven. Though we claim to stand for the light, when the land was in trouble, we stayed here in safety."

"It is in times such as now that Retha, more than ever, needs the light," The paladin said. "And until you delivered Malignus into our hands, we did not see that we were not a safe haven for the lost, but a hideaway in which we, ourselves, were concealed."

"We shall *not* allow that to happen again," the white mage said firmly.

Solus Miles tilted his head and looked thoughtful at the mage's words. Pax, however, ruffled one set of his wings and imperiously peered down at them.

"Which is why I say, on behalf of the White Veil Nunnery, that we will join you," Sister Miriam said.

Kit paused. "Join me in what?"

The novice laughed. "Why, in your quest to defeat Lord Valdis, of course!"

How can they know already that I'm gunning for Valdis? Is this EC's doing? "How do you know I mean to fight Lord Valdis?"

Sister Miriam removed her hands from Kit's shoulders and instead reached up to lightly touch her cheek. "Because, my child, you are a Hero of Retha. You stood against Malignus when no one else could. You fought a fight everyone was afraid to enter. As a child of the light, I know you will not stand to let Lord Valdis pollute this land. And we will not let you heroes go alone this time."

"When it is time to fight against Lord Valdis, call us," The paladin said. "We will fight with you. Everyone in the White Veil Nunnery shall enter battle with you."

As Kit's mouth dropped open, a popup screen flickered to life in front of her.

You have secured an alliance with the White Veil Nunnery.

There was additional information Kit would have to glance over later, but the screen told her something of vast importance: EC was right. The NPCs could be recruited...and at a much larger scale than she had estimated.

During her brief time outside the game, EC employees had gone over possible tactics with her. They had instructed her to go after the big groups: the dwarves, elves, fae, and the remnants of the Solis Empire. While they would provide the greatest numbers and best partnerships, this offering from the White Veil Nunnery changed the game.

If I can recruit the whole nunnery...does that mean I can secure alliances with other, smaller NPC groups? Though they didn't have the same numbers, there were organizations of werewolves and shifters, the Court of the Rogue, and tribes of horsemen who rode the best mounts in the game. Recruiting them would give her an even greater tactical advantage!

The buzz of excitement that invaded Kit's thoughts subsided when a new coughing jag burned her lungs and sent her to her knees, her body wracking with the force of her coughs.

"You poor child," Sister Miriam clucked. "How thoughtless

of us to keep you standing here when you clearly need the guidance of the light."

Kit almost threw up from the force of her coughs, but the burning eased as Sister Miriam clasped her hands.

"May the light of heaven shine upon you, brightest of the elves. May it guide your actions and keep you safe as you venture into the darkest of battles," the nun said.

A beam of light sliced through the sky, encircling Kit with warmth. The little skull icon beneath her name disappeared, and Kit found she could breathe more easily. A bell tolled crystal clear in the bell tower, its ringing echoing in the courtyard.

She boosted herself to her feet, wiping a bit of blood off her lip and smiling when she could breathe deeply. "Thank you, Sister."

Sister Miriam smiled serenely. "You're very welcome, child. I do have something additional I wish to discuss with you."

Kit raised her hand in farewell as the paladin bowed and strode off, the white mage bounding behind him. "I'm all ears," she said.

"Because of your bravery and great deeds, I wish to give you a recipe," Sister Miriam said.

Kit focused in on the nun with great zeal. *This must be the recipe Prowl mentioned. I bet it's going to be the most amazing candy ever! Even if it's for reputation only, if it tastes great, I can give it out to other players!* "A recipe? I would love to hear it!"

Sister Miriam patted Kit's hand. "I knew you would appreciate such an opportunity. It is a candy recipe that has been guarded by the White Veil Nunnery for hundreds of years. It is a carefully kept secret, one that has never been seen even by you heroes."

I hope it's something chocolate. I could use a good chocolate candy! Kit swallowed at the mouthwatering thought. "I am very honored."

The novice nodded. "You should be."

"This candy has been sought by many. Indeed, so many have searched for the recipe, none here in the White Veil Nunnery dared to utter its name, lest we birth a frenzy for it again," Sister Miriam continued.

"Uh-huh?" Kit rubbed her hands. *Oh man, it must be a powerful reputation booster! I wonder if I could mass produce it and sell it in the player market?*

"This sacred candy recipe, this gift to mankind...we entrust to you." Sister Miriam held out a ragged rectangle of parchment. The ink was so faded and the handwriting was so intricate, it took Kit's elf knowledge a moment to kick in so she could read it.

You have learned the recipe for: Holy Hard Candy!
You can judge the purity and piety of this recipe by the way it sticks to your teeth.

"Holy Hard Candy?" Kit blandly said. *Well. Hopefully the effect is more impressive than the name. I mean, at the risk of sounding ungrateful...hard candy?!*

Somewhere off to the side, Solus Miles coughed suspiciously, his armor creaking as he turned away from her.

Sister Miriam smiled brightly as she folded her hands together. "Indeed. I trust you will put it to good use, child of the light."

Kit stared at the recipe card. "Yep. I'll try." She raised her eyebrows before pushing a smile on her face and discreetly opening storage so she could tuck the tattered card away. "I thank you for your esteem and kindness in sharing this treasured recipe with me."

Sister Miriam bowed her head slightly. "It is only proper. Now, did you need something more, child?"

"No, but thank you, Sister Miriam."

"Of course. Call us when you have need of us, Kitten Lovemuch!" The nun winked, then floated off to bestow her presence on another player.

Kit rubbed the back of her neck and watched her go. Next to her, the novice who constantly toted the coffer shifted, making her coins rattle. "Oh, sorry," Kit said. "I forgot. Let me get a donation for having my curse removed..."

The novice took a step backwards and shook her head. "No, I shall not hear of taking money from you—not this time, at least."

"What happened to the cathedral's new roof?" Kit asked. "A generous donor?"

The novice made a face. "I pray for it, but, no. You are a true hero, Kitten Lovemuch. In honor of what you have done for the White Veil Nunnery, I cannot ask you for more."

"But I didn't really do anything." Kit propped a hand on her hip and stared up at the cathedral, her eyes roaming over the white stone and colored glass windows. "It was you all who killed Malignus."

"As a necromancer, Malignus was a terrible enemy, for he opposed order, bound creatures to his will, and performed terrible dark arts," the novice said. "Though we all longed to attack him in the name of the light...we remained here, in the sacred safety of the nunnery." The novice shifted her gaze to Kit, her eyes surprisingly intent given that she was an NPC.

"It was our mistake," she continued. "We stand for the light, and the light should *not* hide itself. Yet, you delivered our enemy into our hands and gave us the chance to stand for what we believe in. You made us see what we must do now that Lord Valdis has returned. Which is why it will be our honor to fight beside you, again, on the day you attack the greatest darkness this world has ever seen."

Kit slowly nodded. "I think I get it. Thank you."

The novice bowed slightly. "I am glad I could help. I wish you safe travels in your future, Kitten Lovemuch. May the light guide you and protect you. Now, if you will excuse me, I see that Sister Miriam has delivered another disciple of the light." Grinning, the novice adjusted her grip on her coffer and trotted after the nun with a spring in her step.

Kit watched her go, unmoving even when Miles stepped closer.

"It seems you found your first NPC ally," he said.

"Yes...surprisingly so."

"Oh?"

Kit finally peeled her eyes from the novice and nun and met Solus' gray eyes. "I didn't think they would be so grateful. And I never even thought of recruiting them."

"I'm glad they offered," Solus said. "It will give you even more legitimacy when you speak to the guilds." He hesitated. "Are you ready to go?"

Kit squared her shoulders. "Yep! This answers my questions. Let's head out. Pax, we're leaving!" She led the way back through the cathedral gates and across the white bridge once more, her ears twitching at the soothing flow of the river that passed below. Pax flew ahead of them, then landed on the white marble railing of the bridge, slightly extending his wings.

"The recipe was for defeating Malignus?" Solus asked as he strode along with her.

"Yep. Riko and Prowl each got one for the crafting class they are highest in as well," Kit waved to Pax as they passed him, but the winged warrior was too busy looking handsome and gazing off into the distance to acknowledge her. "I got some really nice accessories and some gorgeous dancing swords as drops, too. Do you want to see?" She grinned widely, unable to suppress her glee.

"You mean to say you will no longer be using a grossly underleveled weapon?" Solus asked.

Kit shook her head and sighed. "Of course that would be the information you latch onto. But I have a new belt—and swords!" She clapped her hands in glee and bound the last few steps across the bridge. "In fact, I'm going to try them out now! I want to see how much they improve my dance buffs."

Humming under her breath, Kit opened her storage and brought up her character screen, piling on the new equipment she had gotten and swapping her fans for the swords.

Instantly, Caolan's Sorrow and Caolan's Agony popped into existence, secured to her belt. Kit pulled them from their hilts and twirled them prettily before she began the first few steps of Battlefield March.

There was a low whistling sound, and Kit's movements slowed as her body felt heavy. It was almost as if she was wading through a pool of molasses. "What the..." She glanced up at her name, the blood draining from her face when she saw a new icon under her name—one of a white mask shaped in a screaming grimace. "No, no, no."

It was a curse: *Surrender to Sorrow*.

Solus Miles folded his arms across his chest and leaned against Sinistre as Kit, still moving at a snail's pace, opened her character panel. Eventually she managed to bring up the swords' information.

Again she skimmed the information about the swords' origins and scrolled down to the bottom of the screen. There, at the very base, it read:

Due to the nature of these swords, they have been cursed with the heartbreak of Caolan. Every use of them chances triggering a curse that inflicts the crushing grief of Caolan upon the user. The effects of the curse and the chance of the curse being casted are greatly increased for a Hero with holy affinity.

Kit stared at the screen and inhaled deeply, then exhaled slowly in a high whining noise not unlike a squealing balloon.

Pax muttered something about a "noisy buffoon," as he landed next to Sinistre and tucked two of his four wings to his back.

"What is it?" Solus asked.

"The swords are cursed," Kit said. "Because they're named —and from some tragic story—they've got darkness attached to them. If I were any race besides elf it wouldn't be a big deal, but because of my holy affinity and terrible reaction to darkness...I won't be able to use them. They cursed me just from that short dance I did."

"If they're cursed, can't they be purified?" Solus asked.

Kit tried to raise a hand to rub her eyes and tisked in irritation when it took several long seconds for her limb to make the journey. "Yes, but it is time-consuming—and I'm supposed to be in Luminos, like, *now*—and costly, which is super not helpful as this character is dead broke."

Solus raised an eyebrow. "Even after slaying Malignus?"

Kit cocked her head. "Well, that's a good point, but I haven't had time to cash in anything yet. But it doesn't matter because you specifically *have* to have a reputation level of 'honored' with the Imperials in order for a cathedral to even accept your request, and as the Imperial guards only just stopped killing me on sight, that's not gonna happen for a while."

"Since you are obviously disinterested in fixing them, can you give them to me?" Solus asked.

"Too late, they're already bound to my character. They can't be given or sold anymore." Kit said as she slowly—almost painfully so—swapped out the swords for her old fans. She couldn't help the droop in her shoulders as the scimitars disappeared and her fans dangling from silken cords looped over her wrists once more.

Solus pushed off Sinistre—pausing to pat the dragon's nose when he rumbled—and ambled closer to Kit. "Yes, but as I am your pledged, you can give them to me in spite of being bound."

Kit paused. "Really?"

"Yes."

"We can share items bound to our characters?"

"Yes, but you have to give them to me through an exchange window. I can't go to your home and use whatever I like." Solus made a few flicking motions—probably as he paged through his own character panel—and moments later, a new window popped up in front of Kit.

Solus Miles would like to trade with you.

Kit accepted the offer and dragged the priceless but equally useless scimitars from her storage panel to the trade panel. "That's pretty nifty! Does that mean I can use your stuff?"

"Unlikely," Solus said as they finalized the trade and the popup screen faded. "Most of my armor and weapons are meant for knights, and the few things that aren't are too high leveled for you. Unless this means you would like to level grind—"

"*No,*" Kit said firmly.

"I'm sure I have many useful things I could give you if you gained another thirty levels."

"Forget I asked." Kit slowly turned her back to the royal knight and plodded back in the direction of the White Veil Nunnery.

"Where are you going?" Solus asked.

"To get this curse removed," Kit called over her shoulder. "And then we'll be off to Luminos!"

3

THE ELITE GUILDS

PAX AND SINISTRE landed just outside the west gate of Luminos, making the ground quake. The dragon snorted, making his nostrils burn bronze like his eyes, and turned his massive head to watch Kit and Solus make their descent down his leg.

"Thanks for the ride," Kit said as she tugged on her skirt and fixed her glove—which had started to slide down her arm. "Did you want to come with me?"

"No," Solus firmly and emphatically said.

Kit grinned. "What, talking to a bunch of high-level guilds doesn't appeal to you? I'm sure they would respect you."

Solus narrowed his eyes. "The less I talk to such people, the happier I am."

"Woah, someone has baggage," Kit said.

Solus placed a hand on one of Sinistre's obsidian claws. "No. I've just been endlessly hounded by members of elite guilds to join them."

Kit squinted up at Solus' nameplate. "Oh, yikes. I never thought about that. Now that you mention it, I haven't ever seen such a high-level player without a guild."

Solus grunted.

Kit bit her lip. "But you're going to help me recruit NPCs, right?"

"Yes," he said, assuring Kit.

Though it had only been a short time, Kit was badly missing the bickering chatter that Axel, Luther, Vic, Cookie, and Gil had kept up in the party chat channel. While she still had Riko and Prowl, it was reassuring to know the taciturn royal knight had her back when necessary—even if he was overly invested in level grinding.

"Remember, don't hesitate to use my name to push the guilds," he said.

Kit pushed a strand of her champagne pink hair out of her face. "Is that really okay when you're trying to fly under the radar with them?"

He shrugged. "You're our best chance at getting out of here. I can suffer idiots for you if it helps."

Kit snorted. "You're such a romantic. Are you going to hang around outside the city?"

"No. I have an errand to run."

"I see. In that case, I'll hopefully see you soon. I'm trying to be an optimist and hope the guilds won't keep us chatting for days, but only time will tell."

Solus bowed slightly. "Good luck."

"Thanks!" Kit waved to him as she walked backwards towards the city, watching while he climbed back up Sinistre's shoulder. As she turned around to face the gate, she beamed. "For the first time on this character, I get to march straight in! No worrying about soldiers capturing me, no fears of the Court of the Rogue stabbing me—this is going to be a great day!"

Pax, hovering a few inches above the ground, made a noise of disagreement. "This city smells."

"Yes," Kit said patiently. "We've already covered that you

greatly dislike Luminos. Are you ready to return to your eg—er —center?"

Pax slightly inclined his chin, making his nose stick up in the air. "No."

Kit paused just outside the gates. "No?"

"No. I will remain outside," the winged warrior announced.

"And all the people won't drive you nuts?" Kit asked.

Pax scoffed. "I am above letting gnats affect me."

"You just complained about the smell, like, three seconds ago."

"I'm staying out!" Pax said, his voice as tight as a violin string.

I guess it's not a big deal. I don't have to worry about being discreet anymore now that my reputation levels have been reset, and I'm actually trying *to get attention this time with the big guilds now.* "Okay." Kit started for the gates again. "Suit yourself. Let me know if you change your mind."

Pax finally let his feet touch the ground, and he strode next to Kit—giving everything within sight a withering glare.

Great. We're going to make so many friends this way. Kit automatically held her breath as they walked through the open gates, passing numerous soldiers.

The Imperial guards only glanced at her as they stood in formation, carefully watching the stream of players entering and exiting the city.

"I did it!" Kit pumped her fist into the air as she bound several steps into the city. "This is the best thing to happen to me since entering Retha."

"Incorrect," Pax said. "*I* am the best thing that has ever happened to you."

"The jury is still out about that," Kit told her pet before she switched to the party chat channel. "Riko? Prowl? I'm in Luminos—by the west gates."

"You made it through without getting apprehended?" Riko asked. "How exciting!"

"I know, right?" Kit squealed.

"Ugh, save the screaming, would you?" Prowl asked. "Riko and I are enroute. I see your dot on our mini-map; we'll reach you soon."

"Great, thanks." Kit strolled up the main road, reveling in her unhurried pace. Though she enjoyed not having to peer over her shoulder every minute, she did keep an eye on the other players, trying to gauge the city's temperment.

When she had last been in Luminos, most of the large and elite guilds had their members out on city patrols to keep the peace. While there hadn't been any riots in Luminos, the city of Torvel had been damaged when two guilds fought.

Panic had been Kit's main worry. But though the players were markedly more reserved than usual, the frantic hum of terror didn't buzz in the streets. *Good. Fear I can deal with—it can be used to push others and make them move. Panic, though, drives people to do irrational and dangerous things.*

As if EC could tell what she was thinking, a pleasant, computerized voice boomed above the streets.

Attention, Heroes. Retha is still experiencing server difficulties. Log off capabilities are temporarily unavailable. EC is working to rectify the situation. Please remain calm. Thank you for your patience.

"I should have told them to change that," Kit muttered as she jostled into an offended Pax to avoid getting run down by a player riding a giant wolf mount.

"Did you say something, Kit?" Riko asked over the party chat.

"No, sorry, just talking to myself," Kit said. "Though this does remind me: have either of you heard from the GMs yet?"

GMs—or game masters—were EC employees who were in

the full submersion video game. They were essentially administrators and enforcers. GMs would hunt down and punish players who broke EC's rules—spammers, cheaters who used bot programs, and even players who were serial player killers. Occasionally they also served as customer service representatives to whom players could report bugs and glitches.

"Nope," Prowl said. "Not a word."

"When I was being put under again, I was told they would directly contact you, Kit," Riko said.

"That's what I was told as well, but since I haven't received anything, I thought I would ask," Kit said.

"There are GMs online?" Solus asked, startling Kit as she had half-forgotten he was a member of their party.

"Two," Kit said. "Both of them are recent transfers from other games, and they're the enforcer-type GM, so they're considered secret. Even the other players they interact with don't know they're EC employees."

"Let's get talking to the guilds first," Riko said. "If you don't hear from them by the time we're done, then we can think it over. Now, could you wave your hand or something? Our mini-maps say you're right in front of us, but I don't see you."

Kit turned around. As an elf, not only was her eyesight keener, but she was taller than most of the crowd and was easily able to see over most players. "I see you guys!" She slipped through the crowded streets, whistling when she reached Prowl and Riko.

Riko's new robes were an earthy green that complemented her tawny colored skin. Unlike her old robes—which were reminiscent of medieval monks'—the upper body of her new robe was fitted and fastened across her neck. It was ruffled, slightly, around the shoulders, to make it resemble leaves. The robe also cinched tight at the waist then flared out, revealing dark brown trousers and boots. Her new staff was still wooden, though it was topped with a golden crescent moon and a white crystal that hung from the top tip of the moon like a teardrop.

Instead of a shirt that was decorated with too many buckles, Prowl now wore a fitted coat that was a deep blue and fastened diagonally across his chest. The collar was popped and slightly larger than average, and little black chains draped across his shoulders.

"Looking good, you two!" Kit said.

Riko twirled, making the skirts of her robe swirl around her legs. "Thank you! Frankly, I'm thrilled. This is almost better armor than my main character has!"

"Yeah, yeah, life is a fashion show, and this is the catwalk. If you two don't mind, we have people to see?" Prowl reminded the pair.

"Give us a moment to preen. We just got some ridiculously good drops!" Riko poked her guildmate in the shoulder. "And you're not fooling anyone. I saw you posing in the mirror when we first logged back in." The druid returned her attention to Kit. "Though he does have a point—they're waiting on us right now. Did you need anything, or can we head straight to the guildhall?"

Kit sighed and rubbed the black tattoo on her cheek. "I dearly want to stop at a barbershop—now that I finally won't be shot on sight—to get this thing removed, but it will wait. We need to get the guilds moving."

Riko reached up to sling an arm over Kit's shoulders. "Don't worry. The guildmasters and guildmistresses we're going to talk to will understand."

Prowl snorted as the trio forged their way through the streets. "I wouldn't count on that."

"Do we have a good turn out?" Kit asked.

"Yes," Riko said. "An extremely impressive one, actually. You'll be speaking to all the highest leaders who are in-game."

"Our friends in the Silver Army messaged us as soon as we got back on," Prowl said. "Once we explained what happened, they connected us straight to their guildmistress, White Lady herself. She's how we got so many powerful people together."

Kit sniffed deeply—inhaling the scent of fish, fresh bread, and roasting meat as they passed by the player market, making their way north to the Guildhall. "Any feel on the game itself? While things seem more somber here in Luminos, I'm not sensing too much tension."

"Luminos is fine," Riko said. "As are all the big cities run by nonhumans—so the dwarf, elf, and fae territory are quite safe."

"I'm sensing a however in this?" Kit asked.

Prowl snorted. "It's one heck of a however. Smaller guilds have been feuding, and players are starting to fight in villages and less-populated cities. The guilds have been able to stamp out all unrest in the bigger cities, but the smaller ones that don't have direct teleportation gates are trickier to get to. Some players have been using loopholes to fight each other before the big guilds can react."

Kit winced. "How bad is it?"

"Nothing horrible so far. No one has been caught in the crossfire, and the fighting ends almost as quickly as it starts," Riko said. "It's been mostly isolated incidents—all much less serious than that fight that tore Torvel apart. But I'm thinking it's only a matter of time before something worse happens."

"How cheerful," Prowl grumbled.

"We need to get word out about Lord Valdis and logging off to give players something to work towards," Kit said. "If we give them an enemy to beat, they might stop fighting each other."

Prowl shrugged and folded his arms behind his head. "Fear does weird things to people."

"They're scared for their lives, Prowl. That thought would do weird things to anybody," Kit said.

They reached the long pathway that led straight into the snowflake-shaped Guildhall. As they marched towards the main body—the cylindrical center part from which halls and towers broke off like branches—Kit glanced back at Pax.

He followed behind her, though the expression on his face was filled with enough hate to melt ice.

"It should get better in a moment, Pax," she called back to her pet. "Though this next crew might gawk at you more."

"Of course." Pax's upper lip curled up as he scowled at an open-mouthed spirit weaver who stared at him. "I've learned not to expect anything better from you *heroes*."

"Excuse me, Kitten Lovemuch?"

Kit swung her attention forward again and smiled pleasantly at a female hunter and an elf ranger. "Yes, that's me."

The ranger smiled briefly, but his eyes didn't reflect the gesture and bore dark circles—a rarity for elves. "We are from the Silver Army and have been sent by White Lady to guide you to the meeting room."

Prowl whistled. "We get an escort now? Kit, you're moving up in life."

"Would you please keep your snark to yourself for the next few hours—or at least limit it to the party chat?" Riko rolled her eyes.

Kit ignored the squabbling pair and smiled at the hunter and ranger. "Thank you for your thoughtfulness. Please lead on."

The ranger nodded his head and took the lead. The hunter waited, smiling pleasantly, until Pax, Riko, and Prowl passed her before bringing up the rear.

"The guilds have already assembled," the ranger explained.

"I hope they haven't been waiting for me?" Kit asked.

"Not very long."

Kit grimaced. *That's not a great start. If they really are repre-*

sentatives of elite guilds, they likely won't take well to waiting on a level 50 elf dancer. But compared to facing Malignus, peeved players really aren't so bad. Kit raised her eyebrows as she followed the ranger up a flight of marble stairs. "I'm realizing this game might be warping my personality into an eternal optimist," she said into the party chat.

"You always were an optimist," Prowl replied in the chat channel. "Because let me tell you, anyone else who had been stuck with the rot that is your character probably would have sat down and rage quitted, refusing to move an inch until someone else solved the bizarre issues with this game."

"Thank you!" Kit said brightly.

"See?" Prowl asked. "Case in point."

"Stop talking," Riko panted in the channel. "I can't take it with all these stairs."

Kit laughed and switched the party chat off. "Can you tell me what guilds have sent representatives?" she asked their guides.

"Oh, they didn't send mere representatives," the female hunter piped in from the back.

"Really?" Kit blinked as she glanced back at the hunter. *I thought for certain I would have to talk to a bunch of representatives first, and maybe a first officer or two.*

"Yes, the guilds who are in attendance are all represented by their guildleaders *and* their first officers."

If Kit had been anything but an elf she likely would have tripped and fallen flat on her face, but instead all she did was daintily waver for a moment. "The guildleaders and the first officers?" she asked somewhat timidly.

"Yep," the hunter said.

Kit pressed her lips together and mentally began altering the speech she planned to give. First officers were the second in command of guilds. They were the de facto leaders if the guildmaster/mistress was not present, and they worked in synch with the guildleader to handle guild business.

Speaking to elite guildleaders straight off is a bit of a shock, but to speak to both guildmasters and their first officers? That means the guilds are far more serious and willing to listen than I estimated. It's a good thing...but it also means if I mess up and make them angry, it will be very hard to fix it in the future.

When they reached the top floor, the ranger left the staircase and strode down a side hallway that wrapped around the circumference of the building. "This way."

Riko gazed with deep appreciation at the marble walls, gold leafing, and the stained-glass windows that showed off images of long-forgotten heroes from the first battle against Valdis. "I've never been on this floor of the Guildhall," she said. "It really is nice."

"You've never been up here because we'd never be able to afford anything here," Prowl snorted.

"There aren't any guild zones up here. It's all meeting rooms." Kit glanced over her shoulder, intending to smile at Riko, but Pax and his massive wings blocked her view as he followed directly behind her.

"Kitten is correct," the ranger said. "This floor is filled with meeting rooms of various sizes—though they're all quite costly to rent out."

"I think there's even a dining hall," the hunter said thoughtfully from the rear. "I know a few players who have held receptions here after taking their vows as pledged in the cathedral."

"It's also been used for parties thrown by players who have gotten their legendary hero class," the ranger said.

"How did you know about the meeting rooms, Kit?" Prowl asked.

"When Milk Crown disbanded, we rented out most of this floor for our farewell celebration."

"The *floor*?" the elf ranger yelped.

Kit shrugged. "We weren't going to be playing anymore, so we blew our guild budget—though by now it has probably recovered with all the properties Milk Crown held."

"I've never heard of Milk Crown," the hunter said.

"I'm not surprised. We disbanded five years ago," Kit explained. "We had been an elite raid and PVP guild. We were smaller compared to most groups, but every member pulled their own weight and then some, so there was never a problem with it."

"So that is how you got the raid experience to pull off your battle against Malignus with such a ridiculously small group?" the ranger asked.

Kit blinked in surprise at his knowledge.

"We're friends with Luther," the hunter was quick to add as they came to a stop outside a set of massive double doors. "It's why we volunteered to escort you here."

"Oh." Kit smiled. "Then yeah. I'm not a seasoned leader, but I do know raids from my years with Milk Crown."

"I hate to break up such a delightful conversation," Prowl drawled. "But is this the place?"

The ranger snapped to attention. "Yes, sorry. We'll take you in and introduce you to White Lady."

As the ranger and hunter opened the doors, Riko skirted Pax so she could nudge Kit. "Don't you know White Lady? I thought you said she played and had already founded the Silver Army when Milk Crown was in its heyday?"

Prowl raised his eyebrows so high, they almost disappeared under the black goggles strapped to his forehead. "Heyday? Really, Riko? That is an old-lady word."

"I never knew her personally, but I knew of her...and she probably knows of me." Kit shifted her weight from one foot to the other. "I was...um...personally responsible for killing her whenever we faced Silver Army in PVP."

PVP referred to player-verses-player mode—which was basically a competition between two teams battling it out to see which was strongest.

"Ahh, yes. Azarel the over-powered echo of arcane strikes again," Prowl said, referring to Kit's old character.

When Kit played with Milk Crown, she had specialized in a heavy-damage-dealing character that could take down anyone—though she paid for it by being ridiculously easy to kill. The transition to being a dancer—a character who was best used in the thick of things so her buffs could affect the entire party—had been somewhat rough because of the great difference in playing style.

"Hush," Riko growled as the hunter and ranger pushed the doors open. "Chin up, my fellows. We're going in."

Prowl muttered something under his breath about old hags, but he squared his shoulders and lifted his gaze as they followed the hunter/ranger duo inside. (Pax lagged behind them, sticking to the edge of the room as they ventured farther inside.)

Though Kit made her feet follow along, she did not hide her attempt to peer around the chamber.

It was unlike any meeting room Kit had been in, mostly because it lacked proper walls. It was rectangular in shape, though most of the chamber jutted away from the main building, and only marble pillars held up a roof that consisted of mostly skylights.

Banners of gold cloth that sparkled in the sunlight were hung between the pillars and fluttered in the slight breeze, creating the only real semblance of walls. Gold suns were etched into the marble flooring, the giant stone table at the center of the room, and in the ornate sculpting of the ceiling.

White Lady—the only player not seated at the table—smiled

kindly at Kit. "Welcome Kitten Lovemuch, and Riko and Prowl of La-Lune. Thank you for accepting our invitation and coming."

"Not at all." Kit glanced back long enough to see that Pax still hung back, even as the huntress and ranger shut the doors again. "We should be the ones thanking you!"

The guildmistress motioned for them to stand at the head of the rectangular table. "Everyone is now present, so I will begin with some introductions," White Lady said as Kit—flanked by Riko and Prowl—peered up and down the table.

"Of course there is my guild, The Silver Army, a mostly PVP guild. We are represented by myself and my First Officer, Waffle." White Lady gestured to a blue-haired male naiad, who smiled and waved. He sat beneath a pennant that displayed the Silver Army's symbol—a silver sword and a harp.

"Corporate Force is next. We are lucky to have both Guildmaster Phizzy and First Officer Nyxiane with us today. Corporate Force is a raid guild."

Kit smiled and nodded as she met Phizzy's gaze. Though he was a cheerful gnome and appeared to be perfectly harmless with his large, styled mustache, Kit felt she could detect a certain amount of ruthlessness behind his golden spectacles—a feeling that was matched by his human first officer. Though Nyxiane smiled politely and adjusted her silver glasses that made her look like a librarian, Kit was willing to bet the duo was a powerful combo. Both of them seemed to look straight through her. (It took Kit a moment to realize they were staring at Pax, who, though he stood in the shadows, still stuck out like a star with his glittery armor and white wings.)

Intellectuals, Kit internally labeled them to help her keep them straight among the incoming rush.

"Tainted is another PVP guild. They're on the smaller side, though they hold some of the best PVP scores for the year."

White Lady nodded at a pair of humans. "It is led by Guild-master Ryunosuke and First Officer Reynard." The guildmaster —a shorter male who had blue-black hair and was almost entirely covered by black fabric—was clearly a ninja, and the first officer—with his hands covered in fancy gauntlets and his clothes in Imperial colors—had to be a royal assassin.

Cut-throat, Kit decided.

"The Killing Squad is mostly known for raiding—" White Lady started.

"Though we never back away from a challenge!" the guild-master—a werewolf—growled.

"Yes, the whole server knows that," White Lady acknowl-edged with a sweet smile. "Guildmaster Half-Fang and First Officer Long Claw are representing it today."

Both the guildmaster and the first officer were male were-wolves, though the guildmaster was so scarred, he looked like someone had shoved his wolf-face into a blender on more than one occasion.

Bloodthirsty. Definitely bloodthirsty.

"Brave Heart Company is here, represented by Guildmaster Saint George. They are mostly a raid guild as well," White Lady continued.

Though Prowl coughed to cover up his snort at the guild-master's pretentious name, Kit studied Saint George, taking in the way he impatiently tapped his fingers on the table and raised an eyebrow at her.

He might be difficult to bring around, though the Killing Squad will probably be worse...

"The Observational Fiends—who play PVP *and* raid—is represented by their First Officer Teara Karma, who is also their acting leader. Their guildmistress was forced off with the massive log off that happened when we were locked in the game."

White Lady turned slightly so she was speaking directly to Kit, Prowl, and Riko. "There are actually a number of other elite guilds that have some players in-game, but most of them have a fraction of their usual players, and many are missing their guild-master and their first officer. Most of those guilds already had alliances in place, though, so as a result, they have joined forces with the guilds that are present."

"I'm hurt, White Lady. Have you forgotten about us?" asked a woman sitting casually beneath her guild's banner.

"How could I forget you, Alistair? Lastly, we have KOS, represented by Guildmaster Gared and First Officer Alistair Lionward," White Lady indicated to a paladin who sat next to a cavalry knight.

Recognizing the name as a prestigious guild from when she had played, Kit eagerly leaned forward to study them and was surprised.

The first officer was a female cavalry knight with blue-black hair that was pulled back into a high ponytail and crowned with delicately crafted blue and gold metal petals. Her chest-plate was almost corset-like, but it was the same blue and gold as her hair piece and was crafted so it looked like a lotus flower encircled her waist. She wore soft white trousers and blue and gold metal boots that extended the lotus flower motif.

The guildmaster wore a much less eye-catching outfit: a chain mail hauberk with a red and gold surcoat, along with layered metal boots, heavy gauntlets, and large pauldrons that were molded to resemble roaring lions.

Kit blinked. *I remember KOS is under new leadership now, but I feel like I know them.*

The First Officer smiled and cushioned her chin on her hand. "We meet again, Lady Kit!"

Kit snapped her fingers and brightened. "Alistair, the knight who saved me from that Court of the Rogue assassin! I didn't know you were with KOS!"

Alistair laughed—a breezy sound. "Yes, you've found out my secret. If it got out that I'm the first officer of KOS, I don't think I would be half as popular."

Gared snorted. "Cut the act, Alistair. Everyone knows you're the first officer. Hello, Kitten."

"It's just Kit, please." She hesitated. "What happened to Belmont and Goshin400?" She asked, referring to the priest first officer and the huntress guildmistress who had founded the guild.

Gared scratched the back of his head. "They got married out of the game and had a kid two or three years ago. They passed KOS off to Alistair and me before quitting Retha for good."

Kit laughed. "In Milk Crown, we always said they had a thing for each other."

"Leaders—and first officers—this is Kitten Lovemuch, Riko, and Prowl. They are the renown players who took on Malignus and won," White Lady said, gently interrupting the small talk. "With all the introductions made, I believe we should begin."

"Of course," Riko said smoothly. "May I assume based on those who are present that none of the big RP guilds are on?"

Half-Fang—the bloodthirsty guildmaster of The Killing Squad—released a bark of laughter. "Are you kidding? Why would we invite those pansies?"

RP stood for role play. In the video game world, it meant a player who was into RP usually tried to play/live through the game as if it were real life. RPers usually played in groups and spent their time in-game acting out anything from the mundane —like going to a tavern together—to traveling across the world and acting as their characters would. (So a dwarf RPer would not be friends with an elf RPer unless it was a gradual occurrence, and no real RPer would ever acknowledge modern technology or even anything outside the game while they were "in character.")

Tainted's leader spun a dagger on his fingertip. "The world could die around them, and they would still be locked in their world of pretend."

Kit barely refrained from pointing out they *all* were locked in a world of pretend, and instead switched to party chat. "Riko, do you have any RP contacts?"

"Not really. I'll get on that once we're out of here, but I wouldn't get your hopes up," Riko said. "I asked because I was hoping someone here had contacts with the RP guilds."

"RPers generally don't mix much with the rest of us," Prowl piped in, his voice making the party chat channel stir a breeze across Kit's neck.

"Yeah, it was the same back when I played," Kit acknowledged. "But we need help from anyone willing to lend a hand."

"Glad I'm not the one stuck talking to them," Prowl muttered into the party chat channel.

"Lady Kit," Alistair—the lady knight and first officer of KOS —smiled beautifully. "We all know due to the announcement that was launched after the defeat of Malignus that you successfully led a raid against him and won. Additionally, we've all received messages from The Silver Army that explained your situation. You are a veteran player from Milk Crown—a guild that is familiar to several of us, though I believe White Lady is the only one who has had the pleasure to ever play with you."

White Lady laughed. "Oh, we might as well call it as it was. Milk Crown frequently thrashed my guild. Kitten—Azarel, as her character was called—is very skilled."

"Yes, the recorded stats from the Guildhall agree with you there." Gared folded his arms across his belly and peered thoughtfully up at Kit. "If you don't mind giving us a brief explanation, what took you from the excellence of Azarel to your...dancer?" he asked, his gaze lingering on Kit's tattoo.

Kit rolled her shoulders back and sighed. "Please, call me Kit. And it was supposed to be a joke," she started in on her often-repeated speech. "My cousin—who was also a member of Milk Crown—now works for EC. He designed this character and made a note in my user profile that, regardless of what game I chose the next time I went to an EC arcade, I should be given a session in Retha and use this character. He made her as awful as possible because he thought it would irritate me. Unfortunately, I logged in shortly before the power surge that trapped us all here."

"Yes." White Lady flicked through a message screen. "I believe you told one of my guildmembers that your cousin said the power surge made all home rental units disconnect, and all arcade full submersion units switch to the backup server, which unfortunately has corrupted files, and it is backup servers that keep us from logging out?"

"That is correct, Guildmistress," Kit said. "My cousin told me that—just as he told me it was possible to beat Malignus, and that beating him would force us to automatically log out of the game so the system could check to make sure we hadn't cheated."

"And you beat him and were logged out?" Nyxiane—from the intellectual Corporate Force guild—asked as she adjusted her silver glasses.

"Yes," Kit said. "Our raid of nearly seventy players was forced to log out and was successfully freed."

"Yet you're back in the game?" This came from Teara—the First Officer of the Observational Fiends, who appeared to be understandably tired given the absence of her guildmistress. A glance at her nameplate revealed she was a falconer—a ranger legendary class.

"EC spoke to us—Riko, Prowl, and me—and asked us to come back," Kit hesitated, unsure how much she should tell them, how much fear she should use to drive her point home. "It doesn't look good. They aren't very hopeful that they'll be able to purge the backup servers of the corrupt code before we *need* to get off. Which is why they sent us."

Kit discreetly nudged Riko with her elbow, prompting the druid to speak up.

"If we fight Lord Valdis and win, the game will again need to check our work and make sure we haven't cheated in some way. EC has informed us that this means *every* player on the server will be forcibly logged out," Riko said.

Saint George—the impatient leader of the Brave Heart Company—narrowed his eyes. "Did your EC employee cousin give you *him* as well?" he asked, pointing to a spot behind Kit.

Kit twisted to look over her shoulder and was surprised to see that Pax was no longer standing on the ground but hovering slightly, all four of his wings unfolded and looking as magnificent as possible.

He's preening for the players, I guess. She cleared her throat. "No. I found Pax in the goblin fortress in the Soggy Swill Bog. It was sheer luck—and perhaps the game's attempt to balance out my character, as I've had pretty bad life skills so far."

"Right," Saint George said, his voice biting with sarcasm.

Several other guildleaders exchanged quiet whispers with their first officers, seemingly in agreement.

"He doesn't listen to me," Kit said. "He won't, either, until I reach level cap."

"Moving on," Phizzy—the Corporate Force Guildmaster—said with a cheery smile. "Why did EC decide to send *you* back?"

Kit mentally fumbled. *How on earth am I supposed to respond to that?!*

"Probably because she beat Malignus with a shoddy raid, when none of you could do it with parties of hundreds of players all above level 100," Prowl snorted. He grunted in pain when Riko ground her heel into his foot.

"Though my compatriot lacks tact, he speaks the truth," Riko said breezily. "Kit comes from an era in which players were far more serious about things like PVPing and raiding. It's been years since some of the raids she ran *monthly* have even been completed. Furthermore, her defeat of Malignus proves her tactical ability."

"The reports say none of you killed Malignus," Teara of Observational Fiends said as she flicked through several iridescent screens. "Didn't you merely transport him to the White Veil Nunnery where NPCs slayed him?"

Prowl rolled his eyes. "Oh, I'm sorry. I must have missed the time any of *you* thought to do that and set a world record and beat Malignus."

Riko switched to the party chat channel, making another breeze brush Kit's neck, and hissed. "Prowl, *stop talking*! If you open your big mouth again, I will shove my staff in it!"

"Names can be changed in this game," Tainted's first officer said in a voice like nails. "How can we be certain you really did all that you claim?"

"Several of my guildmembers joined Kitten Lovemuch's raid. Specifically, Luther was a member of her party when she was still preparing for the fight, and he exchanged several picture messages with my people. She is who she says she is," White Lady said.

Kitten nodded her head in thanks to the serene guildmistress and flicked a droplet of sweat from her forehead. *Sheesh. I knew this would be tough, but I thought they would more object to my character than nitpick everything. If I were anything besides an elf, I'd be sweating bullets right now!*

"Luther is off the game, now," Kit added. "He was in the raid with us. EC asked him to come back as well, but he couldn't due to personal reasons."

Alistair ran a hand through her silky ponytail. "Enough. I met Lady Kit myself before she put the raid together. I can promise you this elf is who she says she is, and we all know it was she who defeated Malignus thanks to the world-wide announcement."

"I still don't like it," Saint George said. "She's a has-been. We saw her records; she and her guild haven't played for five years. Why send an outsider back to save us?"

"Riko and Prowl are not outsiders," Nyxiane pointed out.

Phizzy—Nyxiane's Guildmaster—nodded. "Yes. Plus, I don't know that it's fair to say she's a has-been when—as Prowl so charismatically reminded us—she managed to pull off a feat no one else has."

Teara cocked her head. "So you're siding with her, then?"

Phizzy's glasses gleamed. "It is more that I believe we should hear her out. She's been sent from EC. It would be our loss if we ignored her entirely."

White Lady nodded, then swung her attention to Kit. "I agree with Phizzy. You mentioned we need to fight Lord Valdis, Kit? How do you plan we go about that?"

"We'll need to get as many players and guilds involved as possible. We'll have to get better gear for lower characters and—if possible—organize into fighting raids. I think it would be best if we practiced in smaller groups and ran a few dungeons before we set our sights on Valdis. That's why I approached you all for help. If the rest of Retha sees the top guilds working together for this, they will take it more seriously," Kit said.

Teara—first officer of Observational Fiends—rubbed her eyes. "That's going to be difficult on top of keeping the peace and making our hourly patrols, as well as answering any emergency messages when fights break out. We're already stretched thin."

"I know it sounds tough, but we can't approach this half-heartedly," Kit said. "I spoke with a Retha senior developer. She said the backup server will only last for one big battle against Valdis, maybe two if we're lucky."

"You believe we have *two shots* to get this right?" Ryunosuke, the ninja guildmaster of Tainted, grabbed his dagger midair and snapped to attention.

Kit hesitated. "Yes."

Saint George scoffed. "This is an impossible plan. She's clearly just trying to make herself more important!"

Phizzy held up a hand. "What she says is reasonable enough, George. I imagine the backup servers aren't designed to withstand the long usage we've put them through, and if we really can gather the masses, that's going to strain them even more."

"My name is *Saint* George," Saint George growled.

Waffle—Silver Army's first officer—paused in the act of scribbling out notes. "Gathering as many players as possible for the battle isn't unexpected, either. We'll be fighting on a new scale if we do try to face Lord Valdis."

"Yes," Kit acknowledged. "But that's not all. We also need to recruit NPCs."

"NPCs?" Gared rubbed his chin. "Is that possible?"

"The White Veil Nunnery fought Malignus of their own volition," Riko said.

"And they've already pledged to help me when we fight Lord Valdis," Kit said.

"We've never heard of NPCs fighting with players before. How can you be sure it isn't just empty words meant to immerse us in the world?" Phizzy asked.

"I got a popup screen when they offered," Kit said.

"If you inspect her and look at her character display, at the very bottom there's a little glowing bell symbol," Riko said. "Stare at it, and a new pop up screen will show up, telling you the White Veil Nunnery has made an alliance with her. You can't see another player's reputation levels, so this means it *must* be different."

Half-Fang, leader of the Killing Squad, flattened his wolf ears. "Why would we need help from *NPCs*?" He sneered.

"Other servers have beaten their world's version of Malignus," Kit said. "But no one has beaten their world's equivalent to Lord Valdis."

"And you think *you're* the one who can lead us to victory?" Saint George shook his head. "No. Our guilds are already stretched thin trying to keep the peace. I would consider it if it was Gared or Phizzy, but I will *not* listen to some elf dancer who has too many coincidences going on for her to be a truly skilled player."

"Lighten up, George," Alistair said with a breezy laugh.

"No." The Brave Heart Company's Guildmaster stood and narrowed his eyes. "This is a ridiculous idea. I can't believe any of you are stupid enough to even consider it! This is as doable as..."

"As defeating Malignus, right?" Prowl asked.

Saint George glared at Prowl and snatched up his giant sword that leaned against the stone table. "Laugh all you want, *saboteur*. I'm not going to fall for your little games that distract us from what's important!" He stalked up to Kit—though he had to glower up at her since she was an elf and was taller than he was—and his hand strayed to his giant sword.

"George," Gared barked as he stood, Alistair mirroring him.

Kit met his eyes and forced her spine straight, refusing to back down. She did blink when she felt feathers brush her arm and warmth bathe her back.

When Saint George's gaze strayed behind her, Kit dared to twist her neck to look as well.

Pax stood directly behind Kit, one of his platinum silver eyebrows raised in disdain. "Your name is faulty. You are *not* a saint."

Saint George's eyes widened slightly, and several of the guildmasters and first officers gasped.

"He talks?" Alistair rapidly blinked as she stared at him.

"Yes," Kit said. "Sorry, I forget that not everyone knows much about him." *Especially because he only says mean things. Though I guess it's good to see his distaste extends past me.*

Pax's other eyebrow joined the first in a judgmental stare. "Even a being graced with less intelligence than I could see that what bothers you is not the proposed idea to attack Valdis, but the person chosen to be your leader." He made a tisking noise at the back of his throat. "It displays just how shallow your self-confidence is and conversely how deep your ego goes."

Saint George gripped his sword with such strength his hand turned white. "Brave Heart Company will *never* stand beneath you, Kitten Lovemuch. I will die before I see that happen." He stalked from the meeting area, throwing open one of the wooden doors with more force than necessary, so it cracked against the stone wall.

"Saint George, please do not be hasty," White Lady called after him.

"I will not be talked down to by a washed-up player," Saint George snarled. "*Don't* message me again over this stupid matter. If you try to bring it up, I will pull Brave Heart Company out of its patrols and fortifications." With this last threat, he stomped into the hallway, disappearing from sight.

4

ENTER PLAYER TWO

THE ROOM immediately fell into silence, though Kit could see everyone's mouths move as the guildmasters and first officers spoke to each other either through PMs or party chat channels.

Kit scowled at her pet as she tilted her head and listened to Saint George's heavy footfalls. "Pax, thank you for...that, but do you think you could just *not talk* for the rest of the meeting?"

The winged warrior looked away. "Hmph."

Wind stirred the golden cloth banners, briefly chilling the meeting area as the sun slipped behind the clouds.

Alistair stood, smiling charmingly as she held her arms wide. "Friends," she said. "We must discuss this calmly. I know we are all concerned, and we are all experiencing pressure, but Lady Kit is the best lead we have—not to mention she clearly has the backing of EC."

Gared nodded in appreciation and rested his elbows on the table as he watched his First Officer.

"I believe," Alistair continued, "if players know we're working towards an exit, things might calm down, and they might more easily listen. You all know trying to keep the smaller guilds from fighting has been a bear of a task. If they are forced to focus on preparing for Lord Valdis, they'll be too busy to slug it out."

Visibly, the other leaders began to relax. Phizzy nodded his head in agreement, and White Lady's smile turned more genuine and less strained while the first officer of Tainted nodded and leaned back in his chair again.

Only Teara Karma bit her lip and still looked indecisive.

Alistair sat down and eagerly turned to Gared. "Didn't I do great? I spoke just as heroically as you told me to."

Gared rolled his eyes. "You did, but it kind of ruins the effect when you say so out loud."

This exchange squeezed a few chuckles from around the table, until Teara stood.

"I'm afraid I have to leave this meeting as well." Teara cocked her head as she studied Kit. "I actually believe you, and I believe what you've told us. But frankly I don't think it's feasible. Trying to organize a bunch of panicked players to defeat a boss that no other server has successfully faced? You would have to be a genius in tactics and have the charisma of Alistair, combined with the leadership skills of a general."

Kit winced at the harsh truth in the first officer's words.

"That, combined with the difficulties we guilds are facing, and I'm afraid I don't have the energy to even give it a go. Trying to hold my guild together and keep riots from tearing Luminos apart is the best I can do right now." Teara glanced around the room. "I won't criticize anyone for wanting to try, but I think it's going to be a waste of time and resources."

"It's the only possible way out at this time, Teara," Phizzy pointed out. "Doesn't that make it worth an attempt?"

Teara sighed, and her shoulders slumped. "No. I'm tired and beaten. I can't do more than this. I won't make myself do more than this. Maybe that will change in the future, but I doubt it." She shrugged and made for the door. "Good luck to you all." With that, she was gone—much more quietly than Saint George, but she had also probably done far more damage.

Kit could see new signs of indecision on her audience's faces. Ryunosuke and Reynard of Tainted had their heads tipped together as they also started to speculatively study the door. The werewolves of the Killing Squad were nodding, and they started to gather up the small arsenal of bladed weapons they had plopped down around their chairs. Even White Lady bit her lip, her forehead creased in thought as her elf ears twitched.

A breeze brushed Kit's neck.

"This is bad. We just lost two of seven guilds," Riko said in the party chat channel.

"If we lose even one more, that will be too close to the halfway mark, and then everyone except KOS and The Silver Army will probably fold," Kit guessed.

"Probably," Riko agreed.

"Watch out for the Killing Squad—they're getting ready to leave," Prowl piped in.

Kit's heart pounded faster as Half-Fang stood, his wolf ears twitching.

What do I do? How can I stop them?

Flicking her party chat channel off, Kit blurted out, "I know Solus Miles!"

Everyone stopped what they were doing and looked at her.

"I don't believe you," Half-Fang declared.

Why did I have to say that so desperately? Kit cringed. "He's my friend. He knows what I've been working towards."

Phizzy took off his gold spectacles and cleaned them. "Are you sure you know what you're saying, Kit? All of us here, at one point or another, have tried recruiting Solus Miles. He's the best player of the server; he doesn't befriend just anyone."

Ryunosuke—the ninja guildmaster of Tainted—snorted.

"What you really mean is he has the worst lone-wolf complex out of all of us. I'm with Half-Fang on this one. I smell a bluff."

"He has partied with us," Riko said.

Nyxiane smiled serenely. "If that is so, then he should be willing to speak on your behalf, wouldn't he?"

Kit hesitated.

"Kit, what are you waiting for?" Riko growled into her ear.

"I wanted to do this without flashing his name around," Kit whispered back.

"Look, I get it. I also think it's asinine they'll only believe you if a *male* stands with you," Riko said hotly.

"Uh, I think it's more than that, given that they don't care what I say either," Prowl said.

Riko ignored her guildmate. "But didn't Solus *tell* you to ask him if you needed help?"

A breeze brushed Kit's neck again.

"Hey, Solus," Prowl drawled. "You feel like coming in for show-and-tell? These idiots don't believe Kit, and they want you to back her up."

"Prowl!" Kit said in their chat channel, her voice overly pleasant. "If you could *shut your trap*, that would be stupendous!"

"The guilds are giving you trouble?" Solus asked. (Hearing his voice over the party chat channel still came as something of a surprise to Kit.)

"Um, just a little bit," Kit said.

"Summon me."

She blinked. "Sorry, what?"

"Use Love's Call, and summon me."

Kit's eyes momentarily bugged. Sensing gazes on her, she smiled at the guildleaders and held up one finger, then turned her back to them. "Are you sure about that? I'm in here surrounded by Killing Squad, The Silver Army, KOS, Tainted, and Corporate Force. They're going to be all over you once you're here."

"Then I'll be able to tell them to listen to you. Or else," Solus said.

I swear I can hear Sinistre growling in the background. She shook her head slightly. "I don't want to pressure you into this, Miles."

Prowl rolled his eyes and pantomimed gagging—until Riko kicked him in the shins.

"You forget, I have a vested interest in this as well," Solus replied. "And if we don't work together, as a server, it's unlikely we'll be able to defeat Lord Valdis."

Kit inhaled deeply. "Okay. Hold on, I'll summon you in one moment." She spun back around to face the guilds and flicked off her party chat channel. "He has agreed to come, but I need to step out into the hallway for a moment."

Because there's absolutely no way I'm summoning him with those cheesy, awful lines in front of these people. They'll never be able to take me seriously again!

White Lady nodded and opened her mouth to agree, but Half-Fang cut her off.

"No," he growled. "You, Kitten Lovemuch, are as shady as Lord Valdis himself. I wouldn't put it past you to slip off and run away while we wait for Solus Miles, who isn't really coming. You stay right here."

"Agreed." Ryunosuke nodded.

Kit gulped and switched back to the party chat channel. "Um, Solus? You're going to have an audience for your entrance."

"Stop wasting time and summon me," the royal knight flatly stated.

"Okay then," Kit said into the party chat channel. "Thought I would save you some embarrassment, but I guess you don't care that everyone is about to find out we're pledged."

She paused, waiting for Solus to change his mind.

"Why have I not been summoned yet?" he asked.

"Okay, okay, I'm getting to it." Kit switched out of the party chat channel and gave the door one longing glance.

Half-Fang nodded, and his first officer skulked over to the door and stood in front of it.

Kit sighed. "Here goes my reputation—with players anyway. How can anyone stomach saying this anyway?"

"Kit, just do it," Riko prompted.

Half-Fang narrowed his eyes. "Do what?" he demanded.

Kit squared her shoulders and activated the skill. "Love's Call!" Her arms moved on their own as her hands clasped the spot over her heart. "Though our hearts are apart, they beat as one!" She twirled in a circle then held out her hand. "Come to me, my sweet honey!"

A door of light appeared next to her outstretched hand, and Solus' arm suddenly thrust through it and clasped her hand. Kit stepped back, drawing him out.

She heard the gasps behind her and couldn't help the slight smile that curled on her lips. Eager to see their reactions, she released Solus' hand and spun slightly so she could face them.

Half-Fang's muzzle hung open, and his wolf ears were flattened against his skull. Ryunosuke of Tainted was so shocked, he dropped the dagger he'd been flipping around. Even the lady knight Alistair blinked in surprise.

A bird actually flew through one side of the open-air meeting room and out the other, and still no one uttered a word.

Kit opened her mouth to speak, but snapped it with an audible click when she felt Solus step closer to her and slide a possessive arm around her waist, resting his fingers on the belt of her skirt.

"I hear you've been troubling my pledged?" Solus said in a dark and wintery voice Kit had never heard him use before.

Even she blinked in shock when she felt him brush his lips against her cheek. Riko, on the other hand, could scarcely contain her glee, and instead happily clapped her hands and even jumped in place.

"Solus," Kit whispered in the party chat channel. "What are you doing? I thought we would tell them we were accidentally pledged?"

"Why explain when you can use me as a trump card?" Solus asked, his lips still brushing her cheek as he spoke.

It made sense. If they thought Kit had Solus' full support, they might find it easier to follow her. *Still, this seems to be taking it a bit far...*

Half-Fang looked back and forth between Kit and Solus. "You got hitched to *her*? Out of all the girls in Retha, *this* is what you wanted?"

Solus narrowed his eyes. "If you're wondering why I chose her, you're obviously an idiot; in which case, there's nothing I can do to help you."

Kit tried to smack him but only succeeded in bruising her knuckles on his armor. "Miles!" she hissed.

"He's really Solus Miles, royal knight." Ryunosuke peered at Solus from his chair and shook his head as if he could barely believe it himself.

There were a couple of long moments of awkward silence as the guildmasters and first officers gaped at Solus Miles in disbelief.

Alistair laughed, lightening the atmosphere. "Consider me convinced." She stood only so she could give Kit an elaborate bow. "Lady Kit *must* be our leader. Not only has she defeated Malignus, she has successfully collared our server's most famous —and eligible—bachelor."

"Have you been...pledged long?" White Lady pleasantly inquired.

"Long enough to be angry that you've treated her like dirt," Solus put bluntly. He looked at every individual that stood around the table. "As my pledged, Kit has my full support. Where she goes, I go. Anyone who questions her is also questioning me. Understood?"

Alistair looked down at Gared. "I don't think I've heard him speak so many words in a row before."

"Quiet," Gared barked to his first officer.

"Very well. With Solus Miles in the picture, that makes quite a difference, doesn't it?" Nyxiane said to her guildmaster.

"It does." Phizzy rubbed his large mustache. "We can use Solus as a rallying cry of sorts. He's widely admired by all. If we say he is with the group leading the charge against Valdis, I'm certain we'll get more cooperation. That is, if you don't mind, Solus?"

"Kit will be the leader," Solus said. "All decisions are up to her."

"But you don't mind if we use your popularity?" Kit asked.

Solus, his arm still settled around her waist, fixed his attention on her. "I already told you to use my name and image however you want."

Kit gulped under the intensity of his gray eyes. "Okay. Thanks," she said weakly.

"Excellent. This will give us the perfect starting point to begin recruiting players to our cause," Nyxiane declared happily.

"I was hoping you larger guilds would start getting the word out among the players, but I still want to send a party out to recruit NPCs," Kit said.

"You will lead it?" White Lady asked.

Kit nodded. "Yes. As I already have an alliance with the

White Veil Nunnery, I think I can recruit the dwarves and possibly the fae without too much trouble."

Ryunosuke eyed her. "You're only level 50. We should send an escort with you."

"Good idea." Gared stood and slapped his gauntleted hands on the back of his wooden chair, producing a loud crack.

"Might I suggest that, if it is possible, we send our first officers to travel with Kit?" Phizzy asked.

Half-Fang snorted. "You've gotta be kidding. With all the crap we're trying to keep up with in Luminos?"

"But that's why they must go," White Lady said. "Because it will be a show of faith; players will realize we're quite serious if the first officers travel with Kit."

"Alistair can go," Gared volunteered.

Alistair whipped around so fast, it made the tail of her ponytail stream behind her. "But Captain, I couldn't possibly leave you!"

Gared rolled his eyes. "There's no reason to be dramatic, Alistair."

"Without me, who will reach the top shelf for you in the guildzone?"

Gared glared at his first officer. "If you want a broken limb as a going-away present, keep talking."

"Reynard?" Ryunosuke asked, looking to Tainted's first officer.

"I'll go." The assassin ran his fingers over his daggers.

"As will I," Nyxiane pleasantly chimed in.

"I can go," Waffle—White Lady's first officer—said. "I'll just need a bit of time to train a few other guildmates so they can take over some of my duties."

"Thank you, Waffle," White Lady said gently. "Half-Fang? Will you allow Long Claw to join?"

Half-Fang growled and scratched his ear much like a dog. "I

still don't like this. But without Long Claw, you stand a bird's chance in a cat's den. He'll go with ya."

Reynard frowned. "That offends me," he said.

"Don't care," Half-Fang growled.

"Is there anyone else we can take as well?" Kit asked, fishing for more help. *While this would be a great group, we* still *don't have any healers!*

White Lady nodded. "Yes, looking at the party, I can see there is no dedicated healer—something that will be very much needed to make certain Kit remains unharmed."

Gared sighed. "I know a guy. I'm not sure he'll be willing to help, but I'll see if I can contact him."

"I would also like to take several other players—specifically those who fall between level 52 and 60," Solus said.

Half-Fang frowned. "Why?"

Solus raised one of his intimidating eyebrows and somehow managed to look down on the werewolf. "Does it matter?"

I wonder if Pax learned the eyebrow thing from Solus? Kit thought, before the royal knight's request caught up with her. "Wait, you just want lower-leveled players so you can stop us to level grind."

"You're level 50," Solus said. "You cannot lead us against Valdis at level 50."

Nyxiane was typing out a message in a popup screen. "Solus Miles is correct. It is in our best interest to get you to the level cap—to make it harder to kill you, if for no other reason."

"KOS has a few experienced players who were on their alternate characters when this mess went down. A few of them are around that level range," Gared said.

"Same for Corporate Force," Nyxiane said.

"Excellent!" Phizzy clapped his hands and smiled. "Let's start writing down names and make sure we're building a balanced party. Kit, do you have any specifications you'd like known?"

Kit hesitated. *I want to say no. I want to let them do whatever they want...but I should probably establish an interest so they don't think I'm Solus' puppet.* "Yes, actually. Could we get all the levels and classes written down? I would like to go over my options."

Phizzy patted the table. "Pull up a seat, and we'll get started. I can't wait to see what kind of party you build."

"Indeed," Nyxiane added in an almost purr.

Kit flashed them a smile as she crossed the room, glancing behind her to make certain Pax followed. She met Solus' gaze and offered him a grin. "Thank you."

Solus nodded and took up a position so he stood in the shadow of a support pillar, leaving Kit to work out the details of their newest adventure.

———

Luther—or, in reality, Luke—rubbed his aching head and stifled a yawn. He glanced down at his sleeping two-year-old and smiled, then softly stroked her forehead with his thumb. His other daughter—a five-year-old—was surrounded by toy horses. She changed her voice's pitch as she played by herself.

I'm out. I'm out of Retha.

It felt too good to be true—like waking up after a long nightmare. He released a shuddering breath, disturbing his beautiful wife who was nestled into his side.

"Are you okay?" she asked.

Luther draped an arm across her shoulders. "I'm perfect," he said.

She smiled up at him and kissed his cheek. "I'm so glad you made it. I was so frightened..."

Careful not to disturb the two-year-old, Luther pulled his wife closer. "I know."

The moment was broken by the irritating ring of the video conferencing app on his tablet.

Luther groaned and tipped his head back so it rested on the back of the couch. "Leave it," he told his wife when she pulled away and picked the tablet up. "It's probably just another nosy relative."

"No..." His wife shuffled back to his side. "I think this is for you." She winked as she passed the tablet off. "I'm going to heat up something the neighbors brought over. Enjoy."

Confused, Luther took the tablet, his heart freezing at the words on the screen.

Invitation to video conference with: Axel Talbot, Gilbert Gray, and Victoria Samn.

Luther quickly swiped yes, and his smile grew when four familiar faces filled his tablet screen.

"Hi Luther," Cookie said. She leaned into Victoria as the pair shared a tablet. "Thanks for taking our call!"

Luther raised an eyebrow. "You thought I would ignore it?"

"Mm, yeah," Axel said, as blunt as ever. "You were super reluctant to give us your real name before we got off that conference call EC set up."

Luther adjusted his two-year-old and leaned back in the couch. "That's because you're all young. You might not want an old man like me hanging around."

"Oh, my gosh," Vic rolled her eyes. "You're like, thirty-five. That's not *that* old."

"How is your family?" ever-thoughtful Gil asked.

Luther's lips softened into another smile. "Fine," he said, briefly pointing the tablet down so the camera could pick up his adorable daughter that was drooling on his stomach.

"She's so cute!" Cookie cooed.

"She's going to ruin your dress shirt," Vic said.

Cookie pulled away from her friend. "Vic! How could you say that?"

"Well, it's true," Vic said.

"Given what we just went through, I don't imagine he cares much about his shirt," Gil gently pointed out.

Vic flattened her lips in thought.

Luther adjusted his daughter so she wasn't in danger of slipping off, then used both of his hands to hold up the tablet. "I assume whoever started this call did so for a reason?"

"That was Vic," Axel tattled.

"I started it, but Cookie was the one who insisted on it," Vic stressed.

"Yeah, I wanted to make sure everyone was doing okay, and..." the cheerful college student paused, pushing a lock of her blonde hair out of her face.

Vic nudged her. "Just spit it out. They'll understand."

"What is it, Miss Cookie?" Gil asked.

Cookie scratched her nose. "Well...I don't really know how to say this...but I was wondering if anyone else was dissatisfied about the way things ended—with sending Kit, Riko, and Prowl back, I mean."

"We can't go in there after them," Luther said before she could say anything more.

"I know. It's more like...isn't there something we can do to help them?" Cookie looked at the camera with such hope, Luther felt a little bad for his hurried statement.

Axel squinted. "I don't see how. They're in the game and cut off from the rest of the servers, so it's not like they can even check the community tab for help."

"Axel is right," Luther said. "As much as it bugs me to say it, there's no possible way we can reach them. Only EC can establish contact—and that's pretty sketchy, too."

Cookie sighed. "Yeah, that's what I thought."

There was a moment of silence before Gil piped in. "I am glad we did not sign those confidentially agreements and non-disclosure agreements on Riko's advice."

"It's been unsettling how little EC has shared," Luther said. "There are news articles and coverage on the lockdown, but it seems that they've only shared the basics."

"My parents knew we were locked in because of a power surge and faulty coding, but that was it," Vic said. "They thought we got out because EC managed to disconnect us, not because of our fight with Malignus."

"Yeah, Vic and I are neighbors, and my parents thought the same thing," Cookie said.

"It's somewhat maddening," Gil said mildly. "For it means Miss Kit, Miss Riko, and Prowl aren't getting any recognition for their bravery in returning."

"We can tell the world!" Axel beamed. "That's why we didn't sign those boring papers. Besides, the payout they were offering was pretty pitiful anyway." He snorted to illustrate his disdain, briefly shaking his camera so his image on Luther's tablet shook.

Luther blinked. "Payout?"

"Yeah, didn't you guys get an offer? It was, like, $1,000 or something ridiculous like that in exchange for my recorded footage. As if *any* amount of money would make me part with my video—I hiked a cliff while poisoned in Retha!"

"You didn't hike. You went up some stairs, and the poison wore off when we weren't even one-fourth the way up," Vic sourly said.

"Same thing," Axel said.

"No, it's not," Vic said.

"Wait, Axel, you still have your video footage?" Luther asked.

"Yep. I already checked on it and have it backed up on my external hard drive just in case they decide to 'accidentally' erase it." Axel gave Luther that same cocky smile he used to flash around in Retha—though it looked more sassy than cocky on his sixteen-year-old face than his game persona. "I've already been making some compilation clips!"

Luther shifted his tablet to one hand so he could rub his chin. "Then I take back my previous statement. There's still no way for us to help Kit, Riko, and Prowl in the game, but if Axel has his video footage..."

Vic smirked and folded her hands together. "Okay, now you have my attention."

Everyone—Luther included—moved closer to their camera. He paused as he tried to organize his thoughts into a cohesive plan. "How about this..."

5

FAME AND FORTUNE

KIT TROTTED down the sparsely decorated hallway of the Guildhall, letting her feet carry her to what she had once considered her home away from home, the Milk Crown guildzone.

"This is going to be *amazing!*" Riko followed so closely behind her she almost stepped on the back of Kit's foot.

Prowl muffled a yawn. "Personally, I'm more interested in the bodyguards they're sending with us."

Kit tossed a glance back over her shoulder. "Which are you more excited for, Miles?" she asked her pledged.

Solus glanced briefly at the ceiling. "Both will be interesting to witness."

Prowl snorted. "All that means is you can't decide if your hero-worship of Milk Crown or the ability to drag Kit through more level grinding with a better party is more exciting."

"Prowl," Riko warned.

"What?" Prowl complained. "I think it's better we put it out in the open so Kit doesn't get fussy when Solus stops us to level."

"Hm," Pax said at the mention of leveling. (Kit didn't know whether that was a noise of discontent or of approval.)

Kit narrowed her eyes and was about to respond, but a popup screen interrupted her.

> *You have a private message from: Halbryt*
> *Accept message?*

She frowned briefly. *Why does that name sound so familiar?* She hesitantly accepted the message.

"*Kittredge?*" a male voice inquired.

Though he couldn't see her face, Kit smoothed her expression. "That's me. I assume you're one of the two secret GMs?"

"*I am. Do you have a moment? I would like to meet you and introduce you to my coworker.*"

"Can we meet in a few minutes? I'm about to enter a guild-zone in Luminos right now."

"*Sure. My coworker is in Luminos, so I would prefer to meet there anyway. You're getting ready to go recruit NPCs?*"

"Yep. Do you have any advice?"

"*Sorry, but no. The option to recruit NPCs only opens up after Malignus is defeated, so I don't know anything about it.*"

Kit sighed. "It was worth a shot." She came to a halt just in front of a huge, gold-gilded door. A crown was emblazoned on it, as were the words "Milk Crown" in a fanciful script.

"I'll message you when I'm finished in the guildzone?" she continued.

"*No need. I'll be waiting outside the Guildhall entrance. Swing by when you're done.*"

"Great, thanks!"

"*Yep.*"

Kit waited a moment to make sure they were disconnected before she switched to party chat. "One of the GMs that EC told us about just contacted me. I'm going to go talk to them after we finish in the guildzone."

"Good. That's one less thing to worry about." Though Riko was replying to Kit, her eyes were hinged on the gold door, and she rubbed her hands.

"It's about time they reached out to you," Prowl said. "What were they doing until now? Rearranging their inventory alphabetically?"

Kit placed her hand on the door, making a new screen appear before her.

Speak the Password to Enter.

She briefly turned away from the screen. "If you don't mind, Miles, we'd like to keep it on the down-low that we're in contact with the GMs. For now, anyway. They're secret GMs, and while they'll eventually come forward, I would like to wait until we have more players united so they don't get swamped with unnecessary questions and angst."

"Understood," Miles said.

"Ready to go in?" Kit asked.

"Yes!" Riko cheered.

"Why do you keep stalling?" Prowl asked suspiciously. "Have you forgotten the password again?"

"My memory isn't *that* bad." Kit cleared her throat and addressed the door and prompt, which displayed the same message: *Speak the Password to Enter.*

Kit cleared her throat. "The Password."

The door clicked and swung open.

The group was quiet for a moment.

"Seriously?" Prowl finally complained. "That's your high-level password you couldn't remember?"

"I didn't use it that often," Kit defended herself as she pushed the door farther open and entered the guildzone.

Inside, the air was warmer and thick with the scent of greenery and the loud tweets and chirps of birds.

It took Kit a few moments to let her eyes adjust to the sunlight, but she smiled when she heard Riko behind her.

"Oh my," the druid gasped.

The main room of the guildzone was a beautiful mash of elven and Imperial architecture and design. The room was three floors tall and rectangular. The far end of the room was made of three windows that nearly stretched as high as the ceiling. Each window had blue and gold glass arranged in the shape of a crown. Stairs—flanked by two white marble statues of winged warriors—led up to a small dais where two beautiful golden chairs were placed.

The ceiling almost resembled a honey comb, and multiple chandeliers hung from it, casting rainbows across the floor.

A rug of the same blue with gold edging ran the length of the room, and stone walls and tear-drop shaped arches were cut into the walls of the first floor. The second and third floors were also cut into the sides of the room, so the main room was accessible no matter which floor you stood on. The left side of the chamber led into a maze of rooms, whereas the right side overlooked a sun-bathed garden that contained trees, flowers, and a small waterfall.

Prowl whistled. "You guys must have sunk some *serious* cash into this place."

Kit smiled as she stepped farther into the room. "We had to do something with all our PVP prizes." She straightened with surprise when Pax strode past her, making a beeline for the giant winged warrior statues at the far end of the room. He gazed up at them, his wings momentarily folding tight against his back.

The pound of running feet filled the air, making Solus and Prowl grab for their weapons, but Kit merely grinned.

Two humans—a male and a female—came zipping onto the third-floor balcony. They elbowed each other—each trying to be in the front—as they raced down the stairs. They skidded to a stop just before Kit and the others, their shoulders heaving as they took in great gulps of air.

"Welcome to the guildzone for Milk Crown—ack!" the male said before the female rammed him from behind, shoving him out of the way.

"How can I help you?" The female beamed.

Kit laughed. "Hi, Fame. Hello, Fortune."

The male popped upright, joining the female. They looked so similar, they could have been twins. They tilted their heads before brightening and declaring, at the same time, "Azarel!"

They tackled Kit in a flying leap, smashing her between them.

Fame, the girl, actually started crying. "We've been waiting here *forever*, but nobody comes anymore!"

"It's been so boring and lonely—why did you abandon us?" Fortune asked, scarcely less upset than his sister.

Kit wriggled in their grasp so she could turn around and address her friends. "Guys, I'd like you to meet Fame and Fortune, our guild NPCs. They're supposed to be siblings, if you can't tell. Fame, Fortune, this is Riko, Prowl, and Solus Miles. I give them visitation rights and permission to take any item that is not bound. The celestial being admiring the statues is my pet, Pax, so he gets visitation rights, as well."

Fame held the edges of her blue, knee-length dress, making the gold embroidery on her hem flash. She curtsied, and her curled pigtails of red hair slid over her shoulders. "A pleasure to meet you."

"We hope you enjoy your stay in Milk Crown's guildzone,"

Fortune finished, bending over in a bow. He was dressed similarly—in black trousers and a blue shirt with a gold vest—and his red hair was also perfectly in place.

Together, Fame and Fortune smiled benevolently, making their oddly colored eyes twinkle. (Fame's left eye was gold while her right was blue, whereas Fortune's left eye was blue and right was gold.) A moment later, they crowded Riko and Prowl.

"What can we do for you?" Fame asked.

"Do you want new armor? I can fetch what is most appropriate for you or tell you what your ideal set would be," Fortune said.

Fame yanked him backwards by the collar of his shirt. "Forget that! I can tell you where you should level, and what monsters you should concentrate on for the best drops or exp."

"They need better armor *first* so they can go level," Fortune insisted.

"No, they need to level and get good drops so they can afford the expensive armor you always recommend!" Fame snorted.

"Fame, I need all the maps you can bring me for the mountains and dungeons around Brunascar," Kit said, interrupting the pair. "Fortune, please check and see if we have any dancer gear."

The pair saluted Kit. "Yes, Azarel!"

Fortune elbowed his sister to get in front of her on the staircase, so Fame grabbed him by the vest and yanked him backwards.

Kit squinted as she watched them race to the top floor. "I'm starting to feel really bad about leaving them here. They weren't so desperate when Milk Crown was active..."

"How did they know it was you?" Solus asked.

Kit nodded to a chalkboard nailed over the entrance, which held a list of player names and little symbols placed in front of them. "Our permissions setting. Our guildmistress and guild-master had it set so we could come here with any of our alternate characters—though Fame and Fortune only recognize me because they're advanced NPCs."

"How did you get them?" Solus asked.

"The higher rank of a guild you have, the more stuff you can get. It's why our guildzone is so big, too. You can get one guild NPC pretty early, but we ranked high enough so we could have three," Kit explained.

"But you only have the two?" Riko asked.

Kit laughed sheepishly. "Yeah... Regular guild NPCs are little more than mascots or storage holders that follow the leaders around. But you can buy skills and improvements for them."

Solus tilted his head. "Really?"

"Yeah," Prowl popped a mint leaf in his mouth and chewed with an unimpressed expression. "With real-world cash." He raised an eyebrow at Solus. "How do you not know this?"

"I've never been in a guild," Solus said.

Prowl rolled his eyes. "That explains it."

"Fame and Fortune seem unbelievably advanced," Riko said. "Most guild NPCs I've seen are far more robotic."

"Yes, all of us guildmembers ponied up and bought the most deluxe skills we could get—they were sort of our thank-you gift to our guildmasters. They can recognize me because both of them have slightly less extensive permissions than a Fibbit NPC Banker. They can access information on my entire account, but they can't make any trades." Kit motioned for the trio to follow her deeper into the guildzone. She momentarily raised her voice. "Pax, we're going to one of the armories. Since this is the guildzone, you can explore however you like; you don't have to follow us," she shouted.

Pax ignored her and turned to face the open corridor that led to the gardens.

Kit shrugged and resumed her explanation. "Both Fame and Fortune have specialties, though."

"Like what?" Riko asked.

"Fame can tell you anything you want to know about any monster in Retha. She also has every single available map—even ones we as players don't have—so combined with the monster database she has access to, she can tell you where certain monsters are more likely to be, what the chance is they will drop certain items, how long you would have to play before you would likely get a level or receive a certain drop—basically lots of useful stuff for raiding and leveling," Kit explained as they left the main chamber for a small hallway. "That's why we named her Fame. If you follow her advice, she'll make you famous."

"And Fortune?" Prowl asked.

"Ah, yeah. We jokingly called him that because if you listen to him, he'll *cost* you a fortune. He specializes in armor and weapons. He can look at the gear you have on your character and tell you the best combination for your playing style. He can also suggest armor in different price ranges that would best suit you—though he is always most excited about the expensive sets or the ones you can only get by raiding. He can even help you make custom armor sets. My guildmaster used him whenever he put armor sets together for me."

"So he's basically a walking weapon and armor database," Prowl said.

"Those must have been *expensive* skills to buy," Riko said.

"You're not kidding," Kit grumbled as she stopped outside a wooden door. "Originally we were planning to get a third sibling—another girl—and name her Knowledge. She was supposed to have the item database skillset. But after paying for

these two, none of us had the real-life cash to pay for a third."
Kit cleared her throat, then spoke in a slightly raised voice. "Fortune, we're going into the bottom armory."

"I AM COMING!" Fortune shouted with great zeal.

Kit opened the door, revealing the honey-comb-shaped room. It was lit solely by torches, but every inch of wall space in the room was covered with armor, swords, bows, quivers, maces, lances, and every weapon imaginable that glittered and reflected the light. Stacked chests were placed flush against the wall, and the black and white tiled floor was littered with standing models of horse armor sets, clawed tips for hawk talons, collars for various pets, staffs for magic-based players, and more.

"Okay, now *this* is going to be fun." Prowl adjusted his goggles as he strode up to the wall and started peering at a set of daggers.

"I'm sorry, did you say *bottom* armory?" Riko asked.

"Yeah, there's one on each floor," Kit said.

Riko reverently closed her eyes. "I love you. I love this guild. I love your guildmasters. Both of them."

"You guys can take anything that isn't already bound to another player. It will be easy to tell—you won't be able to pick it up," Kit said.

"How do we get the stuff off the walls that's higher up?" Prowl asked.

Fortune banged into the room. "I will assist with that!" He bound up to Kit and bowed. "Here, Azarel, is the list of dancer armor sets we have in stock." He passed Kit an impressively long —and detailed—list.

"Is there anything that doesn't leave a gaping hole over my belly?" Kit asked.

Fortune blinked. "No."

Kit sighed. "I don't know why I keep hoping for something logical. Thanks, Fortune. Go ahead and help Prowl.

"With pleasure!" Fortune hurried to join Prowl at the wall, pausing just long enough to grab a rolling ladder.

Kit studied the list and glanced up to smile when Solus joined her.

"Anything you can take that will be better for you?" he asked.

"A few jewelry pieces—nothing better than the anklet I got from Malignus, though. It looks like there are two full armor sets I will soon be able to use—one that will be useable at level 60, the other at level 75," Kit said.

"Take the one for level 75," Solus said.

"You aren't seriously thinking we'll be *level grinding*?" Kit asked. "I mean, yes, I figured doing a little was unavoidable, but I'm only level 50 right now. That's a twenty-five-level difference!"

Solus Miles shrugged. "We'll be going to locations you have not yet journeyed to as Kitten Lovemuch. That means we'll have to travel there by foot."

"Yes, but we'll be dragging a number of first officers with us. I can't imagine they'll really be thrilled to stop and watch me level grind," Kit said.

Solus folded his arms across his chest. "That's why we're taking lower-level players from their guilds, as well. They won't complain if their own guildmates are benefiting from the grind."

Kit pinched the bridge of her nose. "You know, if you were half as sly in leading raids as you are at sliding in opportunities to level, you would be better at it than I am and have to lead this raid against Valdis."

"Your habit of tramping into areas far above your level offends me," Solus said.

Kit brandished the armor list at him. "It's not like I have a choice."

"You do," Solus said stubbornly. "You could level."

Kit sighed as she watched Fortune dump three different armor sets on top of Prowl—who shouted in pain and offense. "Why do I even bother trying to show you reason?" she asked dryly.

Solus Miles shrugged again.

Kit shook her head, then paused. "I know I asked earlier, but are you certain about our image as pledged?"

"I promised I would do whatever it took to help you," Solus said.

"Yeah, but once this is all over, when you come back into the game—*if* you come back, because I'm willing to bet some people won't—your reputation is going to be ruined," Kit said.

Solus raised an eyebrow. "I'm far more concerned with getting us off the game safely and as swiftly as possible than I am with the wagging tongues of gossips."

Kit pressed her lips together as Fortune swiped a bracelet out of Riko's hands and replaced it with a different one. "Then thank you for your help, for being willing to speak to the guilds."

"It hasn't been settled yet," Solus warned her. "You're going to have to do something about The Killing Squad and Tainted in particular—and I don't think Corporate Force is nearly as cooperative as they would have you think."

"I'm hoping that by recruiting NPCs, I can prove myself," Kit said.

"You'll prove you're competent," Solus said. "You won't prove that you really are better than they are at leading raids."

Kit sighed. "You're probably right, but I can't help but hope it will go better than that." She glanced at her friends—Fortune was attempting to yank Prowl's goggles off his forehead, and the saboteur was resisting and kicking at the NPC.

"Riko, Prowl," Kit called. "I'm going to see if I can rustle up any cash for this character. Just shout on the party chat channel if you need me."

"Got it!" Riko said. "Oh, Fortune!" she purred. "I need your help—can you tell me which shoes would be most beneficial?"

"Certainly. If you would just *let go*, sir," Fortune grunted as he still tried to wrestle with Prowl over the goggles. "I can provide you with a much better pair of goggles."

"No way! These have sentimental value. Back off," Prowl snarled.

"Fortune, once you've finished helping Riko and Prowl, could you come find me?" Kit asked. "I want to snag one of the dancer armor sets you found, and I would like to know if we have any dancer fans."

"Certainly, Azarel!" Fortune said in a sing-song voice.

"Ouch! That was my hair you pulled," Prowl yelped as Kit and Solus slipped from the room.

"Where are we going?" Solus asked.

"To the main treasury," Kit said.

"Are there three treasuries as well?" Solus asked.

Kit laughed. "No, just this one and then a storage room. Truthfully, they're mostly just filled with valuable junk our inner hoarders wouldn't let us sell or stuff that was bound to our characters that we didn't want to use."

She led the way back to the main chamber, and together they climbed the spiral staircase before entering the maze of rooms on the second floor.

"Here we go," she said when they reached the only door in a small side-hallway. Kit opened the door, and for a brief moment the room was lit only by three flower-shaped windows at the far side. After a moment, ornate oil lanterns shaped like crowns sputtered to life.

The treasury was constructed almost entirely of white marble veined with gold streams that cut smooth lines and circles through the floor and twined around the support pillars. Shelves were built directly into the marble walls—the edge of each one sported a flourish of some sort. The shelves were covered with items—everything from gem vases to gold tiaras to a spyglass that glowed blue in the dim light. Chests were placed at every available bit of wall space that was not claimed by shelves, and there was a marble staircase that led to a platform.

For a moment, memories made Kit freeze. She could almost hear her guildmates laugh as they tried to cram more items on shelves that were already filled. She could almost see them march past her as they accused each other of hoarding or relived their most recent raid.

Instead of bringing her pain, as they once would have, the memories made Kit smile.

Solus shifted.

"I'm fine," Kit said, interpreting his silence. "Just...remembering." She strode into the room, her eyes combing the shelves for less valuable items she could sell to NPCs.

"I guess money isn't a problem for your character anymore," Solus said.

"Mmm, not quite," Kit said. "Most of this stuff sells for only a few coins to NPCs. It's players who would find it valuable. I don't have time to set up a market stall, so I'm somewhat limited on the actual funds I can get." She kicked a chest open and used a black unicorn horn to dig through the items.

Solus was silent as he gazed around the room, occasionally pausing to peer at an item on a shelf.

Kit had a nice little stack of tokens—proof that raids had been completed, and one of the few items received on raids that NPCs would actually exchange for quite a bit of money to serve as a sort of reward—when Fame zipped into the room, her arms filled with rolled-up scrolls.

"The maps you've requested, Azarel." Fame handed off the first of the scrolls, which Kit unrolled. It was a map of the lower mines of Brunascar. It took a moment of staring before the map flashed and was added to Kit's character map database. She rolled it shut and swapped it with Fame for the next one.

"Thanks, Fame."

"Is there anything else I can get you?" the NPC asked. "Any more maps? Perhaps some research into the monsters around Brunascar?" Fame looked so hopeful as she clutched the maps, it almost hurt to look at her.

"Yes, could you mark on the map where the spider nest in the lower mines is?" Kit asked.

Fame beamed as Kit's map database updated with the next map. "Of course!"

"Thanks." Kit handed the map back, glancing up when Fortune came skidding into the treasury room as well.

"I have several dancer fans around your level, Azarel," Fortune cradled a bundle of fans in various styles and colors. "There's one that will be useable in five levels that is *much* better than what you have now. I have two sets of fans you may use now—otherwise there is a dancer hammer in the upper treasury."

"I'm really only interested in fans—unless we have dancing swords?" Kit asked hopefully.

Fortune stood up straight and blinked. "There are no dancer swords inside the guildzone. Dancer swords are a rare drop. There are only fifteen mid-level dancer swords that are rare drops from various monsters, and only six sets of named swords that are unique and of the highest level. The easiest dancer sword to obtain would be the Dragon's Bane set, which are drops from dragons—"

"Vindict Dragons," Fame chimed in. "Which live in the Sky-Break Mountains. The chance of a Vindict Dragon dropping Dragon's Bane swords is .0023%."

"Okay—thanks," Kit hurriedly said before the pair could

rattle off any more depressing stats. "I'll just take the best fans we have on hand that're available for my level."

Fortune brightened. "Ah, yes! That will be this set, Azarel." He set the fans down and rummaged through the pile for a few moments before brandishing a set of white and gold fans. They were beautiful—though rather delicate with gold work and beads making the base spokes—though each spoke ended with a knife-tip that jutted out at least two inches past the fan's paper.

Kit swapped out her old set—enforced by dwarven smithy work—for the new fans and tried flicking them open and shut several times. "They're lighter and more ornate—but these knife spokes are wonderful!"

"I'm glad you approve," Fortune said. "Though there are better fans for you that cannot be found in the guildzone—"

"It's fine; thanks, Fortune. Would you see if there's anything in any of the other treasuries that would be better for Riko or Prowl?"

"Of course." Fortune glanced at Solus Miles, looking him over from head to foot. "Shall I grab a few things for Solus Miles as well?"

Solus shifted. "My equipment is better than anything here."

Fortune smiled almost gleefully. "I regret to inform you, you are incorrect. We have a great many more appropriate accessories for you. They will be underleveled, but it won't matter given the terrible accessories you are carrying now and how little they improve your stats."

Solus frowned.

"Yes, grab a few of the best options for Solus, Fortune. Thank you!" Kit hastily said.

Fortune bowed a little, then trotted off.

Solus watched him go with furrowed brows. "All my gear is top rated."

"I'm sure it is, but you forget: we ran raids weekly. We have some rare stuff that probably isn't available often these days," Kit said.

"If it's rare, then I should pay you for it," Solus said.

"No, no, no," Kit winked. "You've bought me so much, this is the least I can do to repay you. Besides! You're my pledged."

"If Solus Miles is pledged to this alternate character, would you like to give him permission to enter and use your bedroom facilities, Azarel?" Fame asked.

"NO!" Kit shouted. "No. No!" She held a finger out to Fame, then turned to Solus Miles. "I mean—sorry, um."

Solus Miles cracked a smile. "I understand. Shouldn't you continue looking for tokens? We have to meet the first officers in an hour."

Kit winced. "You're right. Sorry—Fame can show you around if you're bored."

Fame stood on her tip toes. "I can show you the strategy room," she offered.

"It's just a library," Kit said. "But it's pretty neat. You'll probably like it."

Solus nodded. "Sounds fine."

"Great!" Fame clapped her hands. "This way, please. We must go to the top level of the guildzone," she explained as she led Solus from the room.

Kit shook her head slightly as she returned to digging through the chests. *I never thought an NPC would be just as unhappy about the guild disbanding as I was.*

6

RP AND GOSSIP

"LOOKING GOOD, YOU GUYS," Kit called out to Prowl and Riko as they joined her and Solus in the main chamber. Fortune followed proudly behind the pair, smiling as he pointed to Prowl's new goggles—which were rimmed with gold and glowed a little.

Riko wore a new jewelry set and shoes, while Prowl looked like he had been stripped of just about everything except for his new shirt and boots.

"I can confidently say between the drops we got from Malignus and all the new stuff Fortune found for me, I don't think I've ever been this well geared," Riko said.

Prowl sulkily adjusted his goggles. "I guess."

"Is everyone ready to set out?" Kit asked.

Solus nodded and rested his hand on the hilt of his sword. Past him, waiting at the door, Pax shifted his wings and looked at Kit as if she were a bug.

"Yep, let's go!" Riko said.

"Wait, you're leaving?" Fame asked, her eyes wide.

Kit winced. "Yes, sorry, you two. We'll try to be back soon."

"Take us with you!" Fortune begged.

Kit smiled sadly. "I wish I could, but only the top officers of Milk Crown have permission to take you from the guildzone."

"But you *do* have permission!" Fame zipped over to the chalkboard by the entrance and tapped it.

Kit joined her after a moment, blinking when gazing at the chalkboard brought up a popup screen.

Like the chalkboard, it listed the names of the players in the guild, as well as their guild rank. Kit furrowed her brow in surprise when she saw that every player in Milk Crown who was not already an officer had been promoted to the level of "Junior Officer," a position whose permissions included removing NPCs from the guildzone.

"When did that happen?" Kit asked.

"The Guildmaster and Guildmistress were the last to enter the guildzone," Fortune said. "Before they left, they switched all permissions."

Fame clasped her hands behind her back and stared at her feet. "And then no one came back for many, many years."

Kit played with a lock of her pink hair. *Did they make the change in case any of us came back and wanted to play again?* She shook her head to clear her thoughts and smiled. "Okay. Then Fame, Fortune, as a Junior Officer of Milk Crown, I authorize you to leave the guildzone and travel with us...though I would appreciate it if you call me by my alternate's first name."

"Yes, Kitten!" the NPCs chorused.

Prowl rolled his eyes. "Great, so the know-it-all Bobsy twins are gonna tag along. *Now* can we go?"

Kit nodded. "Yes—we should hurry, or we'll be late to meet the rest of our party."

"And we only have one chance to make a first impression, so let's go!" Riko opened the door and stepped into the hallway of the Guildhall.

Kit and the others followed her—though Fame and Fortune

tried to squirm through the doorway at the same time and ended up nearly tripping each other. "We're supposed to meet everyone out front."

"Yes, ma'am." Riko winked playful and turned in a circle. "Then we need to go this way!" She strode down the hallway with great confidence.

"I'm not sure I believe you," Prowl said as he skulked along behind her.

"Whatever," Riko said. "I'm not the one that got owned by an NPC."

Prowl squawked in outrage, and Solus frowned thoughtfully as he watched Fame and Fortune fall in line behind the pair. "What will happen to them when we're in combat?"

"Fame and Fortune? Nothing. The monsters don't register them as being targets, and they can't do anything to help us— even if we die," Kit said, perhaps a little bitterly. (She had more than one memory of Fortune lecturing her about her armor as she faded off into oblivion.)

Solus nodded. "Even so, they still seem like they'll be useful to have around."

"Oh, yeah," Kit agreed. "Fame's especially useful to take when you're venturing into new areas. Don't tell Fortune I said that, though. He's a bit sensitive about it." She winked at Solus, who raised a black eyebrow at her.

Kit shrugged and glanced at the NPC siblings. They were intently staring at Pax, who narrowed his eyes at them. "What?" he snapped.

Fortune looked crestfallen. "Your armor can't be upgraded. That's a shame. You'll never get stronger than you already are."

"*Excuse me?*" Pax growled, but he had already lost Fortune's attention as the NPC trotted ahead.

Fame, however, squinted up at him. "You're not a monster,

either. Just a pet. Boring!" she declared in a sing-song voice before chasing after her brother.

Pax glared at the siblings with murder in his eyes as Riko led them out of the Guildhall.

The sky was still gloomy, and Kit could see rainclouds on the horizon as she scanned the gardens around the Guildhall, searching for her future party.

"Lady Kit, over here!" Alistair waved, a sincere smile brightening her face. Behind her were the first officers of the five guilds that had agreed to work with Kit, and a mixture of lower players. At her side was Gared and a human male Kit didn't know.

"Hey there, Kit," Gared greeted. He had his arm thrown over his friend. "This is Noir—he's a priest with the legendary class of holy oracle. That's the top healing class in the game. He's going to accompany you and serve as your personal healer on this journey."

Noir had to be good at his job—either that or his guild was extremely wealthy. He wore a cream and gold robe that had long, elaborate sleeves that nearly trailed on the ground and revealed a white undershirt that came to his wrists. A red sash with gold tassels was tied around his waist, and a gold hood covered his head, though his dark purple—nearly a shade of midnight—hair peeked out beneath it.

Ironically, though he wore clothes to fit his role, his attitude and expressions were quite opposed to the usual serene healers. Although his skin was a healthy copper color, he had dark bags under his eyes, a flat expression, and narrowed, moon-yellow eyes. And at his feet, sitting on its butt, was a fuzzy—and rather portly—raccoon.

Interesting pet choice. It's usually thieves who get racoon pets, not priests. Kit pushed the odd match from her mind and smiled. "It's a pleasure to meet you, Noir. Hopefully you won't have to do much during our trip."

Noir eyed Kit and leaned into his staff—which was taller than him and topped with a star. "Yeah, we'll see about that. And its Noir Nohealz4U," he said, adding his unfriendly last name.

Well, I'm Lovemuch, so I can't really point fingers. "Great," Kit said, keeping her smile in place.

Gared—his arm still thrown over Noir's shoulders—rocked the holy oracle a little. "Don't worry about him. When battle comes, he'll heal—and if you're half as good as I think you are at tactics, you two should get along fine."

"You owe me *big* for this," Noir growled.

"What, don't you want to get off the game?" Gared asked.

"Doesn't matter," Noir said. "You still owe me."

"Stop griping, Noir. This is going to be fun!" Alastair laughed as she slapped the priest on the back, knocking the air from him.

Riko tapped the tip of her staff on the ground. "Are we taking *everyone* here with us?" she asked.

"What?" Alistair glanced over her shoulder at the gaggle of players and laughed again. "Goodness, no. It's just that Corporate Force, Killing Squad, and Tainted sent more players than necessary so Solus Miles can pick and choose a party as he wishes."

Solus glanced down at Kit. "Do you care whom we take?"

Kit was momentarily distracted when she got another popup message.

You have a private message from: Halbryt
Accept message?

"Um, I want a solid party, like the one I outlined back in our meeting with the guildmasters... Riko can help you. I have to take this private message. Riko—make sure he doesn't take a bunch of DPS to level grind, would you?" Kit asked as she flicked yes.

"You got it! Come on, lover-boy. Let's go make your pledged proud." Riko waded into the loud crowd of players—that only grew louder when Solus Miles joined her.

"Fame, Fortune, stay with Prowl, please," Kit said before twisting her attention back to Gared, Alistair, and Noir. "I'm sorry; I'll be one moment."

Gared waved her off, so Kit scuttled away with Pax on her heels. "Hello, Halbryt," she said when she stood alone next to a bush. "I just got outside. Can you tell me where you are?"

"Just keep walking south, towards the market," Halbryt instructed.

Kit trotted along, blinking when she saw a vaguely familiar beast tamer who sat on top of a black cat. She snapped her fingers. "I *knew* I recognized your name. You're the flirty pirate's friend!"

Halbryt stroked his cat. "Yes."

"Does your guild know you're a GM?" Kit asked.

"No. Joining the guild is part of my cover story," Halbryt said. "Each of us enforcer-type GMs are plugged into a different community. I keep an eye on the smaller guilds."

They exchanged handshakes.

"I wish I could say I'm happy to meet you, but these circumstances aren't quite what I wished," Kit said.

Halbryt shrugged. "Have you explained the situation to the top guilds?"

"Yes. I'm getting cooperation from five of them, for now. I'm hoping to branch out, but first I want to recruit some NPCs while the guilds start to spread the word."

"You won't start to gather players to your cause?"

"I'm hoping that by using the big guilds to do the legwork, I'll be able to collect everyone faster than doing it personally," Kit said. *Besides...at this point, I don't know what I would DO with the players I managed to unite. I can't even comprehend prepping to fight Lord Valdis, yet.*

"Fair enough," Halbryt said. "I'll help as much as I can by spreading word among the smaller guilds, but really you need Shashanna's help."

"Shashanna?" Kit asked. "Is he—or she—the second GM in the game?"

"She. And yes. If possible, I'd like to introduce you to her now." Halbryt glanced back at Kit's friends and future party members.

"I could probably swing that," Kit said. "You're positive we need to keep your identities a secret still?"

"Those are my orders from EC."

"Bryce said as much, too, when we were talking about this, but I was hoping for an easier way out." Kit scrunched her eyes shut and scratched her forehead. "It's fine, though. Everyone else will hopefully be busy getting ready—and I *really* want to get this horrible tattoo off my face. I can say I'm visiting the barber to get it removed. One second, and we can be on our way."

Halbryt nodded.

Kit trotted back to the group, Pax on her heels, and switched to party chat. "Hey guys, I'm heading out with one of the secret GMs to meet the other one. I'm saying I need to get my tattoo removed—can you cover for me?"

"Sure," Prowl said.

"You got it," Riko chimed in.

Solus Miles didn't say anything, but Kit didn't expect him to.

She made sure she slapped a smile on her face as she trotted up to Gared, Alistair, Noir, and Nyxiane—the Corporate Force first officer who had joined the trio in her absence. "Hey guys, since Solus and Riko are taking care of the final party selection, I'm going to run off and get this tattoo removed. Okay?"

Nyxiane nodded. "That is an excellent idea—and will likely go far to improve your overall image and increase the respect you receive from others."

Gared eyed the first officer. "No need to be so blunt about it, Nyx." He switched his gaze to Kit. "Give KOS a shout if you run into any trouble."

"I could come with you if you like, Lady Kit," Alistair offered.

"No, it's fine! I'll have Pax with me," Kit said.

Pax sniffed. "You think *I* would step in to aid *you?*"

Kit kept her smile in place as she kicked backwards, nailing the winged warrior in the knee. Pax only scoffed.

"Right, then. We're going. Send me a PM if you need me!" Kit glided away before anyone could stop her, but she celebrated her exit a little too soon, as there was an additional set of footsteps trailing her.

Kit glanced back and was shocked to see Noir—his eyebrows and mouth flattened in displeasure—following her. "Um...?" she started.

"I'm coming with you," Noir said.

"There's no need to," Kit said. "I'm just going to the barber's."

"And I need to avoid Nyxiane," Noir said. "So I'm coming with you."

Kit glanced at his nameplate and saw that, like Solus Miles, he was not part of a guild. "Ahh, she's been trying to recruit you?"

"No," Noir said. "She's a stats junkie and keeps pressing me to let her run some tests on me to see what the top healing number I can get is and with which buffs." He scowled as he adjusted his hood.

Shoot. I don't think I'll be able to give him the shake-off. Well, at worst I'll just have to talk to the GMs through private messages. Kit shrugged her shoulders. "I think I understand. But I hope you don't mind, we're going to take a brief fieldtrip," Kit said as they joined Halbryt.

"Where?"

"My friend, Halbryt, is taking me to meet some more... potential allies," Kit said, thinking fast.

Halbryt nodded. "RPers."

Noir raised an eyebrow. "Really?"

Kit blinked. "Shashanna is an RPer?" she asked. "That is...unexpected."

Halbryt shrugged. "Like I said, we're responsible for different areas."

Noir shrugged. "They can't be worse than noobie players who follow me around to ask for heals and buffs. Let's go."

Halbryt patted his giant cat, then led the way south. They wound through the market, past the shopping district, and up to a somewhat shady-looking two-story building.

A wooden sign that hung at a tilted angle declared "The Broken Drum Tavern—it can't be beat!" Even standing on the street, Kit could pick out the scents of burnt meat, cheap ale, and the raucous shouts of the tavern's customers.

As if on cue, a door flew open, and two players tumbled out, exchanging punches.

"Charming," Noir said.

"When we go in, everyone will be acting in character," Halbryt warned. "They won't openly talk about the game—or being stuck on here."

"Wait, you're serious?" Noir asked.

Halbryt nodded. "They take RPing seriously."

"But now, even while the game is splintering before us?" Noir shook his head.

"Yep," Halbryt said.

"Got it." Kit glanced back at her pet. "Are you sure you don't want to retreat to your center for this one, Pax?"

Pax snorted derisively. "I do not *retreat*."

"Suit yourself," she said. "Lead on, Halbryt."

Halbryt opened the door and strode in.

The tavern was like many of the hundreds scattered throughout Retha. There was a bald, red-faced barkeeper, several barmaids who served food and drink and put anyone stupid enough to try to touch them in a headlock, rows of dilapidated benches and tables, and a floor that was liberally coated with a year's worth of crumbs, dried ale, and other questionable substances.

A few NPCs were seated at the bar, but the biggest group of customers were a bunch of players who sat in a ring of tables at the back of the tavern.

Scanning them over, Kit could see they were all a part of the same guild: Defenders of Talith. It was a mixed group, both in ethnicity and levels. Interestingly, the majority of the players were over level 100, but no matter the level, all of them were tricked out in fancy—and eye-catching—armor.

"There's Shashanna." Halbryt pointed to a female dryad—a level 91 Alchemist—who sat near the center of the ring.

He had to be talking with his fellow GM somehow, as almost immediately Shashanna looked up from her lounging position and grinned. "Halbryt—you rascal. What brings you to these parts?"

Halbryt wound his way through the maze of tables. "Hello, Shashanna. Just thought I'd drop in."

"The young beast tamer has returned," declared a female night elf who was dressed in boots plated with gold, gold gauntlets, and a rakish hat that had a giant feather stuck at a jaunty angle into its brim—a duelist if there ever was one. "Welcome back. Sit and have a pint or two—you must have a new story to share of the adventures you've been on?"

Halbryt shrugged. "I've been here and there, just exploring bits of Retha," he said.

"And what of your companions?" a werewolf boomed. His ears flicked as he studied Noir and Kit. "A priest and...if my eyes don't deceive me, an elf dancer?" He gave Kit a disapproving glare. "Odd company. I never knew an elf who could swallow their pride to dance so openly."

Ahhh, yes. Of course RPers would disapprove of me because elf dancers break the world lore. Fabulous. I'll just have to unleash the greatest weapon in my arsenal—even if it will make him prissy. "I, unlike the rest of my kinsmen, cannot resist the call of music and song." Kit tossed her hair over her shoulder. "Though you might scoff, it has won me the recognition of a celestial being—a *winged warrior*—who has vowed to be my companion."

She stepped to the side so Pax was more visible. He glowed in his silver and white armor in the shadows of the tavern and was too busy scowling at the sticky floor to have noticed Kit's boast.

The RPers fell silent as they noted the pet's presence. Most of them stared in surprise at the pet, and a few actually leaned across their tables, squinting to get a better look.

Please don't let Pax open his insolent mouth and choose to insult me right now—pllleeaasssee don't let him notice our conversation at all! Kit internally prayed.

She was extremely relieved when the duelist whistled and renewed the conversation. "I don't think I've ever seen a winged warrior walk with any adventurer before. Well done, miss...?"

Kitten struck a dancer's pose with her hand over her heart and one foot artfully balanced behind her. "Kitten Lovemuch."

The duelist grimaced slightly, and Kit could see distaste spread through the RPers again, so she quickly added. "My name is a curse I must bear. But one day I hope to be free of it."

Pax ruffled his wings and said under his breath, "Doubtful."

"Can it, Paco," Kit hissed.

"*Paco?*" Pax made offended noises at the back of his throat.

"Please," Kit said, ignoring her pet, "I insist you call me Kit."

"Then, Kit, welcome to our fellowship," the duelist said, spreading her arms wide. "I am Nùrthel, the leader of this little band."

"Thank you for your kind welcome," Kit said.

"And who is this?" Shashanna asked, motioning to Noir.

"Noir," Noir said flatly. His expression dared them to ask for his last name.

"Welcome, Noir. Was Ice-Paw correct? Are you one of the blessed and divine healers?" Nùrthel asked.

Noir eyed her. "For a price you can't afford."

Kit winced. "Do you really think *they* of all people will harass you for help?" She whispered.

"It's been my experience that everyone will harass me if they think they can wear me down," Noir said.

A mage sat back in his chair and brushed food from his expensive silk robe that was decorated with elven script which seemed to move across the cloth. "A priest and a dancer—that's a strange combination with which to explore Retha."

"We just met here in Luminos," Halbryt said smoothly. "Some dark circumstances have forced us to throw our lot together on behalf of Retha."

Oh, he's good, Kit admired as some of the RPers perked up.

A dwarf dressed in green and gold armor rested his hand on the giant royal axe he propped against the table. "On behalf of

Retha? Pah. You're chasing the impossible, lad. Folk can't work together."

"We believe they can," Halbryt said.

A few of the RPers rolled their eyes and whispered to each other.

"Indeed," Kit said. "We believe they have no other choice."

Shashanna cocked an eyebrow. "Then what, pray tell, are these dark circumstances?"

"Lord Valdis," Kit declared, making sure to pose with Pax at her back to look extra striking.

The tavern fell silent.

"Lord Valdis can't be beaten," Nùrthel said.

"Says who?" Kit asked.

The werewolf—who was decked out in all black armor that made no noise even when he stood—growled. "Our ancestors. Even with the power of the Solis Empire at its zenith, and with the weight of the dwarves, fae, *and* elves thrown in, they were unable to kill him."

"It was said Malignus could not be defeated either, and yet he has been slain," Kit said.

A gnome sat up straight, throwing back her heavily embroidered hood so she could get a better look at Kit. "That's where I heard her name! Guys, she led the raid that—!" She turned red and abruptly cut off. "I apologize for my outburst," she muttered.

I don't think she meant to say that, but I'm going to use this to my advantage! "It is true. I led the heroes who defeated Malignus." Kit smiled proudly. "And with your help, I think I can do it again."

Half of the RPers stood, all speaking at once in a rush of noise that made Kit reflexively clamp her hands over her tapered ears.

Most of them spoke to Nùrthel—or were trying to—but

Shashanna caught Kit's eyes and winked, then flashed her a subtle thumbs-up.

"Laying it on a little thick, aren't you?" Noir grunted—Kit wouldn't have heard him if she didn't have her elf hearing.

"If it gets them to stand behind us, sure. Though the big guilds might think they're unnecessary, I'm not convinced," Kit said.

Noir eyed them. "You sure about that? I don't understand how they can sit here and RP while the world burns around them. It seems weird."

"Maybe so," Halbryt said, joining their whispered conversation. "But they're the games' biggest gossips, and they know just about *everything* that happens here. The information they'll be able to provide is worth the effort."

"Yeees," Kit said carefully. *Getting them to spread the word and tattle back to me will help, but even more than that...they couldn't have gotten that fancy of armor at a market. Stuff that fanciful can be gotten only as raid drops. And if they're good enough players that they can get that kind of armor in an age where raids are a lot smaller, they might lend us more firepower than people think. I won't be able to know for sure, though, until I let Fortune get a look at them.*

"Great job, Kit," Halbryt said, interrupting her thoughts. "Nùrthel is going to give you an invite to a private chat channel. Accept—and you can talk frankly with them there. But don't lose track of the RP conversation," Halbryt said.

"A private chat channel?" Kit asked. Private chat channels were alternate—nonverbal—chat channels players could be invited to. They let players communicate en masse outside of guilds, raids, and parties

Halbryt shrugged. "They like to role-play, but they have to communicate normally somehow."

"Kit—leader of those who slew Malignus," Nùrthel announced. "It seems we have much to discuss.

As Halbryt warned her, a popup screen appeared.

You have been invited to the private chat channel: RP Forever 2.
Accept invitation?

Kit tapped the yes button, then adjusted her settings so she could open up the chat channel by looking at the image of a little logbook that appeared by her health bar. Instantly, a large popup window appeared, filling with words faster than Kit could read.

Ice-Paw: I heard Brave Heart Company's Saint George walked out on her when she met with the top guilds.

Nùrthel: That surprises you? Lol!

Ai'lan'therristos: Yeah, Georgie can be such a stick in the mud, particularly when no one is cooing over him.

Ai'lan'therristos: Observational Fiends said no to helping as well—but I heard it was more that Teara can't handle anymore right now than that she didn't believe her.

Lillith: Omgosh I can't believe she got a winged warrior pet. Totally jealous~!

Ai'lan'therristos: It gets better—she's Solus Miles' pledged! I was starting to think the guy was a monk in-game and out of game, but I guess he's got a thing for pink-haired elves?

Ice-Paw: Or maybe he values her tactical genius?

Lillith: No, he's a guy. It has to be that she's a pink-haired elf. Glad to hear she doesn't willingly look like that—her character is such an eyesore.

It took Kit a couple of moments to adjust to the conversation, and when she finally realized what they were talking about, her jaw dropped. "How can they possibly know all of this?" she muttered.

"I told you: they're the game's biggest gossipers," Halbryt whispered.

Shashanna: Hi, Kit, welcome to the chat channel! Drop in whenever you have a question—or any great info to share.

The chat log suddenly filled with text as all the RPers welcomed Kit to the channel. Kit looked from the popup screen to the RPers—who were still chatting amongst themselves as they continued to role-play. It took several long moments for Kit to realize they used the text-to-speech function and hid their mouths whenever they chimed in on the chat channel.

Maybe I was wrong, Kit wondered. *Perhaps their information alone really will make them incredibly valuable.*

"Come, Kit. Please let me buy you a drink," Shashanna said as she grabbed Kit by the elbow and pulled her away. "Do you want anything, Halbryt? Sullen priest?"

Noir narrowed his eyes at the female gnome smiling charmingly at him. "No," he said.

Shashanna didn't wait for Halbryt to answer and led Kit to the NPC-populated part of the tavern. "That was pulled off well, Kittredge," she said. "I thought I would have to walk you through it, but you did great."

Kit shrugged. "After being cross-examined by medium and large guilds, this wasn't so bad."

Shashanna laughed. "Probably. I did want to talk to you a bit—EC has asked for a status report. I've heard you've got five of the major guilds following you, and the White Veil Nunnery has already given you their alliance?"

Kit nodded. "Yep. I'm thinking of targeting White Needles Dwarves in Brunascar next. I know Brasil—the dwarf king—and I'd like a few easy wins to start."

"You're letting the guilds spread the word about your mission?" Shashanna asked.

Kit stifled the desire to cringe. *These GMs are ruthless!* "Yes.

I would rather get NPCs behind my name to help back me up and let the big guilds use their own reputation to draw in the first wave of players."

Shashanna nodded. "Not a bad plan—that will give you time to decide how to organize the raid. I'll send a report back."

"Thanks," Kit said.

Shashanna nodded. "It seems like you've got enough muscle behind you, but if you need more help, Halbryt can recruit his guild. I'm afraid I won't be much help there. We RPers specialize in information, so we'll throw ourselves into getting rumors out about you. Could you check in whenever you get a major win? We can make sure the whole world knows."

"Sure," Kit said. "If you learn anything you think might be useful, will you let me know?"

"Absolutely," Shashanna said. "Don't be afraid to use Halbryt as your errand boy, by the way. I've been sending him across the map to see for himself how the players are lasting."

So that explains why he and the flirty pirate seemed to pop up everywhere.

"There's been a marked uptick in tension. It started before you beat Malignus, but it's gotten stronger since you logged off," Shashanna added.

"That's just grand," Kit said dryly.

Shashanna shrugged. "It could be worse. I'm hoping if we can get your name out—and proof that you're getting ready—fast enough, it will keep things from escalating. But I'll keep you read into the situation. Speaking of which, you said you're heading to Brunascar next, right?"

"Yes. I'm meeting up with my party after I run to the barber's to get my tattoo removed."

"Good. There's a pack of brimstone chimera that a small guild summoned with a Cuckoo Toadstool out by the White Needles Mountains. They've been slaughtering nearly all the lower-level players who have been trying to get to Brunascar. Since you have Solus Miles and Noir in your pocket, I'd suggest you take them down. It will be a good PR chance."

Kit slowly nodded. "Okay...Thanks for the info. I'll take a look at my party and see if we can swing it." Kit said.

Shashanna winked. "Of course. Now, what do you want to drink? You have to order something, or our RP won't appear legit."

7

PARTY POLITICS

"I DON'T GET IT. Why are we doing this?" Long Claw—the first officer of the blood-thirsty Killing Squad—grumbled as the party hid behind an outcropping of rocks that was nestled precariously into the mountainside.

"If we wipe out the chimeras, it will build respect with the lower-level players," Kit said as she watched a few brimstone chimera sniff around the rocks—their snake-headed tail hissing.

The chimera's lion bodies were thick with muscle, and their coats were an ashy black color—though the snake scales that made up its tail were edged with red. Even from this distance, she could smell the strong sulfur odor they shed.

"But what do we care about lower-level players?" Long Claw frowned as he scratched his head.

"Just because they're lower level doesn't mean they don't deserve help," Waffle—The Silver Army's first officer—frowned.

"Spoken like a true bleedin' heart," Long Claw grunted.

"If we can gain the respect of players—no matter their level —it means we're a step closer to gaining the respect of the server," Kit said. "While we might be focusing on getting NPCs to stand with us, eventually we'll have to move on to the players.

If we can build a positive image before then, we'll find it easier to get players to join us."

"Not a bad plan," Nyxiane—or Nyx as she asked to be called—said.

"Are we going to attack the chimera, or what?" Noir impatiently asked. He sat with his back against the outcrop, his racoon pet—Trash Panda—plopped in his lap, gripping his fingers with its little clawed paws.

Fame and Fortune—who trailed after Kit with Pax—watched the racoon pet with interest. They appeared to only half listen to the conversation as Kit had already told them to stop rattling on about the chimeras' potential drops and the superior armor party members might receive for fighting them.

"That's the plan," Kit said, "but brimstone chimera usually travel in huge packs. So far, we've only seen a dozen. I'd like to know where all the others are."

Solus shrugged. "Even if more show up, it won't be a problem. They're only level 60."

"And half of the party are between level 50 and level 58, as per your request," Kit pointed out.

Solus tilted his head back. "So they'll have the chance to gain exp. I'll tank—and I can easily outlast a pack of chimera."

"You're a DPS character—not a tank," Kit pointed out.

Solus shrugged. "With my superior armor and legendary class, it doesn't matter."

"Actually," Fortune said as he tore his gaze from the portly raccoon, "your armor isn't *that* superior."

"What can you tell me about brimstone chimera, Fame?" Kit asked, quickly intervening.

"They don't have high attack power, but they can attack from the head or hindquarters due to the snake-headed tail," Fame rattled off. "Combine that with their great numbers, and they can reduce an adventurer's health quickly. They possess no

Area of Effect attacks or magic-based attacks. They only have physical attacks, and they're highly susceptible to physical or magic damage."

"Okay," Kit glanced back over the party—besides the first officers, there was a handful of DPS classes—both physical and magical based—and a few support type classes. *No tanks, of course.* "Here's what we're going to do."

"Arrr-yah!" Long Claw shouted as he raced to the two chimera Kit could see from her vantage point. As a level 115 warrior, he easily cleaved through both of them, making the chimera roar before they faded away.

Long Claw turned around. "All your worrying was for nothing." He didn't have time to flick one of his triangular wolf ears before four chimeras jumped him—three of them biting down on his arms, and the last one raking its claws across his back.

"I think he might have the worst of Axel combined with the worst of Luther in him," Riko said thoughtfully.

"Hey, that's mean to both Axel and Luther," Prowl snorted.

Chimera flooded the rocky valley in a blanket of black. There had to be at least 150 of them—and each one foamed at the mouth and ground rock beneath the claws of their paws.

"If he does this the whole time we're partied, I'm going to set Solus on him." Kit sneezed at the now suffocating odor, then shouted over Long Claw's howls. "Wizards, mages, anyone with magic attacks: hang back behind the rocks and stay on the mountain side. DPS, move forward but stay back-to-back—if you wade into the pack on your own, they'll eat you alive!" Kit turned to Solus, who unsheathed his sword but hadn't yet left. "Can you use your AoE attacks? You'll take out more much faster."

Solus cocked his head. "It will rob those in your level range of exp."

"I don't care. I'm looking to finish this as quickly as possible."

Solus shrugged. "I suppose they aren't ideal monsters to use for level grinding."

Before Kit could lecture him, he was gone (tapping his incredibly useful lifeskill that let him make huge jumps) and landing near Long Claw.

Kit watched for a moment as Prowl, Reynard of Tainted—the royal assassin—a swordsman, and a scout joined Solus and Long Claw. She flicked her fans open, then jumped over her rock shield. "Come on, Noir. We're getting closer," she called to the priest.

"What?" Noir grumbled.

"We have to get closer," Kit repeated.

"*Why?*" Noir demanded.

"So I can use Battlefield March. Fame, Fortune, stay here by the rocks."

"Yes, Kitten!" the NPC siblings chorused.

Kit offered them a wan smile, then began picking her way down the mountainside. "Pax, please try not to gather too much aggro," she pleaded with her callus pet as she hopped over a head-sized rock.

Though Pax descended the mountain with her, he pointedly gazed over her head at the valley below.

"A support character who insists on being as close to harm as possible? You are a healer's worst nightmare," Noir grumbled as he skidded after her, his raccoon hanging from his arm.

At the base of the mountain, Kit stepped into her Battlefield March skill, twirling and leaping with more grace than she had in real life. Kit nodded in satisfaction when she saw the buff appear under the DPS players' name—and was happy to see her range was strong enough that Riko and a few of the other magic users got it as well.

Alistair—mounted on her cavalry horse—plowed into the chimera, twirling a spear overhead as her horse ran the monsters through with the horn affixed to its plated face armor.

"Waffle, Riko, focus on the chimera that are at least two rows past our DPS line," Kit called over the party chat. "If you attack too close to them, you'll just double-kill the monsters, and I'd rather not waste our efforts."

"Whom would you like me to weave together?" Nyx asked. As a specialized support class—a spirit weaver—Nyx could tie multiple players together so they could share skills. It worked best if the players had the same class, but tying similar classes together worked nicely as well.

Kit glanced over the party, trying to think. *Reynard, Solus, and Alistair are all level cap and performing at the top of their skills—plus their classes are all a little too different to get much of a bonus. DPS is already getting a bonus from my battlefield march, so...* "weave the magic classes together, Nyx. Use your best judgement on who it should be," Kit said, then shouted. "Long Claw, fall back! You're getting too far away from the party!"

The warrior werewolf plowed his way deeper into the swarm of chimera, laughing as he wildly swung his jagged saber.

"Idiot," Noir snorted as he clasped his hands together. They glowed gold before he pointed to the werewolf, healing him.

"Siren's Storm!" Riko shouted, unleashing her powerful AoE skill over the chimera pack as Waffle—a summoner—set a griffin loose. The winged creature took out a cluster of chimera with a piercing hawk's cry. Just past them, a mystic used a skill to clobber two chimera together, and a spellbinder wove two spells together to trap a chimera to the ground and then set it on fire.

Kit glanced at the party health bars, her heart leaping into her throat when she noticed that Prowl, the swordsman, and scout—who all stood on the front lines—were down to one-third their health bar.

Panicked, she searched for and spotted them on the battle-field, fighting to keep the chimera from completely over-whelming them.

Kit swallowed as she calculated a fast plan. "We've got trouble. Prowl, Arild Edge, and Hide_N_Seek are getting pummeled! Solus, Alistair, work on opposite sides of the valley—with you two stopping the flood, we can slowly funnel the chimera to the lower-level DPS players. Reynard—you're with Solus."

"Moving to follow orders." Alistair's voice was serene and held a bit of a chuckle in it, even as she speared a chimera in the throat and drove her horse across the valley.

"Solus doesn't need help," Reynard said—his voice barely audible over the roars of the chimera.

"Alistair has her horse—which is almost as good as another player. She'll be able to crowd-control better than Solus can by himself," Kit said, then glanced at Long Claw—who was still wandering around in the middle of the chimera. "Long Claw, get back here!"

The warrior werewolf either didn't hear her or didn't care.

Kit sighed as she twirled prettily, making Pax swerve to avoid colliding with her.

"Do we need to review what you learned with Luther?" Prowl drawled over the party chat channel.

"Luther wasn't a problem once he learned to respect me," Kit said.

Prowl stopped a chimera in its tracks with a fistful of pepper grit and a well-aimed dagger. "Then teach him why it's in his best interests to listen."

Kit exhaled sharply through clenched teeth. "Noir, stop healing Long Claw."

Noir swung around to face her, his expression unreadable. "Really?"

"Yes."

A smirk crawled across his face. "With pleasure." He turned his gold-laced heals to the lower-level DPS players.

Kit let herself relax for a moment and just danced. The funnel was working—even with Long Claw wandering off like an idiot. The chimera pride was starting to thin, and they were no longer able to rush Prowl and the lower-level players. Better yet, Riko with Siren's Storm, Waffle with his magically summoned creatures, and the rest of the magic users were able to kill off the first layer of chimera before they even reached the blockade of Solus, Reynard, and Alistair.

Fame picked her way down the mountainside, smiling brightly when she reached Kit.

"What is it, Fame?" Kit asked, knowing the NPC wouldn't disobey an order and come down the mountain just to gawk.

"Though it is giving you a sizeable amount of trouble, this is a small chimera pride," Fame announced.

"No one asked you, Fame!" Prowl shouted as he threw three traps down in a row to halt the oncoming tide of chimera.

"How much smaller than normal is it, Fame?" Kit asked.

It is approximately two-thirds the size of an average pride," Fame said.

"She's an NPC, so I'll never have to heal her, even if players attack her out of rage, right?" Noir asked.

"Correct—but Fortune's way worse." Kit posed artfully on the tip of one foot as she stretched the other up behind her in a back bend. Her tapered ears twitched as she heard several rocks skitter down the mountainside. As she flicked her fans open and shut and twisted, she craned her neck to glance up the mountain.

Chimera crept soundlessly across the sides of the mountain,

stalking towards the party's magic users—who were oblivious of the danger.

"Great gaping goats!" she uttered.

Congratulations! Your life skill, "swear proficiently," has risen to level four!

Kit pushed the notification away with an impatient flick of one of her fans. "Magic users, behind you! Solus—help them! Reynard, stay where you are."

With a few careful jumps, Solus reached the first line of chimera before they could pounce on Waffle and Riko—who stood side-by-side.

"I need a heal!" Long Claw shouted.

"Too bad. You're not getting one!" Kit snapped. "Waffle, Riko—all magic DPS start to fall back down the mountain, towards me. We can't let the chimera divide us."

Kit—still dancing—tried to split her attention between the two fronts. Noir was able to keep the DPS alive—but when a chimera pounced on Nyx, it made Riko's and Waffle's spirit weave buckle just as they were in the middle of striking together, about to unleash Siren's Storm on a sea monster and a clot of chimera.

Nyx, Riko, and Waffle slowly trekked backwards, but the spellbinder and mystic tarried.

"Glowrious, Lumina Myst, get out of there!" Kit shouted after glancing at their names. "You're going to get your hides handed to you!"

The spellbinder finally ran, but the mystic jutted her lower lip out and stayed where she was.

A chimera skirted Solus by climbing higher before skidding down the mountain, landing almost on top of the mystic.

Kit pointed to the mystic. "Riko!"

"On it. Nature's Bindings!" Riko ensnared the chimera and hauled it off the mystic.

"Griffin incoming," Waffle said cheerfully.

"Lumina Myst, get down here, or next time we'll let you die," Kit said.

The mystic scowled at her, but she hurried down the mountainside after she boosted herself to her feet.

Kit glanced at her pet, hoping he might be moved into a rare act of aid, but her winged warrior pet was too busy hovering in the sky and looking regal to acknowledge their struggle.

Why yes, she thought dryly as she kept dancing. *I'm so glad I have an ultra-rare and powerful pet. He's been such a boon to this character.*

Riko and Waffle reached Kit, joining her as Solus still tangled with the second flood of chimera.

The only good thing about this is the chimera can't move very easily on this kind of incline, so they aren't able to rush us like the ones in the valley.

Kit kept at Battlefield March, breathing a little easier when the valley chimera slowed to a trickle. She ignored the glare Long Claw sent her as he chugged a health potion. "Alistair, do you need Reynard, or can I send him to back up Solus?" Kit asked.

"Unless these cats are hiding more somewhere nearby, I think me and Trust can handle this," Alistair said.

"Send Alistair," Long Claw growled. "I can hold them myself—*without* heals."

"You seem to forget that Alistair is a cavalry knight. She's most powerful with her horse—which cannot climb mountains like a goat," Kit said tightly.

Nyx laughed. "A set-down given with obvious information. I applaud it."

"Me, too," Riko grinned as she held another chimera captive

with Nature's Bindings. "I can't *wait* to see what Solus does with him after this is over."

Kit spun, then again peered between the two fronts. There were less than two dozen chimera in the valley, maybe even as few as a dozen. The chimera on the mountain, however, were strewn unevenly across the rock and still numbered in at least forty. "All DPS except Prowl, switch your attention to the chimera on the mountain. Prowl—stay behind and use traps to keep the remaining chimera from jumping Alistair."

"Sure," Prowl threw a trap so it hit a chimera in the face, making it roar loudly in anger.

Kit switched from Battlefield March to Serenade of Magic, increasing the magic attack power of the party.

"Here we go," Riko whooped. "This is going to be fun—let's go, Waffle! Loading Siren's Storm—bring on the sea monster!"

Reynard slipped from shadow to shadow, dropping chimera with one swipe of his bladed gauntlets. The scout followed him—marking a path for the swordsman to more easily follow.

With their physical attacks combined with the increased magic attack power, the mountain chimera—moving slower, making them easier targets—were easy to thin.

"Siren's Storm!" Riko shouted.

They were almost clear when Alistair's horse neighed loudly.

"Kit, look out!" Prowl shouted.

Kit dropped out of Serenade of Magic so she could turn, spinning just in time to see the chimera as it sprang at her. It slammed her into the unforgiving rocky ground with a clawed paw to her chest.

Kit could see her health drop, and it felt as though her lungs would collapse under the monster's weight. It lowered its lion head towards her face, and a glob of foam dripped from its teeth and landed on her cheek with a wet splat.

Thankfully, her arms were free. So Kit cringed as she raised one arm above her head, and pointed at the chimera with the other. "Triumphant Echo," she wheezed.

Golden bubbles popped around her, before a matching shimmer appeared over the chimera. A moment passed before the monster's limbs moved so it held one paw out. That was when Kit saw the fatal flaw in her plan.

"Murderous muffins," she said when the chimera—forced by the skill—lifted his other front paw to try and copy her, leaving him without any way to bear the weight of his front end. It landed on top of her, crushing her beneath its massive weight and smothering her face into its matted mane.

The five seconds of Triumphant Echo ticked past quickly, and soon Kit could feel the chimera's jaw press into the top of her skull as it snapped its mouth open.

"This might end badly—ack!" Kit coughed when she inhaled its mane.

The chimera picked its head off her just enough so it could target her throat. This close, its hot, sulfuric breath was overpowering, and Kit couldn't breathe.

"Beloved's Guard!"

As the chimera lunged for her, a black mass hit it, throwing it off with such force that it smashed into a rocky outcrop and faded, its health entirely sapped.

Kit gasped for air as the tingling sensation of a strong heal flooded her. "Thanks, Solus, Noir."

"Have you become overly fond of Triumphant Echo since you brought Malignus down with it?" Solus asked as he offered her a hand.

"No, it was an impulse attempt to keep myself alive." Kit gave him her hand and yelped when he pulled her up with such strength she smacked into his chest.

As she peeled herself off, Noir frowned sharply at her. "I had you," he said. "You weren't going to die."

"I should have remembered that, but old habits die hard, and I've been offed so much as this character it's almost a knee-jerk reaction now." Kit rubbed her chest, nodding in thanks to Noir as he cast another heal that made the skin of her chest—sliced when the Chimera first tackled her—mend.

"Using Triumphant Echo was not a bad idea," Nyx said. "It was just poorly executed."

"Right," Kit coughed.

"It is rather unexpected, however, that your pet did not step in," Nyx continued.

"That's not expected at all," Kit laughed. "We have a very independent relationship, meaning Pax doesn't help me if I want him to, or even if I don't want him to. Isn't that right, my dearest Pax?" Kit called up to her pet—who was still hovering above her head.

"It's a shame you didn't die," Pax said.

Kit considered throwing his egg at him but decided that would be a tad childish—and she'd probably miss anyway. So instead, she looked up at the mountain (where Reynard sliced through the last pocket of chimera) before directing her gaze down the valley.

"I apologize, Lady Kit. That was my fault," Alistair apologized as the silky black tip of her ponytail fluttered in the breeze. She and Prowl had vanquished nearly all the remaining brimstone chimera—Long Claw was still fighting a few—so she dismounted her horse and patted its shoulder. "I thought I could kill it before it reached you, but my throw went wide when a chimera unexpectedly smashed into Trust."

"No worries," Kit said. "I survived, after all."

Prowl threw down a trap, freezing a chimera that escaped Long Claw. He darted towards the monster, ending it with a stab to its chest. "Yeah, this is probably a record for you. You've gone how long now without being killed, maimed, or cursed?"

Kit grinned and was about to reply when Long Claw released a brutish roar that made her ears ring.

Steeling herself for the worst, she swung her gaze to the werewolf.

Trash Panda, Noir's racoon pet, held the werewolf's tail in his black paws and bit the end of it.

As Long Claw howled in pain, Trash Panda yanked his head back, ripping a tuft of fur from the end of the werewolf's tail.

Long Claw tried to kick the racoon, but Trash Panda was too fast. He zipped across the field with surprising agility given his girth as Long Claw took out his aggression on a chimera.

"I think I'm starting to see why you chose a racoon as a pet, instead of something more typical for a healer—like a phoenix," Kit said.

Noir patted his racoon on the head when it waddled up to him, then held out his hand so Trash Panda could deposit the tuff of fur on his palm.

"Well done," he told his pet. "That *is* a prize worth stealing."

Trash Panda chattered happily and plopped down on his rear.

"You crazy nutjob!" Long Claw bellowed across the battle-field as he stabbed a chimera. "Control your rabid rat!"

"I *was* controlling him," Noir said. "Why else do you think he would do that?"

Long Claw growled and killed the last chimera, but Kit ignored him and scanned the battlefield. "We're all alive; the pride has been taken care of; players will now be able to reach Brunascar...all in all, I'd call this a successful mission."

She cracked a smile when she spotted Fame and Fortune

loudly reproaching the stubborn mystic for her armor and lack of maps.

"It wasn't too bad of a fight considering it was our first one," Solus said.

"I survived only because I drank a potion. Our healer didn't heal!" Long Claw complained as he joined them.

"You disobeyed orders and ran off into the middle of the pride when I specifically said to come back," Kit said. "If you decide to do your own thing, you aren't going to get the benefit that comes with being a part of the party that *is* working together. That goes for *everyone*," Kit said, turning to face the mystic who had resisted retreating.

Lumina Myst glanced past Kit to Solus Miles and blushed bright red, then immediately lowered her gaze.

"I know my limits better than you do," Long Claw growled.

Prowl adjusted his goggles. "Sure you do—that's why you almost died out there."

"Is everyone ready to head out?" Kit asked. When everyone nodded, she led the way down into the valley. "Then let's call our mounts and move on to Brunascar."

"Yeah, let's recruit some dwarves!" Riko shouted.

"They have good food in Brunascar," Waffle said.

"I guess—if you like meat smothered in gravy." Reynard's upper lip curled slightly as he sheathed the blades on his gauntlet.

"They also have great meat on a stick," Waffle said.

"And some good candy," Kit added.

"Candy?" Nyx asked.

"Didn't the recipe to your rock crystal candies come from the dwarves of Brunascar?" Solus asked.

"Yeah, and I'm hopeful they'll have a new recipe for me to try. The last one I got was kind of...disappointing."

"I'm aware. I was there."

"Play nice, and I'll make some for you."

"I'll pass."

"Come on," Kit grinned as she reached the bottom of the mountain—or at least a stretch where the incline was flat enough she could summon Chester, her pony. "I need *someone* to play guinea pig."

"That's not part of being pledged," Solus said dryly before he summoned a large black horse that was decked out in fancy tack and barding.

"Now *I'm* curious. What recipe did you get, Kit?" Riko asked.

"Holy Hard Candy."

Prowl laughed. "Are you serious?"

"Deadly."

"I was thinking your character seemed almost cool with that gaudy face tattoo erased, but go figure, the curse of Kitten Love-much strikes again," Prowl laughed and elbowed Reynard. "Am I right?"

"That character definitely is a curse," Reynard agreed.

"Yes, I get it! Can everyone summon their mounts? I'd like to get to Brunascar before dark," Kit said, whistling for Chester.

"Lead on, maker of holy hard candy," Prowl said.

"Hey, Fortune," Kit called as the NPC summoned a nondescript horse. "Prowl says he wants to hear in detail about the shortcomings of his armor and what new pieces he should get to improve."

"Okay, *that* was uncalled for," Prowl said.

"Oh, Prowl, I am so glad you asked!" Fortune beamed widely and completely ignored the saboteur's protests. "Let us begin with your pauldrons..."

8

EVENT IN BRUNASCAR

"FAME, how many minutes until we arrive in Brunascar?" Riko asked.

"The City of Brunascar—home of the White Needles dwarves—is a ten-minute walk if we continue at this pace," Fame reported.

"Good." Long Claw kicked a rock, which rolled down the rocky tunnel. "We've been walking forever."

Besides the roar of the occasional underground waterfall, the tunnel was fairly quiet. But as they marched towards the city, Kit could have sworn she heard the occasional dwarvish war cry and clang of weapons. She tilted her head and strained her ears. "Waffle, as a dryad, do you have better hearing?"

The summoner nodded. "A little better than humans."

"Do you hear anything?" Kit asked. "Like...shouts?"

Waffle stared up at the ceiling, which twinkled with unmined gems and ores, then shook his head. "No—but as an elf, your senses are no doubt superior to mine."

"What do you hear?" Solus asked.

"It sounds like a fight...but I must be wrong. Brunascar is a fortress—there's never any fighting near it." Kit snuck a peek at Pax to see if he seemed concerned.

Though the winged warrior practically glowed in the dark with his dazzling armor and sparkling wings and hair, he didn't seem particularly unrestful as he trailed behind her.

Long Claw snorted. "Can't make sense of your own character's senses, but you think you can boss us around?"

"Can *you* hear or smell anything?" Reynard asked as he flexed his hands, making the knives on his gauntlets pop free.

Long Claw scoffed, but his triangular ears twitched and rotated as he listened. "The space is too enclosed," he finally said.

"Brunascar should be visible shortly," Nyx said. "This tunnel will spit us out onto a rocky ledge. We can see it from there."

Kit had to stare down the tunnel for a moment so her eyes could adjust—having Pax so close on her heels kept throwing off her night vision. "I see it. I'm going to run ahead and look."

"I'm not following you," Noir warned her. "I don't run."

"It's fine. There shouldn't be any monsters in the tunnel anyway." Kit smiled, then trotted ahead. She wasn't too surprised when Solus Miles jogged after her, easily settling into the pace she kept.

"Does anything feel off to you?" she asked.

Solus shrugged. "We've run into an unusually low number of monsters while traveling into the city."

"You know, my guild could have saved loads of money on tricking out Fame if you had played with us," Kit joked. Her laugh trailed off as they neared the end of the tunnel, and she could no longer pretend her ears were playing tricks on her. The sickening crunch of metal puncturing flesh and the shouts of the dwarves were too loud to mistake.

She sprinted the last few steps and almost skidded straight

off the side of the ledge at the end of the tunnel. "Fudging fishcakes..."

Brunascar was a regal city, built straight out of the innards of the mountain and bearing the intricate geometric design of the dwarves...and it was overrun by spiders.

Arachnids—ranging in size from that of a small dog to a pony—crawled along the city walls and scurried in the streets, which were draped with webbing.

Usually, Brunascar was quietly lit by glittering crystals, but as she stared down, Kit could see the pinpricks of torches as the dwarves charged around their city, brandishing their weapons as they collided with the swarm of spiders.

"Guys," Kit said into the party chat. "Hurry up. Brunascar is under attack."

"That's impossible!" Long Claw snapped.

"Who's invading?" Nyx asked.

"Spiders," Solus said.

"Of course it would be spiders," Prowl growled.

Riko sighed. "It's a shame Vic won't be here to fight with us. Her rage seemed to increase the power of her fireball."

"I don't get it, what's going on?" the order-ignoring Lumina Myst asked. "Nothing like this has happened before!"

"Better get used to it," Noir said dryly. "Malignus is dead. We're playing in a new age of Retha now."

The fighters of the group—Reynard, Long Claw, Prowl, Alistair, and more—arrived first, but a glance down the hall proved Riko, Noir, and everyone else weren't far behind.

Kit scratched her nose, trying to block out the putrid scent of smashed spider innards. "Solus, do you think we could survive skidding down the side of this cliff?"

"Probably," Solus said. "Those who didn't would respawn inside the city."

"That's too reckless," Nyx panted as she finally arrived.

"Why?" Kit asked as Pax peered over the side of the ledge. "We might lose a bit of experience, but it's nothing worth crying over."

"We can't throw ourselves into the city without a plan," Nyx said.

"Though I appreciate the thought, Nyx, Kit's right. We need to get down there immediately." Alistair peered over the edge of the steeply inclined cliff. She glanced behind her to wink at Kit. "As always, I am yours to order, Lady Kit."

Kit gripped the base of her fans and flicked them open and shut. "Then let's go." She stepped around Pax to join Alistair at the side of the ledge, took a breath, then stepped over the edge and skidded down the incline.

"God bless America!" she screamed as she went whizzing down the incline. She leaned back and landed on her butt—which frankly felt like it was on fire as she slid across rock, but it was better than going face first. (Even with her elf grace, Kit was not willing to risk that extremely painful possibility.)

Next to her, Alistair hooted—going down the incline with one leg crouched beneath her and the other extended out in front.

When the incline briefly curved up, Kit was thrown into the air and collided with a stalagmite.

"That hurt," she grumbled as she peeled herself from the wet, stony surface. Secured for the moment, she twisted around to look back up the ledge.

The rest of the party reluctantly followed her down the incline—though they did it with markedly more finesse.

Waffle summoned his griffin—which carried both him and Riko down to the base. Prowl, Reynard, and a couple of the lower-level players went down, riding shields like metal sleds. Fame and Fortune fared the best, using an actual *toboggan* Kit vaguely remembered Milk Crown receiving as part of a winter festival.

The mystic teleported, and Nyx came down riding on Long Claw's back as he ran on all fours and jumped down like some kind of demented mountain goat, laughing wildly.

I'm glad someone is enjoying themselves.

Kit winced as she adjusted herself—she had badly bruised her butt and had taken a fair chunk out of her health bar—but waved to Noir as he rode past, sitting astride a log he had probably removed from his inventory.

"I guess I should have thought more before jumping over the side," Kit sighed.

"Yes," Solus Miles agreed as he landed from one of his impossibly high leaps directly behind her. "You are regretfully impulsive considering how intelligent you are." Wedging his feet against the huge stalagmite, he scooped her up.

Kit yipped when he leaped into the air, easily clearing the remaining bit of the steep incline. "Seriously? It could have been this painless? Why didn't you offer sooner?"

"You threw yourself over the side before I had a chance," Solus said wryly.

They landed with a swift jolt.

Solus carefully tipped her out of his arms, and she ran a hand over her smooth hair—as perfect as always.

"Thank you, Miles," she said.

Solus slightly inclined his head, acknowledging her thanks.

Kit waited for Pax to fall in behind her before addressing the party.

"Until we get a better handle on this, I want us to stay together," she said. "Let's move in a tight, diamond formation. Magic DPS in the center, fighters and tanks on the perimeter. Alistair, I want you leading us with Solus taking up the back."

"My pleasure, Lady Kit!" Alistair winked, then summoned

Trust with a special horn. A whirl of golden light burst into existence next to the knight, then burned away to reveal the cavalry horse.

Alistair vaulted on her horse's back and twirled her spear. "Let's go!"

The group slowly took the shape Kit requested—though Pax flew above them rather than join Kit on the ground.

"Fame, what can you tell me about these spiders?" Kit asked.

Fame intently stared at Brunascar as they crept towards it and watched spiders launch themselves at hollering dwarves—who cut the over-sized monsters to bits. "They are cave arachnids and range from level thirteen to twenty-five. The most susceptible parts of their bodies are the front of their heads—where their eyes are—and their abdomens. They are most weak against piercing weapons and fire or light."

"Level twenty-five? This will be a cakewalk," Long Claw snorted.

"Maybe, but I still want us in a group for now. Look sharp—and watch above. They might try to jump down on us," Kit called out as they approached the city walls.

Brunascar's entrance was covered with webs that smoldered and turned into sticky puddles when lit with fire.

"Into battle we ride!" Alistair shouted as she charged forward on her massive horse.

Long Claw howled, and his eyes gleamed with bloodlust as he unsheathed his saber. "The Chief is gonna be mad he missed this!" He declared as he jumped on the back of a spider and stabbed it.

"Nature's Bindings!" The vines of Riko's magic curled around a spider, holding it secure until Prowl finished it off with a flick of a dagger.

"Burn, Igneous!" Waffle shouted as he summoned a fire

goat. The creature snorted and stomped a leg, then charged straight into a clutch of spiders.

Kit—standing in the center of the diamond formation—felt a bit like a prairie dog sticking its head out of its hole as she scanned the fighting dwarves.

I don't see any I know. Maybe I should have Riko try to get their attention? Wait—there! Kit cupped her hands around her mouth to make her louder when she saw a familiar dwarf shouting as he whirled hand axes around him like a murderous whirlwind. "Drust!" she shouted.

The dwarf hacked through another spider, then squinted, his eyes barely visible beneath his bushy eyebrows. "Kitten Lovemuch—the not-a-true-elf—that you?"

"Yes!" Kit directed the party to fall in line with Drust and his fellow dwarves. (Long Claw, of course, did not follow. He was scaling a wall, slicing through spider egg sacs.)

"Welcome back to Brunascar." Drust threw a hand axe and hit a smaller spider. The monster fell over with a twitch and disappeared. "I trust ye had a pleasant journey?"

"What's going on?" Kit asked.

"This small skirmish?" Drust asked. "'Tis nothing!"

The mystic screamed when a giant spider launched itself off a wall and sprang at the group. Unfortunately for it, it nearly fell directly on top of Pax. The winged warrior thrust his sword up and went from glowing prettily to blazing like a star.

The spider shrieked as it collided with Pax and burned to ash in his blaze.

"I'm not great with words," Prowl shouted above a dwarf war cry. "But I'm pretty sure this constitutes as something more than 'nothing.'"

Drust nonchalantly waggled his axe. "It's merely a bunch of wee spiders—you can hack right through them! They're not nearly as pesky as rock dragons."

Fame nodded knowingly. "This is true."

"But what happened? Why did the spiders suddenly go on a rampage?" Since they had stopped running through the city, Kit took the moment to launch herself into Battlefield March. It was difficult to perform the dance in the confined spaces of their diamond formation, but the buff was worth it. "I know they live in the lower tunnels and will eat any who venture into their nest, but I've never heard of them attacking Brunascar before!"

"It's only the work of that wretched Lord Valdis," Drust said offhandedly as he slammed one of his axes into the head of an oncoming spider.

Kit blinked. "I beg your pardon?"

"It's as Noir said before," Solus Miles effortlessly sliced through two spiders with one swipe of his sword. "Retha isn't the same since you've slain Malignus. It has moved on to a new era."

"Yep, that about sums it up—my admiration and respect on offing that dusty necromancer, by the by," Drust agreed. "Since you've done that, all sorts of monsters and crawlies are popping up across the land, spurred on by the power of Lord Valdis. Here in Brunascar, we get spiders. Mind you, your fussy kinsmen in Fione Forest? As far as I hear, they've got nothing plaguing them. Bunch of prancing pansies," he grumbled.

"Have you been fighting these spiders since Lord Valdis returned?" Kit asked.

"Nope. They come in waves—you just happened to arrive in time to enjoy this battle. But it's a great way to practice fighting, eh?" Drust's beaming grin was barely visible through the braids of his beard.

Long Claw jumped off a city wall and landed on top of a spider, smashing it. "As if Kitten Lovemuch ever fought a day in all of her existence."

Prowl threw down a trap to stop a spider that was making a beeline for Noir. "Just like you and thinking, huh?"

"Where is King Brasil?" Kit asked.

"What?" Drust shouted. "I can't hear you."

One of his fellow dwarves—bearing a sword bigger than he was—came jousting down the street in a minecart, sending spiders fleeing the area. "By the hammers of luck!" the dwarf shouted as he whizzed past.

Kit stopped dancing so she could crouch slightly and shout directly into Drust's ear. "Where is King Brasil?"

"Gone hunting, of course." Drust squinted at her as if she were crazed.

"Hunting *what*?" Kit asked.

Drust stepped back to let the fiery goat Waffle had summoned again charge ahead. "The spider queen. He's trying to find their main nest so he can kill her and put an end to this."

"By *himself*?" Nyx asked, her eyebrows forming a sharp V of displeasure.

"Yep!" Drust said cheerfully.

"Reynard, incoming above," Kit called to the royal assassin seconds before a spider popped out of a building window and sprang towards the group.

Reynard pulled a dagger from his belt and flicked it at the spider, nailing it in the eyes. When it landed, he lunged underneath it, raising one of his dagger-covered gauntlets to slice its abdomen, instantly killing it.

"Thank you!" Kit called out to him before she returned her attention to Drust. "Can you tell me which direction he went?"

"He took the western tunnels, but you won't be able to follow him on foot," the dwarf warned her.

"I see. Thank you." She nodded her head in respect—a gesture Drust returned before he, much like Long Claw, hefted his axes over his head and chased after a dog-sized spider.

"So, leader, what's the plan?" Riko asked.

Kit opened and closed her fans as she tried to organize her thoughts. "We're going to divide up into teams."

"Good call. Smaller teams would be able to move more quickly and could push the spiders from Brunascar faster than if we travel as one party." Nyx's skin took on a blue glow as she used her spirit weaver powers to bind attacks by the mystic and the scout.

Kit opened up the party panel and converted their group into a raid so she could organize the party into small groups. "Waffle is going to lead The Exterminators. Nyx will lead The Bug Killers, and I'll lead the Queen Squashers."

"Being a glory hog, aren't you?" Long Claw snarled before he bit a spider's abdomen.

Kit shivered in revulsion at the sight, but added, "No, it's because I'm the one with a healer."

"He could leave you," the swordsman, Alrid Edge, scratched his ear.

"No, *he* couldn't," Noir snarled. "I'm guarding Pinkie because Gared asked me to. The rest of you could rot with Valdis for all I care."

"Gared will be glad to hear you view him so loyally." Alistair wheeled her horse around so it crushed an egg sac that was starting to hatch. "Though I feel obligated to let you know I'm his favorite."

"I wouldn't be so sure about that, Alistair," Riko said before she pointed to the mystic. "Nature's Blessing!"

"Yeah," Prowl chimed in. "I'm pretty sure he only puts up with your swashbuckling antics because he can use your pretty face for marketing and PR purposes."

Kit finished divvying out the top players of the party—sending Long Claw and Alistair to go with Waffle, and Reynard to back up Nyx—then split up everyone under the level of 60.

In the end, her party was made up of Riko, Prowl, Noir, and Solus. *We might be a bit overpowered since we have Solus and Noir, but I want this taken care of as quickly as possible. We're going to speed through this.*

"Terminators, I want you to trace over the southern half of the city," Kit said. "That area has more flat pathways and open spaces, so Alistair and Waffle should be able to do more damage. Bug Killers, take the northern area—and be sure to go *all the way* north. There are some tunnels up there where the spiders might try to hide. Flush them out," Kit said.

"All right, Terminators, let's go!" Alistair whistled, and her horse reared. "Party leader, would you like to ride with me?" she asked with a dazzling smile.

"No," Waffle said. "Definitely not."

"Bug Killers, this way." Nyx gestured for her team to follow her as she started to walk north. "Reynard, I want you to scout ahead..."

Soon, Kit stood alone with her party.

"Where to, Kit?" Riko asked.

"West," Kit said, "to the tunnels Brasil took."

Solus nodded and led the way, his cloak flaring behind him.

"Drust mentioned we can't go by foot," Prowl said. "What do you reckon that means?"

"Probably that we need a mine cart," Riko said.

"Maybe..." Kit glanced back at Fame and Fortune, who trailed her. "Do you know why some tunnels would be considered impossible to pass by foot, Fame?"

Fame gloatingly elbowed her brother, then hurried ahead to walk at Kit's side. "It's impossible to say why without knowing which tunnel," she happily reported. "Some can only be entered with a dwarf guide; others require the use of a boat, as they pass through an underground lake, and others require alternative traveling methods."

"So you'll be able to tell when we get there?" Kit asked.

"Yes, Kitten."

"Great, thanks. How are we doing, Solus?" Kit called up to the royal knight.

"Honor's Judgement!" Solus shouted. Ahead of them, a sword the size of a school bus popped out of the ground, sending no less than eight spiders flying and killing them all.

"This is going to be easy," Prowl said.

"Stay on your guard," Kit warned. "You never know when someone might pop out of the shadows to curse you."

"That only happens to you," Prowl said.

"If anyone is cursed, I can easily dispel it," Noir said.

Kit stopped walking. "Really? *Any* curse? I thought there were some that are too powerful for players to remove."

Noir raised a purple eyebrow. "Not for me."

Kit clasped her hands together and pressed her fists to her chin. "Truly?"

"I'm a divine oracle. There's not a curse in the game I can't remove—though I can't help you if being in a specific location gets you cursed, as it will immediately recast," Noir said.

"I don't care; just removing it is plenty." Kit closed her eyes. "Thank you, Gared. Thank you, thank you, thank you for finding me a divine oracle. Noir, I am so glad you exist."

"Better watch out, Solus," Riko called after the quiet knight. "Noir might steal Kit from you at this rate. He can heal her *and* take off her curses—the two things she prizes most in this world."

"I'm not worried." Solus flicked his eyes back and forth across their crumbling path as they followed it out of Brunascar and across a couple ravines.

Riko grabbed the hem of her new robe before she stepped across a crack in their rock path. "Why not?"

Solus glanced back at her. "Because, as you say, I have more money," he said before facing forward and pointing his sword at an incoming swarm of spiders. "Honor's Judgement!"

Riko laughed. "This is fantastic news, Kit. It looks like your pledged might be developing a sense of humor!"

"Yeah, except I don't care about money." Kit purposely refused to look down as they passed over a bottomless ravine and kept her eyes on the glowing tunnels that weren't too far away.

"I don't get it," Noir frowned. "Aren't you two supposed to be deeply in love or something?"

"Um," Kit stammered. "Uh. Love is a *complex* thing."

"We would be more in love if she would actually level," Solus said.

"Hey!" Kit barked, ripping her eyes from the tunnel and fixing them on Solus' back. "That's it. I'm no longer accepting your complaints about leveling. I've got a pet angel; no one is shooting me on sight—I think I'm doing pretty well for myself!"

"She's right," Fortune piped in. "Rather than levels, she really should focus on her armor instead."

"Fortune, do *not* start!" Kit warned him with a pointed finger.

Fortune gave Kit a dimpled, unafraid grin. "Yes, Kitten."

"We're here, finally!" Riko cheered when they reached the western wall...where six different tunnels split off. "But which one do we take?"

"Hmm, that's a tough call," Prowl said. "Why don't we just *take the one that has all the spider bodies in it*?" He pointed to a dim tunnel that was littered with smaller spider carcasses.

"Retha can be heavy handed in its directions," Noir said.

Kit approached the tunnel. "Hey, Pax, you want to play flashlight and float ahead in there and light it up for me?"

"I do not know what a flashlight is, but I am not a tool for your convenience." Pax landed so he could fold one of his two sets of wings against his back and cross his arms across his chest.

"No, I suppose that's true," Kit said. "You're really my *pet*—which means you're supposed to be a recipient of all my love. Wanna hug?"

Pax scrunched his face up at the thought and held a hand out in front of him, shooting a globe of light down the hallway.

"Soda-sipping grannies," Kit said. *I didn't think that would actually work!* She crouched as she watched the light race down the hallway, flooding it with light and revealing the occasional spider body. "Yep, I'm pretty sure this is it. That floor looks awfully rocky, though."

The ground was uneven and covered with pebbles, rocks, and the occasional boulder or stalagmite. Trying to walk it would be slow going—even for Solus.

It's not impossible, but the tricky thing is the timing. Drust said the spiders attack in waves—will they retreat if we don't reach King Brasil in time? Kit tapped her fan on her thigh as she thought. She suspected the spider event was directly tied to their chances of convincing Brasil to stand with them against Lord Valdis. If they didn't help him this time, would they have to wait around for the next wave of spiders?

Prowl knelt next to her. "Yeah, there's no way we can walk this. The old hag would fall flat on her face."

"What did you call me, pervert?" Riko growled.

"Pervert?" Prowl squawked. "What happened to juvenile delinquent?"

"That was before Cookie. Now, *what* did you say about my age?" Riko dragged Prowl into a standing position by yanking on his ear.

Fame joined Kit at the tunnel opening. "Ah, yes. This tunnel requires riding a mountain sheep to pass."

Kit glanced up at the NPC and smiled. "Of course, the

mountain sheep! I had almost managed to suppress them from my memory, but I guess it's for the best. Is there still a stable just north of here?"

"Yes," Fame said.

"Hmm, can't say I'm thrilled to ride one again, but it will be a lot faster than forging ahead ourselves." Kit popped to her feet and turned to the rest of the party. "Have any of you guys ridden mountain sheep before?"

"I have," Solus Miles said. He and Kit shared a grimace.

"It's the fastest method to get to King Brasil," Kit said.

"I know," Solus said.

Kit started to shuffle in the direction of the stable. "It's the best plan."

"It is," Solus said grimly.

"Why do you two sound like you're trying to convince your-selves?" Prowl asked.

"It's reasonable, given what the animals are like," Riko said.

"You've ridden one, too?" Kit asked.

Riko nodded. "For a quest I vowed to never repeat no matter how many secondary characters I made."

"It can't be that big of a deal," Noir said. "I've heard of them —and even seen some before."

"We'll have to wait and see, I guess. Come on, let's go get some mountain sheep." Kit started towards the stable in earnest, shaking her head with a thin smile when she heard a sheep baa.

"Mountain sheep? Not a goat?" Prowl asked.

"Yeah, goats are too smart of animals to want to live in the mountains. The livestock that best adjusted to life in here are a particular breed of oversized mountain sheep," Kit explained. "They're the only animals stupid enough to live underground and eat moss—though the dwarves do keep other animals in their mountain pastures."

"Or maybe it's because a mountain goat would be too

cliché as a mount, and while EC embraces many traditions of fantasy, it loves to be a special snowflake in other ways," Noir grumbled.

"These sheep must be huge," Prowl said. "And why haven't I seen any before? A sheep sounds like something a druid would want as a mount."

"They're dwarf animals that you can only ride around Brunascar while you're here. Not that many would *want* to do that," Kit said.

"Players cannot own one. You cannot collect a mount medallion for one," Solus added.

Kit raised an eyebrow at the royal knight. "Do I sense a completionist in you that made you *try* to get one of those stupid beasts?"

Solus shrugged.

Kit shook her head as they ambled up to the stable—a homey, wooden structure with a straw roof that looked as though an animal had tried sampling it numerous times. "When this is all over, Miles, I think you need to have your priorities reevaluated."

Solus smirked slightly and stepped into the stable.

Sheep the size of Kit's pony startled and baaed at their entrance. They were so covered in fur, they almost looked like stuffed animals. Their fur was snowy white, and their black faces and ears were so fuzzy, you couldn't see their eyes. Even their cloven hooves were covered with black hair.

"Aww, I forgot how cute they are," Riko cooed.

"I think it's a defense mechanism," Kit said as she slipped over the wooden fence that contained the sheep in the stable. "They're so cute, it makes you feel bad for wanting to wring their necks. Okay, we'll let the sheep out one-by-one—the last thing we want is a stampede. They have little rope loops around their necks. Grab your sheep by the rope loop—it will follow you easily enough. Do *not* mount them! We'll lead them right up to the tunnel we want to take and get on there."

"Fine. Hit me with my sheep of terror." Prowl stood in front of the swinging gate and wriggled his fingers.

Kit escorted a sheep to the gate—which Solus opened.

The fuzzy animal trotted into the stable—its hooves tapping the ground—and baaed in Prowl's face, gently butting him with its balloon-shaped head when the saboteur dug his hands into its coat to grab the rope.

A breeze brushed the back of Kit's neck as the raid chat activated.

"Reynard, where did you go?" Nyx asked.

"I'm taking care of a spider swarm in an armor shop," the royal assassin said.

"That's four blocks away," Nyx said, her voice stiff with disapproval.

"You're level 108. The spiders only get as high as 25," Reynard said. "You'll be fine."

Kit switched to the chat channel as she pushed another sheep to the gate for Riko. "Reynard, stick with Nyx."

"There's no need to," Reynard argued. "She can kill anything in this zone with ease."

"Are you just ignorant in character classes, or are you so driven to prove your angst-filled superiority you say stupid things?" Nyx demanded.

"*What* did you say?" Reynard snarled.

Kit finished herding a pair of sheep for Fame and Fortune, then flicked her pink hair from her face. "Renard, Nyx is a spirit weaver—she's a support character. She can't fight very much on her own; she needs other players present so she can bind their attacks and stats. You're the only other high-leveled character in her party, so you've just cut her attack power greatly," she explained as she selected another sheep. It butted her in the stomach, making her hack. "Get back to your party," she wheezed.

"I know what her class does! You're just worrying over nothing—her level is too high for the spiders to do much damage to her," Reynard said.

Kit passed off the sheep to Noir, who led the prancing beast outside. "Reynard, spiders are swarming Brunascar. We have no idea what this event entails. None of us have ever experienced it before, and we don't know what will happen if we fail to help the dwarves exterminate the spiders. It's not worth it to risk all of that just for the sake of killing the spiders a bit faster. Get back to your party."

Reynard sighed in annoyance.

Interpreting the sigh as reluctant agreement, Kit switched out of the chat channel as she dragged a sheep to the door for Solus.

"Do you want me to find Reynard?" Solus asked as he took the sheep. "I wouldn't mind the temporary player-killer label."

Kit laughed. "That is tempting. *Really* tempting. But it's not worth getting upset over. I just assumed players from the top guilds would understand how crucial teamwork was. I didn't think..."

"They would let pride and petty politics get in the way of their survival?" Solus asked, watching as Kit selected a sheep for herself. "No one can accuse humans of being smart and good natured in their drive for survival."

"Yeah, my bigger concern is that they need to learn this before we fight Valdis." Kit grunted as she led her chosen sheep to the gate. "If the guilds all act out of synch and do whatever *they* think is best, we won't stand a chance against him."

Solus maneuvered his pony-sized sheep so he could open the gate for Kit—firmly shutting it behind her before any of the other creatures could escape. "You need to be firmer."

"I need a lot of things," Kit said grimly. "Shall we go?"

Solus motioned for her to leave the stable first.

Kit walked back to the tunnel—her sheep marching at her side. She glanced up at Pax—who had dimmed his glow back to the level of a firefly instead of a star. "You think you'll be able to keep up with the sheep?"

Pax scowled down at her and let himself sink and eventually land. "Something as banal as *livestock* cannot outpace me."

"I wouldn't be so sure of that, Paco," Kit said cheerfully. "In fact, the one bright spot in this will likely be that you'll be taken down a peg."

"My name is *not* Paco—and as limited as your cranial capacity is, I am certain you are aware of this!" Pax snarled.

"You're right, but you seem to be more of an ornery and verbally abusive parrot than something as beautiful and helpful as a winged warrior. So Paco the Parrot suits you way more," Kit said.

"I hope a spider bites you," Pax said.

"Your mercy and compassion astound me, as usual." Kit winked, then addressed the rest of the party when she caught up with them at the mouth of their tunnel. "Everyone ready to go?"

Prowl pulled his goggles down over his eyes. "Sure."

"Then lead your sheep right up to the entrance—*don't* get on until you are practically standing in the tunnel. Then...hold on for dear life." Kit's sheep turned to nuzzle Solus Miles' sheep, nearly yanking her over in the process. "Hopefully they'll stop when we find King Brasil. Any questions?"

Riko shook her head. "Lead the way, Kit!"

Kit scrunched her nose slightly. "I have to lead?"

"Yeah. If you go in, the glow-worm will follow you so we'll actually be able to see," Prowl said, nodding at Pax.

Air leaked out of Kit in a squeaking sigh. "Right, right. That makes sense. Okay." Kit reluctantly led her sheep to the tunnel. It baaed cutely as it walked behind her. She led it all the way into the tunnel so the others could crowd in behind her, waiting for her to mount up.

Kit ignored her sheep as it chewed its cud almost directly in her ear and instead stared into the dim light of the tunnel. *Prowl had a point—it would be creepy to gallop through this place without Pax lighting it up.* She shook her head. *No more distractions—I've got to keep focused. If the queen spider gets away from Brasil before we arrive, this might all be in vain.*

With that thought propelling her forward, Kit jumped onto the sheep's back and held its rope neck-strap in a death grip.

9

BOSS BATTLE

THE SHEEP TOOK A STEP FORWARD, then lunged into a heart-stopping, scream-inducing gallop. It wasn't smooth and even like a horse's stride, but bouncy and filled with hops as the sheep switched between bouncing up and down and leaping in a sideways bend—as if it wished to kick itself in the face with its own hind feet.

Kit screamed when it nearly collided with a dead spider body, and she almost fell off when the sheep bolted and abruptly changed directions. It charged head-first towards the wall. Instead of smacking into it, it *jumped*, momentarily landing sideways before using the wall as a spring board and zooming back across the tunnel.

"Sodding, suffering, suicidal sheep!" Kit shouted when she felt her grip slip a little.

Moving as fast as Chester could at a full gallop, the mountain sheep zoomed back and forth across the tunnel like a snowboarder going down a half pipe.

Somewhere behind her, Kit thought she could hear Pax swearing in an angelic language, which was almost covered up by Riko's shrieks.

By the light of Pax, Kit saw Noir and his sheep race past, only to nearly smack into them moments later when Noir's mount hit the brakes and skidded to a stop just so it could turn ninety degrees and nearly impale itself on a human-sized blue crystal that jutted out of the side of the tunnel.

Prowl's sheep bucked and kicked as if it were a wild bull, and it nearly dumped him when it fell onto a dead spider's head.

The rope bit into Kit's hands as her sheep hopped up and down, kicking up its heels and tossing its head. *I hope this doesn't last much longer!* She yelped when the sheep daringly scaled a pile of boulders that almost reached the ceiling, then jumped carelessly over the edge before Pax could catch up and shed his light on the darkened side.

"I hate you!" Kit shouted at her oblivious mount as they fell. "Go live in a petting zoo, you over-grown wooly jellybean!"

They landed with a jolt, and off the sheep went again—jumping and sprinting, barely avoiding smashing head-first with Fortune's sheep.

Kit nearly cried with relief when—between gut-wrenching spins and more halfpipe jumps—she caught sight of a glittering light at the end of the tunnel.

"We're almost there!" she shouted to the others—yipping when her mount almost tossed her into a wall. As if it understood her, Kit's sheep course-corrected and barreled straight for the end of the tunnel. It exited the tunnel and flung itself over another spider body.

Kit's grip finally gave out, and she slid off the sheep's side, managing to land in a crouch—though she barely avoided being run down by her mount when it happily circled her twice.

Prowl shouted as his sheep raced past. He had slid off the animal's back and was clinging to its side, though when the sheep made a sharp turn to avoid a mine cart, Prowl was thrown off.

He smashed into the mine cart with a painful crack and slowly picked himself off the ground. "I'm going to eat mutton, *lots* of mutton, when we get back to Brunascar," he vowed.

"These are the devil's sheep," Kit agreed. She turned around in time to see Pax fly out of the tunnel. She couldn't help smirking at him. "You know, Paco, you were right. You really kept up with these *banal* creatures."

"Your mother is a banal creature," Pax muttered.

Kit snorted. "At least I don't have a pair of wings popping out of my a—" she cut herself off when Solus Miles and his sheep came bursting out of the tunnel. Solus coolly disembarked from his mount with a jump, his cape picturesquely fanning behind him as his sheep ran off.

"Show off," Prowl grumbled.

Riko arrived next—with a lot of screaming—and a whooping Fame and Fortune were on her heels. Though the NPCs slipped off their mounts with ease, Riko clung to hers until the sheep saw itself in a reflection on a crystal and charged it head-first, knocking itself silly.

The sheep staggered a few steps and shook its head as Riko slipped from its back. Unfortunately, she was nearly run down by Noir and his sheep.

Noir fell off the side and groaned. "These things need to be exorcised. No domesticated animal should move like that." He glared as his sheep kicked up its heels and jumped into another one of the rider-less mounts, sending them both tumbling.

Kit glanced around the cavern in which the sheep had dumped them. It was circular in shape, though there was a steeply sloped hill in the center. The cavern wasn't completely enclosed—the very center of it was open, letting a thick beam of sunlight crack through the shadows of the cavern and bathe the top of the hill in light.

Above the baas of the sheep and the groans of her friends, Kit could hear a dwarf roar.

"Come at me, you craftless, toe-biting spawn of shadows! You shall find your doom at the edge of my blade!"

"That'll be Brasil. Come on everyone—up the hill." Kit hurried up the incline, her elven agility letting her keep pace with Solus and Prowl, even as Noir, Riko, and Fame and Fortune fell slightly behind.

Kit steeled herself for the worst as they crested the hill.

Brasil stood alone before a giant spider that was easily the size of a horse. Spread behind it—glowing in the shadows—was a massive web that was dotted with what looked like wispy puffs of cotton but wriggled with the telltale signs of an egg sac.

"This isn't so bad." Prowl slipped a dagger from his belt and held a trap in his free hand. "She's smaller than Brutus," he said, referring to the giant spider Kit and the others had faced in a previous questline.

"Yes," Kit agreed. "But Brutus was not a proud mother." She pointed to the wriggling egg sacs with a shiver.

"Okay, what's the plan?" Riko asked, panting slightly when she and Noir caught up.

Kit glanced at the queen spider. "Fame, want to read me in?"

"Yes, Kitten!" the NPC smiled, and the red coils of her pigtails bounced. "Rathshi, the queen spider, is a level 30 mob boss, weak to physical strikes to her head and abdomen. Fire and light are also effective against her."

"Thanks," Kit said, her mind whirling. *Though she's low-leveled, mob bosses are always harder to kill. Still...with Solus and Noir on hand, it should be a snap.* Kit pointed to the spider. "Solus Miles, I choose you! Go—use One-Shot!"

Prowl stared at her. "Please tell me you don't think that was legitimately funny."

"You're a killjoy," Kit complained.

"A killjoy with a refined sense of humor—unlike you."

Before Kit could come up with a retort, Solus sprinted across the hill and leaped, landing on the queen spider's back. He plunged his sword into her abdomen—which took a good 5% off its health bar.

The spider made a rattling, hissing noise and writhed, throwing Solus Miles off her.

Riko whistled. "This is a strong spider. Even though it's a boss, I thought he'd get her in one shot."

"Yep, we better head in." Kit jogged ahead, leaping into Battlefield March as soon as Solus fell in range. "Greetings, King Brasil!"

"Kitten Lovemuch!" King Brasil boomed. "You are looking markedly less gaudy than when I last saw you, unlike your perfumed-stinking kinsmen."

I guess that means he approves of my armor? "Gee, thanks," Kit said.

King Brasil didn't seem to hear. "You are back in Brunascar?"

"Yes, I thought I'd come see the sights, kill some spiders, you know, the usual." Kit nodded to Noir when he took up his post next to her. Riko settled in a bit behind them and began loading her Siren's Storm spell.

King Brasil laughed. "We must celebrate your return! Tonight, the ale will flow thick." He raised a giant hammer above his head, blocking the spider when it tried to spear him through with a wiry leg.

"That sounds delightful, but perhaps we ought to take care of the threat this spider serves, yes?" Kit asked.

"I guess I wouldn't say no to your help, lass. Not that I'm in any danger, but this wicked, cave-slinking beastie always crawls away just before I've gotten the best of her."

"Hear that, Riko?" Kit called. "Once you cast Siren's Storm, be on standby with Nature's Bindings."

"Right-o!"

Kit turned back to Brasil, but the dwarf king had moved on, swinging his hammer over his head as he ran at the spider boss. "Try to bite me again, you rickety bug, and you'll rue the day. By the hammers of my father!"

Kit glanced at the queen spider's health bar—she was at roughly 70%. *Not bad. I actually think we've got this in the bag... for once.* Kit dropped her gaze past the spider, and her keen eyes picked out the handful of spiderlings climbing from an opened egg sac.

"Prowl, take care of those baby spiders before they cause problems, would you? And then take down all those egg sacs if Siren's Storm doesn't kill them."

"'Kay."

"Casting Siren's Storm!" Riko announced. A torrential storm opened up over the spider, hammering it with rain before the clouds crackled with electricity. Lightning struck the spider again and again—making its legs spasm. The grand-finale lightning bolt hit her in the abdomen, crackling with power and magic before the storm dissipated.

"That took out the spiderlings but not the egg sacs," Prowl announced. "I'll take care of 'em."

"Thanks, Prowl," Kit said.

Noir leaned against his staff and yawned. "I like the way you play, Solus Miles," he said.

Kit grinned and—in between the twirls and leaps of her dance—glanced at the Royal Knight.

He moved faster than the spider could track—circling her head and sliding under her belly to stab her before she could react. He popped back to his feet and paused just long enough to slice straight through the leg the spider queen was trying to use to run Brasil through.

The spider shrieked, and Brasil roared happily.

"She's down to 40%—Riko, look lively; you might be up soon," Kit said.

Before the druid could reply, another breeze brushed the back of her neck.

"You idiot!" Nyx shouted on the party chat channel. "We wiped—against level 20 spiders—because of you, Reynard!"

Alarmed, Kit glanced up, toggling the health bars of the raid.

Several members of Nyx's party were at zero, until they joined the spirit weaver in respawning. *This is certainly going to be a fun and happy reunion...*

"It's not my fault you can't handle a few spiders," Reynard argued.

"No, it seems it is my fault for believing you're actually a decent player who knows basic party tactics!" Nyx seethed.

Kit sighed and stopped dancing. "Guys, keep up hacking at the queen. This might take a moment."

Riko waved—though she didn't remove her eyes from the spider. "Good luck."

"Thanks. Fame, Fortune, stay with these guys. I'll be right back," Kit said.

"Yes, Kitten!" the NPC siblings chorused.

Kit retreated a few steps so she wouldn't be in the way and toggled the party chat. "What happened?"

"Reynard regrouped with us, only to chase after two wayward spiders by himself," Nyx started, her voice withering. "A nearby web covered with egg sacs erupted, dumping hundreds of small spiders on us. Without his added DPS, there were too many for us to kill. Lumina Myst and Glowrious couldn't even get their spells off, as the spiders kept interrupting them."

"Reynard, why didn't you stay with your party?" Kit asked, moving even farther away from the fight when Brasil's shouts nearly drowned out Nyx's explanation.

"Because this is a lower-level zone. It shouldn't have been a problem," Reynard argued.

"And yet we wiped," Nyx said.

"Anyone from *Tainted* would have been able to handle it. We're better trained," Reynard said.

"Oh, please." Nyx laughed harshly. "The only reason you survived is because you ran away with your tail between your legs! The spiders would have swarmed you as well if we'd left you alone here."

I guess Nyx really *doesn't like dying,* Kit noted. "We'll discuss this after this mission is over. For now, Reynard, regroup and stick with your party. Have I made myself clear?"

"Yes," Reynard growled.

Kit turned off the party chat channel and sighed. *I put Reynard with Nyx because I thought he would stay with her. He was fine when we fought the chimeras, so what caused this? Is there tension between Corporate Force and Tainted I don't know about?* She groaned and rubbed her eyes. "I don't even have a plan for Valdis, but that doesn't matter if we can't work together!"

She shook her head to clear her mind, glanced at the spider queen—who was down to approximately 10%. She started to walk back to the group, when something snagged her by the waist and yanked her backwards.

She screamed—or tried to—but a black gauntlet covered her mouth, muffling her scream so it couldn't be heard over Brasil's roars and Prowl's cheers while they carved the last bit of health points from the spider queen.

Kit struggled, wrenching herself sideways with the plan to stab one of her bladed fans into her captor's side, but when she saw what held her captive, her muscles slackened.

A black spirit knight—one of Valdis' creation from the ages past—held her. A black spirit knight was—for lack of better words—a spirt embedded into a set of armor. They were powerful, and the one that held Kit could crush her skull like an egg before she blinked.

This particular knight was bigger than Solus Miles. Its spiked armor was dingy gray—though it was spattered with dried blood—and inside the open visor of the helm was not a face, but a glowing ball of orange light threaded with red.

Kit wriggled in the black spirit knight's unmovable grasp and nearly impaled herself on a spike of his armor. She twisted her neck to peer at her party and tried screaming, but Riko was holding the spider queen captive as Solus finished it off. *If I could just get their attention...* Hopeful, she glanced up at Pax—who was flying just above her.

The winged warrior stared unhelpfully down at her, occasionally shedding a feather and doing nothing else. Fame and Fortune had noticed Kit's plight, but as non-combat NPCs, they didn't register the danger and just smiled and waved to her.

It seemed Kit was on her own.

Well, it was a good run, she thought ruefully as she jabbed her fans at the glowing ball of light with no success, *but I guess it's about time I died. I haven't gone this long without getting shot or stabbed in ages.*

A little icon of a glowing black helm appeared by Kit's health bar. *Touch of Death,* it read. *Oh, so I'm cursed now as well? Such a surprise!*

The knight—using his grip on Kit's mouth and waist—picked her up and held her over his head in some weird sort of embrace.

Despite Kit's reluctant acceptance of her impending doom, her heart beat oddly in her chest. *This is it.* She squeezed her eyes shut and tried to get one good kick to the knight's head before he finished her off.

She felt the black spirit knight move, and the world seemed to swirl around her.

A moment passed...and nothing happened.

Kit popped her eyes open and furrowed her brow. The knight was slowly ambling down the hill. She couldn't even see her party any more.

What is going on? Why hasn't he killed me already? Does he have to do it on stable ground? Or is he—

Kit caught sight of the boney, lizard-like creature that waited at the cave entrance with a spiked saddle tied to its back.

Kit's heart started to beat faster and faster, and her breath suddenly seemed suffocating. *He's not going to kill me; he's carrying me off.*

Renewed vigor surged through her limbs as she struggled and kicked—trying to make the knight release her. When the drops notifications filled her screen—Solus must have successfully finished the spider—she impatiently swiped them out of her face.

If I could just get on the ground, my cowardly leader skill would never let him catch me! Even though she kicked the helm clear off the glowing ball of light, the black spirit knight's grip never wavered.

A breeze brushed the back of Kit's neck. "Hey Kit, where are you off to?" Riko asked.

"Probably going to wring Reynard a new one," Prowl laughed. "But wow—that was a fun fight! It seems like for the past few weeks Kit's been throwing us into impossible battles—this was awesome!"

They were almost to the lizard mount. The beast smiled at

Kit with a mouth full of blackened teeth. The overwhelming rotted-meat scent of its breath made Kit's stomach heave. Her desperation growing, she shoved one of her shut fans between her mouth and the knight's hand—not even flinching when she cut her own face.

Using the fan like a lever, she pressed down on the heel of the fan, making the other end pop up and peel the knight's hand from her mouth.

"*Miles!*" Kit screamed with all her might before the knight grabbed her again, this time by the throat.

Though he squeezed her neck, she could still manage a wheeze of air—just not enough to rally another shout. *I don't know what's going on—monsters never did anything like this before! What's happening?*

She started to shake as the black spirit knight stopped next to the lizard. Blood pounded in her ears, and she could feel the sting of tears in her eyes. *This is terrifying!*

Just as the knight started to slide onto his mount, a wall of crackling light smashed into him.

Kit felt herself yanked from the black spirit knight's grasp. It took her a moment to realize Solus held her secure against his shoulder. She twisted around just in time to see Solus stab his sword straight through the black spirit knight's breastplate. The sword flared with light, and the glowing ball of the knight's bound spirit shuddered before it, the armor, and the lizard mount were burned away in the fire of Solus' attack.

Kit clung to Solus' shoulder as she tried to assure herself. *It's over. I'm safe.*

Solus awkwardly tried to juggle holding his sword and supporting Kit as she leaned into him. "Are you okay?"

"Thanks," Kit said. She had to speak quickly or her chattering teeth would betray her. "For saving me."

"What happened?" Riko shouted as she skid down the hill, nearly running Noir over in the process.

Prowl was the first to reach them, his eyes pinched with concern as he pushed his goggles up his forehead. "I saw the death knight—it didn't kill you?"

Kit shook her head and tried to breathe deeply. *I have to be calm. That was frightening, but this is still a game. EC wouldn't create a monster that would mentally scar a player—even if that was terrifyingly realistic.*

"It seemed like it intended to carry her off," Solus said.

"A *black spirit knight*?" Noir flicked his robes as he thought. "Bandits and goblins will drag players back to their camp, and I've heard of the occasional player getting taken back to a monster nest to be slain, but a black spirit knight? A monster supposedly loyal only to Valdis and his followers?"

Riko opened her arms, and Kit—realizing Riko's soft druid robes would be a great deal more comforting than Solus' armor—pulled away from the royal knight and walked into Riko's hug.

The druid smelled of forests and flowers, which reassured Kit's elf senses. "I think it has something to do with the return of Valdis." She took a deep breath and stepped out of Riko's hug, offering her a smile in thanks. "It's something we'll have to warn everyone else about—though it might just be because we were facing the boss, and I happened to be standing away from everyone."

Prowl smiled crookedly. "You are, as Axel liked to say, shark-bait."

Kit felt her skin crawl, and the world turned cold and sepia-toned for a moment before some of her health bar was sapped. "That's right—I got cursed. Could you get that off me, Noir?"

Noir slapped his hands together in a gesture of prayer. "Yeah. I charge extra for curse-removal blesses, though." The slight smile that tugged at his lips betrayed his humor, drawing a chuckle from Kit.

"Oi!" King Brasil shouted as he made his way down the steep hill. "Why did you all run off? You need to learn to properly celebrate a battle that's been won," he complained. "We should have opened a keg of beer!"

Prowl peered at the dwarf king with interest as he marched down the last of the incline. "Do you just happen to carry a keg of beer on you at all times for battle celebrations?"

"Of course!" King Brasil puffed his chest up as he trundled up to them. "And in case a babe is born, or someone dies, or it's someone's birthday, or if there's a festival I don't know of but would be happy to observe."

"Raging alcoholics," Noir muttered as he reached out and prodded Kit on the forehead. "Angelic Touch."

Kit relaxed when the curse icon disappeared. "Thanks, Noir."

Noir shrugged slightly. "That's why I'm here."

Yep, I'll have to send Gared a thank-you message! Kit filed the note for later and eagerly swung her attention to King Brasil. *Now, for the main event...* "Honorable Brasil—King of the Dwarves—I am glad we have crossed paths once again. I very much wish to speak to you."

"Sure, sure. We can do that back at Brunascar." Brasil tapped his leg with the head of his hammer and licked his lips. "But first...we celebrate!"

10

EVENT REWARDS

KIT CRADLED a pint of mead in her hands as she scanned the Brunascar feasting hall in search of her party members.

Once the spiders were completely flushed from the city, Brasil ordered everyone to convene on the feasting hall to "strengthen ourselves with sustenance!"

The dwarves brought forward so much "sustenance"— mostly roasted mutton, smoked boar, and lots of gravy, though there were also nutty rolls, mountain berries, cheese, and cheese-stuffed pastries—that they broke two of the serving tables.

After that, Drust started rolling the kegs in, and when they opened the famous Firebrand Keg, all pretenses of sobriety were dropped.

Kit's gaze lingered on the two dwarves who were sitting on a chandelier made of axes. "Axel will be sad to find out he missed this."

Solus—the only member of her party not raising trouble with the dwarves—dipped a roll in gravy. "Axel...the warrior who always wanted to test his strength? Red hair—"

"With a man-bun? Yep, that's Axel. When we got the

dwarven seal, he was sad we couldn't stop to join in the fun." Kit sipped her drink and watched the mountain sheep one of the dwarves had brought into the feasting hall for a laugh sit like a dog and lick Long Claw's furry face.

"Why were you in such a hurry *then*, but don't act with the same urgency now?" Solus asked.

Kit avoided Riko's hand when the druid flailed—laughing so hard at a joke Drust told, she almost fell off the bench.

"I really *want* to move at a faster pace, but I recognize we're facing a much more difficult task..." Kit trailed off with a sigh, unwilling to yet again force herself to face the enormity of everything. "The bottom line is we can't rush. We're dealing with thousands of more people—from players to NPCs. Though I *do* want us off as soon as possible, I recognize that if I act with the same singlemindedness, I'm more likely to throw everyone into a panic."

Solus nodded. "Possibly."

At the far end of the feasting hall, Fame, Fortune, and a young dwarf gathered around the Firebrand Keg and filled their mugs.

Fame took a gulp of it, then belched out a ball of fire. She grinned, then coughed a puff of smoke into her brother's face.

Fortune shook his head, then chugged half his pint. When he finished, he paused for a moment and puffed up his chest, then breathed fire for a good ten seconds.

Not to be outdone by the siblings, the young dwarf tried to chug his pint as well. Unfortunately, he swallowed wrong and hiccupped, making tiny flames that a baby dragon would have scoffed at. Fame patted his back while Fortune lectured him— probably telling him that he lacked fire-resistant armor.

Though normally such a sight would have made her laugh, the reminder of Valdis and her responsibilities made her sigh.

She ran a hand through her silky pink hair. *I can't let myself despair over this. If I think about it too much, I'm just going to freak out, and I already doubt I can do this...*

"What is wrong, not-an-elf-elf-friend?" King Brasil boomed as he made his way to Kit and Solus, passing by Alistair and Prowl, who were dancing on top of a table. (That the well-made dwarven furniture didn't break under their weight, but two had cracked due to the burden of the food was a testament to how many platters the dwarves had brought out.) "Though we are celebrating a great victory, you look as though someone has shaved your beard," the dwarf king said.

Kit grinned at Brasil. "It is nothing. I merely feel a little fatigued."

She was distracted for a moment when Pax crowded her space as a female dwarf with impressive biceps swept past, carrying a tray of food. (The only reason the winged warrior wasn't airborne, Kit bet, was the dwarves hanging from the rafters and chandeliers.)

"There were a lot of spiders, I suppose," Brasil said doubtfully.

"It was not the spiders..." Kit started, then paused. *Wait, I could use this to my advantage!* She brightened and struggled to hide a smile. "Battling Malignus put a strain on my soul that I have not quite recovered from."

"I would expect so." King Brasil grunted as he plopped down on the bench across from Solus, Kit, and Riko. "Necromancy is a dark thing. You have my respect for his defeat."

Riko pulled her attention from the other celebrators and turned—all smiles and total professionalism with her charm on max—to the dwarf king. "I am glad we have your esteem—though we must thank you for giving us the dwarven seal. If you had not, we would not have been able to approach Malignus!"

King Brasil tugged on one of his beard braids. "I was glad to be rid of it—I thought it might ease the forces of darkness that poked round here, but it seems it didn't help much. Now we just have spiders—though I think with the spider queen's death, we have put a stop to it." He peered over the table, looking at Kit's waist. "I couldn't help but notice your belt, elf-friend—it's a splendid thing! As are your robes, Mistress Riko."

"Hmm? Thank you. I was given it as a reward for killing Malignus." Kit glanced down at the belt—which was beautifully crafted, golden metal with a ruby-encrusted buckle.

"My robes are the same," Riko added.

"I expected as much!" King Brasil paused to chug his entire pint in one breath. When he finished, he wiped his mouth and froth-spattered beard off on his arm. "You should wear them always, so those who see it will know your great deeds!"

Kit exchanged looks with Riko. "Sure," she said, not really certain what to do with the unusual fashion advice.

Solus stirred at her side. When he had her attention, he raised an eyebrow, then looked at the dwarf king—who took a newly-filled stein from another dwarf and passed off his empty one.

"I'm working on it," she whispered to him, then returned her attention to King Brasil. "As I'm sure you know, King Brasil, Lord Valdis has returned."

"Of course." King Brasil scowled fiercely. "He is responsible for emboldening the spiders!"

Kit licked her lips. *Here goes nothing!* "We, the Heroes of Retha, mean to march against him."

King Brasil took a swig of his new drink. "That's a tall order —many times more difficult than your fight with that crusty necromancer."

"I am aware of the impossibility of our mission," Kit said. *Seriously, dude, you have* no idea *how aware I am of it.* "But it's our only chance for survival," she said grimly. The truth of her words made her want to cringe.

"Does that include you, Master Solus?" King Brasil asked.

Solus Miles tightened his grip on his pint. "Yes—along with everyone who arrived here with us."

"Hmm? I can't recall ever seeing you play nice with another," King Brasil said.

"There is too much at stake," Solus shrugged. "If we fail to defeat Valdis, we will die."

Kit finally let her grimace surface. *Way to make a dark situation even more grim, Solus.*

"But though I believe we need to fight Lord Valdis, I am here because of Kitten Lovemuch," he continued. "She is my pledged, and she is the only one I trust to lead us into this fight."

His words warmed Kit's heart until King Brasil raised an eyebrow. "Not-a-true-elf? She's your pledged?" He scratched his beard. "I won't lie to you, lad: you have strange taste."

One of Kit's eyebrow's twitched. *It's one thing to hear that from other players and another to be told that by an NPC.* She rested her chin on her fist. "Excuse me for being strange."

Riko cleared her throat. "We're currently gathering our forces. But though we are heroes, our numbers alone will not be enough to defeat Lord Valdis Moarte."

Kit forced herself to sit up straight and adopt her elven grace. "We came here to ask you, King Brasil, for an alliance with the White Needles dwarves—for a promise to go with us when the time comes and fight the darkness that is once again encroaching upon this land."

King Brasil opened his mouth, but Riko beat him to it. "Already the White Veil Nunnery has pledged to join us—and as we said earlier, we shall continue to seek out allies."

King Brasil drank while Riko spoke, then peered at the bottom of his stein. "Are you done?" he asked.

Kit exchanged nervous glances with Riko and Solus. "Yes... so what do you say?"

King Brasil snorted. "Of course we'll join the fight! You two are among the heroes who slew Malignus, and you helped my people here in Brunascar. Who could reject legends such as that?" He leaned across the table and winked. "Plus, a true dwarf never runs from a fight!"

King Brasil staggered to his feet and hopped up on his bench, garnering the attention of his subjects. "We, the White Needles Dwarves, will march with the Heroes of Retha to fight Lord Valdis. We'll give him what-for! By the forges of Brunascar —he'll regret waking from his extended nap!"

The dwarves roared with enough force to shake the squat stone building and slammed their mugs and steins on the tables, sloshing ale everywhere. Kit took in a shaky breath, encouraged by their response, but was a little puzzled when a notification didn't pop up, informing her of the new alliance.

King Brasil grinned as he plopped back down on his bench.

"I am so glad you have agreed to aid us," Riko said. "And we cannot thank you enough for your support."

"We wouldn't miss it," the dwarf king assured her. He turned his gaze to Kit and leaned back speculatively. "Though there's something that must be done before we make this all official."

Solus tapped the side of his beer stein. "Spit it out, King."

"Yes, Yes." King Brasil took another swig of his drink, then announced, "Kitten Lovemuch, as the leader of the heroes, you must first show that you have the courage and mettle of a dwarf before we agree to follow under your flag."

I don't know that I like the sound of this. "Oh?" Kit politely enquired.

"Oh, no," Riko groaned. "Not—"

"Indeed," King Brasil rubbed his hands together in glee. "You must ride down Tremblebach Falls in a barrel!"

———

Kit dug her heels into the rocky riverbank. "Does it *have* to be me?" She grimaced at the water. Her heart had been beating nervously in her chest throughout the long, winding walk up to the top of the falls—during which she had gotten *Swear Proficiently* to level five.

"I'm afraid so, Lady Kit." Alistair smiled sadly as she placed her hands on Kit's shoulders. "Brasil said so himself—though I wish I could spare you this."

"Even if he didn't say it had to be you, no way am I trading with you." Prowl folded his arms across his chest and snorted. "I've already been down the falls once, and it was awful. Ouch!" The saboteur winced when Riko pulled Prowl's goggles by the nose strap an inch or so off his head and then let them go so they hit his forehead with a snap.

"Stop. You're making her feel worse," Riko said.

Prowl adjusted his goggles with a grumble that was barely audible over the dull roar of the falls. "I wasn't particularly *trying* to make her feel better."

Kit eyed her friend. "Rest assured, Prowl, you'll pay."

Prowl narrowed his eyes. "What, are you threatening to tell Cookie?"

"No." Kit let a smile so large it was creepy settle on her lips. "I'll tell *Vic*, who will tell Cookie—likely with some strongly worded advice about you."

Prowl made choking noises and glared at Kit until Alistair moved to stand between them.

"At least I can promise, Lady Kit, that you won't die," Alistair said. "You'll get wet, but I think it's impossible for a player to die going down the falls—I don't believe the game is coded to allow it."

"I'm not scared of dying," Kit said plainly. "I've gotten that fear out of my system after playing as Kitten."

Pax—who stood behind Kit in all his shiny glory—made a scoffing noise in the back of his throat.

Kit ignored him—while secretly hoping his fancy armor rusted—but continued, "I'd just rather not be traumatized and scared out of my mind."

"You're gonna hate this then," Prowl piped up from behind Alistair. There was a pause, a crack of something snapping against skin, then an angry hiss. "Ouch—stop snapping my goggles!"

"Then stop baiting her," Riko said.

Alistair rolled her eyes heavenward, then glanced at Solus Miles—who was standing slightly apart and staring out at the frothy, churning river like some kind of moody hero. "Solus, don't you have any encouragement for your pledged?"

Solus reluctantly turned from the water and blinked at Kit. "Once you get this over with, you'll have dwarf minions to boss around."

As strange as the comment was, it did make Kit perk up a little. *He's right. I just have to remember that even if this is terrifying, it will net me a lot of allies in the long run.*

Alistair pressed her palms to her forehead. "I'm starting to think Gared may be the only well-spoken, intelligent male in the close companions of my heart."

Prowl snorted. "I'm pretty sure he would have some *not* well-spoken things to say if he knew you counted him as a companion of your heart."

Alistair started to protest as Kit slipped past her and joined Solus on the shore.

Solus rested his hand on the hilt of his sword. "Sorry. I couldn't think of anything helpful to say," he said.

"No, that actually did make me feel a lot better," Kit said.

The river kicked a fine mist into the air, slightly dampening her hair. Kit rubbed a tendril between her fingers. "I just hope my heart doesn't stop halfway down, killing me, so Brasil insists I have to do it over again."

One of Solus' rare smiles tugged at the corner of his lips. "You'll survive. It's like riding Sinistre. When he's free-falling."

Kit hunched her shoulders up, sucking her neck down. "Sounds like a smashing good time."

"Pinkie, they've got your barrel ready," Noir called as he picked his way across the shore.

"That we do!" King Brasil grinned widely as he strode next to Noir, a handful of grizzled dwarves trailing in his wake.

"Oh...yay..." Kit said with zero enthusiasm.

King Brasil laughed and smacked her on her lower back with enough force to make her take a staggering step forward. "You'll be fine, lass. Mark my words, you've got more dwarf than elf in you!"

Kit smiled wanly. "I'm glad *you* think so."

"Now, off to the pier. This way!" King Brasil strode towards the wood-and-rock pier that jutted almost halfway out into the river. Two dwarves were already stationed there, holding ropes that kept a large barrel pressed against the pier.

"We'll send you off up here, but there's another party at the bottom to greet you and witness your great courage. The rest of your party—along with those chatty twin servants of yours—are with them," King Brasil said. "As is my wife. She'll be waiting for you with a cup of tea to warm you after your, uh, dip." Brasil removed his golden crown so he could scratch the top of his shaggy head. "She claims it's good tea—worthy of an elf—but if you need something stronger, one of the lads can give you a nip," he winked as they tromped across the pier.

She glanced over her shoulder to check on Pax. She was surprised to see that, in addition to her ornery pet, who was strutting for the sake of the admiring dwarves, Solus Miles followed behind her, carrying a second barrel.

When he caught her eye, Solus shrugged. "I may as well come with you. It seems cruel to make you go alone."

She paused. "Really?"

He nodded.

Kit opened her mouth, but she didn't know quite what to say. Going over the waterfall wasn't deadly or anything, but she already felt better knowing Solus was going with her. "Solus, I..."

"What a splendid idea!" King Brasil thundered, interrupting her muddled thoughts. "Such a show of devotion. In fact, why don't you all go over the falls with Kitten Lovemuch?"

"What?" Prowl howled. "*No!*"

Alistair rolled her shoulders back and laughed. "If you have a barrel to spare, I suppose I shall go as well. Let it never be said those of KOS are faint of heart!"

"Come on, Prowl," Riko said. She followed Alistair down the pier as the lady knight rolled a barrel along. "Don't be a *cowardly* delinquent."

"Why do I have to do this again?" Prowl complained—though he reluctantly followed. "I already proved I have dwarf-like courage and all that crap."

Noir stayed on the shore and waved what looked like a handkerchief. Trash Panda sat at his feet, waving his stolen tuft of Long Claw's tail. "Have fun. Bon voyage. Trash Panda and I will witness your act of bravery."

"You aren't going to go with them, lad?" Brasil asked as he stomped his way back down the pier so he could grab a barrel for Riko.

"I'm a delicate healer. They can't risk losing me," Noir said.

"Pansy," Prowl muttered.

"Guess what, Prowl?" Noir said with a large smile. "The

game—meaning I—have altered your fate. The next battle we fight in, you will *die!*" He tipped his head back and laughed deeply.

Kit squinted at the divine oracle. "Healers are scary."

"Yes," Solus agreed as he tucked his sword into his character storage.

"Everyone into your barrels—it is time for you to test the falls of fortune!" King Brasil declared with a savage smile.

Kit reluctantly climbed into her barrel, which bobbed under her weight.

"Didn't you go down the falls as Azarel?" Riko asked as she lowered herself into a barrel held secure by a brawny dwarf.

"Yes, but as an echo of arcane I may or may not have triggered an ice spell while going over the side and gone down it like a sledding hill," Kit admitted.

"Why?" Solus asked—he barely fit in his barrel and had to take his cape off so it didn't drag in water behind him. "You aren't afraid of heights." Solus frowned at his chest for a moment before he brought up his character panel and removed his black, metal armor until he wore only black trousers and a white linen shirt.

Kit tilted her head as she watched him. "No, but I *am* afraid of falling. Why are you switching armor?"

"So I don't drown."

"Good point, Sir Solus," Alistair shouted from down the line. "I had best swap armor as well, or I'll sink like a stone if I fall out of my barrel."

I guess I'm glad I've only played characters that have light armor. Kit glanced up at Pax. "Are you just going to fly behind me, Paco?"

Pax flapped his wings, shedding a few feathers.

Kit rested her chin against the rough rim of her barrel. "You know, it's beyond me how you don't resemble a plucked chicken with the number of feathers you lose every day."

Pax glared at her. "*What* did you just say?"

"Everyone in?" King Brasil boomed. "Comfortable? Yes? Good! Loosen the barrels, lads!"

At their king's command, the dwarves let go of the ropes that held the barrels against the pier.

Instantly, the current swept the barrels up, carrying them down the river.

"This is crazy!" Prowl shouted above the roar of the river as they were tossed along.

"I think it could be a theme park ride," Riko said.

"Maybe." Kit's barrel bobbed up and down, and she rammed into Riko.

Alistair laughed. "It is a rush, for sure. Forward—into glory!" She pointed ahead, to the edge where the falls began and the water roared as it plunged. Her heart slammed into overtime with such force, Kit could hear the pounding of her blood in her ears.

"Brasil, you beer-brained, toad-licking weasel!" she shouted shrilly. "I hope your axes break and you drop your hammer on your foot!"

"Ooh, someone is mad," Riko laughed.

"I am, too, and I don't even have to be here!" Prowl snarled.

Kit's barrel slammed into a rock, making her spin wildly. "Shut the front door, Prowl!"

Congratulations! Your life skill, "swear proficiently," has risen to level six!

She pressed against the back of her barrel and kept spewing the nonsensical curses as the river dragged her into the lead of her motley group. "Fffffrig! Frig on you, frig on you!"

"Here we go," Alistair shouted somewhere behind Kit.

"Go bald, King Brasil—gah!" Kit screamed before she switched to cursing in elvish—spitting out words so fast her character knowledge couldn't even translate them.

The riverbed fell out, and Kit—with several tons of water—tumbled over the overhang and plunged down. Icy cold water pummeled her, spattering her face with a stinging force. She could barely see and nearly choked on water as she kept up her stream of alternate expletives.

Congratulations! Your life skill, "swear proficiently," has risen to level seven!

Her stomach flipped as she free-fell, and the wind flung her soaked hair into her face. Between the rushing air and the needle-stinging spray of water shooting into her face, she could barely see clearly enough to spy the base of the falls until it was almost upon her.

She yelled off one more line of curses, then pinched her nose before her barrel hit the water-filled gorge with a tremendous crack that rattled every bone in her body.

The barrel smacked the water with such velocity, it plunged beneath the water, which embraced Kit in a cold hug. The river still flowed with enough force it yanked Kit—underwater as she was—forward.

Her fingers tingled—either from the death grip she had on the barrel or from the cold—and the barrel bobbed towards the top of the river.

Kit surfaced with a gasp, her hair plastered to her skull and her body, shivering with adrenaline. She coughed as she pushed her sopping hair out of her face. *I guess even the elf race trait of Perfect Hair couldn't beat back Tremblebach Falls*, she thought as she turned around in her water-filled barrel.

Solus bobbed to the surface, holding to the side of his barrel.

He looked different without his armor, and his smile seemed to come a little easier when he met Kit's gaze.

Or maybe he's just amused I look like a sewer rat.

Beyond Solus, Alistair had slipped out of her barrel. She held onto her barrel with one arm and punched the other in the air. Though she shouted, Kit couldn't hear her over the roar of the falls.

Just behind the cavalry knight, Riko and Prowl surfaced—sputtering and shivering like Kit.

"Well done, Kitten Lovemuch!" King Brasil shouted.

Kit wiped water from her face. *I'm surprised I can hear him at all over the water—but he does have a healthy set of lungs on him.*

"You have proven yourself. The White Needles Dwarves will be proud to march with you!"

Kit beamed when a new popup flickered to life.

You have secured an alliance with the White Needles Dwarves.

"We did it!" Kit shouted—though she couldn't tell for sure if her friends heard her or not.

Alistair cheered, and Riko clapped, though Prowl—visible from only the bridge of his nose up—looked murderous as he dog-paddled in Kit's direction.

Kit tilted her head at him until Solus pointed past her and motioned for her to turn around.

The crowd of dwarves and other players were just behind her, waiting on a platform cut into the rock of the riverbank.

Kit tipped her barrel over and started swimming towards them, her elven knowledge taking over so she used gliding, powerful strokes. She rolled her eyes when a beautiful feather swirled through the air and landed just in front of her.

Holding her head above the water, she glanced up at her

winged warrior pet—who looked none the worse for the wear. In fact, the mist of the falls settled on his hair, giving him a disgustingly handsome rainbow effect. "Did you have fun?"

Pax lifted his chin and didn't look down at her. "I will forever delight in the memory of you—red-faced and screaming like an ugly newborn."

Kit skipped her arm across the top of the river, showering Pax's feet with icy water, making the pet scowl and fly higher. Smirking, Kit shouted after him. "Yeah? At least I'm not a vain, clay-brained parrot!"

Congratulations! Your life skill, "swear proficiently," has risen to level eight!

———

Luther stifled a groan as he stumbled downstairs. The house was dark and silent, and his cellphone said it was 4:32 am. After everything he had gone through, Luther wanted nothing more than to sit in his bed with his wife and just *be*...but Axel had sent him a rather enthusiastic and urgent text, demanding he log in for a video conference.

Not much could get Luther out of bed, but a message from a fellow Desperate Quest party member would do it.

This had better be worth it. Luther wiped sleep from his eyes as he snatched his tablet from its charging station and plopped down on the couch. The screen cast a soft blue light across the room as Luther jabbed at apps and logged in. Immediately, the call popped up.

Invitation to video conference with: Axel Talbot, Gilbert Gray, CookieMonster28, and Victoria Samn.

Luther accepted the invitation. "This had better be good, Axel," he growled, his voice still rusty from sleep.

"It is!" The red-haired teen assured him. "I finished the Retha gameplay compilation of Riko, Prowl, Kit, and us. You gotta see it before I upload it."

Ahh yes, time to see if it's useable or if I'll have to put out feelers and find someone skilled at video editing. When Luther shared his idea—to create a compilation of the best moments from the footage Axel had recorded and release it to the Retha community to get the word out about Kit's mission—Axel had offered to edit the footage himself.

As it was the teenager's recording, Luther didn't really feel like he could say no and just ask for the footage. *Besides, no matter how skilled or unskilled he is, it should at least be a good starting point. Right now no one knows Kit is leading everyone in the fight for their lives.*

Luther cleared his throat. "Great—let's see it."

"Sending the file," Axel said.

The video conferencing application asked Luther if he wanted to accept the shared download. While he plugged away on his tablet, he was vaguely aware of Cookie chatting in the background.

"I'm impressed you got it done so quickly—you had *hours* of footage to sift through," she said.

"Yeah—I pulled an all-nighter since my parents already said I don't have to go to school today." Axel slightly puffed up his chest and arrogantly tipped his head up. "Besides, I have loads of practice."

"Practice?" Gil asked.

"Got the video. I'm minimizing so I can watch it," Vic announced.

"Same here," Luther added. His tablet screen turned black as the video filled the screen.

"Malignus stands on the threshold of returning Lord Valdis to his rightful throne, and when he succeeds, chaos and darkness shall descend upon Retha, and all heroes shall be slaughtered," a rattling voice hissed—one Luther faintly recognized as the Shadow Reaper that attacked players during the quest for the four seals.

"Killing Malignus is impossible!" someone shouted, the screen still black.

"Dozens of guilds have banded together to try and defeat him, but no one has managed it," another voice chimed in.

"It's a throwaway quest!"

A light bloomed on Luther's screen, and Kit's melodic voice filled the air. "I know why you all think it's impossible. But if we try to attack Malignus, we won't lose out on anything. But if we don't...

The light made the screen blaze as orchestra music in the background swelled. Footage of Prowl attacking a dragon, Riko holding an umbra-nox captive with a vine spell, and the party running from the giant spider in the City of Wizards flashed.

Axel used a soundbite of Kit to voice-over the action. "There was a power surge, and our server went down," she said. "Unfortunately, there were corrupt files in the backup server. That's what's preventing us from logging off."

Clips of the Aridus Plains, Elba, Luminos, and the Igneo Desert sped across the screen, fading away to reveal an image of Malignus laughing at the sky, his putrid magic swirling around him.

The screen blinked, switching to show Kit—in her pink-haired, elf-dancer glory—standing in the wastelands, staring the necromancer down. "Command Party—attack at your leisure," she said. "Knock the smile off that son-of-a-sick-snake."

The screen went black for a moment, before the image of a popup screen came into focus.

*Congratulations. You have completed the world quest: Curse of
the Necromancer.
You have defeated Malignus.
Auto-log off in 10 seconds.*

The screen switched to a clip of Kit, climbing the stairs of
the Solis Sentinels. Golden letters burned in the sky
above her.

*She freed a raid of players and broke out.
But she's put her life on the line and returned to Retha again, this
time to free the server—but she's not alone.*

"Beloved's Guard!"

The video switched to an image of Solus Miles holding a
sword and standing between Kit and a shadow reaper, his gaze
steely.

Luther whistled. "You've got more marketing chops than I
gave you credit for, Axel," he said as he watched a few more
video clips of Kitten, Prowl, Riko, and Solus fighting and
standing together. "To plop Solus in this video was genius. His
name alone will get this clip a ton of views."

"Of course," Axel snorted.

The screen faded to black again, and golden letters glittered
once more.

Kitten Lovemuch: the real Hero of Retha.

The music cut, and the video application minimized,
pulling up the video call again.

"That was good," Vic said, her forehead wrinkled slightly.
"Like, *really*, good!"

"You did a fantastic job, Axel," Gil chimed in.

"I'm impressed," Luther said. "It's really great. How did you come up with the idea?"

Axel smugly folded his arms across his chest. "It was easy for me. I have a video channel and stream gameplay compilations of Beast Master. I even have some subscribers!" He scowled a bit. "Getting stuck on Retha screwed up my release schedule, though. I better not have lost anyone as a result!"

Luther played the video again—at a smaller size so he could still see the video chat—and only half-listened as the others kept up the chat.

"Is that why you recorded everything?" Cookie asked. "Because you were planning to post it on your channel?"

"Yep," Axel said. "I was trying Retha to see if I wanted to move to it now that Beast Master is shutting down."

"You had *hours* of footage to go through—how did you find those bits?" Gil asked.

Axel shrugged. "Retha doesn't load them to your account as one single file, which made it easier to sort. Plus, I was just looking for the best bits—if possible, I want this to go viral. *That* will show the world what's really going on and what Kit, Prowl, and Riko are doing."

"This is perfect, Axel. You did great—thanks for staying up to do this," Luther said as he watched the movie through again.

Axel grinned as he scratched his nose. "Just you guys wait until I can make a gameplay compilation of us as a party!"

Luther was pulled from his revere when a light flicked on, and his wife swept down the stairs. She smiled at him but didn't stop, and instead made her way to the kitchen.

Luther considered shutting the tablet down and following her—being in-game and away from her and their girls as long as he had been was nothing short of torture—but forced his attention back to the tablet.

"Go ahead and upload it to your channel," Luther said.

"Text me the link when it's done, and I'll pass it on to my Silver Army guildmates."

"Sure. I'll ask my subscribers to pass it around as well." Axel grinned broadly and knocked over several empty cans of energy drinks as he tried to stretch his arms out in front of him.

Gil sighed. "I'm afraid I don't have many gaming friends, but I can still send it to a few when you're done."

"I'm part of a chat community; I can spread it there," Cookie piped in.

"I feel like there's one very obvious group we should try to contact, though it might be...difficult," Vic said carefully.

"Who is that?" Luther asked.

"Milk Crown." Vic's black hair tumbled over her shoulder as she tilted her head.

"They would have more pull and affluence—and probably more contacts—but how can we reach them?" Luther asked. "None of them are a part of Retha anymore."

"Before we parted, Kit mentioned Bryce had given her information from Milk Crown, so he has a way to contact them," Gil pointed out.

Luther grimaced. "I can try to talk to him, but we'll have to be careful. We don't want EC aware of what we're doing until it's too late to pull it, and even if Bryce agrees to keep it a secret, he might get fired."

"I'm fairly certain his job is already on the line given that he leaked information to Kit and sent her back into the game without the approval of top management," Gil pointed out.

"Kit's his cousin," Vic added. "He's loyal to her. I don't think he's going to squeal on us."

"And what do we have to lose?" Cookie asked.

"Besides my amazing and awesome video skills," Axel added.

"All right, I have Bryce's contact info. I'll try calling him at a more reasonable hour." Luther glanced up when his wife crossed the living room, carrying a steaming cup of coffee. "Anything else we need to share, or can we break up this *delightful* morning meeting?"

"Nope, nothing here," Cookie said.

"Me, either," Vic added.

"I should probably get off anyway." Axel muffled a yawn. "If my parents realize I've been up all night, they'll kill me."

"Take care, everyone," Gil said.

"Bye-bye!"

"Yeah, bye."

Luther smiled at the camera, then exited the program. He put the tablet aside and took the coffee with a grateful sigh. "You're an angel," he said to his wife.

She smiled as she joined him on the couch. "How did the video turn out?"

"Great," Luther said. "The kid is amazing. I didn't think anyone as obsessed with manliness and strength like he is could pull off such a difficult project, but he nailed it."

"Good." His wife snuggled closer and sipped her own cup of coffee. "You deserve to get your story out—and your friends deserve the recognition for what they're doing."

Luther draped his arm over his wife's shoulders. "I only hope it works."

11

LEVEL GRINDING, AGAIN

KIT STARED out at the dreary Aridus Plains and flicked a rain-drop from her forearm.

With the White Needles Dwarves won over, it was time to review what they had learned and move on to the next target. The wisest thing would have been to hold the strategy meeting in Brunascar, but whether it was because the elf in her needed it, or the darkness of being in the mountain was too much for her, Kit opted to take her raid to the surface first.

She frowned up at the cloudy sky, and a few raindrops spattered her face. *I do regret it a little...but it's not like we can return to Luminos. If we go back there, the first officers will likely abandon us to check on their guilds, which will waste a huge chunk of time. Now that we finally have a better idea of how this should go down, I'd really like to ramp up the speed.*

Prowl slouched past Kit, carrying an armload of firewood. "Camp's almost made," he said. "Alistair has a pole tent—for reasons I can't understand—that she and Reynard have pitched. If you join everyone in it instead of standing like an idiot out here in the rain, you'll be more comfortable."

Kit grinned. "Yes, but I'm finally outside, and I can see the sky...as cloudy as it is."

"You sound like an elf," Prowl shouted back to her.

"Thank you!" Kit turned around, looking back at the White Needles Mountains so she could call after him.

Alistair's tent was a large and flashy affair. It was made of elaborately carved wooden poles and bright blue and white fabric accented with silver flourishes and dangling tassels. It was more than big enough for the entire party, even with Alistair's cavalry horse taking up an entire corner of the tent by itself as it chewed on a bale of hay.

Pax stood at the edge of the tent—standing beneath its cover as he peered up at the sky. Long Claw sat not too far away from the winged warrior, and he eyed Alistair's horse as he set about making a fire. (Waffle had reported to Kit that he had no problems with Long Claw listening to orders...after Alistair and her horse ran the werewolf down. Twice.)

"How do you have this much personal storage?" Riko asked the lady knight as she stared up at the canopy. "Do you know how many drops you could carry instead of this thing? You could make a killing in high-income drop areas!"

Alistair laughed. "I'm afraid I don't carry this—Trust does. All cavalry horses carry basic tents, but you can upgrade them if you're willing to spend the money." Alistair winked.

Nyx peered up at the tent and rubbed the beads of what appeared to be an abacus. "Gared bought it for you?"

Alistair beamed. "How did you know? He did—he said something about aesthetics and the guild's image."

"I imagine it was a sound marketing investment," Nyx said.

Kit flicked more raindrops from her brow and started for the tent, pausing when a popup screen appeared.

You have a private message from: Shashanna

Accept message?

Kit turned back to the drizzling Aridus Plains. "Hello, Shashanna."

"Hi, Kittredge. Is this a good time?"

Kit's ears twitched at the steady pitter-patter of the rain falling on Alistair's tent. "Yes, it's perfect timing, actually. We just secured the allegiance of the White Needles Dwarves and were about to hold a strategy meeting."

"You won Brasil over already?"

"Yes. There was an event we had to deal with—a spider invasion—but I don't think that will happen anymore since we killed the queen spider and got King Brasil to agree to fight with us."

"A spider invasion?" Shashanna said, sounding thoughtful. *"I hadn't heard of it—but that might be because the chimera were keeping the lower-level players from entering Brunascar."*

"Probably." Kit's nose twitched at the scent of wet dog— Long Claw, probably, based on the direction from which the scent wafted. "And it's not like high-level players go to Brunascar often given that it's one of the lowest zones in Retha."

"True. Regardless, well done! The guild and I will start sending out rumors about your win in Brunascar."

"That would be great. I was going to ask you, though, if you've heard of any other unusual events—like the spider invasion."

"Since you killed Malignus, you opened up the next chapter of Retha. There're a lot of new and unusual things going on."

Kit squeegeed water out of her hair. "Yes, but I'm specifically wondering about any in the big cities—like Lèas in Fìone Forest or Tìr Nog. I'm pretty certain we had to clear those spiders to get King Brasil to join us. I'd like to know in advance if the elves, fae, or Imperials have similar situations."

"I see. Tir Nog itself is fine—but I heard the goblins have left Soggy Swill Bog, and a bunch of lake monsters moved in. Technically Lèas is fine as well."

"Only technically?"

"They've increased the amount of reputation required to get into Lèas, and the elves themselves are upset, but there are no additional monsters. Elba is a different matter."

Kit cringed. "I guess one out of three isn't too bad. What's happening in Elba?"

"Every few weeks a bunch of goblins and bobokins sail up Nignay river and launch a siege. It lasts a fair amount of time— about a week or so—but it's a pretty vast force based on the screenshots and reports I've seen."

"Great, I guess we know what major race we're recruiting last."

Shashanna laughed. "There's no rush to secure Elba. There're hundreds of smaller pockets of people and organizations you can recruit."

"Yes, I've been trying to decide what the next targets should be."

"Go somewhere fun," Shashanna suggested. "If you hit everything too hard, you'll burn yourself out."

"I'll keep that in mind. Was there anything you needed?"

"Just remember to PM me whenever you win over a new group—or you can announce it in the RP chat channel."

Kit glanced up at the logbook icon by her name. "Sorry, I should have done that."

"No worries. Oh—I did want to let you know, though, there's been a bit of fighting between the middle-level guilds."

"What do you mean by 'a bit'?"

"Nothing as bad as Torvel yet, but the elite guilds have their hands full trying to stamp out the infighting. I don't think we're far from repeating it."

Kit sighed as the rain trickled down her back. "Okay. Thanks for the heads up."

"*Of course.*"

"And thanks for spreading the rumors—I mean news—too." Kit blanched, then blinked when she heard the faint squeak of armor and wasn't too shocked when Solus joined her. She was surprised, however, that he held an oil paper umbrella over her, shielding her from the drizzle. *I've got to give him credit. He is a devoted fake video game boyfriend,* Kit thought.

Shashanna chuckled, puncturing Kit's musings. "*It's my job. Take care, Kittredge.*"

"You too, Shashanna." Kit glanced up at the oil paper umbrella and grinned when she could make out the dragon pattern through the material. "Thanks, Miles," she said after ending her private message.

Solus shrugged. "Though you accuse me of acting like a moody hero, at least I don't make it a habit of standing out in the rain."

Kit cracked a smile. "I was talking to Shashanna—the GM who is stationed with the RPers. She helped me figure out what I want our group to do next." She meandered towards Alistair's monstrosity of a tent, and Solus mutely followed, still shielding her with the umbrella.

"Have you gotten wet enough today, or do we need to go back to Tremblebach Falls?" Noir asked as he cuddled Trash Panda.

Fortune shook his head in woe. "You would not get so wet, Kitten, if you bought an armor set with water attribute."

Fame nodded absently in agreement as she shuffled through a bunch of rolled up maps she had pulled out.

"Thanks, Fortune," Kit said wryly as she stepped under the protection of the tent.

Solus Miles shook out his umbrella and slipped it back in his inventory before joining her. "Everyone has gathered," he said, nodding at their unusual party.

"We have." Alistair raised a golden goblet of some sort of fruity, fizzy juice. "Tell us our next target, Lady Kit!"

Kit bit the inside of her cheek. "We're going to split into two groups and go after different targets."

Alistair frowned. "Is that truly wise? You're the leader of this movement. Shouldn't you be there for every alliance made?"

Kit shook her head. "Maybe in a storybook, but we haven't the time. If we split our group in half and go after the easier targets to start with, we'll get more allies at a much faster rate. We'll have to join up again, later, but there's no point in moving as one large group if it's not needed."

"It's the best use of our resources," Nyx acknowledged. "Particularly given that Kit is our greatest resource in this fight, and the faster we make our alliances, the sooner we free her up."

Long Claw sharpened his saber with a scowl. "She's not our best resource. She can't even fight."

Nyx rolled her eyes. "I wouldn't expect someone from the Killing Squad to understand the details of something as complex as economics and strategy."

Kit cringed at the spirit weaver's comment. *While I can understand her disdain of Long Claw, I wish she wasn't so derogatory. Inflaming him isn't going to help.*

"Are you calling me stupid?" Long Claw snarled.

Nyx sniffed. "I'm impressed you caught even that much."

"Why you—"

"Enough," Kit said. "Nyx, please. We have to respect each other, or we'll never even get to fight Lord Valdis because we can't agree on anything."

Nyx shrugged and seated herself on a plush cushion.

Kit glanced around the party, but no one raised any further

complaints. "We'll keep the raid but split it into two parties." Kit pulled up the party panel and began rearranging everyone as she spoke. "Who has the highest reputation level with the elves?"

The tent bubbled with talk for a moment as the players compared their levels, while Kit mentally tabulated the groups.

"Waffle will lead the first group—Player One—and Nyx will serve as the group spokesperson for the NPCs. They'll be going to Lèas."

Waffle and Nyx should be a good combination. Waffle is a more laid-back leader and is less likely to ruffle players from other guilds. Nyx, on the other hand, has more cunning, so she is needed to deal with the NPCs.

"Reynard, as well as half of the lower-level players, will also be a part of Player One," Kit said as she started dividing the players into the appropriate party.

"I'll run the second group: Player Two," she continued. "Noir and Solus will stay with me, as will Alistair and Long Claw."

"You're crazy," Noir muttered next to Kit. "Dump the werewolf on the other group!"

"It's already going to be a struggle to get the varied guilds to work as a cohesive group," Kit whispered to him as the players started to change spots in the tent, moving to stand by their new party members. "I'm not going to make it extra difficult for them —that's my duty as the leader. Plus, he doesn't have very much reputation with the elves. I doubt they would let him in Lèas."

Noir shrugged. "Your grave."

Kit continued to divide out the players, pausing when she reached Riko and Prowl. "Either Riko or Prowl should go with party Player One."

"Why?" Reynard asked as he cleaned the blades on his gauntlets.

"Besides me, Riko and Prowl are the only two on the server who beat Malignus," Kit said. "The request for help might have more weight if they're there."

"We're talking to NPCs," Nyx pointed out. "I don't think we have to be quite so heavy handed."

"Maybe." Kit pressed her lips together as she stared at her friends' names. *I can't tell if Nyx sounds right just because I don't want to send them away from me, or if it's because it's really a reasonable assumption.* "I don't think either of them will have enough reputation to get in Lèas anymore, anyway."

Riko—who had been reclining on a cushion and nibbling on grapes—sat up. "What?"

"I just spoke with a contact of mine. She said the elves are now requiring a higher reputation level before they'll let you in Fìone Forest," Kit explained.

"Why am I not surprised," Prowl said sourly. "Considering they're as interesting as *paint chips*, they seem pretty paranoid about letting others in."

"In that case, Riko and Prowl should probably stay with you," Waffle said. "We can send for them if we don't get anywhere with the elves."

Riko dusted off the hem of her fancy robe. "Sounds good to me!"

"Okay," Kit nodded. "Waffle, you officially have the title of party leader. Organize Player One however you like and leave for Lèas when you want."

Waffle nodded and exchanged glances with Nyx. "Thank you, Kit. We won't fail you."

Kit smiled. "Thanks for trying this."

"Of course," Nyx nodded.

"Party Player One," Waffle said, turning to his group. "We're going to set out now. We'll go back to Brunascar and use a teleportation gate to get to Fìone Forest. We'll walk on foot to Lèas from there."

While the Player One party picked up their stuff and pulled on hooded cloaks, Kit joined Long Claw at the fire—which merrily popped and crackled with warmth. *Yep, Long Claw is the wet dog smell.* Kit smiled slightly at the realization.

"Good luck, Kit," Waffle said once his group mobilized.

"You too. I'm counting on you, Waffle, to hold the group together, and you, Nyx, to bring the NPCs around." Kit said.

The pair nodded and stepped out into the rain, leading the way back to Brunascar.

Kit stood so she could wave and didn't sit until the party rounded a bend in the road and disappeared behind a mountain rim.

Noir rubbed Trash Panda's head. "So where are we going, oh-venerated-leader?"

Kit grinned like a Cheshire cat. "Kamoi: King's Land."

———

Kit's forehead glistened with sweat, and she leaned against a tree as she heaved in great gulps of air. "I'm dying," she declared with great certainty. "Noir, don't resurrect me; just let me be dead in peace."

Noir extended his hand to heal Arild Edge, the lower-level swordsman. "Tell that to your boyfriend."

Kit glanced at the party—which fought with a flock of brightly colored, reptilian birds, and a small herd of forest bulls. The forest bulls resembled giant warthogs, but they also had thick exoskeletons that were covered in moss and greenery.

One of the forest bulls headbutted Prowl, sending him flying. He hit the ground not far from Kit with an audible crunch.

Kit and Noir peered at his prone, splayed body for several moments.

"Noir?" Kit prodded.

"Oh, yeah. I guess I can heal him," Noir said.

"This is your doing, Kit," Prowl growled as Noir cast the healing spell. "You were the moron who agreed to Solus' idea to level our way down to Kamoi!"

"I thought Alistair or Long Claw would stop us." Kit tugged on her belt, trying to hitch it higher up her hips. "In fact, I was banking on it."

"Alistair would never step down from a possible adventure —particularly given that Gared isn't around to force her to focus," Noir said dryly.

Kit sighed. "Yeah, I figured that out now."

Beyond them, Alistair rode on the back of one of the forest bulls—whooping with glee. (When Solus had first used Call of Contest—his skill that lured enemies to him—and summoned at least thirty of the forest bulls, the cavalry knight had flattened part of the forest trying to ride the monsters.)

Prowl stood and dusted himself off. "I think you have brain damage, or you would have remembered the exhausting non-stop push that was the *last* time we leveled with your significant other."

Kit reluctantly threw herself into Counterdance when one of the reptilian birds began a shrieking song that raised the flock's defense. "We had to travel by foot to Kamoi anyway. I don't have the teleportation gate—and I'm not the only one with that problem, so sending Solus ahead to summon me wouldn't have worked. Besides, Solus mentioned earlier that if I level, the other players might believe me a little more when we fight. I didn't think it would be a big deal, but after the fun times we had with the chimera and the spiders..."

Prowl snorted and twirled his daggers before leaning his

back against a squat, half-chopped tree trunk. "Sure—it's not just because you can't say no to him."

"Prowl, I wouldn't lean against that if I were you," Kit said. "This is the fae forest, and the last time I sat on a tree trunk it—"

Prowl yelped when a leering face appeared in the bark of the trunk, and bark started to form on Prowl's back. He leaped away from the tree, glared at it, and loped back into the battle, throwing a dagger at the first reptilian bird to swoop at him.

Sweat soaked Noir's dark-purple hair, and he pushed his hood off with a grimace. "I hate every part of this game right now, but your pretty-boy does have a point. The more levels you have, the better off you'll be—and if you get enough so you can use your winged warrior pet by the time we have to face Valdis, *I* certainly won't cry."

"His heart is in the right place," Kit agreed. "But we walked all the way from Brunascar to the fae forest, and we'll still have to skirt the sea monsters in Soggy Swill Bog and go farther south to reach Kamoi. That's a lot of territory to cover."

Solus Miles held his sword out—tanking five of the forest bulls at once. One of the bulls charged him—ramming its ivy-colored tusks into the blade of his sword.

Solus kept his stance, but the monster pushed him back several feet so the royal knight's boots made trenches in the dirt. When another forest bull rammed him, he held his ground and actually turned slightly to talk to Kit as the creature tried to push against him.

"Did you say sea monsters?" he asked.

What the pancakes? Does he have elf hearing, or is that another one of his ridiculously helpful life skills? "Yeah. I heard the goblins have moved on, and there are sea monsters in the bog instead."

"Good thing you got Pax when you did," Riko grunted. "Earthen Pit!" She opened a hole under one of the forest bulls that swallowed it up, then ducked to avoid a bird. The scout leaped out of the trees and made quick work of the bird, then turned around to face three of the shrieking things.

Solus gazed over Kit's head. "You're level fifty-five now. I imagine by the time we make it to Kamoi, you'll be nearly sixty."

Kit flicked her fans open and switched back from Counterdance to Battlefield March. "If we walk the whole way there, we're going to seriously tick Long Claw off."

Solus shrugged slightly—even as a forest bull attempted to ram him. "Long Claw is always angry. The Killing Squad doesn't have a reputation for being stable." He peered over the back of the forest bulls that huffed at him, nodding to the glowering werewolf, who was taking out his aggression on a forest bull of his own.

Solus scanned the area—probably noting the depleted number of attacking monsters—and raised his sword.

"Can we take a short break before you call in the next wave?" Kit was quick to insert. "Several members of the party are about to run out of mana."

Solus nodded. "The scout can build a fire and make some camp rations while we wait so we can have a buff for the next wave."

Kit sagged in relief, and Noir flicked her a thumbs-up. "Good thinking," he said as Solus waded back into the fight.

Noir peered down at his pet raccoon, which sat on its rump eating some kind of berry. "Go on, Trash Panda. Take whatever thing is most expensive."

The raccoon set his snack aside and scurried off into the fight, disappearing among the forest bulls' thick legs.

Kit shook her head. "You are extremely creative in the way you use him."

"Thanks. I like his skills enough. But really, I don't want to imagine how bad the requests and demands for heals and buffs would be if I had a phoenix," Noir grumbled.

Kit laughed, but due to her dance, she was unable to duck when one of the sharp-clawed birds divebombed her. She grit her teeth as it raked her back with its claws and nailed her in the head with a wing.

Prowl and the scout, Hide_N_Seek, double-teamed to take it down in a heartbeat, but her back burned until Noir set a warm heal on her.

The last forest bull snorted when Riko felled it with Earthen Pit, and the remaining flock of reptile birds scattered when Long Claw whirled his saber above his head.

Slowly, everyone looked to Solus, as if afraid of what he might do.

The royal knight sheathed his sword. "Break time."

The lower-leveled party members collapsed. "Thank goodness," the swordsman, Arild Edge, groaned as he plopped down. "I don't think I've seen that many monsters in one place ever before."

Riko gazed out at the crater-riddled meadow they had made their stand in. "Ahh, so young, so innocent. Just you wait until we get to an area that isn't forested."

The spellbinder, Glowrious, sat pretzel style as he tried to regain his mana. "But how can Solus Miles tank that many? He's a DPS knight—not a tank."

Prowl stuck a finger in the air. "Behold: the abilities of an over-powered legendary class."

"He knows how to attack monsters to take the best advantage of their weaknesses," Fame added, smiling like a proud mother. (Though this made her brother roll his eyes.)

Kit breathed a little easier now that the monsters were gone. She turned in a circle. "Does anyone see Pax?" She narrowed her eyes as she looked for a trail of shed feathers but didn't see any.

"No, but he can't have gone too far." Riko stretched out her legs, then glanced at the scout. "Do you mind making a fire like Solus Miles suggested? I have some camp rations that will boost our stamina so we don't *die* before we make it to Kamoi."

"Sure." Hide_N_Seek went to work and within moments had a cheerfully crackling fire. "Is Kamoi really going to be worth all this work?"

"This and more," Kit promised. She shifted her gaze to the sky, still searching for her unhelpful pet. "It's pretty much paradise—or at least as close as you can get in Retha. It's tropical, warm, and it has more coconut- and melon-flavored drinks and food than you can shake a stick at." *We should have told Vic about Kamoi when she brought up the idea of VR tourism. She would have loved it.* "I'm going to search for Pax, guys. I'll be just in the trees. Fame, Fortune, you can stay here."

Fame—who had been talking to Solus Miles—nodded. "Yes, Kitten!"

"As you order," Fortune added.

"Fortune, I've been meaning to ask you," Glowrious scooted closer to the NPC. "I have two different staffs—can you tell me which one is better for me?"

"With *pleasure!*"

Kit slipped past the first layer of trees—giving the stunted tree that had almost eaten Prowl a wide berth. Her tapered ears twitched when she picked up the sound of rustling wings, and she raised her gaze to the treetops.

Pax was perched in a large tree, artfully splayed over a branch and leaning against the tree trunk as his lower wings cascaded behind him.

"Pax, we're taking a quick break, but we'll be moving on soon. Okay?" Kit called up to him.

The winged warrior did not deign to acknowledge her; instead, he picturesquely held out his hand for a tiny fairy to land on.

Kit squinted up at him, then shouted. "Hey—Paco!"

Pax nearly fell off his branch in his outrage as he glared down at her. "What?" he demanded with a scowl.

"Just make sure you keep pace." Kit turned to return to the camp but paused when she saw Solus leave the meadow for the forest as well. "Is everything okay?" she asked as he approached her.

Solus nodded. "It occurred to me something might kill you while you searched for Pax."

Kit chuckled. "Camp is, like, fifty feet away."

Solus shrugged. "You find trouble wherever you go. And if there isn't any, you make it."

"I could take offense to that, but I'm going to be a reasonable adult and overlook it—I won't even threaten to sic Fortune on you."

"How mature."

Kit grinned a little. *He does put up with a lot. He doesn't seem to dislike it, but...* She wrinkled her forehead with concern. "Are you okay with all of this?"

"With leveling? Absolutely." Solus Miles gave her a business-like nod.

"That's not quite what I meant—but yes, I guess with the leveling, too. Are you okay with the assumptions everyone has made, with being a leveling tank, and with serving as our main DPS?" Kit asked.

Solus shrugged. "DPS is my thing."

"Yes," Kit drawled out her response. *I'm not getting through to him...how to reword this?* "But you don't feel like a tool, or something I use however I want, right?"

"I *told* you to use me however you want."

Kit grumbled in aggravation. "I *know* you did, but that doesn't mean that's right. You're as close to a celebrity as this game gets, yes, but I don't want you to feel like I value you just for your levels and fame."

Solus thoughtfully studied her, his brow puckering slightly. "What else is there to value?"

Kit stared at him. "What else?" she repeated.

He nodded.

Kit felt her eyes bulge. *Oh my gosh. He must have it worse than Noir. Does he seriously not see why people would like him?* "You're thoughtful, for starters—or really I should say chivalrous since you're a knight. Like going down Tremblebach Falls with me. No one else offered—no one else would have gone, either, if you hadn't."

Solus said nothing, but Kit was *very* aware that he was still watching her.

"And though I complain about leveling, I know you do it because you're trying to shield me from scorn." She fussed over one of her earrings to give her hands something to do. *I really hope he doesn't fear I'm transforming into one of his fangirls, or something.* "And...um..." Kit finally glanced at him.

The very edges of Solus' lips quirked—but Kit wasn't sure if he found more amusement in her awkwardness or her praise.

Someone—a nearby forest bull perhaps—please drop by and end me from my misery. This is so embarrassing! "Yes," she finished.

One of Solus' eyebrows quirked up, giving his light smile a rather sarcastic edge. "Why haven't you invited me to your guild?"

Kit blinked. "Did I miss something in this conversation, or...?"

"If you like me so much—"

"Can we *please* say admire, or value?" Kit protested. "Or at least establish I'm not one of your moony-eyed fans?"

"If you like me so much," Solus repeated, "why haven't you asked me to join Heroes of Retha."

"Because I'm not actively recruiting for Heroes of Retha?" Kit said.

Solus lowered his black eyebrows—this time in a slightly judgmental slant. "Prowl is in the Heroes of Retha."

"Yeeesss," Kit slowly agreed.

"Invite me," Solus said.

"No," Kit refused.

Solus stared at her. "No?"

Kit hunched her shoulders and shrank a little under the weight of his icy eyes, but she nodded. "I won't invite you."

"Why not?" Solus asked.

I can't tell him why. I can't! I'll lose all his respect! "If you joined, everyone would want in."

"Not true," Solus said. "The vast majority of players have guilds—particularly the ones we're interacting with now. In fact, joining Heroes of Retha would make it easier on me, as I would stop getting private messages about joining other top-tier guilds."

Kit momentarily straightened, her embarrassment forgotten. "Are they seriously still trying to recruit you *now*? When our lives are at stake?"

Solus shrugged. "Not all see me as personally as you do."

"No wonder this has been a struggle—these people have screwed-up priorities!" Kit grumbled. She sneezed when one of Pax's shed feathers twirled through the air and brushed the tip of her nose.

"So invite me," Solus prompted.

Kit rubbed her nose. "No."

Solus leaned back a little, his surprise showing in the set of his mouth and the tilt of his head. "If you don't invite me, I'll have to conclude you only tolerate me and that the guild is some secret passage of friendship."

"It's *not* a secret club," Kit said. *He's not going to let this go, is he? Why didn't he show this kind of persistence in searching for Jehoshaphat, the Hermit of Singleness? Not that I'm complaining, but he's never been this stubborn!*

"Then invite me."

"*No.*"

"Why?"

"Because it's a stupid name!" The reason exploded from Kit's mouth before she had a chance to reel it back in, and it seemed like it was the cork out of the bottle; Kit couldn't stop her rant after that.

"Heroes of Retha is like *the* lamest guild name ever—though it might tie with Killing Squad. It's pretentious, unoriginal, and super big-headed," Kit scowled. "And if I see it after your name, I just might *die. You* don't care about your reputation, but in Milk Crown it was pretty well acknowledged that any PVP battle was at least one-fourth intimidation. And tying such an uninspired guild name to you? Ugh! No! I won't stand for it! Forget all your fans and your fame—it would be a tragedy to have you join Heroes of Retha just based on your power and dignity as a player." Kit shivered in distaste at the very thought.

Solus slightly narrowed his eyes. "You won't invite me because your guild name is awful?"

"Yes," Kit grumbled. "And no matter what you say, I'm not going to budge on this."

Solus grinned—as in a smile that actually flashed his white teeth and removed the icy edge he seemed to constantly wear. "You're a very interesting person, Kit."

Kit folded her arms across her chest until she realized she

resembled a pouting doll and then switched to put her hands on her hips. "Sorry—we can't all be as noble as you."

Solus' grin grew a little, and Kit almost gaped at him.

Holy Hills—he's about a million times more lethal when he's in a good mood than when he's off brooding.

Solus took a step closer to her. "That's forgivable. You're—"

Pax touched down on the forest floor with only the softest crunch of leaves. He tipped his head back and gave Kit a contemptuous sneer that curled his upper lip. "I've decided I would rather follow after you like a puppy while you fight than listen to this poor attempt at a courting ritual."

Kit felt her face turn bright red. *"What?"*

Solus' grin quirked slightly, getting a mischievous edge to it. "Though I *am* enjoying our conversation, it is a rarity that your winged warrior is willing to cooperate, so it's probably best if we take advantage of his obedience. We can finish talking about this later." He turned and stalked back to the meadow.

Kit was frozen in a mixture of embarrassment and a desire to strangle her own pet, then stumbled free when the rest of Solus' words caught up with her. "No, actually, we don't have to talk about this again."

"It's a good conversation."

"No, it's *not,*" Kit said. "Not at all. Do we agree?"

Solus didn't say anything as he slipped through the trees.

"Solus?" Kit trotted to catch up with him. "Do we agree?"

Solus turned to face her. Though he was no longer smiling, his eyes seemed lighter than before. He slid his sword out of its scabbard. "Call of Contest!"

"You jerk!" Kitten called before she was almost mowed down by a forest bull that charged the royal knight.

"What happened to noble?" Solus asked—within hearing range of the group.

"Be quiet!" Kit yelped as she felt the heat of her blush

spread through her body. "Everyone, gear up. Solus decided it's time to level again."

The party groaned.

"Give me a moment, and I'll have a good-sized mob," Solus said.

"That probably means we should start attacking now," Riko said as she popped to her feet, "or we'll be overwhelmed."

Alistair stood. "I agree. I'm always up for a rousing adventure, but Solus' idea of leveling is a little too close to lunacy even for me."

"You hear that, Solus?" Prowl drawled. "If *Alistair* thinks it's reckless, you know it's gotta be bat-crap-crazy."

"Call of Contest!"

12

WELCOME TO KAMOI

BY THE TIME Kit and her party had almost reached Kamoi, they were a tired and dirty mess. Solus had pushed them to such an extent that Kit had reached level 61, and even *he* looked a little worse for wear. His armor was a little scratched and dented from the forest bulls and the many sea monsters they had encountered as they followed the Blue Scale River through fae lands and down to Kamoi.

"We're so close," Kit promised Riko. The druid had her arm thrown over Kit's shoulders, and Kit half-dragged her along. "Just hold on until we arrive."

"Just put me on the beach—I can sleep in the sand," Riko mumbled as her head lolled forward.

"We'll have to get rooms at an inn as soon as we arrive." Alistair led her cavalry horse, who was slowly picking its way across the rocky road. Hide_N_Seek, the scout, was thrown over the horse's neck, already unconscious.

Almost everyone in the party dragged with exhaustion from the frantic leveling pace. There a few exceptions: Kit, because as an elf she had greater stamina than any of them; Long Claw, his werewolf strength gave him an edge; Solus, who probably was sadistically gaining energy from the levels Kit was getting; and Alistair, as the knight had taken care to guzzle stamina potions the whole way down.

"Kamoi is just between these cliffs." Solus nodded to the twin peaks that were staggered before the road.

"If anyone wishes for a detailed map of Kamoi, I have plenty to share—should Kitten give you permission," Fame said with an annoying amount of exuberance as she trotted along, her arms filled with rolled-up parchment.

"Please don't be under attack," Kit whispered as they rounded the bend in the road. "*Please* don't be under attack!" She strained her ears, but all she heard was the soothing roar of the ocean and the piercing call of seagulls.

She took a gulp of air and held her breath as they passed between the cliffs and entered the village of Kamoi.

Unlike Luminos and Elba, where the cities were contained within massive walls, Kamoi sprawled from the cliffs all the way down to the golden beach. Waterfalls spilled down from the rocky ledges, and palm trees and greenery erupted from every nook and cranny.

The village was tropical themed with wooden walkways, bridges, and docks zig-zagging everywhere. Most of the houses were wooden with thatched roofs and open-air sides, but some of the buildings had oil cloth and canvas awnings and wall coverings. The buildings down by the docks were all built on stilts, and many of them were constructed out of ship parts. There was even a pub Kit used to frequent, The Salty Parrot, that was actually a beached ship.

"Great, we're here." Noir dropped to his knees, then fell face-forward onto a fern. "Goodnight."

"Come on, Noir," Kit said as she dragged Riko toward the village. "A bed at the inn will be much more comfortable."

Noir grumbled in protest but pushed himself to his feet.

The inn—an airy and bright structure that was located by the pool from the biggest cliffside waterfall—was thankfully the first building they encountered.

It didn't take long to pay for the many required rooms and guide the rest of the party to their beds.

Kit stifled a yawn as she poked her head in the last room assigned to their party. It was a double room shared by Prowl and Alrid Edge—who were both passed out and hanging half out of their beds.

She slipped into the room long enough to push their limbs back onto their mattresses, then crept out and pulled the door shut behind her with a click.

She trotted down both the hall and the winding staircase that led to the main floor of the inn, waved to the innkeeper—who was chatting with Fame and Fortune—and wove around a giant anchor that served as a coat-rack of sorts for weapons, and made her way outside.

I'm doing fairly well—energy-wise anyway. I should see if I can get anywhere in convincing the people of Kamoi to ally themselves with us.

Kamoi was rather unique in the world of Retha. Though it was technically under fae rule, it was more of a utopian resort town populated with fae, naiads, mermaids, humans, and even a clan of werewolves that were responsible for the village's protection.

Officially, Kamoi was run by the village chief—which was a rather tourist-trap-y way of saying the village mayor. As long as Kit could remember, the post had been held by a sly and older male naiad named Pacifico.

Kit tilted her head up to soak in more of the sun and twitched her nose at the salty scent of the sea. She cracked an eye open when she felt a feather brush her arm.

Pax, who had previously picturesquely placed himself on

the inn's thatched roof, touched down next to her. He studied her from head to toe. "You could use a bath," he said.

Kit rubbed her gritty eyes. "Later," she said. "Though should I thank you for actually paying attention to me?"

"You need to rest, as well. It won't do the group any good if you collapse," Solus said behind her.

Both he and Alistair exited the inn, squinting slightly in the brilliant sunlight.

"Your pledged speaks the truth, Lady Kit." Alistair slapped dust from her cape. "Plus, it would sadden me to see you drive yourself to such lengths," she winked.

"I'll rest tonight," Kit said, "when the villagers are sleeping. For now, I need to track down Chief Pacifico."

Solus nodded. "If you're to have any hope of convincing the people of Kamoi to join you, Pacifico will need to approve first."

"Right?" Kit twitched her nose at the sour scent of fish that filled the air. "Tracking him down is going to be a pain in the butt, though."

Though Pacifico held the role of village chief, he abandoned his duties as much as possible and actually spent most of his time avoiding work while his competent-and-increasingly-stressed daughter handled the village.

"Not at all!" Alistair said cheerfully. "At this hour, Chief Pacifico is down by the beach, drinking alcoholic beverages from a hollowed-out coconut shell."

"He should be giving out daily quest rewards," Solus added.

"I forgot about that. Have you two done a lot of those quests?" Kit turned to follow the path deeper into the village, where it shifted to a wooden walkway. Houses and shops began to sprout around her with greater regularity.

"Yes," Solus said.

"Nope, not at all!" Alistair brightly responded.

Kit glanced back at the cavalry knight. 'Then how did you know where he would be?"

"I come to Kamoi whenever I can slip my KOS leash. Many of my friends usually come with me, and they always want to spend time on the beach," Alistair explained.

Kit kicked a fallen coconut off the path. "Hopefully his daughter will show up, too. She's the one we really need to agree to help us."

"You'll be able to manage it," Alistair declared. "You are our brave and intelligent leader—it's only a matter of time before Atlantia folds before you."

"Thanks for the vote of confidence." Kit jumped the short length of stairs and landed on the warm sand. She shielded her eyes with a hand as she gazed up and down the gorgeous shore.

Laughter and lively music radiated from the Salty Parrot— the ship-turned-pub. Behind it, the docks stretched out into the cove, so ships could dock and the mermaids and mermen could conduct their business with the rest of the villagers.

The rest of the beach was golden and untouched except for the occasional shell. The ocean was a stunning aquamarine color, and for a moment, as the beach wind ruffled her hair, Kit let herself enjoy the beautiful sight.

"There he is." Alistair pointed to a wiry, grandfatherly man. He was a naiad, so though he was mostly human in shape, his fingers were slightly webbed, and he had fin-like ridges that extended past the tips of his ears, sticking out of his unruly white hair. His eyes were the same stunning blue as the ocean, and he had a beard that was thick enough to garner a dwarf's admiration.

A small sea snake hung around his neck, eagerly looking out at the villagers and players who walked the beach and hissing whenever Pacifico accidentally bashed him with his coconut cup.

He was exactly as Kit remembered from her time playing as Azarel, though the way he squinted out at the ocean with a worried, furrowed brow seemed new.

When he caught sight of them, however, he brightened. "By the seas—is that you, Alistair Lionward and Sir Solus Miles?"

"It is!" Alistair said with a booming laugh. "How are you, Pacifico?"

"I could use another drink, but as we have peace for the moment, I cannot complain," Pacifico said. His sea snake pet momentarily disappeared into the mop of his hair. "Who is your friend?"

Alistair glanced at Solus, who shrugged slightly. "This is my pledged, Kit—short for Kitten."

"Ho-ho-ho! What's this? You finally got yourself an anchor?" Pacifico leaned forward so he could speculatively study Kit. "Hmm, an elf? Perhaps it is the reverse, and it is you who are anchoring her? No matter—I'm glad you are honeymooning here in Kamoi. You haven't gotten a room at the inn yet, have you? I can make sure my Atlantia gets a honeymoon suite for you!"

Kit made a strangled noise, which made Alistair grin.

"The elf is a bit of a shy lady," Alistair said.

Pacifico rolled his eyes. "Elven sensibilities—makes one live forever and be afraid to so much as fart in public."

Kit didn't know whether to laugh or puzzle over his strange yet somehow poetic statement. But Pax's not-so-quiet scoff prodded her into action. "We're actually not here for our honeymoon."

"Oh? Been pledged for a while? Where did you go, then? Better not be Torvel—city of canals my snake's tail end," Pacifico grumbled as his snake popped its head out of his beard. The naiad took a slug of the fruity-smelling drink and smacked his lips. "Nothing quite like a coco-loco-pineapple-slam! They don't have *those* in Torvel—let me tell you!"

"Uh, we haven't gone on a honeymoon," Kit said.

"No honeymoon?" Pacifico gasped, then narrowed his eyes at Solus. "Sir Solus—I never took you to be a miser! How can you deny your beautiful pledged a honeymoon!"

"At the time most would be honeymooning, my beautiful pledged was slaying the dreaded necromancer Malignus," Solus said dryly.

Pacifico immediately swiveled back to Kit. "You're *that* Kitten? Kitten Lovemuch?"

Kit nodded.

Pacifico turned to the Salty Parrot and shouted with the strength of a fog horn. "Louis—bring me two more coco-loco-pineapple-slams! We've got the slayer of Malignus visiting!"

A faint "Come get it yourself, you old geezer!" came from the creaking pub.

"And walk all that way? Waves no! Send your old cabin boy out with them!" Pacifico complained.

"My old cabin boy is your son-in-law, ya salt-crusted idiot! And he's gone minding his children 'cause Atlantia is off doing your duties!" The barkeeper appeared at the doorway of the Salty Parrot, an accordion in hand.

"It's good for him!" Pacifico tipped back the rest of his drink, then shook the empty coconut cup at the barkeeper. "It keeps him involved in his children's lives!"

The back and forth continued for a bit, and Kit glanced at Solus, pressing her lips together as she considered him.

The royal knight noticed and shifted slightly. "What?"

"I was just thinking how fascinating it is that NPCs seem prone to razz you about your love life," Kit said.

Solus shrugged. "I have a high reputation level with nearly

every race, organization, and location in Retha. As such, the NPCs are fairly informal with me."

"Your completionism doesn't surprise me," Kit said dryly. "It's more that I find it hilarious that no player would dare call you out, yet the NPCs crack jokes about us."

"I think the key is no player would *publicly* call Solus Miles out," Alistair chimed in. "KOS blazed with gossip when everyone realized he was taken. Some of the lovely ladies in my guild have been sending me updates, and apparently there's been public mourning. You had a fan club, Solus. Did you know that?"

Kit squinted. "A fan club?"

Alistair winked. "It's not terribly rare—I have one as well! But Solus' is probably among the biggest—or it would be if he'd just smile more."

Solus shrugged slightly, then nodded in Pacifico's direction. "I think they're done arguing."

The barkeeper—a large, swarthy man who was heavily tattooed and rivaled Long Claw in the thickness of his shoulders—stalked across the sandy shore, carrying a tray with several drinks. He eyed Kitten and clutched the tray to his impressive pecs for a moment. "You're really Kitten Lovemuch—the elf that led the heroes who slayed Malignus?"

Kit nodded. "I am."

His mouth twisted in disbelief as he looked her up and down before his eyes settled on her belt.

Remembering King Brasil's fascination with the belt, Kit tugged on the buckle so she could angle it properly. "I received this after fighting Malignus."

The barkeeper nodded, and the suspicion in his face faded before he beamed. "Then here—a coco-loco-pineapple-slam on the house. May you and the heroes you fought with live on in good health!" He offered Kit the same fruity beverage in a coconut cup that Pacifico guzzled.

Kit took it and, after noticing the barkeeper's expectant gaze, took a sip of it. The taste—creamy and sweet—reminded Kit of the many drinks she consumed at post-raid and post-PVP celebrations with Milk Crown. Instead of making her homesick or sad as she might have previously been, it warmed her. She lifted her chin and raised the coconut in a cheer. "Thank you for the drink—it's delicious."

"Of course!" the barkeeper said. "Whenever you or one of your comrades want a drink, come to the Salty Parrot. It will be on the house!"

"Thank you. Two of them are traveling with me—though they aren't here at the moment. I will pass on word of your generosity," Kit smiled.

The barkeeper grinned in return, then caught sight of something behind Kit. "Here's your drink, Pacifico. Next time, come get it yourself." The barkeeper practically shouted the words over his shoulder to the older naiad as he hurried back to his tavern.

"Where are you going?" Pacifico shouted after him. "Skittish fellow," he grumbled as he peered at the pub. "Always running—" Pacifico cut off with a shout when a lady performed a flying kick, nailing the village chief right between the shoulders and sending him soaring.

The woman—who looked about Riko's age and sported the same webbed fingers and fin-crested ears as Pacifico—planted her hands on her hips. "Father," she growled. "I've been looking for you all morning. You have two disputes to settle, one request to build a property you have to approve, and Sea Wolf and his crew are expecting to meet you in one hour for the defense inspection...and you were out here *drinking*?"

Pacifico spit out sand as he stood and brushed himself off.

"Atlantia—my charming daughter! You have impeccable timing —and kicks—as usual! I want you to speak to an important hero." His pet snake eagerly slithered down his arm and extended its head towards Atlantia.

Atlantia took the snake, who twined around her wrist like a bracelet, blinking happily when she rubbed the top of its head. "Cut the act, Father. We don't have time to waste."

"But it's not an act—for once," Pacifico said. He shook his head, creating a sandstorm from the sand grains in his hair and beard. "You remember Sir Solus Miles?"

Atlantia spared Solus a glance and nodded deeply. "I do. Welcome back, Sir Solus Miles—and you as well, Alistair Lionward. I hope you enjoy your visit to Kamoi and find it restful and enjoyable so you tell all your friends."

"Yes, yes," Pacifico impatiently said as he fished his coconut cup out of the sand, his lower lip jutting in sadness when he realized his drink had spilled. "Greet them like a good girl—but listen to this! Sir Solus is pledged—to Kitten Lovemuch!"

Atlantia turned to Kit and bit her lip. "The same Kitten Lovemuch who led the heroes that killed Malignus?"

Kit shrugged uncomfortably. "I led them, but it was those at the White Veil Nunnery who actually defeated Malignus."

Atlantia shook her head. "I disagree—they never would have done so if not for you and the other heroes of Retha."

Pacifico fished a shell out of his shirt and rejoined the group. "I was thinking perhaps—since she's here with Sir Solus and Alistair Lionward—we ought to ask for their help."

Kit stood taller. *Help? Is this another event that we use to bargain for their help?* She exchanged glances with Alistair and Solus. "Why do you need help?"

Atlantia sighed. "Since the return of Lord Valdis, our shores have not been as safe as they once were."

"Previously, we only had to defend ourselves from the occasional pirate attack," Pacifico frowned. "But now the ocean writhes with sea serpents."

"They plague our cove and rivers as they travel upstream," Atlantia explained. "According to Sea Wolf—the leader of Kamoi's defenses—he and one of his men followed some of the serpents all the way to the Soggy Swill Bog."

"It is true the serpents have nearly taken over the bog since the goblins moved on," Alistair said. "We passed the edge of the bog on our way here, and we encountered many sea serpents in the rivers."

Pacifico sighed. "They breed here in the cove and then travel upstream, so they trouble not only our sea activities—fishing and the like—but our whole village as well. It is no longer safe to do something as simple as gather water without Sea Wolf or one of his werewolves, and that hurts our entire town. We're a resort village, but visitors won't come if we can't keep 'em safe."

Atlantia pointed to a pair of werewolves who patrolled the beach, walking ankle deep in the ocean as they scanned the waters. "Fighting the serpents requires all of our warriors, which means the pirates sail our shores unchecked. Furthermore, we don't have the strength to entirely eliminate the sea serpents. If we could clear them out of the cove, I believe we could end this fruitless cycle. But Sea Wolf and our town forces can only do so much."

Yep, this has got to be our way in. It makes me wish Riko was here, though, to help me with this. Kit cleared her throat. "I can see what dire straits this has placed you in. The return of Lord Valdis has affected us all. My party and I just returned from helping King Brasil purge Brunascar of spiders."

Hope burned in Atlantia's lake-blue eyes. "You aided the White Needles Dwarves."

Here we go! "Yes," Kit said carefully. "I'm part of an effort to rally the peoples of Retha to fight against Lord Valdis. We wished to recruit the White Needles Dwarves—but obviously Brasil could not leave his people plagued by spiders, so we helped."

Pacifico eyed Kit. "Will you help *us*?"

How do I phrase this without coming off like a jerk? Kit tucked some of her Champaign-pink hair behind her ear. "We will," Kit said. "But darkness is flooding these lands, and Retha will not last if we do not face Lord Valdis and fight him. If we help you today and slay the sea serpents, I expect we will have your support for our coming battle," Kit stated the question more than she asked it but looked back and forth between Pacifico and Atlantia, trying to judge their reactions.

Pacifico tossed his empty coconut over his shoulder. "Of course! Kamoi would never stand to let Lord Valdis take over Retha—we'd lose our customer base!"

"We don't have many soldiers, but if you can save us from the serpents, our boats and provisions will be yours," Atlantia added.

Pacifico nodded. "Yes! In fact, may it be said that the village of Kamoi backs the Heroes of Retha, and once all the sea serpents in our cove are killed, we would be proud to answer the call of Kitten Lovemuch and give you our allegiance."

Kit breathed out a little easier and relaxed her shoulders. There wasn't a popup screen, but Kit was willing to bet it would show up once the sea serpents were cleared. "I am glad you are willing to help us fight. We need every warrior and every bit of help we can get. Thank you. Once my party has rested, we will begin our fight against the sea serpents."

Atlantia reached out and grabbed Kit's right hand, holding it between her own. "Thank you, Kitten Lovemuch." Her snake-turned-bracelet tested the air with its tongue as it adjusted itself on Atlantia's wrist. "Our village will not forget this—nor will we forget any of you," she said, speaking to Solus and Alistair.

Alistair winked. "The honor is ours."

Solus said nothing, but he did nod his head slightly.

"Sea Wolf will take you out to the cove—most of the sea serpents are out at the entrance of the cove—by that cropping of rocks." Pacifico pointed across the blue-green waters to some large rock formations. "There's some sandbars there as well, so you won't be as confined as it looks."

"I'll let Sea Wolf know," Atlantia said.

"Good!" Pacifico beamed. "Then I'll go get us some refreshments."

Atlantia grabbed her father by the collar of his shirt. "No refreshments."

"But we ought to drink to our new alliance!" Pacifico complained.

Atlantia set off in the opposite direction of the Salty Parrot, dragging her father behind her. "No. We can celebrate tonight. For now, you have two disputes to settle."

"But the heroes..." Pacifico complained.

Alistair released a peal of laughter. "We'll be fine, Chief Pacifico. As Kitten said, our companions are rather fatigued. We will not be able to do battle until tomorrow at the earliest."

"If Atlantia tells Sea Wolf, we would like to speak to him tonight," Kit added. "But Alistair is right: we all need to rest."

Pacifico grumbled. "You all work too hard. You need to embrace the peaceful and relaxed spirit of Kamoi!"

"Come along, Father," Atlantia said as she mercilessly dragged him along.

Alistair laughed as she watched the father and daughter stride out of hearing distance.

Kit stretched her arms above her head. "That's another ally —once we take care of those sea serpents, anyway."

Solus nodded. "It is a lucky thing we're only dealing with sea serpents—not pirates."

Kit winced. "Yeah, pirates are a lot harder to fight."

"This should be a fast win, though. We can handle the sea serpents—we killed enough to make serpent-skin armor for each of us on our way down here." Alistair tapped her lower lip in thought. "Though I won't be able to use Trust—which is a shame. Although I do wonder if I can ride a sea serpent..."

Before Kit could respond, she felt a breeze brush the back of her neck.

"Kit?" Waffle asked over the party chat. "Do you have a moment?"

Kit glanced at Alistair and Solus who—being part of the raid —heard the comment.

Alistair swatted her hand at Kit with a smile, and Solus stared out at the sea.

"Yes, I can talk." Kit wove around Pax as she turned to trek up the beach. "Did you win over the elves already?"

"Not exactly..." Waffle trailed off.

"They aren't willing to talk about an alliance," Nyx piped in. "We've sat through several meetings with the elf queen, and we've gotten nowhere."

Kit flicked her fans open and shut as she thought. "Is there an event you need to complete first, like the spiders in Brunascar? We've got the people of Kamoi lined up to join us, but we have to clear a bunch of sea serpents first. Maybe you have to do something like that."

"It's possible based on the information I've received from Corporate Force," Nyx said. "But I believe there's more to it."

"We think they might be avoiding the topic because neither Nyx nor I—nor anyone in our party—were part of the raid that beat Malignus," Waffle explained. "They treat us the way they have always treated us, but I noticed in Brunascar, the dwarves seemed a lot more welcoming and interested in you, Prowl, and Riko. You said yourself that we might need a member from your raid present to get anyone to agree to an alliance."

"I guessed on a hunch," Kit said. She wove her fingers together as she thought. *Killing Malignus was a world quest, and I know there have been other, long-standing, positive repercussions from being involved in world quests. Bryce didn't mention it, but there were a thousand other things we were trying to cover before I came back...*

She shifted her gaze to the cloud-less sky. "It's unfortunate that hunch turned out to be right. But I'm not coming. I don't want to travel in one big pack if I can avoid it—splitting up means we're covering twice as much ground. Plus, even though I'm not despised by the elves, I'm still not on good terms with them. I'll send Riko to you, instead, as I first suggested."

"That's precisely whom I was going to ask for," Nyx said with satisfaction.

"Thanks, Kit!" Waffle said. "Hopefully once she arrives, we'll finally get things moving."

"Yes, but she's not going to arrive for at least a day. She's sleeping right now, and I don't want to wake her up just yet," Kit said.

"Ahh, yes, exhaustion can hit you hard in this game," Waffle said sagely.

"Yeah," Kit said, though she privately thought, *Forget exhaustion—I'm not poking her awake just to tell her she has to go play nice with the elves! I'll be lucky if she doesn't murder me when I drop this bomb on her after she wakes up.*

"Was that all, or did you guys have anything else you wanted to talk about?" Kit asked.

"No, we're doing fine beyond the elves' conversation-rejection," Nyx said.

"Good," Kit said. "I'm fine with dodgy conversations—I just

hope we don't have to do a special event for every group we want to recruit."

"One can hope," Nyx said. "You will tell us when Riko is on her way?"

"*Riko* will probably tell the whole raid when she's on her way," Kit said wryly. "But, yeah. If she doesn't announce it on the party chat, I'll let you know. If you guys have time, you might want to gather up some of the reputation drops for her, as I don't think she has high enough affinity with the elves to get in with the new restrictions."

"We can do that," Nyx said firmly.

"Yes. Good luck with the sea serpents!" Waffle said.

"Thanks," Kit said. "Let me know if you have any other problems."

"Will do," Waffle promised before the party chat fell silent.

Kit dug her feet into the warm sand, stared out at the ocean, and sighed.

I don't really want to send Riko out, but we can't afford to move slower than we already are. And if things are getting tense like Shashanna said, we will need all the allies we can get to back up our plans.

Besides, at least I'll have Prowl, Noir, and Solus with me. The thought of her fake pledged made Kit relax marginally. *Solus is a much bigger support than I thought he'd be. Though I shouldn't be surprised—he did promise he would do everything he could to get us free.* The thought made her pause. *Actually, that's probably his motivation—as charming as he is. Maybe he's like Luther, and he has a wife or girlfriend waiting for him outside the game. When we were first pledged, I asked if I had to be worried about a jealous girlfriend, but he might have inter-preted that as a jealous in-game girlfriend and not a real-life one...*

The thought bothered Kit enough that she shook herself loose and glanced over at Pax, who was grooming his wings.

When he realized she was looking at him, he scowled. "What?"

"Are you unfriendly because I'm lower-leveled or because you were programmed to have a rotten personality?" Kit asked.

Pax's scowl was twisted with confusion as he lowered his silver eyebrows. "What?" he repeated, sounding much more confused than crabby.

"Nothing; don't trouble your pretty head over it, Paco. Come on. Let's head back to the inn."

Pax breathed out loudly through his nose. "You are as poor-mannered as the divine oracle's raccoon."

"I actually like Trash Panda a lot," Kit said. "So thank you!" She turned her back to the sea and reluctantly began the trek back to the inn.

13

UNUSUAL NPCS

"YOU SOLD ME OUT!"

Kit squinted, trying to make out the shapes of her fellow party members in the thick fog, but even her elf eyes couldn't properly discern them. "I did not."

"You did," Riko said stubbornly. *"How could you send me to the elves?"*

"You've already asked me that at least a dozen times," Kit said.

"Maybe if you gave me a satisfactory answer, I'd stop asking!"

"Look at it this way: at least you won't have to deal with Long Claw anymore." Kit wobbled for a moment when she leaped from one slick rock to the next, doing her best to perform a makeshift rendition of Battlefield March.

"I guess. But you sacrificed me—and why do I have to come alone? You could have made Prowl tag along at least."

"I *had* to send you because getting Prowl anywhere near Lèas would be disastrous, and he'd likely get you all thrown out."

"Yeah, that sounds about right."

"Hold on one second." Kit switched out of the private message and shouted, "Long Claw—don't venture any farther away." She studied her mini-map, where the dot that represented Long Claw skirted farther and farther away from the group.

"I say let him wander," Noir grunted as he scrambled up Kit's rock formation. "Serves him right if he gets himself killed."

Kit twirled picturesquely, then nimbly leaped to another large boulder. "Maybe, but he's great at tearing through the sea serpents, so I'd like to keep him going instead of wasting time waiting for him to respawn and rejoin us." She lifted her right leg up behind her and held it there—almost touching the back of her skull—for a moment.

Fog blanketed the cove. Kit couldn't even see the torches and fires of Kamoi, much less the ocean waters that writhed with sea serpents.

She could see the rock formation behind her and ahead of her, and the occasional sea serpent that twined around the rocks; otherwise, she mostly had to depend on her hearing—which was barely any better. Though she could hear splashes, all noise was muffled, and things seemed to echo oddly, making it difficult to pinpoint the exact location of her teammates.

"Maybe we should have waited for the fog to clear before we came out here," Kit said.

Noir snorted as he frog-leaped to her boulder, clinging to the rock's slick side. "Why would we do that? There are a lot of sea serpents, yeah, but they're all lower-level. Trash Panda, come on," he called, twisting back and holding out his arm. His racoon jumped and caught Noir's arm, but the pet was so hefty, he nearly wrenched Noir off the large boulder.

"Yeah, but I still don't like this weather. The fog seems...

suffocating." Kit tucked her chin as she again tried to listen for the other party members. She could hear Prowl grumbling as he fought on a sandbar just north of her, and Solus was always easy to tell with his pinpoint—and wordless—fighting precision.

"Good news, everyone!" Alistair whooped somewhere south. "Sea serpents *can* be ridden!"

Kit twirled in time to see the cavalry knight glide past on the back of a sea serpent. She had tied a length of rope around its fanged mouth and fashioned a bridle of sorts, mercilessly yanking on the monster's face in an attempt to steer it as it thrashed and fought her control.

"Be careful, Alistair," Kit called. "Your armor will make you drown if you go out too deep." She flicked her fans out and whirled, then jumped back to the rock formation on which she had originally perched.

"Could you maybe *stop* hopping around like some kind of mountain goat?" Noir grumbled as he skidded down the side of the boulder and flung himself back on Kit's new perch.

"Sorry, I'm enjoying the elven athleticism," Kit said a little guiltily. "I would have broken my neck doing this as Azarel."

"Yes, well, we're not *all* elves," Noir sneered as he flopped onto the rock. Trash Panda leaped after him, landing on his head and shoving it into a sopping pile of seaweed.

Kit cringed in sympathy. "I'll be more careful."

"*Kit?*" Riko asked over their private message.

"Yes, I'm back." Kit switched back to the private exchange. "Are you almost to Fíone Forest?"

"*I'm here, but I still have to make my way to Lèas. I wanted to make it clear, though, that if you're going to shove me out of our delightful little group and lead this second party of self-satis-fied players, I will* not *be the one you stick with all the NPC groups you don't want to meet.*"

"I didn't send you to a bunch of self-satisfied players," Kit protested. "You're going to get along great with Nyx. She *needs* your charisma—she has the tendency to speak her mind, which is admirable, but it also gets her into trouble. And Waffle is a very likeable guy."

"*You still haven't agreed not to send me to the hinterlands to get the NPCs you don't want to deal with.*"

"Is there some place you specifically don't want to go—besides the elves?"

"*None that I can think of at the moment...*"

A strange splashing made Kit spin around. She quickly switched out of the private message. "Miles?" she called.

A wave smashed against the base of her rock perch, and a large sea serpent surfaced. Its eyes glowed in the dim light, and its hundreds of teeth flashed as it hissed.

Kit squeaked when Solus jumped from the gloom of the fog and landed next to her. His cape snapped behind him as he lunged forward and stabbed the sea serpent straight through, making it disappear with a spray of water.

Kit relaxed a little. "Thanks, Miles."

He nodded and disappeared back into the mist as swiftly as he had appeared.

Kit stared at her map again, then shouted, "Everyone needs to circle back to the center. It looks like we're spreading out a little too thin; some of the sea monsters are getting through."

"Okay," the scout shouted somewhere in the mist.

"As you wish, Lady Kit," Alistair said. "But before we finish our fight, would someone help me take a screenshot of my new mount and me? I'm going to send it to Gared."

Prowl snorted. "What, do you *want* him to come down here and drag you back to Luminos?"

Kit wiped sea spray from her face and switched back to the private message. "Well, if you think of anyone you don't want to visit, let me know. I wouldn't have sent you to the elves, but I thought they'd be easy. I guess I should have known better."

"*Yes,*" Riko said sourly. "*You should have.*"

"You could go to Torvel next," Kit suggested.

"*The City of Canals? You must be joking.*"

"It's a beautiful city," Kit argued. "It's one of the most romantic places in Retha."

"*Yeah, and it's run by the Court of the Rogue. No. You're not dumping that one on me.*"

"Fine, fine. We can talk about it when you finish with the elves—or after we finish with the sea serpents here in Kamoi. But I really should go—the fight is getting harder."

"*Good luck.*"

"You, too."

"*Thanks. Hopefully it will be better than when Prowl and I had to listen to them drone on for three days and three nights about the seals.*"

"Look at it this way: at least you'll get free reputation. Waffle and the others have been collecting reputation drops for you so you'll be able to enter despite the new restrictions."

"*How generous.*"

Prowl shouted a muffled oath somewhere behind Kit, and there was a tremendous splash.

"Gotta go, bye," Kit said before she closed the private message. "Prowl? You okay?"

Something creaked, and the ocean gurgled, but Prowl didn't reply.

"Prowl?" Concerned, Kit glanced at his health bar. *He wasn't killed—he still has full health.*

Kit jumped three rock formations, then leaped into the ocean with a splash, landing on the sandbar Prowl was supposed to be guarding. "Prowl?"

The sandbar—or what bits she could see of it—was abandoned. She paced the length of the sandbar, splashing through shin-high water. "Does anyone see Prowl?" Kit glanced up at her mini-map. "It looks like he's just past the sandbar, but I can't see him." She narrowed her eyes and squinted, but she still couldn't make out anything through the thick layer of fog that blanketed the cove.

"I don't see him either." Noir joined her with a tremendous splash, and Trash Panda hung from his neck. "Hey, Solus, why don't you call your pet dragon down from the sky to burn off the fog?"

"You can't burn off fog," Solus said, his voice muffled in the thick mist.

"Prowl?" Kit called one last time.

Sea serpents hissed and splashed water, but there was no other answer.

"Something's wrong," Kit said. "He's not answering—he's not even complaining. Prowl! Can you hear me?"

Her heart thundered in her ears as she strained her hearing for anything odd.

I should call the spellbinder—he might be able to send a bolt of fire or something out by Prowl.

She jumped when a popup screen appeared.

You have a private message from: Halbryt
Accept message?

Kit accepted the invite. "Halbryt, can I PM you back in a minute?"

"*This is an emergency,*" Halbryt said.

Kit tilted her head when she heard another splash. It sounded like someone walking in the water—like her and Noir—but according to the mini-map, no one was close enough. "How bad of an emergency? Because I'm dealing with disappearing party members right now."

"*Large-scale emergency. You need to return to Luminos as soon as possible.*"

"What? Why?" Something creaked behind her, and Kit turned around just in time to avoid a wooden paddle that nearly cracked her in the face.

"Solus!" Kit shouted. She tried to scurry away, but standing in shin-high water slowed her down, and she almost fell as she reeled backwards.

"Look out!" Noir shouted.

Halbryt, unaware of the battle, continued. "*Elba is—*" the rest of his words were lost in the scuffle.

Kit heard the telltale whoosh of air, but she was still trying to correct her balance and didn't shift her weight in time. She took a staff to the head in the prime of a swing and toppled, face-planting in the ocean.

Someone picked her up, and she coughed and spat out salt water. She tried to flick open her fans, but whoever held her put a hand to her forehead. "Sleep," they ordered.

The last thing Kit saw was the black shadow of Solus Miles as he leaped onto the sandbar.

Then everything went dark.

———

Kit awoke with a groan. Her head ached, and the sun blazed with an intensity that made everything fuzzy. Her head sagged forward, but when she tried to raise her hands to rub her eyes, she realized they were tied to her side.

She blinked slowly, and her vision cleared enough for her to realize she was nose-to-nose with a parrot.

She yanked back, smacking her head into a wooden surface

behind her. She moaned in pain as the world tilted on an odd axis.

"The last of them is awake," said a man with a voice much like the deep keens of a whale. "The elf maiden."

"What happened?" Kit muttered as she wriggled in her rope bindings—which did nothing but make the rope dig deeper into her limbs.

"We were captured," Solus Miles said to her left. "By pirates."

"Nooo," Kit moaned. "Not pirates!" She regained more of her bearings and was finally able to look around without flopping over.

They appeared to be tied to the mast of a ship. White canvas sails snapped above them, emblazed with the dreaded black skull of pirates. The ship—a monster of a vessel constructed out of black- and red-painted wood—rocked gently with the waves.

Men crowded the deck, and it took Kit's eyes a moment to properly focus and pick out faces and features.

All of the pirates wore giant gold rings, and most of them had over-sized gold chains, too. They wore their buttoned shirts unfastened almost all the way to their navels—which was a bit shiver-inducing to witness, as the majority of the pirates looked to be in their late forties and sported a bit of a beer belly, the roundness of which could be witnessed from their open shirts.

Though they all sported facial stubble and beards, most of them resembled fathers who had accidentally stumbled onto the ship.

"I can't contact anyone," Solus said, "by private message *or* our party chat. It seems we have been isolated."

"Yeah," Kit sighed. "That's typically how they operate. And as usual, they have the worst timing ever. Just before we were snatched, I got a PM saying we needed to return to Luminos ASAP."

"Why?" Solus asked.

"I was knocked out before he could explain it, but it has something to do with Elba." Kit fidgeted, trying to sooth an itch on her lower back. *Elba...Shashanna said it was under attack by goblins, but that's probably the event we use to get the Imperial Empress on our side. I wouldn't think that would be an emergency...*

Looking out over the deck, she could barely see the gray smudge of fog that was the cove. And though the trees on the shore didn't so much as sway with a breeze, the sails were full, and the ship moved with excessive speed, carrying them farther and farther away.

"Is Prowl here?" Kit asked softly.

"Present," Prowl said dryly.

"If the pirates announce an intention to keep me as a heal slave, I want someone to run me through," Noir announced. He wore a grumpy expression, and Trash Panda—who was positioned between Kit and Noir and was also tied to the mast—chattered angrily.

Kit craned her neck as she tried to peer around the mast. "Is it just the four of us, then?"

"Yep." Noir glared at the pirates as if he could kill them with mental hatred.

"Have you ever been captured by pirates before?" Prowl asked.

"No," Solus Miles said.

"I wasn't asking *you*," Prowl snorted. "Of course you wouldn't have something so inglorious happen to you."

Solus shrugged slightly. "As I was always careful to play in zones appropriate for my level, I was never under the threat of being unable to properly defend myself, so there was no risk of becoming captured."

"Oh my sheep," Kit grumbled. "We're prisoners on a pirate ship, and you're *still* complaining that I wander into zones too high for me? Did it ever occur to you that you should be grateful that's the biggest complaint you have about me? What would you have done if I was one of your fangirls?"

Solus thought for a moment. "Killed you, probably."

Kit leaned away from him as best she could while tied to the mast to gape at him. "*What?*"

"What are you two talking about?" Noir asked.

"Silence, prisoners!" A man boomed like a cannon going off.

The pirates parted for their captain—a stocky man with an especially hairy chest, who sported a fancy blue coat and a black tricorn hat with a ridiculously large feather tucked into its brim.

"Well, well! What do we have here?" The captain swaggered across the deck, making the numerous golden chains he sported jingle. He studied Kit and the others over the tops of black-tinted spectacles and scratched his chest with a dagger.

Solus frowned as he studied the captain, then lowered his head so he could whisper into Kit's ear. "Why do all of these pirates look like the fantasy version of forty-year-olds going through a mid-life crisis?"

"Because they *are* forty-year-olds going through a midlife crisis," Kit said dryly.

"Ahh, so *you've* been captured by pirates before?" Prowl asked.

"More times than I care to admit." Kit scowled. "Bryce always teased me that the pirates knew I was the soundest investment as our guildmasters would pay a hefty fee to get their best damage-dealer back."

"What are you talking about?" Solus asked.

"You'll see," Kit said bitterly.

The captain brandished his dagger at Kit. "Silence—there'll be no more *fraternizing* among ye." He circled the mast, studying Kit and her friends. "An elf maiden, a royal knight, a *saboteur*? Why did you grab a saboteur—everyone knows they never have any coin of their own." The captain scowled at his crew.

A pirate who was standing by ship's wheel—but wasn't doing anything to steer the ship and instead had his hand extended out, palm forward, in front of him—shrugged. "He was the easiest to reach first. Gotta start somewhere."

The captain grumbled and completed the circuit. "And last...a healer, if I'm not mistaken. A divine oracle perhaps? Ho-ho-ho—he'll be a ripe one. Healers always are!" he chortled.

"Their value is rather disproportionate to the average hero," a pirate in a red-and-white-striped shirt said as he moved beads on an abacus. "But I think it is the royal knight who will fetch the greatest price. His armor is quite expensive—his sword especially so."

"What's going on?" Solus asked.

Before Kit could respond, the captain bellowed, "Listen, you scurvy dogs! You've been taken captive by the dreaded Pieces of Eight Pirate Company!" The captain grinned as he planted his fists on his hips. "You are now our *prisoners*."

The pirate with the parrot—which Kit could now see wasn't actually alive but was stuffed and tied on to the man's shoulder —nodded behind the captain.

"You'll be silent and tell my men what they need to know —or you'll be losing a few fingers and toes, and mayhap even walk the plank." The captain flashed a set of perfect white teeth, then strode away. "Schmitty—they're yours to rough up!"

A huge man that looked like he might be distantly related to a troll cracked his hands and grinned. "Aye-aye, Captain." As he ambled towards them, his open shirt revealed a tattoo of the Imperial crest over his heart.

Solus frowned. "Is that man an Imperial *guard*?"

"Was," Kit said. "He was a guard."

The pirate with the abacus folded his doughy arms across his chest and glanced at his troll-like comrade. "Don't touch the elf maiden," he said. "If you rough her up while trying to get information from her, you'll earn us the enmity of the elves. I'd rather not garner their attention with our little operation," the pirate said—sounding more like an investment banker than a sailor.

The trollish pirate grunted. "Start with the knight, yeah?"

"No, see if they'll cooperate first," the abacus-wielding pirate said. "Saboteurs are usually cowards and will do anything to save their skins."

"Hey!" Prowl wriggled in the ropes. "I'll have you know that you can't travel with Kit and be a coward—you'd die more often than she does!"

Kit ignored the conversation and bit her lip. She tried to toggle the party chat, then a PM, but both of them were grayed out. Her guild chat wasn't, but that didn't help at all. She and Prowl were the only members of the Heroes of Retha. She sagged against the ropes. "This is going to waste so much time."

"I'm assuming you don't have an important date, seeing as your pledged was kidnapped *with* you," Noir pointed out.

"She received a message telling her to return to Luminos," Solus said.

"We know that, Mr. I-don't-take-leveling-risks. We were tied next to you when she told you that," Prowl drawled.

Solus ignored Prowl and kept his eyes on Kit. "You don't have to worry. We have a way out."

Kit squinted up at him. *Did the pirates rattle him when they snatched him?* "How?" she asked plainly.

Solus glanced at the puffy clouds in the sky and gave her a meaningful look.

Mystified, Kit stared at him. "I have no idea what that means."

"Enough out of you," the hulking pirate growled. He punched his right fist into his left palm and smiled. "We need to have a bit of a talk."

"I'm too shy to speak—talk to the saboteur first," Noir said.

"I'm going to kill you," Prowl snarled.

Noir rolled his eyes. "Make as many threats as you like. The fact is, I'm worth more than you." He froze, and his bronze coloring paled a little. "I didn't mean that—I meant important! I'm actually poor."

Abacus pirate was back, rearranging beads. "I'm sure," he purred. "Particularly as I look over your armor. The Hood of White Righteous? Because obviously a poor divine oracle can afford such a rare piece."

"It's because I'm bad at budgeting. I don't even have a house. I'm a homeless hipster," Noir said.

Abacus pirate tapped the tool on his chin. "New plan," he told his hulking companion. "Start with the priest."

"Hey, hey." Prowl stood on one leg and nudged the abacus pirate on the thigh with his free foot.

The pirate twisted his lips in disgust. "Stop that."

"Make me." Prowl kicked his leg up extra high and managed to smear his boot on the pirate's shoulder, then groaned. "Oh, that was too much. I think I pulled something."

"Saboteurs are always so gross," the pirate grumbled.

"Yeah, well, you smell like BO," Prowl snorted.

The hulking pirate took his eyes off Noir and circled the mast so he stood before Prowl. "What did you say?" he growled, his voice like the rumbles of a volcano.

"I said you smell like BO," Prowl said.

The hulk cracked his knuckles.

"Which is short for beautiful orchids," Prowl said.

"I bet," abacus pirate said. "And what is your name?"

"Riko hagbreath Macgee," Prowl said.

Abacus pirate nodded to the hulk.

The hulk put his hand around Prowl's throat.

"Just kidding," Prowl gurgled as he kept them occupied. "It's Prowl."

The hulk stepped back and nodded, and he and the abacus pirate continued to question the saboteur, making Noir sag in relief.

"That was close. And unfortunate—I won't be able to let Prowl die on a whim now. At least not until he says something stupid again," Noir said.

Kit shifted so her belt wasn't digging into her hip quite as much. "Try not to mention anything related to money, Solus, or you're going to bring out the exceedingly conniving side of these pirates, as Noir has shown us."

"Why are you all so gloomy?" Solus asked. "It does not seem like they will seriously hurt or injure us, despite their threats. What is so fearsome about them?"

"It's because they're not your standard pirates," Noir said glumly. "They're a thousand times worse."

"Look around you," Kit ordered. "That man up by the ship wheel? He's a wizard. He's casting the spell that keeps the wind blowing in the sails. Abacus pirate is either a merchant or a banker—I can't tell which. And as you observed earlier, our questioner is a soldier."

"If these pirates are really career men, how can they be worse than pirates?" Solus asked.

"Because they're fiscally brilliant," Kit sighed. "They have their brigandry and marauding down to a system. They strike at whatever shipments will bring the highest return. They're still a challenge to fight, as their ranks are populated with soldiers *and* wizards, and they're smart in picking their battles. They strike fast like snakes and are gone before you have a chance to win back what they've stolen."

"Though they usually go after material goods, they also have a nice side business of capturing players," Noir added. "How can you not know this?"

"After doing a basic perusal on the community and learning the advantages and disadvantages of fighting them, I decided it wasn't worth the hassle of attacking them," Solus said.

"You seriously haven't done *any* quests involving these guys, Mr. Completionist?" Noir asked.

Solus shrugged. "They didn't interest me. There didn't seem to be any point in gaining reputation with them considering they're supposed to be among the most troublesome to get, and there isn't even a rich reward for their friendship given that they have no domain or stronghold. They don't even have a direct impact on any world or epic quests."

"Yeah, well don't tell *them* that." Kit trailed off as the pirates moved on to Solus.

"Name?" the hulk asked.

"Solus Miles, royal knight," Solus said.

The hulk grunted and wrote the name out with a piece of chalk on a slate.

"Your pledged is about to get robbed blind," Prowl predicted from the back of the mast.

"Pledged?" Abacus pirate perked with such enthusiasm, it made the beads on his abacus click. "You are courting the royal knight? Excellent!" He turned to the hulk and elbowed him. "Make a note that the knight will be paying a ransom for the elf maiden, as well."

Kit frowned and tried to twist her head so she could see the mop of Prowl's spiky hair. "Thanks, Prowl."

"If you would be so gracious, lady elf, to tell me your name," abacus pirate said.

Kit pressed her lips together. *We're about to be robbed; something is going on in Elba; we can't connect with our party... this is all just* great.

The pirate shrugged a little. "I would suggest you comply, lady elf. Either way, you will be parting with a great deal of money before you step off this ship."

Kit barely heard him as her inner tirade made her think ...*If something is going down in Elba, why did Halbryt have to contact me about it? Why didn't one of the guild leaders say something?* The thought made her frown. "I'm Kitten Lovemuch," she said.

The pirate nodded. "Is Love Much one word or two?"

"One." Kit wanted to rub her eyes. *I thought things had been going so well—Brasil joined us, and it seemed like Kamoi would be ours, too. But I guess the guilds are going to be a bigger problem than I thought.*

Abacus pirate tapped his abacus. "That's Kitten Lovemuch, one word. Thank you. But where have I heard..." he trailed off, then dropped his abacus with a loud crack.

Kit glanced at him, fear unfurling in her gut when his face morphed from shock to a great grin.

"You're Kitten Lovemuch," he said. "The elf who led a number of heroes and slayed Malignus."

Kit licked her lips, afraid to say anything. *Why does that make him so excited, and why do I doubt it's a good thing he's this happy?*

Abacus pirate clapped his hands and laughed heartily. "Captain!" he called. "Oi, captain! We have hit the motherload of treasures!"

The captain strode across the deck, dodging one of the

pirate-wizards who was directing wind into the ship's sails. "What is it?"

Abacus pirate scooped his abacus up. He shook his head as he chuckled. "You will never believe it. We have captured Kitten Lovemuch."

"The one who killed Malignus?"

"Aye!" Abacus pirate motioned to Kit. "We should have known sooner—there aren't many elves daft enough to be dancers."

The captain slapped his thighs and released a great gust of laughter. "She's a legend among heroes, and we've captured her! Well I'll be!"

Prowl craned his neck as he tried to see the pirates. "Does this mean you're going to let us go because you're so grateful to Kit?"

The captain whipped off his hat and scratched his balding scalp. "No, not at all." His smile looked almost shark-like as he settled his hat back on his head. "It means we'll get a ransom beyond our dreams for her."

"What?" Kit yelped.

"We'll have to see if we can get a bidding war going between the elves and dwarves." Abacus pirate tapped his fingers together. "They have the deepest pockets and will likely be willing to pay the most for her."

"What are you talking about?" Noir demanded. "You can only ransom us to our friends—or make us pull money from our own resources."

"Oh certainly—for you regular heroes," the captain said. "But when we have a legend on our hands? I'm certain even the miserly fae Winter King would pay handsomely to see her turned over, unharmed."

"No," Kit whispered, her blood turning to ice.

"The bidding war will likely take a few weeks," abacus

pirate said. "And we'll have to find a safe place to hold her—or else they might wrest her from us before we turn her over."

Weeks? The timeline echoed in Kit's head. If she were tied up for weeks...what would happen in that time? Could the guilds hold everything together—would the NPCs even be *willing* to pay her ransom? *This could ruin us. If the players run wild, it will be that much more difficult to unite them. And how can I expect the NPCs to trust us with leading them into battle when I get myself kidnapped by pirates?*

"You can't do this," Kit blurted out. Her careful control started to fray as her fears careened around her head. "We're trying to rally Retha against Lord Valdis. I know you're pirates, but don't you see the danger in this? If you hold me that long..."

The captain scratched his beard. "Just be glad—sweet elf maiden—that we're looking to auction you back to your allies and not the likes of Lord Valdis himself." The captain's gaze turned hard. "I'm sure he'd pay a pretty penny for you."

For a moment, Kit was silent. She didn't know what to think —she couldn't believe they would even *threaten* something that foul!

"It's okay, Kit," Prowl murmured. "Alistair might be an idiot, but she'll figure out what happened. Gared will come get us— we won't be stuck here that long."

But Halbryt said there was an emergency. Will Gared be able to help us? Kit closed her eyes, despair making her spit sour. *The Killing Squad will never listen to me after this. I'll lose support, all because these pirates are even worse than I thought and because I was stupid enough to get captured.*

Abacus pirate laughed. "That's our captain—so generous. Whom do we contact first, the dwarves?"

"No. First we had best carry our little prize off. Then we can begin the auction," the pirate captain said. "Set it for three weeks from now."

Three weeks...and all of my efforts will go to waste. I'll have come back for nothing. I'll have led Riko and Prowl into a death trap and made no difference at all if they get away with this. Kit snapped her eyes open. *I'm not going to put up with this!*

Her fear exploded into hot rage, and she lunged forward, straining against her rope bonds and making them creak. "You yellow-bellied, bacon-bits-eating, bucket-headed prunes!" she shouted. "I hope you choke on your ale and fall overboard—you toe-kissing, weasel-faced frogs!"

14

SWEAR PROFICIENTLY

THE CAPTAIN BLINKED and stared at her, seemingly surprised by her outburst. "Toe-kissing?" he asked.

"Eat grits, you shitake mushrooms!" Kit snapped.

Abacus pirate squinted at Kit and leaned towards his captain. "She's an elf...is she allowed to say this?"

"You bet your arse I can, you uneducated, boil-popping rat!" Kit shouted.

Abacus pirate clutched his tool to his chest. "I am *too* educated," he muttered.

Congratulations! Your life skill, "swear proficiently," has risen to level nine!

Kit flicked the popup out of her face with a toss of her head. The pirates in the immediate area had all paused in their work and stared at her with wide eyes.

"What are you looking at, ear worm?" she demanded. "Have I offended your mother? You deserve it, you low-level—most likely scurvy-riddled—scumbag. And get a new SHIRT! I don't want to see your nasty, old-man belly button!"

The closest sailor shuffled back a few steps.

Kit's breath came in ragged pants as she glared across the motionless deck—all the pirates had frozen where they stood and stared at her.

"Um, Kit?" Prowl hissed. "I know you're mad, but is now really a good time to go on a swearing rampage?"

Re-animated, Kit shouted at the top of her lungs. "Of course it is! It is the optimum time to swear! I came back to this God-forsaken pit of a game, charged with saving everyone's sorry arses. Guess what—I forgot this game frigging HATES ME!" Kit stared at the sky and screamed. "Well I hate it! It's worse than a one hundred-column Excel spreadsheet, a poorly made Powerpoint, and a picture drawn in *Paint!*"

Congratulations! Your life skill, "swear proficiently," has reached the maximum Life Skill level ten!

Kit glared at the deck as her shoulders heaved up and down.

The captain shifted, and Kit scowled at him. She was about to growl but paused when the captain appeared to wipe a tear from his eye.

"That was *beautiful!*" he declared.

Kit rolled the word around in her mind for a few moments before she realized what the captain said. "What?"

"You have the saltiest mouth I have ever heard," the captain said. "I didn't understand even half of what you said, but it's obvious you are very skilled in creating unusual obscenities."

Noir peered at the captain as if he might have contracted an unknown disease. "Are you daft?" he asked, jolting when Prowl managed to kick the side of his leg.

"We do try to speak the jargon of our occupation," Abacus pirate piped in. "But we've *never* done so with your finesse. We should write some of them down for future use—give me your slate." He swiped the slate from the ex-soldier and started scribbling fiercely.

The captain crossed his arms over his chest and grunted. "You know what this means, lads?"

There was a chorus of "Ayes" from across the deck.

Kit's rage cooled rapidly as the captain sauntered up to her. "*We* don't know. What does it mean?" she asked, straightening up.

She stiffened when the captain drew a cutlass from his belt. *Did I anger him into killing me? I guess that would be one way to escape this...*

The captain raised his sword above his head and swung it down at Kit.

She flinched, but the captain didn't so much as nick her. Instead, he sliced through the ropes that held her tied to the mast.

They fell away, freeing her. Kit blinked at the severed ropes, then glanced at Solus and Noir, who shrugged free of their bonds, as well.

Confused, she swiveled to face the captain. "What...?"

The captain nodded in satisfaction and slid his cutlass into its scabbard. "Only a pirate could have such a foul mouth, and we'd never kidnap one of our own. It's in our pirate code!"

Kit stared at the grinning man, barely able to understand his words. *Wait...they're freeing us because of my tirade? Swear Proficiently is actually useful?* The thought was almost as stunning as the idea that the pirates were freeing them without a fight.

Abacus pirate sadly eyed Solus and Noir. "We assume the gentlemen with you are under your protection and are not available to be ransomed?" he asked.

"Yes!" Kit quickly replied. "They're under my leadership."

Noir picked up Trash Panda—who was chattering and

clinging to the mast now that the ropes were gone—and fluffed up his fur. "She pays me a charming wage of two million gold per month and has given me power over the life and death of her companions—"

Prowl slapped his hand over Noir's mouth before he could continue.

Kit nodded in gratitude to Prowl then returned her attention to the captain.

Abacus pirate used his ancient calculator to gesture back and forth between Kit and Solus. "How did a royal knight and an elf-who-should-be-a-pirate become pledged?"

Kit opened and closed her mouth, at a loss for words.

Solus Miles didn't so much as blink. "She uses me for my body."

Kit, Noir, Prowl, and even Trash Panda, turned to stare in his direction.

Abacus pirate and the captain exchanged understanding glances. "You may be an elf, Kitten Lovemuch, but you've the salty blood of a pirate in your veins!" the captain announced.

Kit felt her face heat with the strength of her blush. "Thanks." She kicked the ropes away to give herself something to do so she didn't have to look at Solus. "You said you *try* to swear for the sake of your occupation...what did you mean by that?"

The captain adjusted his belt. "I don't know if you heard rightly, but the lads and I...we haven't always been pirates."

Kitten falsified surprise. "But you've taken so well to the sea and, uh, plundering."

"Thank ye!" Abacus pirate grinned. "We've worked hard to adapt!"

"We actually were upright men who sweated for a living," the captain said.

"Not me," Abacus pirate added. "I was a banker."

Kit forgot about Solus' quip long enough to shoot him a triumphant *I told you so* look.

"We come from a variety of backgrounds," piped up the pirate with the stuffed parrot tied to his shoulder. "Soldiers, wizards, craftsmen, and more. We've always been a brotherhood, though!"

A chorus of "Aye!" washed over the deck.

"While we plied away in our trades, we each came to the realization that life wasn't quite what we thought it would be," the captain said. "Poring over accounts, cranking out spell after spell, guarding fat aristocrats, none of it was as exciting and adventurous as we thought our lives would be when we were boys."

"So we decided to become pirates!" Stuffed-parrot pirate puffed up his chest in pride. "We've had a right, good run of it, too!"

"Indeed, but we came to our occupation late, so I'm afraid there are things we haven't quite captured yet—like the salty language of a real pirate," the captain said.

"That is certainly a courageous tale," Kit said when the pirates all looked to her, expecting some kind of response. "I don't know many who are brave enough to uproot their lives for such adventure."

Some of the pirates winced, and most of them grimaced.

"It hasn't been easy," the captain admitted. "Some of our families haven't taken kindly to the change."

The troll-sized soldier sighed deeply. "My Mam wallops me with a rolling pin whenever I try to visit her."

Abacus pirate scowled. "My wife won't let me sleep in my own house. And she has the children telling everyone I'm dead!"

"That's the price for infamy, I guess?" Kit tried. *So we're free...sort of. How do I talk them into letting us off the ship now?*

She bit her cheek as she tried to figure out how she could steer the topic.

"Do tell," Prowl said as he propped himself up against the mast and yawned. "Is pirate-life as fun as you expected?"

Kit wished Riko was with them—she would have yanked the saboteur's ear for such a stupid statement. Since he was not within kicking range, Kit settled for glaring at him over Noir's head.

The pirates exchanged glances and shrugged sheepishly.

"Using our knowledge to capture treasures and heroes has been fun," Abacus pirate nodded sagely. "There's a thrill to it my life lacked."

"I love the sea—she's a hard mistress to please, but beautiful all the same!" another pirate piped in. "To smell the ocean during day and see the stars at night—there's nothing like it!"

"It's also been a real pleasure living with my mates like this," stuffed-parrot pirate added feelingly, making the rest of the pirates nod in agreement. "To fight next to each other and work together is far more rewarding than my previous job."

"But," The captain said, scratching at his beard, "there are some unexpected shortcomings."

"Besides your families' disapproval?" Noir asked with an eyebrow raised in judgement.

The captain nodded.

Solus Miles tilted his head. "Like what?"

"The food is fair awful for starters," Abacus pirate tapped his callused fingers on the frame of his abacus and screwed up his lips. "The only things safe for proper sea voyages are salted meat, sea biscuits—which are barely softer than rocks—sauerkraut, and ale."

"Yes!" The captain said with feeling. "I enjoy a good drink down at the pub, but all we have is ale! No elven wines or dwarven brew." He sighed so deeply his shoulders sagged.

"Sometimes my hammock flips me out when I sleep during my off-shift," another pirate said.

"Yeah, and you land on *me!*" someone else piped in.

"I can't even have a real parrot, because Jim Bob is allergic to 'em." The pirate with the stuffed parrot tied to his shoulder frowned.

Kit wrinkled her forehead as a seagull flew overhead. "Allergic to parrots?" she asked. *Obviously the designer responsible for these guys has an interesting sense of humor.*

But the pirates were on a roll now; no one listened as they listed their complaints.

"I miss carpets and lounging furniture and *books*." One of the wizard pirates made a motion of holding a book in his hands.

"Yeah, and if we're not cleanin' the ship, we can only play cards or dice," another pirate complained.

The troll-sized pirate finally spoke. "Not to mention we all *smell*."

"Oh, aye!"

"Too true."

"You can't bathe easily on the ship," the captain sighed. "And using salt water just makes us crusty and dappled like whales."

"Pretty sure the salt water isn't the only problem," Prowl said.

Kit leaned around Noir to peer at her friend. "Are you a worm?"

Prowl frowned slightly. "No."

"Then stop baiting them!"

"So if you are dissatisfied with this life, why keep at it?" Noir set Trash Panda down and nodded to him. The raccoon nonchalantly meandered over to Solus and leaned against his boots.

The captain strode towards the railing of the ship and stared out at the dazzling ocean. "For the sea, for our friendship, for the love of being a pirate." He leaned against the railing, making it creak. "And also, because we still have a loan out on the ship and haven't yet paid it off."

A laugh nearly burst out of Kit's lips before she was masterfully able to turn it into a hacking cough. She spotted Trash Panda make a break for a pirate and planted her foot in his way to block him. *The last thing I need is to get tied up again because of a racoon!* She cleared her throat and returned her gaze to the captain. "That is highly unfortunate. I am sorry to hear of this."

The captain shrugged. "We make do. We finally have adventure, after all!"

Kit smiled pleasantly, then stilled when golden words formed before her.

You have secured an alliance with the village of Kamoi.

The announcement surprised Kit and made her smile morph into a grin. "Alistair, Long Claw, and the others must have killed all the sea serpents."

Abacus pirate tilted his head. "Eh?"

"Kitten is leading a movement of heroes to join together with the people of Retha to fight Lord Valdis," Solus Miles said.

"It seems one of her subordinates got through to the village of Kamoi," Noir added.

"Yes, so while I dearly enjoy your company, my fellow pirate-hearted men, we really ought to go," Kit explained. She held her breath, waiting anxiously for their reply. *Please let us go. Please!*

The captain whipped off his hat. "I see. That's a real sorrow."

Kit nodded. "It is." Though she kept her expression smooth, inwardly she was nearly doing cartwheels. *We just might get away with this! I can't believe my impractical life skill was useful!*

"We can drop you back off at the sandbar where we picked you up." Abacus pirate turned to shout at one of the wizard-pirates who was powering the ship. "Off the foremast to the starboard and..." he trailed off.

The wizard pirate raised both of his eyebrows. "That was gibberish."

"Yeah, but I thought I should try," Abacus pirate sighed. "North, man. Take us back north."

"Aye-aye!"

The captain wiped his sweating forehead with a handkerchief before he plopped his hat back on. "In addition to our shameful inability to swear properly, we also aren't too good with sea-directions."

Prowl suspiciously eyed the sails as the ship started to turn. "But you can still properly navigate and sail, right?"

"Oh, sure." The captain scratched his elbow. "We hired a crew of sailors to sail with us for a few months before we officially became pirates. They didn't often use the right terms, though, on account of calling us land-blubbers near every moment of the day."

"Captain!" Stuffed-parrot pirate snapped his fingers. "Seeing as how she's pirate-hearted and everything, ought we not give her *that?*"

The captain brightened. "That'll do. Go get one fast now!"

The hulking ex-soldier peered down at Kit. "If she's going to be one of us, she needs proper pirate clothes."

Kit stiffened. "Clothes? You mean, like, an armor set?"

The hulk nodded.

One of the more rotund pirates perked up. "I have that set of clothes that I had made up for my wife!"

"Given up hope she's ever gonna deign to wear them, eh?" a fellow pirate chortled.

The rotund pirate scowled at him, then smiled brightly at Kit. "We'll get you kitted up like a real lady pirate! You'll see!" He followed after the pirate who toted the stuffed parrot and trotted for the lower deck.

Abacus pirate started moving beads and wrote out some new numbers on his slate. "Captain, when we drop off Lady Kitten, I think we ought to turn around and sail east. According to our records, there's a shipment of magic-infused silk headed for Atlas Bay to the City of Wizards. If we're fast enough, I think we can catch the ship."

The captain planted his fists on his hips, and his eyes twinkled. "You don't say?"

As the captain and the abacus-wielding pirate began to talk about their new plan, Kit discreetly fell back.

"I can't believe I'm saying this, but I think we're going to get out of this if we don't screw anything up," she murmured.

Noir, who was playing peekaboo with Trash Panda, stopped long enough to snort. "What are you talking about? You've obviously gained max reputation with your swearing skill."

Kit folded her arms across her chest. "That easily, with just a bit of cursing? I doubt it."

Noir fed Trash Panda some kind of cracker. "It's not that easy. I don't know anyone else who has a swearing life skill, so it's not like just anyone could waltz up to the pirates and get accepted."

"If you think about it, it's not too surprising." Prowl rolled his shoulders back and glanced up at the fluffy cloud—the only cloud in the sky—that hovered high above them. "Elves are more prone to look favorably upon bards, and dwarves will accept mastersmiths in a heartbeat. If you can swear like a sailor, why not be accepted by them? They're the only human pirates in the game, anyway."

Kit tapped her fingers on her gold belt. "Still...it seems *too* easy."

Noir rolled his eyes. "They're NPCs, not humans. They're going to be way easier to impress."

"Are you having a hard time believing your life skill was useful?" Solus asked.

Kit couldn't stop the slight grin that flashed across her lips. "A little bit, yeah. I'm just so used to this game kicking me in the teeth, it seems weird that everything worked out."

Solus shrugged. "Even if the pirates hadn't accepted you, we would have gotten free."

"Yeah, but there would have been some pretty dire consequences due to the time it would have taken," Kit said.

"Not at all. We could have been free whenever you wanted," Solus said.

Noir glanced at the royal knight. "How? They certainly weren't fans of *you*."

Solus glanced at the cloud.

"I still have no idea what that means," Kit said.

Solus rested his hand on the hilt of his sword. "Haven't you stopped to wonder where Pax is?"

Kit blinked rapidly, then glanced up at the cloud again. After a few moments, she could just make out Pax—a silver and white smudge against the cloud—and more importantly, she saw the few times Sinistre's black wingtips edged out past the haze.

"Sinistre..." she said.

"Could have rescued us if necessary," Solus agreed.

Kit pressed her lips together. "That would have been really reassuring to know back when I thought I had bungled everything."

Solus shrugged. "I thought you would realize Pax was missing."

"How—or why?" Kit squawked. "When he's silent, I'm *glad!*"

"If you were so certain we could get out of this mess, why didn't you do anything?" Prowl asked.

"I thought Kit would want to try getting the pirates to join the alliance," Solus said.

He was being thoughtful, Kit told herself. *He didn't know the mental anguish I was going through.* Still, Kit had to make herself take a step away from the knight so she wasn't threatened to pinch his ridiculously sculpted cheeks.

"What's the plan when we get back?" Prowl asked. "Are we gonna join Riko in Lèas?"

"Nope," Kit said. "I need to get back to my contact and see what's going down in Luminos—and maybe message Gared to see why no one has sent me a message if it really is that dire."

"Here you are, Kitten Lovemuch!" the rotund pirate smiled widely as he marched up to her, carrying a brown-paper package. "Your proper pirate attire! If you like, I can show you to the captain's cabin so you can change!"

Given that Kit could merely equip and unequip her armor through her character panel, a changing room wasn't strictly necessary. But...*maybe I should see how revealing this outfit is before I parade around in front of Solus and the others.*

Kit smiled. "I would greatly appreciate such a gesture. Thank you!"

The portly pirate grinned happily and bowed a little. "Right this way!"

———

Kit stood in the rowboat the pirates had prepared to take them closer to the sandbar (as they couldn't risk running their not-yet-paid-off ship aground). She had a boot propped up on one of the benches and managed to keep her balance even as the pirates rowed them across the bobbing ocean.

Prowl scowled up at her. "Would you stop posing like that?"

Kit sniffed the salty air and leaned into her propped-up boot in what she thought was a roughish manner. "Why?"

"Because you're going to fall out!"

Kit scoffed. "I'm an elf! It takes more than a rough ocean to make me lose my balance."

"It seems like your wardrobe change has given you a confidence boost," Solus said.

Kit twisted so she could grin back at him. "I do feel pretty jaunty."

Her new pirate armor had quickly become her favorite armor set yet. She got to have sturdy leather boots, a ruffled cream skirt, and a pirate-style red brocade jacket that covered her entire torso—except for, of course, her belly. (Thank you, EC designers.) Add in her white ruffled collar that served as a necklace and an awesome pirate captain hat that even had the requisite feathers, and Kit was feeling pretty happy with herself.

She admired her long sleeves and swished the tail of her coat. "I could get used to this!"

Solus thoughtfully rubbed his chin.

Noir clung to the side of the rowboat, and Trash Panda was seated on top of his head like a living coonskin cap. "Trying to figure out how to use your vast fortune to be a proper sugar daddy, Solus?"

Kit arrogantly tipped her head, making her hat bob. "I beg your pardon?"

Noir shrugged. "Would you rather I call you his tapeworm?"

"Hmph." Kit returned to facing forward as the pirates

continued to maneuver their way to the fog-free sandbar. (Turns out the fog was made by some of the wizards-turned-pirates—a testament to their cunning.)

"I am happy to spend money on Kit whenever she should need it—particularly on her armor and weapons," Solus said.

"Yeah, I get that. But you two don't act like many of the pledged I've seen—particularly given that you're supposed to have some great love story," Noir said.

Kit ignored him and instead adjusted the lapel of her jacket, refusing to rise to the bait.

"What do you mean?" Solus asked.

"As far as I can tell, Kit's the one who gets all the pluses of being pledged. You spend money on her, let her flash your name around however she likes—though she seems strangely prone to keeping your relationship quiet—and guard her while she waltzes around, instigating fights."

"I do *not* instigate fights," Kit said.

Noir rolled his eyes. "What I mean is, what does Solus get out of the arrangement? Protection from fangirls?"

Solus shrugged. "Kit is fighting for our lives. I support her not only because she is my pledged, but because she is doing all of this for us—for the players."

Kit smiled at Solus, relaxing a little. *I might have assumed he is kind of shallow—and he still is—but he's still really a noble guy.*

"Uh-oh," stuffed-parrot-pirate said.

A wave crested at the front of the rowboat, violently rocking the little dingy. Kit took a staggering step backwards and was about to resort to crouching on the floor when Solus wrapped his arms around her waist from behind and gently tugged her back so she fell onto his lap.

"Thanks, Solus," Kit said as she sat on his knees and flicked a blob of seafoam off her new skirt.

Solus looked from Kit to Noir and said blandly, "There are additional bonuses, of course."

Kit blushed and switched her gaze to the ocean, ignoring Noir's laughter. She shifted her legs under her so she could get up, but Solus tugged her backwards. "Do such comments make you uncomfortable?" he asked quietly.

"It's a little embarrassing, but I'd find it hilarious if I wasn't involved," Kit admitted. "I'm glad you are comfortable enough to joke around."

Solus shrugged. "I want to make certain other players know I value you."

Kit pushed a loose strand of her hair behind her ear so it would stop smacking her on the lips. "Does it really matter what they think? As long as the guild masters know you support me, anyway."

Solus stared at Kit and said nothing, though she could tell by the slant of his black eyebrows and the light in his gray eyes that he was thinking.

"Land ho!" the pirate captain called out. "This is where we leave ye."

Kit tore her gaze from Solus and stood—all smiles—to address the captain. "Thank you for the ride. Your ship is a joy to behold, and she is lucky to have such stout crewmen."

The captain laughed heartily. "Not so yellow-bellied now, are we?"

Prowl hopped over the side, making a splash when he landed shin-deep in the water that covered the sandbar. He held the little boat as Noir scrambled out—hissing when Trash Panda wrapped his paws in his hair.

"Before we part, Kitten Lovemuch, the crew and I would like you to take something." The captain nudged the pirate with the stuffed parrot.

He smiled as he secured an oar, then reached behind him

and revealed a gold-and-pink-flecked conch shell that was nearly the size of Kit's head. "Here, it is a conch horn. Blow here —where the tip is broken off—and you can make a true, pure note."

"Thank you," Kit said, surprised by the weight of the shell when she took it. "It's beautiful."

"Tis a sign amongst those of us who are pirate-hearted," the pirate said seriously. "You belong to the brotherhood now, and surely ye are one of us even if ye do not sail with us."

Kit opened her item storage and put the shell away with a wink. "I am honored to be considered a scurvy-sea-dog."

The pirate grinned, but the captain chortled and slapped his belly. "I do like you, Kitten Lovemuch. If you have need of us, call to us with the conch shell," he said. "Wherever there is water, we shall come!"

Solus also hopped out, then turned around and held out a hand for Kit. She took it, but glanced back at the pirate captain when his words finally sunk in. "You'll come?" she repeated.

"Aye! A pirate never leaves his brother behind—at least not in our Pieces of Eight Pirate Company," the captain said.

So Noir is right...I am at full reputation with them. Though she itched to check her character panel, a glance at the beach revealed several figures running up the shore. One of them was Alistair, easily identifiable in her blue and white lotus-themed armor.

Kit hopped out of the boat with Solus' support. Once she was steady on the underwater sandbar, she turned back to the pirates.

"May the sea be kind to you, and the wind be at your backs," Kit said.

"Aye, I hope there's treasure in your future," the captain winked, then turned back to the pirates who had rowed them out. "Back to the ship, men! We've got treasure to claim!"

Kit waved as Prowl pushed the boat off, and the pirates rowed back across the ocean—heading for their ship.

It took only a moment before the party chat channel exploded to life.

"You're back!" the scout shouted. "And the pirates *dropped you off?*"

"That was not the outcome I was expecting," the spellbinder chimed in.

Long Claw snorted. "I'm not surprised you came rolling back after we did the hard work of killing off the sea serpents."

"You said they were easy and not worth your time," the scout said.

"Kit," Alistair was barely audible over the chaos of the chat. "We need to leave for Luminos. *Now.*"

15

TROUBLE IN ELBA

KIT WALKED SO FAST DOWN the hallway of the Guild-hall in Luminos, she was almost jogging. She clutched her hat to her head, ignoring the puzzled looks players cast her way in her hurry. Behind her trotted Alistair, Solus, and Pax. (Well, Pax glided. He wouldn't do anything unseemly like trot.)

"Riko, how close are you to finishing with the elves?" Kit asked her friend in the raid chat channel. A breeze brushed the back of her neck when the druid responded.

"Tough to say," she drawled. "They keep yapping and singing, but I'm betting they can't go on too much longer."

"Stay on standby," Kit said. "Depending what the news is, we might have to pull you into this."

"Is it really that dire?" Riko asked. "I know Gared told you to come back to Luminos immediately, but what's the problem?"

"Infighting." The dirty word fell heavily from Kit's lips as she grimly strode along.

"Between the big guilds?" Riko asked.

"No, but no matter how small the conflict is, it's not good. If we have guilds at each other's throats, people will start picking sides—which is exactly what we *don't* want when we're trying to preach unity." Kit paused outside the meeting room Gared had directed her to in their previous discussion before her party took the teleportation gate to Luminos. "I have to go; I'm here. Ask Prowl if anything comes up."

"Good luck."

"Thanks." Kit squared her shoulders and rapped her knuckles on the door.

"Please, Lady Kit." Alistair stepped forward and pulled the door open with a tense smile. "You're our leader. No door is closed to you."

I don't know about that. Kit gave the cavalry knight a brief smile before she strode into the room, the heels of her boots clicking.

It was a different meeting room from last time—which had been clearly chosen to shock and awe. This room was hexagon shaped with a stain glass window stretching from floor to ceiling on one side. The other sides were dotted with sculptures, treasure, and weapons that were bolted to the stone block walls. A circular, wooden table was placed in the center of the room, and the guild leaders were seated in massive chairs posted around it.

Everything reminded Kit of a castle hall, but she pushed the comparison from her mind as she joined the guildmasters. "Hello, everyone."

"Who called her here?" Half-Fang growled at her entrance.

"I did." Gared stood and moved to pull back a chair for Kit, but Solus was already on it.

Alistair marched up to Gared with a smile. "Hello, Guildmaster!" she chirped, though her eyes glinted as her gaze skipped over the meeting attendees.

In addition to Gared of KOS and Half-Fang of Killing Squad, Phizzy from Corporate Force, White Lady of the Silver Army, and Ryunosuke of Tainted were present as well.

"Alistair, hey." Gared smiled tiredly and lightly slapped her back. "Thanks for seeing Kit here safely."

"Of course, I always attend to my duties," Alistair boasted.

"Oh really? So riding sea serpents is a part of your duties?" Gared asked as he folded his arms across his chest.

"Um," Alistair said.

"Hide_N_Seek, sent me those screenshots," he said, naming the scout.

"Rats," Alistair said.

Kit removed her hat—she didn't want the brim obscuring her view—and set it aside. "Alistair said there was infighting. Could someone tell me exactly what's going on?"

"Of course." White Lady rested her hands on the wooden table. "Are you aware that before you defeated Malignus, Midnight Watch and Steadfast—two medium-sized guilds—fought in the city of Tovel? I believe you weren't in Luminos at the time, but you likely still heard of it."

"Yes," Kit said. "It was still a bit of a hot topic when I put together my raid against Malignus. I thought KOS marched in and stopped the fighting?" She glanced at Gared, who nodded.

"We did," he acknowledged. "But stopping the combat was just about the only measure we could take. We can't do anything about their verbal hostilities."

"Since then, both Midnight Watch and Steadfast have exchanged blows, so to speak," Phizzy said. "A couple of Midnight Watch guildmembers jumped a Steadfast mage, and of course Steadfast retaliated. Then sympathizers for each side got involved and created unrest."

"They haven't done anything in Luminos—or even in the area." Half-Fang growled, and his triangular wolf ears flattened against his skull. "Instead, they fight in outer villages."

"But they still mostly kept it to smaller-scale skirmishes," Phizzy said. "Until now."

"What's happened?" Kit asked.

"Midnight Watch and Steadfast took advantage of the goblin ships that attack Elba—the crown jewel of the Imperial Empress—and have locked the city down," Phizzy said.

"How is that possible?" Riko shook her head. "The teleportation gates mean anyone can get in and out."

Phizzy held a finger in the air. "*Except* when the goblins attack." He sighed and twisted the ends of his elaborately styled mustache. "The goblins attack Elba in waves and stay for days at a time. Based on what Nyx reported back to me about Brunascar, we can assume this is one of the new events dumped on us with Malignus' death. Wiping them out is likely needed to secure the Empress' help."

"I can follow that," Kit said. "It's a special-one-time raid, of sorts."

"Exactly!" Phizzy said. "Unfortunately, it means that there are unusual rules we haven't encountered before."

"Whenever the goblins attack, the city shuts down," Gared said. "The gates close, and there's no way in or out through normal means. Additionally, all Fibbit teleportation services are closed during the siege as well. We suspect it's done to create a feeling of authenticity." He sighed and rapped his knuckles on the table. "Normally, it would be an exciting challenge and at worst maybe hinder players a bit. But the real danger is that, as Phizzy said, Midnight Watch and Steadfast have locked themselves in Elba, and they're duking it out."

"How long does the goblin siege last?" Kit asked.

Ryunosuke balanced a dagger on his fingertip. "Roughly a week. Plenty of time for them to do serious damage. This current attack has been going for less than a day."

"As we are all basically immortal whilst playing, the problem is not that the guilds will physically harm each other in their fight, but that it will have emotional repercussions," Phizzy said.

"The tension caused by infighting will escalate the fear and panic that is already spreading through the server," White Lady said. "If players truly begin to turn on each other, any hope of uniting them to fight Lord Valdis is over."

Half-Fang snorted. "If players start rioting, we'll have bigger problems than suicide runs against Valdis."

Kit pressed her palms to her eyeballs as she tried to arrange her thoughts. *How could this happen? Retha has such an amazing and supportive community—how can it be fracturing like this?*

Solus, as if sensing Kit's thoughts, shifted behind her. "Fear without hope can twist a person."

"Poetic, but true," White Lady said.

Kit straightened in her chair. "What's the plan? Are you going to march on Elba?"

Gared sighed. "We'd like to, but it's too dangerous. We haven't the troops to support such a movement."

Solus Miles frowned. "I thought KOS alone stopped the fighting last time."

"Yes, but we can't pull KOS so far from Luminos," Gared said. "And we already sent two guilds to Elba before it got locked up: Brave Heart Company and Observational Fiends."

Is it ironic that those are the two guilds that refused to join the fight against Lord Valdis?

"Tainted picked up the rumor that there was going to be a fight in Elba, so we sent Teara and Saint George thinking that would be enough to stop them," Phizzy said. "Now with the gates—teleportation and physical—closed off, they're stuck there."

Half-Fang slapped his giant hand on the table and his claws into the wooden surface. "I told you the Killing Squad should have gone," he growled. "If we were there, this wouldn't be a problem."

"I don't understand. Isn't it a good thing Observational Fiends and Brave Heart Company are there? Can't they stop the fighting?" Kit asked.

"They're out numbered," Gared said. "Badly. Based on the rumors we worked off, we greatly underestimated the forces needed to subdue the conflict."

"The rumors were inaccurate." Ryunosuke sat up straight, every line in his body stiff. "It's not my guilds' fault that only incorrect information was spread."

Kit bit her tongue to keep from speaking. *I'd bet Pax that Shashanna and the RPers had a better reckoning of the numbers. I need to bring them into the fold, regardless of how everyone feels about RPers.*

"Ryunosuke is right. The fault lies with no one. It was merely an unfortunate miscalculation on our part," White Lady said soothingly.

Kit nodded slowly. "So what do we do?"

Half-Fang growled. "*We* don't do anything. You don't even have a reason to be here—this fight has nothing to do with your campaign against Valdis."

"Maybe not directly, but what happens in Elba will have repercussions that will affect it," Kit said.

"We'll have to wait for the goblin siege on Elba to end." Gared leaned back in his chair. "Maybe send some auxiliary forces—though I bet as soon as the siege is raised, everyone will teleport out of Elba faster than we can enter it."

"But that means Elba is a free-for-all right now," Kit said.

Ryunosuke shrugged. "It's not like they can do any damage to the city. The game won't allow it."

All the big cities of Retha, like Luminos and Elba, were, according to game lore, still "spelled" by ancient magic that made them impervious to all damage—fire, water, physical, none of it touched the city.

In reality, it was just game coding to keep delinquent characters from trying to wipe out the largest places. The smaller cities, however, were a different case.

"Maybe," Kit said. "But it's not going to help the server's morale."

"We'll just have to crack down harder," Phizzy said. "There are a few medium-sized guilds we can conscript, which will give us more forces to patrol with."

"Forces that aren't nearly as well trained, armored, or leveled." Ryunosuke's voice dripped with disdain as he spun his dagger with ease.

Kit shook her head. "You can't really believe you can properly patrol the whole continent? It's massive!"

"Then we can control the cities that matter and rule them with an iron fist." Half-Fang peeled back the upper lip of his muzzle, revealing his canine teeth.

"Retha is a *game*, not a dictatorship," Kit argued. "We're all players, and we're all stuck here. If you try to assert that much control, you'll only be confirming everyone's fears!"

Phizzy raised his hands, palms up, in a gesture of supplication. "Then what would you have us do?"

"Wipe the goblins out," Kit said. "If you can end the river attack, we'll get the Empress' alliance, *and* the city will open."

Ryunosuke rolled his eyes. "Are you listening at all? Gared said we don't have the forces to do that!"

White Lady held up a hand to stop Ryunosuke's fire-filled words. "And what would you have us do after that?"

Kit fiddled with the lapel of her fancy jacket. "Everyone is fighting because they're scared, right? Maybe we could start hosting raids to practice large-group combat, or just try distracting them by throwing questing parties or something. If you give the players something to *do*, I don't think the server will be quite so self-destructive."

"That's an idealistic idea at *best*," Ryunosuke snorted.

"Can we kick her out yet?" Half-Fang demanded.

"Now, now," Phizzy waggled a finger. "She has a point. We might not be able to do much about Elba, but if we can start planning events and activities, it would maybe build goodwill among players. That used to not be a problem, but since everyone has been left to their own devices for days on end, the community is clearly fracturing."

Kit grabbed her hat and rubbed the brim with her thumbs to give herself something to do. Though she was glad Phizzy saw the reasoning in trying to engage other players, the dismissal of Elba bothered her, and based on Gared's pinched expression, she wasn't the only one.

"Teara and Saint George are getting their asses handed to them," Gared said. "I really don't like abandoning them in Elba."

"They've finally converged to a safe part of the city," Ryunosuke said. "And all of their numbers who wiped have met up with them again. That's as good as you can hope for in this situation."

The statement made Kit clench her hands into fists. *Wiped? That means they were killed—by other players! How can he be so blasé about that?*

Half-Fang braced a knee on the edge of the table. "They're hiding, when they should be entering the battle."

Phizzy slightly shook his head and looked towards the heavens. "Not everyone's fight tactic is to kill everything that moves until you pass out from exhaustion, Half-Fang."

Half-Fang snarled, a sound that came from deep in his throat. "How will anyone take our rules seriously when players from our alliance don't actually fight?"

"Retha is a *game!* There shouldn't have to be rules," Kit said.

White Lady sighed. "I believe the general agreement is that there is nothing more we can do?"

Gared furrowed his brow, but the other guildmasters nodded.

Kit wanted to shout, but what could she do? *I may have some elite players with me, but it's not like Solus can singlehandedly subdue Elba or Pax can flutter his wings and inspire them to fall in line. This is wrong...but what can I do?*

"In that case, the next order of business is to decide what auxiliary troops to send when the fuss is over," White Lady said.

"Corporate Force can send at least twenty," Phizzy said.

Kit slid out of her chair. She moved closer to Gared and whispered, "I'm assuming Elba was the emergency you called us back here for?"

Gared nodded.

"Then I'm going to head out. It doesn't look like there's anything I can do here." She straightened, almost smacking into Pax when she backed up a step.

"Good luck. Let me know if Alistair is too much for you," Gared muttered.

Kit nodded.

"Gared, I know KOS will be patrolling Luminos, but do you have any spare players you can send?" White Lady asked.

Gared returned his attention to the meeting. "I'll have to check, but I can probably send a handful. My people will all need breaks, though, once we're through this mess."

Kit padded across the meeting room, barely aware of Solus, Alistair, and Pax following her. Her heart was heavy with disappointment in her fellow players, their fear, and her own inability to do anything to help them. *I was sent here to help...but I can't do anything.*

———

Kit sat pretzel-style on the marble edge of the massive mermaid fountain placed in the middle of Luminos' marketplace. The marketplace was not nearly as full as it would have been on a regular playing session, but it still buzzed with conversation, laughter, and the pitches of players angling to sell their wares.

A troupe of fire dancers—possibly the same ones Kit's party had seen in Bangle many weeks ago—were performing just in front of her. They whirled, flipped, and threw themselves into awe-inspiring gymnastics as circles of fire flared around their wrists and ankles, and the NPCs' magic conjoined so they could create a moving picture made of fire as they danced and shouted.

Kit stared at them without really thinking of what she was seeing. *Players are fighting seriously against one another...how can you combat that? How can you get everyone to work together? Or maybe the real problem is that I'm failing them, which is why things continue to grow more tense.*

"Everything okay, Lady Kit?" Alistair asked.

"Yes." Kit shook her head, then rubbed her eyes. "Sorry, just...thinking."

"So where are we headed next?" Noir flopped down next to Kit and used a delicate fan—one Trash Panda had likely swiped for him—to fan his face as he sipped a fruity beverage.

"Not the elves, please," Prowl groaned. "I can't handle their stuffy pacifism right now."

"Riko is with the second team working on the elves right now," Solus said. "It wouldn't be efficient to meet up with them."

"We could visit the plainsmen!" Alistair brightly said. "I have quite a few friends among the NPCs given that they were the ones who gave me my cavalry knight legendary class!"

"I have maps for the lands the plainsmen call their domain!" Fame declared with a sparkling smile.

"Thank you, Fame. I know you'll have maps for whatever part of Retha we choose to visit," Kit said.

Fame shot her brother a triumphant look and held an armful of maps to her heart.

Fortune ignored her and instead gave Kit a serene smile. "Please allow me to be of assistance to you, Kitten."

"Er, now isn't really the time to discuss armor, Fortune," Kit said.

"Duh." Long Claw scowled into the marketplace, as if the smiles and looks of awe the fire dancers were garnering were distasteful. (And who knew, given that his guildmaster was as emotional as a honey badger, they might be.) "We should decide where to go and get moving. I don't want to sit around this city all day doing nothing."

Kit offered the NPC siblings a half smile, then let air leak out of her in a gusty sigh. "Give me a few moments to PM some friends. We can decide after that."

"Take your time, Lady Kit!" Alistair brightly gazed around the marketplace. "I think I just might go check—"

"No." Prowl grabbed Alistair by her shoulder. "Gared told me never to let you wander off."

Alistair laughed. "He was exaggerating."

"He said if we let you go, you'll never be seen from again because you'll forget what you're supposed to be doing. Fortune, get over here and tell the lady knight how terrible her armor is."

"Actually!" Fortune started with a bright smile as he waltzed over to them. "Alistair Lionward's armor is level and stat appropriate!"

"*What?*" Prowl yowled.

"She could have better, of course, but her armor is the best in the raid," Fortune continued.

"Gared spares no expense on my behalf!" Alistair said proudly.

"Of course," Noir scoffed. "Any entrepreneur knows to sink money into the marketing plan that works best."

A ghost of a smile twitched on Kit's lips as she brought up the PM screen and filled out the necessary blanks to make a call to Halbryt. *I never did get back to him. I should let him know I heard about Elba.*

Kit sent the message and waited for the GM to accept the request, her gaze flickering from the NPC dancers to Pax—who was watching them with what could be mistaken for intrigue.

When Solus Miles joined her in sitting on the fountain rim, she flashed him a brief smile—though it died when she received a refusal message from Halbryt.

Halbryt is not available to receive your private message.

"What's wrong?" Solus asked.

"I'm trying to get through to one of the GMs, but he's not responding. Let me check with someone else..." Kit trailed off as she sent a PM invite to Shashanna.

Only a moment passed before the GM picked up. "*You heard the news about Elba?*" Shashanna asked, leaping straight into the matter.

"Yes. I just got out of a meeting with the top guildmasters. They don't plan to do anything." Kit rested her elbows on her knees and leaned forward, looking down at her feet.

"*And you agree with them?*"

"No. But I don't really know what to do. Do you know if Elba was what Halbryt messaged me about? He sent me a PM, but I got kidnapped by pirates, and the PM was cut off."

Shashanna was silent for a moment, then sighed. "*I don't know how to tell you this, but Halbryt is stuck in Elba.*"

Kit sat straight. "What?"

"*It's my fault. My guild picked up a rumor about the fight going down. I sent Halbryt there to scout it out and see if he could find any evidence for it—if he did, I planned to warn you. Unfortunately, while looking into it, he and some of his guild- mates got locked in with the goblin siege, and now they're stuck in that bloodbath.*"

Kit pressed her fists against her chin as she tried to think. "Is he okay? Have you heard from him?"

Solus—though he couldn't hear her conversation—frowned as his eyes took in her stricken facial expression.

"*He occasionally gets bits and pieces back to me. It's a madhouse there.*"

"Any idea how much longer the siege will last?"

"*I think it started just when he first messaged you.*"

"Which was this morning."

"*Yes. And it typically lasts almost a week.*"

That's what the guildmasters had said, but I was hoping they were miscalculating. Kit felt her eyes widen in dismay. *Halbryt is a GM—he can't be stuck in there for multiple days!*

Shashanna sighed. "*I'll have to be more careful with my investigations in the future. But I just thought...I never dreamed the guilds would be so set on fighting!*"

Kit stared out at the marketplace, watching other players laugh as they traded, chatted, and watched the fire dancers. "The majority of the players are doing okay."

"*Yes. But if a small but violent minority manages to breed enough hysteria, things will go down fast.*"

Kit groaned and covered her eyes with her forearm. *I'm a tactician—not a sociology or psychology buff! I can't even plan for Valdis, much less try to puzzle through this!* She took a deep breath. "Well...thanks for the info."

"*Of course. Sorry I didn't message you sooner—I tried a few hours ago, but that must have been when you were with the pirates."*

"Yeah." Kit took off her hat and set it in her lap. "Are you going to do anything about Elba?"

"I tried formulating a plan, but I can't come up with anything helpful. My guild is small and deals mostly in information and rumors. We're strong, but not strong enough to face a battalion of goblins—or players."

"That makes sense. Okay—let me know if anything changes."

"Same to you."

Kit sighed deeply when she exited out of the PM.

"Trouble?" Solus Miles asked.

Kit nodded. "Halbryt—you've met him before, briefly, he's one of the GMs—is stuck in Elba."

Solus said nothing, but Kit noticed the set of his shoulders stiffened.

Kit stared at the sky. "I can't help but think that leaving Elba to burn isn't the right decision. Brave Heart Company, the Observational Fiends, and Halbryt and his crew...they don't deserve to be penned in there. But what can I do?"

"They fight because they're afraid," Noir chimed in from Kit's other side. "While rumors of you have spread, no one really believes you can pull off a win against Valdis."

"Great, so at least we're all on the same page," Kit grumbled.

She watched Pax shift closer to the fire dancers—who were building to a climax as they leaped about, creating an image of a dragon with their fire.

"They don't have hope," Solus said. "That's something the guildmasters can't offer—they can only bring protection."

"Are we talking about the fighting in Elba?" Prowl asked.

Kit mutely nodded.

"Your husband-o has it right." Prowl popped a mint leaf in

his mouth and chewed. "Besides KOS, most of the guilds haven't done much to release information about you—and Gared is limited in what he can spread without Alistair around to use her charm and charisma."

"I do make a wonderful storyteller!" Alistair beamed over his shoulder.

"But what do I do?" Kit whispered.

Solus shrugged slightly. "Give them hope."

"But hope for what?" Kit asked.

"Beats me," Long Claw snorted. "You are uninspiring and on a suicide run. Good luck with that."

Alistair tapped a finger against her chin. "That's not true. You're the first player to ever secure the allegiance of three different NPC groups—four if we count the pirates."

Noir took a gold and gem-encrusted ring Trash Panda delivered to him. He shut one eye and held the ring up against the sky so he could study it. "You're also the only active player to have a winged warrior as your pet, plus you're pledged to Solus Miles."

"And you defeated Malignus with less than seventy people," Solus said.

"But that information has spread like wildfire," Kit said. *The Defenders of Talith promised to talk it up.*

The fire dancers started chanting together, then ended their act by building a human pyramid as fire roared around them. Pax must have immensely enjoyed himself, for he went as far as giving them two generous claps with the rest of the audience.

"Yeah," Prowl snorted. "But it's one thing to hear that info in whispered rumors, and another to see proof of it."

But that's false hope! Kit's eyes stung, and for a moment she really wanted to cry. *All that stuff might be true, but it doesn't mean I'm really capable of pulling this off! I feel like such a fraud.* She briefly hunched her shoulders as she thought of Halbryt—who had always been kind, even when she had just happened to encounter him—and exhausted Teara from the Observational Fiends. *But no matter if I can really do this or not...I can't let them rot in Elba. No one gets left behind.*

Kit picked up her hat and settled it on her head. "Okay. I know what NPCS we're going after next."

Alistair tilted her head. "What group?"

Kit smiled. "The Imperial Empire. We're going to Elba."

"I apologize for my forwardness, but could I intrude on your conversation?"

Kit flicked a fan open and shut as she realized the interloper to their conversation was one of the female fire dancers. The NPC bit her lip as her gaze flickered from Kit to Solus and the others.

Alistair gave the fire dancer a sweeping bow. "Of course, talented lady! We welcome your presence—your show was quite inspiring!"

The dancer smiled broadly at Alistair and uttered a quick "Thank you!" before she turned all of her attention to Kit. "I thought I overheard your companions saying you were the one who led the fight against Malignus?"

Kit opened and closed her fan again in her surprise. "Yes, I am."

The dancer brightened, making her bronze-colored skin glow. "Then you're the elf dancer—Kitten Lovemuch!"

I wonder if I can get the allegiance of the fire dancer NPCs... I didn't think of them because they're such a small group, but they are notoriously strong. I wonder if there are other class-based NPC groups like them we could recruit as well. Kit gave the dancer a twitch of a smile. "When I can't avoid it, yes."

The fire dancer actually squealed and stood on her tip-toes, making her red hair dance like flames. "It's such an honor to meet you!" She briefly turned to her companions and whistled. "Family, it's Kitten Lovemuch!"

Instantly the dancers—who had been packing up their performance materials—ringed around Kit.

"An honor!" a male dancer proclaimed as he vigorously shook Kit's hand.

"I never thought I would have the chance to meet you!" One of the older female dancers laughed happily. "You are as graceful and beautiful as the stories say."

Some of the fire dancer children wriggled their way through the press of bodies and popped out at Kit's feet. "Wow," a little boy breathed as he stared up at her. "You really *are* an elf!"

Kit self-consciously shifted and felt her tapered ears twitch a little. "I'm not the only warrior here that was present for the battle against Malignus." She gestured to Prowl—who was in the process of adjusting his goggles. "Prowl fought bravely as well."

Some of the fire dancers smiled and nodded to Prowl, but it was clear Kit was the one they were mostly interested in.

"We were glad to hear that Malignus was overthrown, of course," an older male dancer rumbled as he adjusted the ruby bracelet that was fastened around his wrist. "But to hear it was a *dancer* who led the charge?" He laughed and shook his head. "You have made us proud to share your class, Kitten Lovemuch!"

"This is stupid," Long Claw declared as he folded his arms across his chest and his furry wolf ears twitched.

Everyone ignored him.

"And it is so rare to see an elf dancer." A tiny slip of an elderly woman reached up and brushed the tips of Kit's tapered ears. "Which is a shame—your grace and elegance surpasses all due to your race and training."

"Thank you," Kit said, trying not to blush under their happy attention. *This is a bit intimidating, but it's a thousand times better than getting shot in the chest! Killing Malignus might be the best thing that ever happened to my reputation!* "But I'm not anything special. You all are undoubtedly much stronger than I am—and *far* more capable in battle," she said, trying to keep the bitterness out of her voice.

Fire dancers were perhaps the only type of dancers in Retha that posed a serious threat damage-wise.

I wonder if they are available as a legendary hero class. That would be the ideal class if I was stuck on Kit long enough to reach level cap.

The grandmotherly woman snorted. "Dragon droppings!" she declared. "You have brought more respect to our class than we have enjoyed in years, yet for all your fathomless years as an elf, you are still just a chick."

A younger male fire dancer nodded as he ruffled his flame-red hair. "Indeed. Your future has yet to open up before you, Kitten Lovemuch. One day you will see the chance for greatness."

Kit stared at the NPC, slightly confused. "What?"

The fire dancers ignored her question.

"Did I hear you plan to journey on to Elba?" the original fire dancer asked, her anklets jingling as she hopped from foot to foot.

"Yes," Kit glanced at the rest of her party, silently asking them for help with her eyes.

Prowl held his hands up and backed away, but Alistair took pity on her. "Goblin ships are attacking Elba," the lady knight said. "We aim to stop them."

"What a happy coincidence," declared the fire dancer. "We are traveling to Elba, as well! This was to be our last performance in Luminos," she said, gesturing to the space by the mermaid fountain that they had vacated.

As the fire dancers eagerly stared at her, Kit grappled for words. *I don't get what I'm supposed to do with their excitement.* "How nice?" she tried.

One of the male dancers put his fist to his chest and bowed slightly. "It would bring us great joy—and honor—if we could travel with your party."

Oh. Oh! I wonder if I could convince them to fight the goblins with us! "Certainly," Kit smiled broadly.

A popup screen appeared in Kit's face.

You have received the quest: Caravan of Dance
For quest information and goals, view your quest log in your character panel.

Kit quickly peeked at the quest information and was a little disappointed to see it was just a regular daily quest to travel with the dancers from one location to the next. *Still, if we cruise up, and the city is closed because of the goblins, I can't imagine they would refuse to fight.*

Noir, who was back to fanning himself with his delicate fan, snorted. "Did you fail to hear the part about goblins sieging the city?" he asked the dancers.

They shrugged.

"We have faced many battles before," a male dancer with the face of carved granite rumbled. "Goblins burn just as easily as other creatures of Lord Valdis' creation."

Kit sighed and clasped her hands together. "That bravery is what it means to be a dancer and yet pack a pretty powerful amount of DPS."

"Careful, or you'll start drooling," Prowl said.

"Our plan," the grandmotherly fire dancer started, "was to teleport to Lake Town and follow the road to Elba."

Kit adjusted her hat. *Will we be able to move quickly enough to reach Elba before things really implode? But I don't have any teleport gates that are closer than Lake Town anyway with the Elba gates closed off.* "I think that will work—though we intend to move swiftly."

The fire dancers nodded. "If we follow the road, we can risk traveling at night—though we will be attacked by monsters, I fear," a male dancer said.

"Good," Solus Miles said.

Kit narrowed her eyes at him. "We won't have time to level," she warned.

He shrugged. "Perhaps not seriously, but the monsters in that area should give you good exp."

"Yes!" Fame clambered to get in front of the royal knight. "I can give you detailed information about the monsters in that area, Kitten. Much *better* information, too, so it won't be necessary to listen to vague guesses." She shot Solus a look that clearly communicated she felt he was stepping into *her* territory, unwanted.

Kit twisted her mouth in a quirk of humor, then turned her attention to the fire dancers and the rest of the party. "We will need an hour or so to prepare ourselves," Kit said. "We must inform our companions of our new plan and gather any materials we need for our fight."

Prowl groaned. "Please don't say we're going to have Fortune help us upgrade our gear. Seriously, I can't take much more from the know-it-all-twins."

"You wouldn't have to if you upgraded your armor to the sets I have recommended." Fortune gave Prowl a sunny smile, which made the saboteur flatten his lips like a frog.

"Of course!" the original fire dancer chirped, ignoring Prowl's complaint. "We need to finish packing our equipment and gather our mounts. We will meet you at the teleportation gate in an hour?"

"Yes," Kit nodded. "Until then!"

The dancer laughed joyful. "We look forward to it!"

Kit smiled grimly as she waved farewell. *I wish I could say the same. I have no idea how we're going to take on an entire goblin siege with our small party.*

16

JOURNEY TO ELBA

KIT CROUCHED on a rock and watched the Nignay river churn past, roaring as it spilled over the cliffsides.

She stood on top of the cliffs just behind the Solis Sentinels and watched as the warm rays of the sun peeked over the eastern horizon and cast orange and yellow hues on the stone dragon and winged warrior.

She glanced up at her character information—she had reached level 63—and groaned.

"Are you in need of assistance, Kitten?" Fortune asked.

His twin skirted Pax and peered over the side of the rock bank and into the rushing river.

"No, I'm fine. Thanks, Fortune." Kit pinched her nose, then glanced back.

They were taking a brief break to rearrange item storage, cook some camp rations, and to give the fire dancers a chance to eat. *We've set a good pace, but we're still taking too long! But I guess it doesn't matter how fast we get there, as I have no idea what to do about the siege.*

An invasion alone was going to be difficult to handle given that the attacking goblins and bobokins would be on-level with or slightly above Kit and the other lower-leveled party members. But having the goblins skidding around on *boats* was going to throw a wrench in Kit's usual tactics.

Kit tried to come up with a battle plan as she stared at the frothy water, but it didn't help. *Maybe Solus and Sinistre could attack from the sky...but if we want to hit them with damage, we would need mages, wizards, and rangers—any class with distance attacks. Long Claw and Alistair don't have those, and after Solus, they're our top damage dealers.*

She stifled another groan. *I can't do this. My brain is numb. How can I think that with just my little party I can clear the goblins and open up the city when two elite guilds have already failed at this?*

She bit her lip and considered trying to message Halbryt again. As it was barely dawn, perhaps some of the fighting had subsided in Elba, and he had reached a safe area.

There were shouts back at the temporary camp as three python-sized creatures that were an unsettling cross of a fanged caterpillar and a centipede fell from one of the trees and landed on Noir with a splat.

The scout and spellbinder took them out shortly, and Kit's exp bar crept up a few percentage points.

"Solus!" Noir scowled as he boosted himself into a standing position and brushed dirt from his white linen robe. "You better not be using your taunt skill."

"We're trying to move quickly." Solus shrugged. "Even I am not so obsessed with leveling that I would risk bringing in monsters on this march."

Kit cracked a slight smile and rested her chin on her knees as she remained crouched.

The air in front of her shimmered, and golden letters appeared.

You have secured an alliance with the elves of Fione Forest.

Kit's smile bloomed into a grin, and she switched to the raid chat channel. "Way to go, party Player One!"

A moment passed before the raid channel hummed to life.

"Thank you," Nyx said. "That was a satisfactory agreement —the elves will be a great resource when we fight Valdis."

"They pledged mostly archers," Reynard said.

"Oh gosh, that was bad." Riko groaned. "I don't know how you guys managed to let them yammer on and on before I arrived. Seriously, elves are the most long-winded people ever. And I work in city politics!"

Kit let Riko's cranked voice melt away some of her inner tension. "At least you got it done," she said.

"Yes, having Riko with us definitely made a difference," Waffle said. "If you mean for us to keep recruiting NPCs, I think we will need to have Riko or Prowl with us to pull it off."

"I volunteer Riko," Prowl said, tuning into the raid channel with all due nosiness.

"I'll fight you," Riko said seriously.

"Oh come on! You love this stuff!" Prowl argued. "You're all about trying to be charming and what not."

"*Trying?*"

"Where do you want us to go next, Kit?" Waffle asked.

Fortune strolled past Kit, pausing in front of Pax long enough to eye him critically. "You don't even have stat bonuses," he muttered before ambling on.

The winged warrior, who had been gazing picturesquely off into the sunrise, scowled after the guild NPC.

"About that..." Kit pushed herself into a standing position, taking care to brush off the hem of her jacket. "I'm assuming your guildmasters have read you into the situation in Elba, Waffle, Reynard, and Nyx?"

There was a moment of silence, then Waffle meekly replied. "Yes."

"What situation?" Riko asked.

"Nyx and Waffle can give you details, but basically Elba is locked up in a goblin siege. It's one of the new events that hit Retha with Lord Valdis' return. Because it happens every few weeks, two medium guilds—Midnight Watch and Steadfast, which have already fought and had to be subdued by KOS in the past—planned an all-out brawl when the current siege hit. The city is in an uproar," Kit said.

Riko hissed out a puff of air. "Yikes. The boxing gloves have come off."

"Yeah." Kit held her hat to her head when a breeze ruffled the brim. "Which is why it's perfect you finished with the elves."

"Oh?" Nyx asked.

"Yes. I want you to regroup with us and come to Elba."

"Why?" Reynard asked. "Our guilds aren't going to move against Elba—not until the siege is over."

Kit awkwardly shuffled her feet. "Yes, well, nevertheless...I decided I'm going to do something."

"Do you really think we can do something?" Nyx asked mildly.

"We're going to find out," Kit said flatly. "There are innocent players in that city, and some idiots whose heads we have to crack together."

There was a moment of silence.

"Well, I'm going," Riko said. "You guys can try throwing yourselves at the next target if you like—though, as you've learned, you aren't getting anywhere without me. Ta ta!"

"Wait, Riko," Waffle called. "Kit is our leader. We're all going."

Reynard grumbled over the chat channel but raised no complaints.

"Very well." Nyx said, her no-nonsense business tone back in place. "We will teleport to the nearest city and meet you at Elba."

"Sounds great. Thank you, and we'll see you soon." Kit exited out of the chat channel and glanced over her shoulders when her elf ears caught the sound of pebbles crunching beneath a foot.

Solus strolled across the riverbank, his gaze on Fame and Fortune as the twins clambered across the bank.

"Kitten!" Fame shouted. "There are Silverfin Fish here— their scales are rare drops!"

"Are they used in candy?" Kit asked.

A fine wrinkle spread across Fame's forehead as she stared at Kit. "I am uncertain, as I am ignorant in matters of items and crafting."

"Spoiler: they aren't. So I don't care about them," Kit said. She glanced at Solus, then nodded at the Solis Sentinels—which were now more golden colored as the sun continued to rise. "Beautiful, isn't it?"

Solus nodded. "Everyone is almost ready to leave—Prowl is stirring up the camp rations. He said to tell you to stay away until he's finished so you don't poison everyone."

Kit tried to smile, but based on the slants of Miles' eyebrows, she failed.

"What's wrong?" he asked.

Kit shook her head. "Nothing, really. Ugh, hopefully we won't be attacked too much. I think the road will veer away from the sentinels again, which means going through the forest..."

She trailed off when Solus reached out and brushed her hand. "What's wrong?" he repeated.

She briefly twisted around so she could gaze back at the

merrily crackling fire where the fire dancers and her party chattered and laughed. "I'm a little freaked out right now," she admitted. "I know we need to do something about Elba...but I'm drawing a blank."

Solus moved closer to her so their shoulders brushed. "You're being too hard on yourself right now," he said. "You beat Malignus on your first try because you went in with the attitude that you were going to attempt the impossible. Don't think about how perfect you have to be; try to think out of the box."

"It was a little different then. I was dealing with people who were so desperate to get out of the game, they would have marched with me no matter where I went." Kit rubbed the back of her neck. "It's much more political now."

"Perhaps," Solus said. "But even if they fight, everyone still desperately wants to safely leave the game. They all have a unique reason."

Kit glanced at the royal knight—who at the moment looked like the moody hero Kit always teased him about as he stared out past the sentinels, and the rising sun cast warm rays across his black-and-gold armor. "Do you have someone you are desperate to return to?"

Solus' expression turned thoughtful, and he gave her a half nod.

So to answer my previous musings, yes, he is definitely taken. Out loud, she said, "That's a yes."

Solus glanced at her. "Of a sort."

Kit cleared her throat and nearly scowled—angry with herself for being disappointed. *Flipping Flapjacks, we're fighting for our lives here, and I'm acting like a high school girl with a crush!* She shook her head and continued. "Anyway, in regards to my creativity in taking out Malignus, I haven't been very good at that lately. You were the one who was thinking more creatively. Back when we were on the pirate ship?" She shrugged. "It never occurred to me to tell you to use Sinistre to save us."

Solus raised an eyebrow. "You aren't used to having a pet—a helpful pet."

"Oooh, Pax, did you hear that?" Kit called to her winged warrior. "Solus just insulted you!"

Pax ignored her and instead outstretched all four of his wings, making a few of his feathers fly around the area.

"You have a fire-breathing dragon, and I have a stylish statue that occasionally likes to insult me," Kit pursed her lips. "He wouldn't have done anything against the pirates." She narrowed her eyes at the winged warrior's back.

Solus shrugged. "He didn't have to. You handled it."

Kit sighed so deeply she hunched forward slightly. "More like sheer luck handled it. I still can't believe Swear Proficiently was actually *useful*." She frowned at the thought, then glanced up at Solus to find his icy gray eyes fixated on her face.

She offered him a tired smile.

He nodded once, then briefly slipped his arm around her shoulders to give her a short but warm side hug.

Kit leaned slightly into him. *Even if he's taken, I'm glad he's with me. Even when we were tangled up with the pirates.*

On a whim, she opened her item storage and pulled out the conch shell the pirates had given her. "The goblins are attacking by boat," she said carefully.

Solus dropped his arm from her shoulders. "That's what the guildmasters said at the meeting."

Kit nodded slowly. "I wonder...the pirates said to call whenever I had a need...and they *are* good at fighting." *We're not by the ocean, but they didn't say if I was by the ocean I could call them; they said by water.*

Solus mutely watched her as she puzzled through the situation.

Kit bit her lip, then glanced up at him again. "I'm going to try something."

Solus held his arm out in front of him. "Go ahead."

Kit climbed farther upstream, where the water wasn't *quite* as fast and turbulent. Feeling a bit like an idiot, she held the conch shell up to her mouth and blew.

The shell created one solid, somewhat high-pitched note that sounded a bit like the horrible flutes elementary schools give little kids to toot around with.

When she ran out of breath, Kit pressed her lips together and stared at the shell. "That was pretty unimpressive." She gazed up and down the Nignay river but saw no sign of the NPC sailors.

It was worth a shot, I guess.

Kit turned back in the direction of camp when she heard another yelp followed by shouts from the spellbinder, Glowrious, as he—from the sounds of it—set another one of the caterpillar creatures on fire.

The throaty gurgle of the river changed, and Kit glanced back at the Nignay long enough to see that the area directly next to the embankment on which she stood glowed and bubbled like a hot tub. Narrowing her eyes, Kit leaned closer, then shrieked when a ship shot out of the water prow-first, like a whale surfacing.

She shouted, turned on her heels, and zipped back to Solus Miles' side, her heart pounding at the unconventional arrival method.

As she suspiciously eyed the ship, she realized that though water gushed off the sides, an air bubble seemed to cover the decks where pirates—still dressed in their low-cut shirts and sporting gold rings and necklaces—clung to the masts and railings.

Pirates wielding magic stood at the prow and stern, their

hands glowing as magic runes circled them. When they all made a cutting-off gesture, the air bubble popped.

The captain stood on the railing closest to Kit and hung over the side, clinging to one of the sail ropes. "Ahoy there, Kitten Lovemuch!" he called. "What, pray tell, are you needin' our help with?"

Kit stared open-mouthed at the pirate ship, which treaded water thanks to the efforts of the ex-wizards among the crew, even as the river tried to sweep it downstream towards the waterfall. "You guys are that good at magic that you can teleport a ship through *water*...and you wanted to be pirates?"

The captain shrugged. "We all have dreams, matey—woah!" He yelped as the rope he clung to tightened when a gust of wind filled the sail and tugged on it.

Kit stared and watched some of the pirates rush to support their captain, still a little dumbfounded. "They are so overpowered," she said to Solus. "I mean, players can't do anything like that!"

Solus shrugged. "They are considered a special-bonus NPC group to gain reputation with."

"Still." She shook her head, then raised her voice again. "I called you to see if you could take me and some comrades upriver. We're short on time, and sailing will be faster than riding... or it should be." Kit wrinkled her forehead as she studied the river. "Is it possible to take an ocean ship up a river?"

"No problem!" the pirate captain assured her. "If the river gets too tight, we'll just float over it!"

Solus slightly narrowed his eyes. "If it weren't for their fixation on their pirate dream, I suspect they would be a hellish force to encounter."

"They already are," Kit grumbled. She glanced at Fame and Fortune as the NPC siblings finally joined her.

Fame studied the pirates for a moment, then turned to Kit.

"Sea pirates normally are aggressive targets, but it seems like these are not."

Fortune stood at her side, his arms folded across his chest as he sighed. "Just like your pet, their armor doesn't have stats."

Kit shook her head at the guild NPCs, then returned her attention to the pirates. "If that's the case, then I would greatly appreciate *safe* passage for my friends and me—and we've got some fire dancers we're traveling with, too."

"We've plenty of room for all—provided they are *your* friends," the captain said.

"Oh, yeah. Absolutely. We're very close," Kit said vaguely. *I wonder what happens if they think we aren't friends. Probably Long Claw will find out.*

"Then they are welcome aboard!" the pirate with the stuffed parrot boomed.

Kit relaxed and felt some of the worry loosen in her shoulders. "Thank you—as one pirate-hearted to another," she said, sincerely. *This is going to save us so much time—traveling by the river will be faster because it's a shorter distance, but I suspect it will be especially swift given that they magically power their ship.* She bit the inside of her cheek as she studied the pirates. *Though this is already a huge help, if I really do have a high reputation with them from swearing...maybe I can push for more.* She was afraid to hope, but if something drastic didn't change, Kit and her party wouldn't be able to do much even if they arrived well before the siege was over.

She cleared her throat. "Hey, do you guys think you're up for a ship fight with goblins?"

The abacus pirate peered at Kit across the river. "Are they carrying gold?"

"No," Kit said. "But they've laid siege to Elba, locking the Imperial Empress inside. I imagine she would be very grateful to see their forces defeated."

The abacus pirate scratched his side. "Maybe," he said doubtfully. "She's pretty stingy."

"If you want us to go into battle, as fellow pirate-hearted men, I sup'ose we ought to," the pirate with the stuffed parrot added with zero enthusiasm, which made Kit a bit nervous.

Come on, I need to think more creatively! "Once the battle is over...I will teach you the most foul swear words I know," Kit offered, stiffening herself for a rejection.

Abacus pirate brightened. "Will there be more cursing by the sheets of Excel?" he asked excitedly.

"Sure," Kit said. "And slugs, worms, and sheep."

"You can count on us, Kitten Lovemuch! We're the fiercest pirates in Retha!" the pirate captain bragged.

"Mostly because we use magic," said stuffed-parrot pirate.

"And because the only other pirates are goblins and such, and they're shamefully bad at it," Abacus pirate added.

Kit laughed—whether in humor or sheer relief, she didn't know. "Excellent. Give us a minute to pack up, and my party will be ready to board."

The captain swept his hat from his head and bowed deeply. "Of course. We'll prepare the gangplank!"

Kit waved to them and turned back towards camp, though she paused long enough to glance up at Solus Miles. "This just might work!"

Solus shrugged. "I never expected any less from you."

Kit left him observing the pirate crew and trotted off to the party. "Hey guys!" she shouted. "I have a faster way up-river!"

———

Though the swift trip up the Nignay river was uneventful—and perhaps even a little funny as Long Claw discovered werewolves could get seasick on a river—their arrival at Elba was grim.

The city—still white and shining with gold—glimmered in the early morning light, but the Nignay and the riverport were blanketed in black.

Hundreds of black ships crawling with green-skinned goblins and big-eared bobokins floated on the river. They were all smaller than the pirate's vessel, but most of them were bigger than a yacht and sported crude, bloodied shields bolted to their sides. Goblins and bobokins were packed so tightly in the boats, it was a wonder they could move.

Kit leaned against the railing and tried to keep her face expressionless as she studied the hoard. "I might have underestimated the size of their forces," she said.

Solus said nothing as he stared through a small telescope, but Prowl snorted. "Jeez, you think?"

The pirates kept the ship anchored just far enough down river that they didn't pull aggro on the goblins and get themselves attacked.

Long Claw grunted from his position farther up the railing. He dangled over the side of the ship, and his yellow eyes were half-shut as his tail drooped. "This is why we shouldn't have come," he growled. "But no, Kitten Lovemuch knows better than all the guildmasters of the best guilds in the game."

Alistair sashayed across the deck, her ponytail whipping in the slight breeze. "That's not totally true!" She patted Long Claw on the shoulder when he groaned as the ship rocked with a wave. "Gared wanted to do something. But KOS's hands are tied."

Kit drummed her fingers on the railing of the ship and started mentally sifting through her resources. "We have one ship with a crew of mage pirates, a troop of fire dancers, and a pretty strong party—though we're split at the moment."

A seagull cried, and Kit glanced up at the ship's rigging where Pax was perched, his wings spread out behind him. "We can't count on Pax, but Sinistre gives us a mighty big advantage..."

She looked from her winged warrior to the white city blocked by black. "The city is filled with players who could potentially beat the snot out of the invasion...but Elba *is* our end point. We're here to stop the unrest inside it, but we have to get there first."

She frowned as she mentally repeated the thought. *Does stopping the player violence really have to be the last step? We can't use sheer force—that's just going to escalate everyone.*

"Miles?" Kit glanced at the royal knight and turned her back to the city so she could lean against the ship railing.

"Hm?" Solus collapsed the telescope and slipped it into his item storage.

"Do you really think that lack of hope is the reason for *this*?" She jerked her thumb over her shoulder, gesturing to Elba.

Long Claw snorted. "Are you kidding? Midnight Watch and Steadfast have always had bad blood." He slowly straightened up as if it pained him and grumbled. "This is what happens when you have a has-been running the show. They don't have a clue what's going on. Chief never would have said something so stupid."

Solus ignored the werewolf and stared at Elba. "Panic and raw emotions drive humanity to do dangerous things. That's the difference between a peaceful protest and a riot." He swiveled so his piercing gray eyes settled on Kit. "Think of them as an overly large guild stuck in a raid," he said. "Right now, they have no leader, no idea what the raid objective is, and no hope of getting out."

Kit scratched her cheek absentmindedly. "A raid, huh?"

"With all the usual politics, drama, and elicit romances," Prowl grumbled.

Kit stared down at her feet and scuffed the toe of her boot on the spotless deck. *If we're thinking of this like a raid...then what if stopping the fight in Elba isn't the final goal? What if that's what we have to do first?*

A half-baked idea started to form in her mind—one that was dangerous and likely to be a gamble. *But we're already too late to keep the hysteria from starting. Even if we break Elba open, we'll only minimize the damage. So what if we could instead smite the fight in the city before the goblins are beaten?*

Switching to the raid chat channel, Kit cleared her throat. "Waffle—or Nyx or Riko—how close are you to Elba? You aren't coming from Lake Town, are you?"

"Are you insane? No way am I walking from Lake Town to Elba again!" Riko snorted.

"We're quite close," Waffle said. "Nyx recommended we use a teleportation gate to reach Bangle, then teleport from there to Fory—a small settlement on the edge of the Igneo Desert. From there we ported to Niteo—a satellite city near Elba. We're probably about one hour out from the small forest west of Elba."

The vague plans in Kit's mind started to sharpen and take shape. *Yes...we just might be able to do this—or at least we can get all the way to Midnight Watch and Steadfast. It will be their decision if they want to stop or not.*

She tilted her head. "Hey Alistair, can you contact Teara and Saint George?"

"I can try," Alistair said. "I know Gared said he was in contact with both of them not even an hour ago."

"Perfect," Kit said. "Please tell them to send me a PM...and inform them of our position."

"What, too high-and-mighty to do that yourself?" Long

Claw scoffed—though he clutched his stomach when the ship rolled.

"No," Kit absent-mindedly tossed her hair over her shoulder. "I just know neither of them would accept a PM if I sent it myself." She shoved off the railing and strode away, making a beeline for the husband-wife pair of Fire Dancers that seemed to run the troupe—luckily, they were speaking with the pirate captain.

"Have you come up with something?" Noir inquired as she marched past him. (The priest was seated on a cushioned chair and was splitting a bunch of grapes with Trash Panda.)

"Maybe," Kit said. "But you're not going to like it."

"I don't like any of your plans," Noir called after her. "Except the ones where you let people I don't like die!"

"There will be a couple of perks," Kit called over her shoulder as she climbed the stairs to the upper deck where the captain and fire dancers stood.

"Like what?" Noir sourly asked.

Kit grinned. "You'll get to fly!"

17

INVITE TO RAID PARTY

KIT HELD ON TO SOLUS MILES' waist as she admired the view. Sinistre circled Elba, soaring so high, they nearly touched the clouds.

"Waffle, are you in position?" Kit asked over the raid chat.

"We are," the summoner confirmed.

"Alistair, Hide_N_Seek?" Kit peered over Sinistre's shoulder, catching a glimpse of the secondary party. They were crouched behind a rock formation that shielded them from the goblins and bobokins but was still situated close to Elba's main gate.

"We are here," Alistair declared.

"And we're staying hidden," the scout dryly added.

"I want to again mention how much I *hate* this plan!" Noir shouted over the raid chat.

"But Noir, you're flying," Kit pointed out.

"I am being clutched in a dragon's paw!" he said sourly. "Sooner or later, this beast will have to land, then I will be crushed. Death is imminent."

"Sinistre will land hind-legs first," Solus said.

"See?" Kit said in a soothing tone. "Nothing to fear! Enjoy

the view!"

"That's easy for you to say," Noir said. "You're riding the dragon's back! I'm down below, downwind, and directly next to a werewolf who apparently not only gets seasick, but airsick as well!"

Long Claw made a gagging noise, which momentarily filled the chat channel.

"The bigger they are, the harder they fall," Nyx said coldly.

"Hey, if we're complaining, I get a turn," Prowl said.

"I fail to see how you're in any sort of hardship," Nyx said. "You're standing on a boat with a small army of NPCs, far away from conflict."

"Yeah," Prowl snapped. "Except I have Fame and Fortune with me! Did you know there are twenty different sets of goggles that are better than the ones I have—*and* are level appropriate?"

"You could ask Fame what monsters drop goggles," Kit suggested.

"No!"

Kit smiled as Sinistre circled the city again. "You'll survive. I'm confirming locations with my contact and Teara, then we'll begin. Last chance to check your weapons, eat, or regain your manna."

The raid channel momentarily buzzed with grumbles as Kit switched over to a PM.

"Teara?" she asked.

"*Yes.*"

"Have you successfully made it to the southern armory?"

"*We have—with no casualties.*"

The nerves in Kit's guts eased slightly. *Good—that was a linchpin in this plan. With Halbryt and his guild backed into a corner, we need Observational Fiends' help to reach them.* "Excellent. I'll do the knock when we drop down by you."

"We will listen for it. Have you reached Saint George?"

"He emphatically refused to reply when Alistair asked him to PM me after I spoke with you," Kit said. "Haven't you been in contact with him?"

"Some," Teara said, her voice flat.

"Do you think maybe you could get through to him and convince him to join us?" Kit asked hopefully. "He doesn't have to agree to follow me to Lord Valdis—we could just use the extra power in this fight."

"It wouldn't do any good," Teara said. *"I'm not a guildmaster —I don't warrant the same amount of information and respect. He doesn't have to listen to me."*

Kit frowned. "But you're responsible for Observational Fiends."

"I'm still just the first officer," she said firmly.

Kit shrugged a little—given how reluctant she had been to so much as lead a party when she first got stuck in Retha, she could hardly blame her. "Okay—I've got to go. I need to check in with Halbryt and his guild, then we'll be down."

"Understood."

Kit started to switch messages.

"Everything okay?" Solus Miles asked—outside the raid chat channel.

"I think so—I *hope* so," Kit said.

"It's a good plan," Solus said.

"It's a *risky* plan," Kit said.

"You excel in risky plans," Solus said. "You were the one who decided to attack a shadow reaper that was much higher-leveled than most of the members of your party, and you beat it. I would bring up Malignus, but I'm getting sick of using him as the same example again and again," he added.

"I never denied that I'm prone to suggest risky plans, it's just...this one might actually blow up in my face." Kit briefly rested her head on Solus' shoulder before she remembered herself and snapped to attention. "Before if we all wiped and everyone died, oh well. But if I can't get Midnight Watch and Steadfast to stop fighting..."

"It's a good plan," Solus repeated.

"Let's hope it works." Kit sent off a PM to Halbryt and waited for the beast tamer to accept.

Communication with Halbryt had been rather touch-and-go.

Given the party of Observational Fiends players who had been sent to Elba was comprised mostly of level cap—or near level cap—players, Observational Fiends had been able to escape the conflict once it became obvious they couldn't stop it. They had retreated to parts of the city that weren't yet touched by the battle between Midnight Watch and Steadfast and had been able to set up a guard and protect themselves.

Halbryt and his guild—Fellowship of the Bling—were not so lucky. They were a medium-sized guild to begin with, and only a handful of players were in full submersion units when the server went down. As a result, they were being battered around the city like pinballs in a pinball machine.

They hadn't been able to find a safe hideaway, and they were forever running back to the Elba city spawn point for their guildmates who were slain. Unfortunately, the Elba spawn point was in a cathedral located in the main city square...where the bulk of the fight was.

"*Here,*" Halbryt said, interrupting Kit's thoughts.

"We're about to touch down and meet up with Observational Fiends, then we'll be coming for you. Where are you guys now?"

"*We're trapped in a bakery. There are fights in the alley behind us and outside the front door.*"

"Which bakery?"

There were several moments of silence before Halbryt responded, sounding distracted. *"Jake's Cakes."*

"Okay, try to hold your position. I'll let you know when we're enroute." Kit exited the PM and switched back to the raid chat. "Okay everyone, we're going in. Wait for your signal."

"Sinistre," Solus called to his dragon. "Drop off."

The dragon changed his flight pattern and began a rather steep descent that made Kit's eyes water as the wind whipped around her.

"Remind me again why he can't just land in the city?" Noir shouted over the howling wind.

"It's against the game's rules—dragons can land on city walls for a short amount of time, but not within city limits," Solus said.

"It's probably to keep players from using dragons to level settlements," Kit mused.

Sinistre kept his body in a sleek, downward angle, gliding straight for Elba. Then, he tucked his wings, and the speed of their descent rapidly increased.

"This is it!" Noir shouted. "Death has come—I will die in the inglorious act of being squashed by a dragon. When I respawn in Elba, I won't be able to fight off the hoards with my delicate build and will be taken captive as a heal slave."

Prowl snorted over the raid chat channel. "Only an idiot would want *you* as a heal slave."

Noir went silent—probably with terror—and even Kit's heart beat furiously as they careened towards the city walls with no signs of stopping.

Just before it seemed like they would crash into the city walls, Sinistre unfurled his wings, slowing them just in time. He landed on his hind legs, his claws gripping the walkways located on the city walls.

The black dragon leaned out into the city and opened his

paws, dropping Noir and Long Claw on a thatched roof cottage. He then awkwardly leaned to the side and changed the angle of his wing so Kit and Solus could slide down it.

As soon as Kit's feet hit the wall walkway, Solus shouted, "Take off!"

Kit barely had enough time to scramble away before the giant dragon pushed off the city wall—making it shake—and soared back into the sky where he returned to circling high overhead.

"That was...something." Kit nodded to Pax as he descended and hovered near her—unable or perhaps uninterested in flying off with Sinistre. "Are you okay, Noir? Long Claw?" She and Solus hurried to the edge of the wall and peered into the city.

"I have straw in places where there should not be," Noir announced. When he looked up and spotted Kit and Solus, he waved a hand to them, then picked a piece of straw out of his ear.

Long Claw stood—though with her superior eyesight, Kit could see that his legs shook. "What are we standing around for? Let's go!" he snarled.

"Be my guest," Noir grumbled as he stood up. "No one is going with *you*."

"Let's go," Solus said to Kit.

Kit nodded and—with her elven agility—leaped off the city wall and landed on the thatched roof cottage with a muffled thump. She had to crouch with the force of her land, but Solus—with his enviable long-jump life skill—was fine.

At least Swear Proficiently was actually useful, she reminded herself as she brought up the mini-map. "It looks like the city gates are about three blocks to the east, Long Claw."

"Yeah, I see it," Long Claw grunted.

"Scout out the guard house—if there are too many Imperial

Guards, wait for our arrival. Otherwise, use whatever stun and status ailments skills you have to subdue them," Kit said.

Long Claw rolled his yellow eyes. "I *know*. You went over the plan about a dozen times."

"Something she wouldn't have to do if you actually *listened*," Nyx said over the raid channel.

"Pipe down, *Corporate*," Long Claw snarled.

"Enough," Kit said. "Disagreements aren't an option right now. Focus on the plan. Solus, Noir, we're going north-east from here."

Solus nodded, and Noir flicked another piece of straw off his robe. "Right, right. Lead the way, Pinkie," he said.

Kit sat on the edge of the roof and slipped over the side, falling two stories and landing relatively gracefully.

Noir crawled down the side of the building, scrabbling for footholds and grumbling the whole way, while Long Claw jumped from windowsill to windowsill.

Solus landed at Kit's side with a snap of his cape as Kit reoriented herself. "That way, Long Claw," she said, pointing in the direction of the gatehouse. "Good luck."

The werewolf said nothing as he loped off down the quiet street, his saber unsheathed and his eyes glowing.

As Kit waited for Noir to finish his descent, she tipped her head and listened.

Even from here—the southern-most wall of Elba—she could hear the metallic clang of clashing weapons, the shouted war cries, yells of pain, and the sizzle of magic. The air smelled of blood and smoke, and her heart fell.

I thought maybe it wasn't as bad as everyone said, that maybe Halbryt was just stuck on the wrong side of the fight. But they really are trying to destroy each other.

Noir landed with a plop and sighed. "I miss Trash Panda."

"He'd be a liability in a situation like this," Solus said.

"I don't care. I still miss him."

"Come on, Noir. This way," Kit called as she led the way, striding through the maze of white buildings. The streets were eerily empty, and for the first time Kit could ever remember, the city did not have a constant background chorus of seagulls and birds.

"We're going to the southern armory, yes?" Solus pulled his sword free from its scabbard and twirled it once.

Kit stopped when they reached an intersection and carefully poked her head around the corner. Pax ignored her pause and strode right into the middle of the intersection, making her roll her eyes. Thankfully, the street was empty. "Yes." Her tapered ears twitched when she heard what sounded like a swordfight. "We've got fighters somewhere around here."

"Let them come," Solus coldly said as they turned up a road that ran north to south.

"Easy for you to say," Noir said. "You're not the one trying to keep a level 63 dancer alive."

Kit ignored the chatter as she did her best to silently pick her way up the road. "We have to turn at the next intersection," she said. "The armory will be the fifth building on the left.

Solus nodded, and the trio fell silent as the sounds of the swordfight grew louder.

As she listened to the sounds, her character information kicked in, bringing a rather unwanted and grim enlightenment. *That's more than a two-person swordfight*, she realized. *I hope Solus is up for facing them by himself.*

As they drew closer to the intersection, Kit pressed herself closer and closer to a white stone building. When they reached the corner, she peered around a decorative golden statue carved into the corner and espied two parties of players clashing just outside the armory they needed to reach.

Roughly twelve players were facing off—most of them were

fighter-types, but there was at least one priestess and an alchemist as well. Many of the players were from a mishmash of guilds, but as she stared at the whirl of nameplates, Kit saw at least two members of Midnight Watch and one from Steadfast.

"We'll have to take them out," Noir said as he crouched in front of Kit and joined her in peering around the corner. "Or the second Observational Fiends comes out of the armory, they're going to attack."

Kit bit her lip. "Solus can't stun a crowd that big."

The royal knight shrugged. "So I kill them."

"But then you'll get the player-killer tag," Kit pointed out.

"It is removed once enough time passes," Solus said.

"Besides, no one is going to report him in this kind of situation," Noir added.

Kit groaned. "I know, and it's not like we can subdue the whole city using stuns, but I still feel bad about it."

"I wouldn't have come if I weren't prepared to get the tag," Solus said. "Shall we?"

Kit sighed. "Yeah. Let's go."

Together, they turned the corner and ambled towards the fight. "I'll launch into Battlefield March when it looks like they're going to attack you," Kit said.

"That's not necessary," Solus said as he studied the fight. "If you can call Observational Fiends out, we'll be fine."

"Maybe, but it would make *me* feel better if I contributed," Kit said.

Lagging behind her, Pax made a noise in the back of his throat.

"What?" Kit asked.

"I find it amusing you're under the illusion that you *can* contribute," Pax said.

Kit nearly whirled around to glare at her pet, but Noir

distracted her. "Looks like we've got some admirers," he said, nodding to the group.

A level 30 thief and a level 70 fencer peeled off from their group and charged Solus, Kit, and Noir, with shouts.

Solus swung his sword out in front of him. "Fatal Strike!" He lunged forward as his sword glowed blue and stabbed the fencer, killing her in one shot.

"Guys, I'm going to need help!" the thief shouted to his friends as he tried to stab Solus in the side. His dagger bounced harmlessly off Solus' fancy armor.

"I'm going in for the signal," Kit shouted as she bounded towards the fight. She ducked an acid bomb thrown by the alchemist, but she didn't entirely escape the damage as it spattered when it went off, flicking acid on her bare stomach.

Kit roared in pain as the acid burned her skin and ate away at her health bar. "Why does everything go for my *stomach?*" she growled.

"Did you have to plunge into the thick of things before Solus got more than one attack off? Sanctified Mend!" Noir complained as he cast a heal—warm and soothing—on her.

Kit planted herself against the wall—hoping to escape the chaos of the fight.

The two sides were still fighting, though Solus had already finish off the thief and was stalking toward the main group.

"Charge of Valor!" he shouted. His sword glowed like a star and dwarven scrawl, fae symbols, elvish script, and runes from the ancient Solis Empire twirled around the blade as he plowed into the fight.

Kit rapped on the wooden armory door three times as she watched Solus take out a level 101 night stalker. She waited five seconds then knocked twice more.

The door swung open, and a berserker and a death knight burst out, immediately plowing into the fight. The rest of the

Observational Fiends guildmembers who had come to Elba poured out behind them.

Kit briefly switched out of the raid chat channel when Teara, bringing up the end of the party, skidded to a stop next to her. "Ready?"

"Light it up," Teara said as she adjusted her thick leather gloves—a necessity for her falconer class.

Kit brought up several character panels as she rushed, inviting Teara to her raid under the party name Observational Fiends Friends.

For a moment the raid was silent, then suddenly new names flooded Kit's raid-leader screen as Teara sent the invite out to all present guildmembers.

"Everyone accounted for," Teara said in the raid chat channel.

"We've successfully met up with Observational Fiends," Kit announced in the raid chat. "Play nice, everyone," she warned.

"Hello, First Officer Teara," Nyx greeted.

"Nyxiane—hi. I'm so glad to hear you," Teara said.

"I imagine so," Nyx said.

Kit activated her Battlefield March skill as she watched Observational Fiends crush the squabblers between them and Solus. As Observational Fiends had brought twenty players to Elba, they had roughly doubled the size of the raid.

The death knight grabbed an acrobat by the throat and threw him in a whirling pit of darkness, slicing off half the acrobat's health. When the acrobat tried to retaliate and jumped for the death knight, an Observational Fiends bard bashed him over the head with her lute.

"Long Claw—how's the gatehouse?" Kit asked as she twirled and spun.

"I handled it," Long Claw said.

"Have you?" Alistair said, sounding surprised. "Did we miss your signal, then? The gate still looks closed to me."

"I handled the *guards*!" Long Claw snarled. "I'm opening the gate now—jeez."

The raid chat was silent for a moment, and Kit cringed when a wizard hit her with a fireball.

The attack was short lived—Noir had her fully healed even before Solus headbutted the wizard.

"Gate's open," Long Claw said, his voice short.

"And there we have it! Forward," Alistair laughed. "We must draw the goblin's attention so charming Waffle, beautiful Nyx, and their party can enter first. Let's go!"

"We're in position," Hide_N_Seek said.

"Then we'll move towards the gatehouse," Waffle said.

"We need to move *faster*," Riko said, "or the gate will be open too long. Come on, Nyx. Shake a leg!"

As Kit leaped into the air, a sage started to target her, then paused when he saw Pax looming behind her. His hesitation gave an Observational Fiend ranger the necessary opening, and he was taken down with two well-placed arrows.

Farther down the street, a crusader and a fighter fled, leaving one lone war priest with a quarter of his health. The war priest tried to rush an Observational Fiends mage, but Teara's golden eagle—which was the size of a horse—came screaming down from the sky and took him out with its clawed feet.

"Hurry up," Long Claw said. "The guards are waking up."

"Wow, your stun skill must be really low-leveled if they're coming out of it already," Prowl said.

"Shut up!" Long Claw snarled. "You aren't even fighting!"

"Party Player One is through the gate," Waffle said.

"Don't stop, kiddos, keep moving! We're blocking the gate," Riko ordered.

"Waffle, I'm curious," Prowl said. "How did you manage to

lead your party with *two* bossy chicks?"

"Prowl," Riko growled. "I swear on all my money, when this is over, I'm going to call up Vic and have a long *chat* about how inappropriate you are. We'll see what Cookie thinks about you *then*."

"You're gonna die, saboteur," Noir said. "And for once, your blood won't be on my hands."

"Party Player One is forming a rearguard and backing in," Alistair announced.

"We've cleared up our fight," Kit said as she stopped dancing. "We'll meet you at the rendezvous point and move on to Jake's Cakes."

"Why are we going to a *bakery*?" Teara asked.

"That's where a friend of mine is hunkered down with his guild," Kit said. "We've got to rescue them before we try to take on the main fight."

"Everyone is in," the scout said.

Long Claw grunted. "Gate's closing—and I've lost a crapton of reputation with the Imperials because of this. This had better be worth it, Kit."

"I do believe you are softening, Long Claw," Alistair declared. "That's the first time you've called her by her name!"

"You are a weirdo," Long Claw said.

"Moving to the meet up spot," Waffle said.

"Yes, and we're staying in one group," Nyx said.

"Of course we are—to divide our forces would be to weaken us," Alistair said.

"She was talking to *you*," the scout said. "Because you roam off when distracted."

Assured everyone had made it in and her plan was still moving forward, Kit shifted her attention to her group. "Everyone ready to move out?"

Teara rejoined Kit and adjusted her hawker's glove. "Observational Fiends is ready."

Kit glanced at the guild—who had arranged themselves in a tight formation at their First Officer's back. The group was split with about half of the players keeping their eyes on Teara, and the other half warily gazing around at their surroundings.

Now that is teamwork! Kit admired them a moment before she brought up her mini-map and orientated herself. "Great, then we're heading this way."

Kit pointed up the street, and without asking, Solus and the death knight took the lead positions, acting as shields for Teara and Kit as they started off.

Noir joined Kit and glanced speculatively at Solus' back. "I think his coolness level is compounded whenever he's around a bigger group of people."

Kit blinked and looked up from her mini-map. "...*what?*"

"Solus." Noir nodded his head at the knight. "The more people there are, the more silent-and-brooding he acts. I think it might be because he's secretly shy. That's why everyone has been so wowed with how he treats you—it's because he's comfortable with you."

"Um," Kit said with all intelligence as the party quietly padded down the street.

"I questioned whether or not he really was all he was cracked up to be when I first met him. I mean, why would he tie his paragon of strength to *you* by being your pledged?" Noir continued. "But now I can see it's because he's most comfortable with you. Not only you—he seems at ease with your friends too —but he undoubtedly is the most defenseless with you."

"That is a really deep observation," Kit said carefully. *And I'm not sure how I'm supposed to react to it. I mean, yeah, Solus and I get along great now. But I think he's seeing more to us than there is because of Miles' little act for the guilds and his desire to get home...to whoever it is that he is missing.*

"Which is why," Noir said, "you should take advantage of it."

Kit's fingers itched to pinch the bridge of her nose, but she didn't want to shut her eyes in such a dangerous situation. She glanced at the Observational Fiends guildmembers, but they were either murmuring to each other or still gazing hawk-eyed at their surroundings. "You are just as bad as Riko," Kit growled.

"Oh, I didn't mean you should milk him for money—though I will support such an idea, and it is necessary for me to say I like expensive, spelled-silk robes in shades of white and gold, and I need them in extra tall." Noir flicked a strand of his dark purple hair from his eyes. "No, I was thinking how you could grind Saint George under your heel if you showed your hubby off just a little more."

"Saint George isn't going to follow me just because of Miles," Kit said.

"No," Noir said, his expression gleeful. "But you can humiliate him—which is just as good!"

Kit rolled her eyes then called ahead to Solus and the death knight. "Left turn here."

"You don't like Saint George, Noir?" Teara asked from Kit's other side.

"Not at all," Noir grumbled. "He's overly pushy and doesn't take no for an answer. Plus, he's so *arrogant*—he doesn't believe anyone would disagree with him."

"He tried to recruit you for his guild?" Kit guessed.

"Saying 'tried' implies he attempted once, and that was it," Noir grumbled. "He's never stopped."

Teara was silent for a few footsteps, then she added, "He's rather selfish," with more heat in her words than Kit would have expected.

Kit and Noir exchanged glances, but they didn't have to say anything. Teara railed on without prompting. "I tried to coordinate a retreat with him when I realized we couldn't handle the scale of the fight. We were in the central square of the city at the time, and it was utter chaos. When I finally sent a PM to him, he told me he couldn't be responsible for Observational Fiends as well as his own guild, and it was our fault if we were so incompetent we couldn't retreat without help."

Teara narrowed her eyes. "I'm aware I'm not a great leader—I'm just a first officer. But Observational Fiends is a *great* guild, and we've trashed Brave Heart Company numerous times in PVP. How *dare* he call us incompetent?"

"Is that why your guilds split in separate directions?" Kit asked.

Teara shrugged. "By the time I had cooled my head and realized that even if Saint George is an arse, there's bigger safety in numbers, the central fight had worsened, and it became nearly impossible to reach the north-west side of the city where his guild is."

"I wouldn't blame you if you didn't link up with him just because he's a prat," Noir said.

Kit resisted from agreeing only by forcing herself to stare at the mini-map again. "We're almost there," she said into the raid chat.

"I think you're only a street up," Riko said. "Cuz I can see Pax's wingtips over the building."

Kit glanced up at her winged warrior pet, who was flying at the moment. "Great, we'll make contact shortly." She cleared her throat, then continued, "We're staying in our separate groups as we walk to the bakery—I don't want us to cause suspicion in the city or interest anyone trigger-happy and looking for a fight."

"Are things really that bad?" Waffle asked, concern lining his voice.

"It's a possibility," Teara said. "But even if they get the word out, I don't know if anyone would purposely peel off from the main fight to track us down. They aren't terribly organized."

"I respectfully disagree," Nyx said, her melodic voice grim. "They must be very well organized to dupe our guilds and hold this fight in a time that would make it difficult for us to send troops."

"Kit." Solus stepped slightly to the side so Kit could see between him and the death knight. "I see them."

One street down, Alistair saluted them from the back of her horse, and Waffle waved. Riko adjusted her robes but nodded to them, as the rest of the two parties milled around behind her.

"Great. Since we're all here, I'm combining party Player One and Player Two, and moving Noir, Solus Miles, and myself to party Observational Fiends Friends." Kit brought up the raid panel and started rearranging the three parties, merging the original two. "Waffle is leading the new party, Elba Tourists, with Nyx and Hide_N_Seek in second command."

"Yes, ma'am," the scout said.

"If you think it's best," Waffle said dubiously.

"I do," Kit said grimly. *He's the one Long Claw and Reynard are most likely to listen to.* "Let's start moving west. Give us— party Observational Fiends Friends—a three-minute head start. We're going to circle around the back of the bakery. Elba Tourists should go through the front." She nodded when Solus pointed to the right turn they needed to take to start moving west toward the bakery. "Halbryt said there are players outside and behind the bakery, so expect a fight."

"It won't be a problem," Reynard said coolly.

"I'll slice 'em limb from limb," Long Claw said, "and wear the player-killer tag as a badge of honor for killing idiots like these."

Maybe it's a good thing we're doing this—it will give Long Claw and Reynard a way to channel their aggression. Kit waited until they were about four blocks west before speaking up. "Okay, Elba Tourists, you can move out now. Let me know if you get caught in a fight and need backup."

"Understood," Waffle said.

"Though it won't be necessary," Reynard chuckled darkly.

Kit slightly shook her head at the royal assassin's bloodthirst as she pulled up a PM and waited for Halbryt to answer.

As soon as the beast tamer accepted the message, Kit said, "Hey, we're about four minutes away. You're still in Jake's Cakes?"

"*Yes,*" Halbryt said. "*Be careful—it's mostly silent out front, but someone used powerful enough magic to shake the building just outside the backdoor.*"

"Thanks for the warning. Sit tight—and tell your guildmates we're almost there."

"*Egelthas will be delighted.*"

"The flirty pirate you always travel with?" Kit asked.

"*Yes. He's the guildmaster.*"

"Him?" Kit wrinkled her forehead. "I wouldn't have pictured that."

"*Who else would name their guild Fellowship of the Bling?*"

"Good point." Kit paused for a moment, straining her ears to listen. Though the entire city bubbled with the noise of conflict —clanging weapons, neighing horses, magic, and more—she was able to identify a strain of it coming from the direction of the bakery. "I think I hear the fight near you, so I'm going to sign off. See you soon."

"*Be careful.*"

Before Kit could respond, the beast tamer exited out of the PM.

Kit switched to the raid chat and expanded her mini-map, blocking out most of her sight. She gazed at the dots that represented the other players and started formulating her plan.

"We've almost reached our target. They've confirmed that there are fights behind the bakery—and I can hear them already. Elba Tourists—you're going through the front door. Announce you're with Kitten Lovemuch before you go in, though. When I first contacted him, Halbryt said they had a few people try to break down the door, so the guild is on edge. Observational Fiends—we're going around the back. Watch out for a powerful magic user—Halbryt said they managed to shake the building."

"Understood." Teara turned to briefly glance at her guild-mates. "Is everyone clear?"

The raid chat filled with a chorus of affirmatives, but Kit barely heard it as they drew closer to Jake's Cakes. Her heart thundered in her ears, and her mouth felt dry.

I always was a nervous wreck before a PVP battle. It's easier to face down a monster or even a raid boss, but there's something about fighting other players that is a little more...frightening.

She took one last look at her mini-map, triple-checking the path they needed to take, then minimized it. "Solus," Kit murmured. "Turn up the alley to our right."

The royal knight nodded and took the turn, leading them up a tight inlet. When it dead-ended into a T-intersection, Kit pointed to the left.

As they trotted closer, the sounds of fighting grew louder. The ground shuddered beneath Kit's feet, and the hungry crackle of fire and the smell of ash tugged on her senses.

"We're dealing with a pyromancer," Kit said.

"Any other orders?" Teara asked as they stopped just short of the intersection.

"Tanks and fighters first," Kit said. "All ranged attackers stay towards the back."

Teara nodded as an explosion of fire shook the city block, making silt and fine grit fall from the ancient buildings.

"This is why we can't have nice things," an Observational

Fiends sage grumbled.

"I want to try calling out to them and see if they'll stop," Kit said.

Noir stared at her. "Are you *crazy*?"

Kit shrugged. "By attacking them, we're just assuming they are looking for fights. We're not giving them a fair chance."

"If they weren't looking for fights, they would be trying to hide," Teara pointed out.

"I know," Kit said. "But if we don't offer them the choice, we're no better than they are."

Noir rolled his eyes, but Teara thoughtfully scratched her collar bone.

"Make it quick, and just lean around the corner," Solus said. "Or they'll one-shot you."

Kit nodded and edged her way past Solus and the death knight. She almost choked on her own spit when she poked her head past the corner. She counted twenty-three players engaged in a fight in the dank and putrid-smelling alley.

She switched out of the raid chat channel, then shouted. "Hey, guys, stop fighting!"

The predicted pyromancer paused, but everyone else around her kept fighting.

Kit held up her hands. "I don't want to fight—I'm trying to save players who are stuck here—" She cut off with a yelp when the pyromancer flung a column of fire at her, and Solus grabbed her by the collar of her jacket and yanked her back.

"Well, there goes that hope," Kit grumbled as she switched back to the raid chat and dusted off her jacket.

Solus shrugged. "You tried," he said. "We attack on your mark?"

Kit glanced at Pax as he gave up flying and sat on a windowsill with a bored look. "Yes. On three," she said, having to fight her instincts to keep from whispering unnecessarily in the raid chat. "One...two...," she paused an extra beat, but her ears didn't pick up on the sizzle of fire magic. *"Three!"*

Observational Fiends—led by Solus—burst out of the intersection and plowed into the fight.

Kit moved in the center of the pack, cushioned by tougher classes on either side of her—though she could hear Noir grumble about brutish heathens directly behind her.

Given that the quarreling players were divided, it was easy for Observational Fiends to surge forward. Though the numbers were roughly even, the other players were divided, and Observational Fiends was able to smash the first six players between them with ease.

As Kit carefully picked her way through the Luck-Luck Dance, her eyes traced the fight. The alley was narrow—which was something of a disadvantage as it kept Observational Fiends from completely overwhelming the other players.

Solus and the death knight rammed through the enemy forces, knocking other players over, and the rest of Observational Fiends preyed upon the fallen players.

"They've got an archer standing on a roof, shooting down into the alley," Kit called as she leaped awkwardly to avoid a pile of rotting refuse.

"I've got him." Teara whistled for her eagle, calling the golden bird down from the skies. The bird raked its claws across the ranger's chest and yanked him off the roof. The Observational Fiends bard dove out of the way to avoid him as the sage moved in, finishing him off with a brutal attack of electric blue light comprised of glowing runes and glyphs.

Kit spun and danced as an Observational Fiends rogue and hunter teamed up to take down a crusader.

The rogue whistled, "I am loving the luck boost! Maybe dancers aren't so bad after all," he said as he moved on to his next target.

The pyromancer tried to get off one more fire bomb, but Solus cut his way to her with a single-minded focus. Before she could finish casting the attack, Solus lashed out with a skill of his own.

"Charge of Valor!" he shouted, making his sword glow with foreign scripts as he landed a blow across her stomach.

The pyromancer dropped like a ragdoll, fading into light as she respawned.

A few players fled before Observational Fiends could finish them off. All others were subdued shortly after.

Kit broke off her dance and trotted up to the back door of Jake's Cakes. "Teara, could you send a few of your guildmembers to scout the area out? I want to make sure none of the deserters stick around and get any ideas."

"Konk, Shooty D'Arrow, Metronome," Teara barked. "You're on."

The rogue, hunter, and the female bard split off from the party. The rogue went down the street, the hunter up it, and the bard slung her lyre across her back, then crawled up the slick side of a white stone building with the ease of a spider, disappearing onto the roof shortly after.

"Elba Tourists, are you clear?" Kit asked.

"Just about," Waffle said. "Do you want us to scout the area?"

"It's not necessary," Long Claw said. "We've killed everything."

Kit hesitated. "Scouting is always a good practice."

"For the paranoid," Long Claw snorted. "Or for those who aren't great fighters. *Nothing* escaped us."

"Yes," Reynard purred in agreement.

"All right, then. Give me a moment to get in, then we'll open the door for you." Kit switched out of the raid chat and knocked on the door. "Halbryt? It's Kit. It's safe now."

The wooden door opened a crack, but the inside of the bakery was too dark for Kit to see much before her eyes could adjust, but it didn't matter. After a split second, the door was thrown wide open.

"Miss NPC dancer!" Egelthas declared. "I *love* your new armor set." He winked at Kit and wriggled his eyebrows before puffing up his chest. "Can I correctly interpret this as your declaration of feelings for me?"

Kit whipped her hand up and pointed to her ring. "Nope— still pledged. Happily. Thank you."

"How sad for me." Egelthas opened his mouth to say more, but Halbryt grabbed him by the shoulder and whipped him back.

"Kit, thanks for coming for us," the secret GM said. "We couldn't make it out by ourselves. How are we escaping Elba?"

Kit gave him her best smile. "We're not actually leaving the city yet."

Halbryt frowned. "What?"

"I didn't have enough time to explain everything to you because you were focused on staying alive, but we're actually here to break up the fighting," Kit said.

Halbryt's frown deepened. "Did the big guilds send in more back up?"

"No," Kit said. "Not at all. Can we come inside? The rest of the group should be waiting at your front door."

Halbryt stared at Kit, his forehead wrinkling in confusion.

"Come on in!" Egelthas swept Halbryt aside and beckoned for everyone to enter. "If you have time, buy a slice of cake! For an NPC, Jake makes a mean carrot cake."

Observational Fiends filled the back of the cakeshop, and when Kit made her way around Halbryt's six additional guild-mates, she opened the front door for the Elba Tourists.

"Welcome!" Jake the NPC baker said cheerfully as Kit's

crew filled the store past full capacity. The NPC didn't even blink when several players were forced to join him behind the counter in order to make enough room for everyone.

"So we're not busting out of this joint?" a gnome belonging to Fellowship of the Bling asked.

"No." Kit shook her head. "We've got to bring the fights to a peaceful close, or this could do irreparable damage to player morale."

Halbryt frowned. "They've been fighting for two days. There's no way you're going to talk them down now."

"Agreed," Long Claw grumbled.

"Tut-tut, my friend." Egelthas winked as he leaned against a countertop. "You haven't even heard her plan, yet."

Kit cocked her head. "How did you know I have a plan?"

Egelthas waved his hand around the room at the raid members. "Because they all came inside and are clearly following your orders—even if some of them have the temperaments of bratty kids denied an internet connection."

"She does have a plan," Teara said.

Halbryt frowned. "One you'd be willing to gamble your guildmates' lives on?"

Teara glanced at Observational Fiends, but her voice was firm. "We're Observational Fiends—one of the top guilds. If there's a chance we can stop this conflict, we have a responsibility to try." A ghost of a smile flickered on her face when her guildmates nodded in support.

"Let's hear it, then," Egelthas said.

"The next step is to confront the players fighting in the central city square," Kit said. "We can't subdue them by brute force with these numbers, but we can snatch the two guild leaders and run. If we can convince the guild leaders to stop the brawl, I think we can succeed."

"How will you convince the leaders?" Halbryt asked.

"If you say with spineless peace talks, I'll kill myself just so I don't have to hear you," Long Claw grunted.

"I'm going to prove to them that we have hope," Kit said.

Long Claw rolled his eyes. "It's no wonder you're an elf—tree-hugging brat."

"I have an ace up my sleeve that will help," Kit was quick to say. She pressed her lips together to keep from adding, *maybe.*

Halbryt scratched his head. "I don't think this is going to work," he said bluntly. "We've been stuck in here since the siege started, and everyone is just too far gone. If it were one of the other servers, certainly—the Japan server never would have rioted like this in the first place, nor would Korea. But now..." he shrugged.

"But," Egelthas said brightly, "we'll still give it a try!"

The rest of the guildmates of Fellowship of the Bling nodded as they picked up their weapons, thanking Teara when the Observational Fiends priest cast several buffs on them.

"We are?" Halbryt blinked. "Why?"

Egelthas clasped Halbryt on the shoulders. "Because this is a game."

Halbryt frowned. "What?"

"Retha is supposed to be fun—and it is, most of the time. But while everyone is scared right now and acting stupid, Retha is *still* a game. We can throw our lives away for miss NPC dancer because we'll just respawn. It's not nearly as dramatic or self-sacrificing as you seem to think it is." The pirate swiveled on his heels and smiled prettily at Kit. "That is, unless it impresses you? Then I'm perfectly willing to be painted a sappy, selfless hero."

Kit grinned a little. "What's my name?"

Egelthas sighed dramatically. "You could just take it as a compliment that I so badly want to impress you, but *nooo*, you need proof that I know your name when it's obviously..." the pirate made a show of looking up at her nameplate. "Kitten Lovesmutt. Oops, I meant Lovemuch. Duh."

"So!" The Fellowship of the Bling gnome smoothed his mustache. "Shall we begin?"

All eyes pivoted to Kit, who was frankly surprised the discussion was over already. She pulled her shoulders back and nodded. "Yes, after everyone takes a moment to check their gear and potions. Support—if you would start casting buffs, we'll be off once you're finished," Kit said. "We're going to travel back east and strike them from the south-east corner of the square, though I want to send a few stealth players in first to scope out the area."

Teara nodded sharply. "Sounds good. Observational Fiends —anyone running low on potions should come see me."

"Fellowship of the Bling..." Egelthas paused and tapped his chin. "You look epic," he finished, making his guildmates roll their eyes.

Kit invited the eight Fellowship of the Bling guildmembers and added them to the Elba Tourists group as the raid chat channel buzzed with conversation. *We might have come for Halbryt's sake, but I'm probably most thankful for Egelthas. He's managed to diffuse the tension with his smarmy act.*

"I'm sorry. I didn't mean to question you in front of every-one," Halbryt said.

Kit flicked the raid screen away and smiled at the GM. "It was understandable. I didn't have time to warn you beforehand. I feel a little bad, too; your guildmaster is much smarter than I assumed."

Halbryt shrugged. "He is when he wants to be. Like now. Knowing what I know, it's been easy to forget the base concept of Retha and view it as more of an elaborate death trap."

Kit nodded and lowered her voice. "Have you heard anything from EC lately?"

He shook his head. "I reported in that you had succeeded in getting the White Needles dwarves after Shashanna talked to you, but I haven't heard anything back. Shashanna might have heard from them, though."

Kit shrugged. "Even if she did, it doesn't change matters much." She stared at the far side of the room and narrowed her eyes in thought. "If I can play my cards right, we'll stop the fighting *and* get the Imperials to join us."

"What?" Halbryt asked.

Kit opened her mouth to reply, but Solus joined them—a pathway magically opening up before the royal knight in the cramped space.

"I think everyone is ready," Solus said.

Kit adjusted her elaborate hat. "Then we better head out. It's going to get hot enough to melt the frosting on the cakes if we stay cramped in here much longer."

Lacking Solus' majesty, Kit had to squirm her way to the front door. "We're going to split up again and move in two parties to keep from raising suspicion," she shouted above the chatter, which died down as she opened the door, making a silver bell jingle merrily. She slipped into the street and started to step aside so everyone could file out of the cramped store. "We will meet up at—"

Pain tore through Kit's body as she took a paladin lance to the chest. Her knees gave out, and she collapsed to her feet, tipping over when she didn't have the strength to stay upright as her health bar tanked.

"Kit!" Riko sounded far away, and her voice was slightly warped as darkness invaded Kit's senses.

Kit tried to speak, but too soon, everything faded.

18

ANGRY BUTTERFLY

KIT SNAPPED UPRIGHT, her breath coming in angry pants. *I was killed. By a paladin. I've been one-shotted by a tank! That has to be a new level of humiliation. I mean, I guess I was overdue to be stabbed, and a paladin is a legendary class, but still! I was killed in one hit by a tank!*

"Kit, where did you go?" Teara asked.

Kit boosted herself to her feet and looked around, taking in the pompous majesty of Elba's cathedral—a beautiful melding of white marble, gold leafing, and an overabundance of skylights. "I respawned in the cathedral."

"You were killed?" Alistair asked.

"Yes. By a paladin." Kit had to work to keep the bitterness out of her voice. *When I have a chance, I'm going to give Long Claw and Reynard what-for. They caught every soldier my coat-covered-arse!* "This is going to change our plans a bit."

"Wait, you're serious?" Hide_N_Seek asked. "You really were killed?"

"She was one-shotted," Riko said. "The paladin hit her hard. He's still out there, by the way."

"Good," Kit said. "Reynard, Long Claw, you two go take

care of him. And then *scout* the area out to make sure he doesn't have a hidden party."

The assassin and werewolf both made sheepish-sounding throat noises but didn't actually say anything.

"M'kay. New plan: you're all coming north to the cathedral. Enter from the back doors. We'll rush the fighters from the front door of the cathedral." Kit dusted herself off and glanced at the two dozen players skulking around the church.

Most of them were splayed out in the pews, dosing or yawning. Some sat in velvet, padded chairs while others were sprawled on the floor playing a card game.

They don't seem aggressive...these guys might be some of the innocents caught up in the fight. A surreptitious glance at the various names, levels, and guilds confirmed her guess—none of them belonged to the same guild.

"Street is clear. The paladin fled—Reynard is still chasing him." Long Claw sounded incredibly subdued, and he cleared his throat nervously.

"Good. Go check the back alleyway," Kit said. "Party Observational Fiends, leave out of the front door now. Elba Tourists, wait for Long Claw to clear the area, then head out as well."

"You said come to the cathedral?" Teara asked.

"Yes. We're going to attack from here," Kit said as she strode to the back of the sanctuary.

"That will make the fight a lot messier in comparison to the stealth mission you were originally planning," Riko said.

"It will, but we'll have the element of surprise that we will work to our advantage." Kit strode towards the doors, making for the glass windows with the plan to peer out of them.

"You don't want to go outside," a fae playing cards called after her.

Kit paused and twisted around, switching out of the raid chat. "Pardon?"

The fae studied the cards she held fanned out in her hand. "That brawl out there is out of control. Even if you haven't picked a side and are just a bystander, you'll be killed."

The fae's dark elf companion must have seen Kit's horrified expression as he was quick to add, "Not that anyone would do it on purpose, but there's so many skills and so much magic being flung around out there, you'll get hit by an AoE skill and end up collateral damage." The dark elf drew a card and made a face before he added it to his hand.

"Then you'll just wake up back in the cathedral," the fae sighed. "We got sick of trying to sneak around the city when we kept getting sent back to the cathedral every hour by random fights in the streets. It's better to just stay here. The cathedral is a safe zone, so we can't use weapons or skills in it."

"Thanks for the warning. I was just going to look outside, though," Kit said.

The fae shrugged and went back to her card game.

Kit peered out the decorative glass windows that were taller than she was and only a foot wide, but the glass was artistically warped and swirled so she could make out little besides brightly colored flashes.

Carefully, Kit cracked one of the cathedral doors open, testing to see if she could be hurt through the space.

A bolt of lightning hit a werewolf berserker just outside the door, but the electricity was snuffed out at the cathedral's threshold.

Feeling emboldened, Kit opened the door the entire way and got her first good look at the massive fight.

It was a nightmare—a mess of boiling anger and rage as players shouted at one another and attacked mindlessly. Spells went off everywhere, and the noise of blade meeting blade was so loud and overpowering, it made her ears ache. Though the sky was gloomy and covered with clouds, the courtyard glowed with light from the sheer number of skills being wielded.

When a player fell down, no one stopped to help. Instead, the fight surged forward around them. Wizards called down storms and fires from the skies; knights and assassins cut pathways through their ranks with their glittering weapons, and everywhere she looked, there was fighting.

Kit had played in PVP battles since the week she first joined Retha, and she had never before seen such an unorganized brawl.

This is hysteria, she realized. *This can't just be about Midnight Watch and Steadfast, or they would be better organized. But there are no patterns, no front lines or structured groups...it's just a massive attack-or-die fight.*

It was worse than she expected on the emotional front. Getting the players to stop would be difficult—they were so ramped up, they weren't following basic civility. *But,* Kit thought clinically, *this will make it much easier to snatch the guildmasters. When they are this blinded by their fury that they can't even hold sides, cutting through their ranks will be far more doable. I just hope we can get through to them.*

Kit's view of the city circle was blocked when Pax landed in front of her with enough force to make the ground shake under her feet. She jumped in surprise as he straightened up, tucked his wings to his back, and gave her the stink eye, twisting his handsome features.

"What?" she asked.

Pax's stink eye intensified. "You left me behind."

"A paladin killed me; it's not like I ported away on purpose," Kit said.

"That does not matter. I had to fly at an unseemly speed to find you here." The winged warrior sniffed, returning his regal features to their usual austerity.

Kit rolled her eyes. "Sorry my death was so inconvenient for you."

"As you should be," Pax sneered.

"Well, Paco, if you don't want to be *bothered* by my life and death, maybe you should return to your egg for this next bit," Kit suggested. "Because I suspect I'm about to die a lot, and the last thing I need is you fluttering around me like a grouchy moth."

Pax's wings snapped open. "A *moth*?" he thundered.

"A very pretty moth—unless you would prefer to be called a butterfly?" Kit asked.

Pax slammed the tip of his metal staff on the ground, making it clang. "I am a winged warrior of the seventh circle! You will not compare me to a *butterfly*."

Kit mulishly tucked her chin. "Then don't get crabby when you stand by—as *useful* as a butterfly—and I die, so you have to actually do something besides look pretty!"

The winged warrior actually rolled his eyes and stalked into the cathedral, muttering in his angelic language.

Though Kit still held the door open, she glanced back over her shoulder to watch the celestial being, which was how she got to see nine players respawn in the cathedral.

They immediately got up and trotted down the aisle, ducking through the door Kit still held open and rejoining the fray. The last one to pass through the door was a paladin.

It took Kit a moment to realize it was the same paladin that had killed her. *I guess Reynard caught up to him.*

The paladin paused at the cathedral threshold and stared at her for a moment.

Kit raised an eyebrow at the tank.

He appeared to be talking to someone on either guild chat or party chat as he moved his lips but no sound came up.

Kit frowned slightly as she watched him step back into the

fight, then glanced at his nameplate. *Hoo-boi. He's from Midnight Watch? I hope that doesn't come back to haunt me.*

"Kit?" Teara asked over the guild chat channel. "We're at the back of the cathedral and are coming in."

Kit slightly shook her head to clear her thoughts as she switched back to raid chat. "Great. Elba Tourists, where are you?"

"About two city blocks down," Waffle said. "We'll enter through the back as well."

"Great. I'm by the front doors, but I'll meet you in the sanctuary." Kit finally released the door and turned to stride back into the sanctuary. As she did so, she switched over to the written chat channel she had been ignoring for some time: RP Forever 2.

She blinked at the rush of text that flooded her vision before she switched to using the game's speech-to-text abilities.

Ice-Paw: Yeah, well Fallen Lordz bombed in the new Lost Orbs raid.

Ai'lan'therristos: No surprise there—they have a tiny guild! They were crazy for thinking they could raid to start with. I'm surprised the Killing Squad hasn't deserted their duties long enough to try it.

Shashanna: They have—they've wiped it as well. Though I think they were blaming it on Long Claw's absence.

Nurthel: More likely the problem is that they have no healers. A bunch of DPS junkies if I ever saw any.

Kitten Lovemuch: Sorry for interrupting, but I have a question for you all.

Shashanna: Kit! Welcome, welcome! How is Elba?

Kitten Lovemuch: Terrible.

Lillith: Sorry to hear that—wanna spill and tell us who is there?

Ai'lan'therristos: Ooohh, and who is winning?

Lillith: More importantly who is losing!

Nùrthel: What did you want to ask us?

Kitten Lovemuch: What can you tell me about the guildmasters of Midnight Watch and Steadfast?

Shashanna: You're seriously still planning to get them to stop?

Nùrthel: A worthy act! Though one that will probably be lost on those swine. Guildies, school her!

Ice-Paw: Midnight Watch is mostly a social guild run by an elf named Diablio. He's a level 108 ranger and is usually fairly good at leading his guild, though he is known to be somewhat emotional and thinks pretty highly of himself.

Ai'lan'therristos: Steadfast is headed up by ViolentAlice, an artificer, level 126. He's a GIRL: guy in real life, even though his character is female. His wife designed his character and is in Steadfast as well. Steadfast is medium-sized, but they meet up regularly and quest a lot as a guild.

Shashanna: Steadfast and Midnight Watch have never really seen eye-to-eye because of Diablio's tendency towards dramatics —something ViolentAlice has very little patience for. The current situation only exasperated the problem. The fight in Torvel started because Diablio was rather demonstratively upset about being stuck on here, and ViolentAlice snapped.

Kit waved to the Observational Fiends Friends party as they filed into the sanctuary, then turned her back to them so she could concentrate on the information the RPers had given her. *So ViolentAlice dislikes being emotional, but Diablio seems to thrive on it...how do I use those characteristics to manipulate the future fight?*

Kit set the thought aside for a moment and returned her attention to the chat channel.

Nùrthel: Is that enough information, Kitten? Or do you need more?

Kitten Lovemuch: No...I think I might have something. Thanks, guys. I really appreciate your help.

Lillith: Anytime!

Ai'lan'therristos: Let us know what happens—I can't wait to break the news in Luminos.

Kit closed out the chat tab before the RP guild's gossip could completely block her vision. She was about to turn around to focus on Observational Fiends, but Solus Miles joined her, resting an arm on her lower back.

"I should have gone through the door first," he said.

Remembering his propensity for hugging, Kit stepped closer to him and patted him on the chest. "No, I should have made Long Claw and Reynard sweep the area. But believe me, I've learned my lesson on that," she snorted.

Solus wordlessly linked his arms around her. He gently squeezed her for a split second before relaxing as Kit sagged against him.

"After this, we should go back to Kamoi," she muttered.

"You want to take Pacifico up on his offer of a honeymoon suite?" Solus asked, smirking and raising an eyebrow.

Kit rapped her knuckles on his black chestplate. "You are awful!" she said.

"Just let me go first in this next fight," Solus said.

"Believe me, I will. That lance *hurt*."

"When White Lady first told me you two were pledged, I didn't believe her. I'm sorry for that, now."

Kit pulled back from Solus and blinked as Teara smiled at her.

"You look very cute together—especially now that your face tattoo is gone," Teara added.

Kit awkwardly cleared her throat. "Thank you?"

"Awww, did we miss a cute couple moment?" Riko cooed as she tromped into the sanctuary, Waffle and Nyx on her heels. "That makes me sad—they're just *adorable* to see together!"

"Still laying it on too thick, Riko," Prowl drawled over the guild chat.

"Quiet, you," Riko growled via guild chat. "Our girl has landed the ultimate Retha meal-ticket. I'm going to support her as much as possible!"

(Riko had left La-Lune and insisted on joining Heroes of Retha before they tried to crack open Elba. Kit had wondered why she was suddenly so persistent; she should have guessed it was because Riko wanted to run a commentary no one else could hear.)

Kit refrained from pointing out Solus Miles really was more "on loan" from his possibly-real-life pledged and forced herself to smile.

Noir pushed his way through the crowd of Observational Fiends players and popped out by Kit and Solus. "So what's the next part of the plan?"

"Isn't it obvious?" Alistair asked as she posed picturesquely with her hand on her hip and her ponytail streaming behind her. "We attack!"

"Yes, and no." Kit double checked to make sure she was on the raid channel and not blasting it out loud for everyone in the cathedral to hear. "As I said in the cake shop, we're going to snatch the two guildmasters. Given that it's complete chaos out there, though, we can't do stealth, and we'll strike as one unit."

Kit clasped her hands behind her back. "We'll move in an oval-shaped formation—heals, magic, support, and all squishy players on the inside, tanks and fighters on the perimeter, using a conveyer-belt-caster system. Any questions?"

"Yes. Teacher?" Noir raised his hand. "What the hell is a conveyer-belt-caster system?"

Kit laughed, then paused when she realized no one else was similarly amused. "Wait...don't any of you know what that is?"

"No," Waffle said. "I've never heard of such a method."

"I have not either. Though I am thoroughly intrigued," Nyx added.

"Okay, well...the conveyer-belt-caster system is designed so magic-based DPS classes have time to cast while the party moves forward. Since all high-level magic can't be casted while moving—it's one of the game's checks to keep magic DPS characters from being over-powered—this method works around that by exploiting slow forward progress and a protective perimeter made of the stronger DPS classes."

Kit tugged on the brim of her hat as she struggled to describe the formation. "So if a wizard is moving at the inside front of the oval, they stop and start casting their spells. Given that the raid will have to fight its way forward, they should have enough time to stand in place as the party moves around them and cast the spell by the time the back end of the oval catches up with them. They then step to the side and walk back to the front of the oval —using short-cast spells on the way up that won't stop them— and then bust out another large spell when they reach the front. It's sort of like conveyer-belt sushi, though you have to be careful with the spells you use. Progress won't stall enough for a class like an echo of arcane to cast anything useful."

"I think I've seen that used in a raid once or twice, when we had enough players to make it worthwhile," Teara said.

Kit nodded. "You need a large party or a small raid to make it work, or it doesn't give the casters enough time to do anything useful. Any other questions?"

Several players shook their heads, and no one spoke out.

Kit glanced over her shoulder, at the closed cathedral doors, and frowned in memory of the fight. "We won't leave anyone behind," she added. "This will *not* be a free-for-all. We cover for each other and help each other." She scanned the raid, relaxing slightly when she saw nods of approval. "Okay, line up. I'll place each player in formation while I go over the rest of the plan. Solus and the Observational Fiends death knight—you two are in front."

———

Kit's heart beat uncomfortably hard—so much so it almost felt like it had relocated to the back of her throat.

Is there anything I'm forgetting to tell them? Any precaution or warning I need to pass along? Nothing came to mind, but she wasn't sure if that was a good thing or not.

"Observational Fiends passed the ready check," Teara said.

"As has Elba Tourists," Waffle chimed in.

Kit licked her dry lips and nodded. "Then move out, now."

Solus and the death knight opened the double doors, then nodded to each other.

This is it, Kit thought as they stepped out of the cathedral, their swords raised. *I hope my crazy plan succeeds, or we'll all be in a world of trouble.*

The tougher characters filed out first, creating a triangular shape backed directly against the cathedral doors so the easily-damaged players—like priests and wizards—could file into the center of the formation and fill it without being exposed to the fight. Once all support characters were out, a strand of tanks and fighters filed out behind them, plugging the hole in the formation.

Kit took a quick survey of the raid—which was comprised of nearly fifty players. Everything looked fine. "Eyes on the guild-masters," she called.

"I see ViolentAlice," Teara called. "Far side of the city square—near the carpet shop. Marking him with my red-tailed hawk." Teara held out her glove-covered arm, and a white and red feathered hawk appeared on it. She tossed her arm into the air, flinging the bird into the sky. It screeched—probably audible only to elves above the clangs of battle—before it leveled off in the sky and circled the area above ViolentAlice.

Kit scanned the battlefield, looking for clusters of Midnight Watch soldiers. *Even if they are disorganized and lost to reason right now, Midnight Watch guildmembers would surely try to fight with their leader when possible.*

Kit's eyes skipped over a clutch of Midnight Watch players before she rewound and stared. "I've got Diablio," she called. "He's just north of ViolentAlice with a cluster of his guildies."

Kit's sharp elf eyes brought the guildmaster into troubling focus. He was speaking to an echo of arcane and the paladin that had previously killed Kit as the battle raged around them.

While she watched, the paladin pointed back to the cathedral and Diablio nodded. Together, the paladin and the echo of arcane left, heading away from the conflict and towards the stores that comprised the square's border.

"We're getting attention," Solus grunted from the front of their formation where he fought off a crusader. "How do we move?"

Kit took a gulp of air and tried to calculate their trajectory path, and what would be the shortest, least dangerous route. *If we walked the perimeter of the building, we would only receive fire on one side, but it would take us longer and they would have more time to prep. But it's not like they know we're coming for the guildmasters anyway.* "Forget it," Kit grumbled. "Straight through!" she shouted. "We'll bulldoze everyone—just stay in formation and remember to work like a team!"

Noir scratched his ear. "Spoken like a leader," he said as Solus and the death knight led the charge.

"I was talking to *you*," Kit said. "You have to heal more than just me in this fight."

"Obviously." Noir rolled his eyes. "Even I'm not *that* cold-hearted. Though I will only act on behalf of the players I actually like, which I am not at all sad to report will severely limit whom I can heal."

"I really have to wonder why everyone is so intent on recruiting you for their guild if you are so snide and unhelpful," Kit grumbled as the exterior of the party reshaped to be more diamond-oval shaped.

"It's because having a snide and unhelpful divine oracle is better than no oracle at all," Noir replied.

Kit snorted but couldn't reply as their raid party pierced the lines of battle.

The Observational Fiends bard, Metronome, played as fast as her fingers would move, and Kit, after glancing at her skills list, reluctantly threw herself into the Luck-Luck Dance. (The hopping motions of the dance let Kit keep pace with the party.)

Halbryt nearly fell off his giant cat when he was hit by a basketball-sized rock. He collapsed on his cat's neck, his health bar barely a sliver, but before Kit could blink, Noir had him back to full health.

"Heaven's Hand!" the divine oracle shouted, and Halbryt's health bar shot up to maximum just before an archer shot off a flaming arrow at him—which a Fellowship of the Bling crusader intercepted.

Alistair's horse screamed in challenge as the cavalry knight brought up the rear, her mount spinning and lashing out at any who tried to follow. Alistair, twirling her spear over her head, kept players from trying to bum rush them with her superior reach.

"Earthen Pit to the right," Riko shouted before releasing the skill, opening up a large hole that swallowed up five players and crushed them between slabs of ground.

Kit hopped forward—still performing the Luck-Luck Dance. *The conveyer-belt-caster system is working—I wasn't sure it would when no one knew about it.*

Teara's golden eagle shrieked as it dropped from the sky like a bullet, its wings half extended to give it better velocity. It pulled up at the last moment, ravaging a barbarian in the face with its extended talons.

Solus and the death knight plowed forward, making the seething crowds part as they ruthlessly pushed forward—Solus' glowing sword and the death knight's black magic scattering players before they even neared them.

Sinistre flew so close to the city, his belly nearly scraped the buildings as he roared. Pax was with him—a spot of gleaming silver against the black backdrop of the dragon's scales.

A team of five players from Steadfast rammed into the left side of their raid formation, making their perimeter buckle.

"DPS—focus fire on the left," Kit shouted.

Hide_N_Seek got off four arrows, taking down a Steadfast player, but shouted in pain when a gladiator laid her flat with a brutish chop to her side. The Observational Fiends bard caught her.

"Heal, please," the bard shouted.

"Glorious Mend!" Noir shouted, enveloping the scout in white light and healing her.

"The fight is getting harder," Teara shouted.

Waffle summoned a griffon, which pounced on the bloodthirsty players that swarmed them, fighting with its lion claws and sharp eagle beak that let it ruthlessly rip armor off players with great finesse.

The mystic from Elba Tourists screamed when a dwarf champion nailed her in the shoulder with a hand axe.

An Observational Fiends crusader put a weak heal spell on her as he shoved the dwarf in the chest with the butt of his spear, making her fall on her back. The Elba Tourist spellbinder finished the dwarf off with a spell of ice and lightning that brought a burst of singed earth and minty freshness into the metallic reek of the courtyard.

Though we're holding ground, we're getting hammered. I'm not sure how much longer we can stand.

"ViolentAlice and Diablio are in long-distance range," the scout said.

"Hold the formation," Kit shouted. "We're almost there!"

Then, the ground beneath her feet started to glow.

Kit's heart fell as she looked down at her feet and saw a glowing white magic circle—one that was a beautiful combination of swirls and sun, moon, and star glyphs—and recognized the marks.

An echo of arcane had her targeted with a loaded spell and was about to cast it. There was no way to stop it, no way to survive it, no way to avoid it.

Kit rolled her shoulders back and shouted. "Keep going! I'll respawn in the cathedral and watch from the doors!"

"Kit, no!" Riko shouted.

Solus briefly turned around to peer at her, his gray eyes narrowed, but there was nothing he could do. Even Beloved's Guard couldn't deflect an attack from an echo.

Kit saw fire flare from an open window in the second story of a building, and a beam of blood-red light shot from the window and across the battlefield.

Kit grit her teeth and stiffened herself for the blow.

The beam of magic passed just over Solus' shoulder, cutting a savage path straight at her.

Pax plummeted from the sky and hit the ground, feet first, with enough force to make the cobblestone beneath him crack and crumble. He raised his sword just in time for the fatal attack to strike the beautiful blade.

Kit expected the attack to blast straight through him, but the winged warrior held his ground. His sword burned white hot as the echo of arcane's attack smashed into it. The air heated, and a powerful wind howled, whipping with enough force to make Kit's face sting when it flicked her hair into her eyes.

The beam of red light hummed, and Pax's eyes glowed white, and his four wings extended, half-curling back towards Kit.

She squinted from the intensity of the light, heat, and wind, and fought to remain standing under the pressure of the magic.

Pax stood strong, a silent snarl fixed on his face as he leaned into his shining blade. He moved against the blast, taking one step forward, then swung his sword straight up with a ground-shaking roar.

His sword went off like an explosion, and the red light rebounded off the blade, speeding back the way it had come. It shot back through the open window and hit its new target with so much power, Kit could see a brief blazing inferno of red flames swallow the room, and the whole city block shook.

If not for her elven grace, Kit would have faceplanted. Instead, she dropped to her knee as she realized—jaw gaping—just how *powerful* her pet was.

And I've been calling him Paco the parrot. It's a good thing pets can't attack their owners.

Silence smothered the battlefield as Pax slid his sword back into his scabbard, tucked his four wings against his back once again, and turned around to face Kit. The fierce angelic warrior was gone, and the familiar sneer narrowed Pax's eyes and twisted his handsome mouth. "I am *not* a useless butterfly," he sniffed.

Kit stared at him—still slack-jawed—and shifted to gaze at the stunned battlefield.

Diablio was even more shocked than she was—he had dropped his weapons and had fallen to his knees. ViolentAlice was taken aback—also thrown down by the strength of the magic—and had his arms folded above the head of his female ranger character as if to protect himself.

Seeing the leaders brought a shot of adrenaline to Kit's bloodstream. "Now! Grab ViolentAlice and Diablio *now*! We flee east—towards the harbor!"

19

QUEST LINE: KIDNAPPERS

SOLUS SPRANG towards ViolentAlice with a contingent force of a crusader, Reynard, Riko, and Long Claw on his heels. The death knight went after Diablio with Observational Fiends forces, while the rest of the raid members surged ahead, cutting a path towards the perimeter.

"Noir, get ready to heal me," Kit shouted as she ran up to a sentinel. She flicked her fans open and smacked him in the face. "Violent Outburst!" she shouted.

The sentinel growled and lunged for her, but Kit dodged with ease as her Cowardly Leader skill activated. The agility buff spread to the rest of the raid, and Solus was a blur when he picked ViolentAlice up and threw the guildmaster over his shoulder like a sack of flour.

The death knight slugged Diablio before similarly picking him up and rejoining the main force as well.

"Go!" Kit shouted pointing to the large archway that tunneled under a building and opened up into a main road.

Sped up by their run buff, the raid successfully fled the battlefield.

"Range fighters, cover us! Wizards, mages, block that tunnel," Kit shouted.

Hunters, rangers, and an archer kept up a steady volley of arrows while Observational Fiends guildmembers steadily filled the tunnel with rocks and boulders.

"Great job, everyone. Now for the split." Kit skidded to a stop next to Teara and Egelthas. "Good luck," she said as the Observational Fiend death knight trotted over to join the Elba Tourists.

"Oh, sure." Egelthas waved her off. "This will be a piece of cake. You've got the hard part."

Teara nodded, then pivoted to face her guildmates. "Observational Fiends, get ready!"

Kit hurried to catch up with the Elba Tourists, who were running for the harbor, as Observational Fiends and Fellowship of the Bling tarried. The guilds had volunteered to stay behind and stop any players who tried to immediately follow them, buying them time.

This has to work. And it will have to work fast!

Kit's heart thudded painfully in her chest as she sprinted with the rest of the Elba Tourists.

"We've got to get on the walkway of the wall that overlooks the harbor," Kit said, her breath coming in pleasant puffs as she ran next to Riko—who was panting heavily.

"You need a *view*?" Long Claw snarled.

"Jump off a cliff, Long Claw," Hide_N_Seek snapped. "Kit died because of *your* screwup. Like you really have room to scoff!"

"Why you—" Long Claw leaped for the scout, but Alistair drove her horse between them.

"Now, now, now, Long Claw. You weren't thinking about harming one of my precious guildmates, were you?"

Long Claw growled but kept running, narrowly missing getting his muzzle bopped by Diablio's flailing.

"You gutless jerk!" the Midnight Watch Guildmaster snarled as he tried to kick the death knight and instead bruised his foot on the knight's solid armor. "My guild is going to rip you to shreds!"

The death knight ignored him and followed Solus when they took a sharp corner.

ViolentAlice was strangely silent, though his face was stormy as his gaze slid from Kit to Alistair to Nyx.

"Uh, Solus, not to be a back-seat kidnapper, but do you know where you're going?" Riko called up to the royal knight as they raced up the road, upsetting a flock of pigeons and a guard NPC.

"Yes," Solus said.

Kit's ears twitched as she twisted at the waist to glance behind them. "Observational Fiends and Fellowship of the Bling started fighting—I can hear Teara's eagle."

"We're almost there!" Alistair declared.

"Then you know where we're going?" Nyx asked.

"Not at all," Alistair beamed, "but I imagine it can't be much farther."

Waffle tried to speak, but he was having a hard time keeping up and wheezed instead.

"Congratulations," Noir grumbled as he ran with Kit. "You've found something I hate worse than being a heal slave: running!"

Kit laughed at his cross expression.

"It's not funny," Noir snapped. "I'm a priest—I should be treated delicately. Why can't someone carry me—like Long Claw?"

"Try it and you'll regret it, healer!" The werewolf's voice was extra guttural as he snapped his teeth at Noir.

"Rude, much?" Noir sniffed.

"Your racoon pulled hair from my tail, and you've let me *die!*" Long Claw snarled.

"I hear seagulls," Kit said. "We should see the city wall soon."

"Why are *you* so breezy?" Noir asked.

Kit winked. "Elf athleticism. It's the best part about this race."

"It's a cheap tactic to rely on your race traits," Reynard said.

Unable to stop herself, it was Kit's turn to needle the assassin. "You're right," she said, sounding sorrowful. "If I would have used my elf hearing before leaving Jake's Cakes, I would have realized the paladin was outside because he *hadn't* been run off as you promised. That would have been an unfair advantage."

Even Waffle managed to heave a laugh at that line.

"Stairs," Solus Miles said, effectively announcing they had arrived at the wall.

A stone archway was built into the white wall, revealing a spiral staircase that would lead to the wall walkway.

Solus Miles charged up the stairs with the death knight right behind him.

Though the Elba Tourists were quiet, the raid chat buzzed with short exchanges as Observational Fiends and Fellowship of the Bling fought.

"I hope you can work fast, Miss NPC dancer," Egelthas drawled over the chat. "Because one of your victims is clearly telling his guildies where you are. They keep trying to make a beeline in your direction."

"It hasn't become a problem yet as they aren't acting all that smart and haven't realized there are other exits they can leave through," Teara added.

"Thanks, guys," Kit said, still breathing easily even though they must have climbed three flights worth of stairs.

"I take it back," Noir grunted. "Stairs are much worse than running."

"Light," Waffle wheezed, pointing up the stairs.

"We've reached the top," Solus said. He cleared the last step, opened the wooden door, and popped out on the wide walkway, which wound snug against the wall's jagged crenel pattern and offered a fine view of the harbor.

Solus and the death knight set the kidnapped guildmasters down as Riko and Waffle extended their staffs. Even more intimidating, Reynard lingered near VioletAlice and Diablio and kept toggling the blades on his gauntlets so they popped in and out.

Diablio glared at them and tossed his head to right his dark hair. VioletAlice leaned against the wall and eyed them.

"What's going on?" VioletAlice asked. He spoke in his real-life male voice—a deep baritone—which sounded a little strange coming from his female character's mouth.

Kit glanced at Pax as he—having opted to fly rather than charge up the stairs—landed next to her and settled his wings into a half-extended position. When he pointedly looked away from her, Kit shrugged and fixed her gaze on the guildmasters, switching out of the raid chat. "We need to talk."

"Do your worst!" Diablio shouted. "As soon as you kill me, I'll be back with my guild, and—elite guilds or not—we'll destroy you!"

"I *highly* doubt that," Nyx said, copying Kit and speaking out of the raid chat. "You are so poorly organized, it would be a challenge for your guild to find their way out of a darkened movie theater."

Diablio snarled and reached for his bow—which he had dropped while attempting to bludgeon the death knight with it.

"Maybe *don't* bait him, Nyx?" Kit asked. "We need to be able to reason with them."

Nyx shrugged and fixed a flat expression on her face that clearly communicated she didn't think reasoning with idiots was possible.

"What is this about?" ViolentAlice asked, the difference between his feminine appearance and deep voice was still rather jarring.

Kit set her shoulders. "I'm Kitten Lovemuch—I'm with the elite guilds—"

"We know who you are," Diablio snorted.

Kit ignored the sarcasm and—feeling marginally more confident in her dashing pirate coat—propped a hand on her hips. "You need to call off the fight."

Diablio laughed. "You've got to be joking."

ViolentAlice narrowed his eyes. "Why?" he asked.

"Because it is going to have server-wide consequences," Kit said. "Everyone was on edge before, but this petty fight of yours is going to open the door for rioting and real hysteria."

"We're not hurting anyone," ViolentAlice argued.

Kit stared at the artificer, and even Diablio turned to gawk at him.

"Are you serious?" Diablio asked.

"We're not," ViolentAlice insisted. "Our fight is between Midnight Watch and Steadfast."

"And the hundreds of innocent players who had the horrible luck of being locked up in Elba with you during this fight?" Kit asked.

ViolentAlice shifted and flipped the braid of his hair over his shoulder. "I thought there would be few players here with the siege going on," he muttered.

"Then you admit your little fight has swept up lots of bystanders. There are players who have been killed so often, they're just sitting the siege out in the cathedral," Kit said. "If you really were trying to keep the fight between you and Midnight Watch, you failed. And why fight anyway?"

"He was the one who lost it," Diablio scoffed.

"Because your dramatizing makes this kind of situation even *worse!*" ViolentAlice boomed.

Kit couldn't keep all the anger out of her voice as she studied the two guildmasters. "You are right, ViolentAlice. Your guildmates are frightened. As their leader it is *your* responsibility to get them through this. However, working them into such a frenzy so they fight in the bloodbath that was the city square is *not* something a good, or even decent, leader would do, and it certainly hasn't helped anyone."

ViolentAlice shook his head. "But he—"

"He couldn't have single-handedly arranged such a panic-filled fight like the two of you have produced," Kit said sharply. "I'm not interested in finding someone to blame for the start of this. What I want is for you two to take responsibility and *stop* it."

"Why does it even matter?" Diablio argued. "We're stuck. Who knows what EC is doing, and if we'll survive this."

Good, finally something I can work with! Kit reflexively opened and shut a fan with her free hand. "But we *can* get out. I was in the party that killed Malignus, and we were logged off. I only came back because EC—"

"I know all about your mythical quest," Diablio interrupted her. "Most of the server has heard the rumor about your *special* win and your equally *special* mission to save all the players."

Solus narrowed his eyes and took a step closer to Kit—as if to shield her from the guildmaster's glare. "But you don't believe it."

"It makes her sound like a unicorn!" Diablio snarled. "No one could do what you're aiming for."

Kit was surprised by the ferocity of Diablio's response and turned to ViolentAlice. "And what do you think?"

The GIRL guildmaster shrugged. "At best, you stand for an impossible quest; at worst, you've been sacrificed and sent by EC to stir up false hope while they try to fix whatever it is that has us stranded."

Riko gasped slightly, her expression stricken. "How can you —they wouldn't do that!"

ViolentAlice shrugged. "Morale-wise, it was the best thing they could have done. How could they better calm players than by showing off someone who successfully got out and returned?"

Riko adjusted her grasp on her staff and bit her lower lip, and the rest of the Elba Tourists shifted and tossed worried glances at Kit.

Ah-hah...so ViolentAlice is not alone in this fear. I wonder if that's why the top guilds have been such a pain.

"No," Kit said with absolute confidence. "I didn't come back because of EC. I came back because my cousin—my old guildmate—asked me to save you all. Because he knows you, and you're his players, and he couldn't stomach the thought of anyone not making it out alive. *He* wouldn't have sent me back if there was no hope." Kit took a step closer to them and slightly pressed her lips together. "I know very clearly *why* I am here, and I know just as surely that killing Lord Valdis is possible."

That is the biggest lie I've ever successfully told. Though theoretically we can kill Valdis, I still don't know how the heck we're going to manage it. But that's not important right now, server morale is. And if we can't fix this, we'll splinter, and then we'll never even get a fighting chance.

"I hope things are going well for you," Teara grunted over the raid chat. "We're past our limit. Some of our party members are down, and players are starting to slip past. I'd estimate you'll have company in about three to five minutes."

Kit swallowed at the close deadline and briefly switched to the raid chat so the guildmasters couldn't hear. "Thanks for the warning. Reynard, Long Claw, I want you two on the door to this staircase. Alistair, would you watch the other end of the walkway?"

"On it!" Alistair said cheerfully as she shifted slightly so she could keep the walkway within sight.

Long Claw and Reynard casually moved towards the door for the enclosed stairway.

Please, please let this work. Kit leaned closer to Solus as she left the raid chat. "Can I borrow your little telescope thing?"

"You mean my spyglass?" Solus asked.

"Yeah, whatever it's called."

Solus nodded and opened up a storage panel.

While she waited for the spyglass, Kit folded her arms across her chest and studied the two guildmasters. "I get it. I could stand here all day and talk, but there's nothing I can say that will make you two believe me, right?"

ViolentAlice and Diablio glanced at each other, then nodded.

"You just don't have any proof," ViolentAlice said, almost apologetically.

The guildmaster had so perfectly walked into her plan, Kit couldn't help the broad smile that settled on her face. "Oh, but I do."

Solus handed her his spyglass. She took it and strode across the walkway to join the guildmasters.

ViolentAlice briefly let his hand touch a sheathed dagger, but Hide_N_Seek's bow creaked as she held a knocked arrow in place.

"Best not try it," Alistair said with a pleasant smile. "We

won't kill you, but we *do* know how to inflict enough pain to take you almost to the edge of death." Her smile was beautiful as she set the butt of her spear on the ground.

"To clarify, you want proof that the game is designed so we can *actually* kill Lord Valdis, right?" Kit asked.

ViolentAlice shrugged and Diablio snorted. "Sure," he said. "But none of the new shadow-y prophecies or requests by NPCs to save them count."

"That's fine," Kit said as she stretched the telescope out to its maximum length. She very briefly switched to the raid chat. "Prowl, you're up."

Kit leaned into the city wall so she looked out at the harbor. ViolentAlice and Diablio turned around as well.

The harbor was a rather grim sight as the blue waters were darkened by the goblin ships, and the bobokins' and goblins' high-pitched squeals and shrieks filled the air rather than the cry of seagulls. Even the air was less fishy smelling and had more of a rancid flavor to it.

Kit handed ViolentAlice the spyglass. "Diablio, you should be able to see it with your bare eyes."

"See *what?*" he sniffed.

Kit pointed downstream, where the harbor faded into the mouth of the Nignay river.

Just as ViolentAlice fixed the spyglass to an eye, the pirates —in their magnificent red and black ship—sailed against the rush of the river and glided to the very edge of the harbor.

Though Kit kept her expression mild, she was so nervous her hands shook badly enough that she had to mask it by drumming her fingers on the wall. *This next part is the dangerous bit. It could go wrong in so many ways—they could attract too many goblins; Bozo and Bingo here might not be impressed with just fire dancers and pirates, or their guildies might find us before we're finished.*

She savagely cut the thought off—the last thing she needed was to make *herself* frightened.

Diablo squinted. "What is that?" he asked, pointing to the ship.

ViolentAlice made a noise of recognition. "Those are the pirates who regularly kidnap players and hold them for ransom until they—or their guildmates—pay up."

Diablo leaned out over the city wall with a confidence—or perhaps idiocy—Kit never could have. "No way. What are they doing *here?*"

"If you manage to be one of a very select number of players and get full reputation with them, they are a summonable method of transport." ViolentAlice eyed Kit. "I've never heard of anyone summoning them in a river."

Diablio pointed to ship. "Are *they* your proof? Because having reputation with them doesn't do anything to convince me this really is possible. It just shows you probably have EC greasing your way—which also explains your winged warrior pet." Diablio narrowed his eyes at Pax, who shed a few feathers that tumbled in the smelly breeze.

"No, they're not my proof. Look and see who the pirates are carrying as passengers," Kit said.

ViolentAlice once again fixed the spyglass to his eyes, but it was Diablio who recognized them first.

"Are those...*fire dancers?*" he asked.

Kit glanced over her shoulder when she heard the shouts of incoming players as they raced through the streets. "Which boat of goblins do you want them to take out?" Kit asked.

Diablio stared blankly at her. "What?"

"To prove to you that the fire dancers—and the pirates—are allied with me against Lord Valdis, I'll hold a little demonstration. Pick any ship—within reason, it needs to be a boat they can off easily without getting aggro from all the other goblins and bobokins—and they'll destroy that specific one."

ViolentAlice shook his head. "That's impossible. You can't boss NPCs around. Even when you're on escort missions, they do their own thing."

Kit stared him down and didn't so much as blink when her ears picked up on feet pounding up the stairs. "Pick a boat, and I'll prove you wrong," she said calmly.

"We've got incoming," Long Claw growled.

"That one." Diablio pointed to a black longboat so far across the harbor that it was almost run aground on the opposite shore.

"Nice choice," Kit said. "It's at the back of the pack, so singling it out won't be a problem for the fire dancers. Yet, because it's on the opposite side of the river, the pirates will have to change course to reach it, proving they're really doing this at my command and not the whim of their coding."

"We're heading in," Reynard said in raid chat. "I'd suggest you have the death knight watch the door once we're in."

Long Claw threw the wooden door to the stairway open and marched in. Reynard followed after him, whipping the door shut behind them.

Kit smiled and magnanimously ignored the strangled shouts that radiated from the stairway, though she did glance at the death knight and nod.

The death knight casually leaned against the door, his dark magic swirling at his fingertips.

ViolentAlice shrugged. "Works for me."

"Excellent! Please, gentlemen, observe." Kit gestured at the harbor scene while she switched to raid chat. "Okay, Prowl. They've picked out a target. They want the longboat on the far side of the river. It's almost on shore; it has...four goblins and seven bobokins."

"That's a really great description that is super helpful and sure to set it apart from all the other boats," Prowl said dryly.

"Um...Miles, can you have Sinistre circle over it or something?" Kit glanced at her pledged.

Solus Miles nodded. "Sinistre!" he shouted as he pointed at the ship.

Kit cleared her throat and exited out of the raid chat. "Solus is going to mark the ship with his dragon so we can be *certain* we're attacking the ship you want."

Diablio nodded. "That's fine. It won't make a difference to the NPCs."

ViolentAlice folded his arms across his chest and squinted at the sky, watching as the black dragon banked and made three lazy circles above the selected boat.

"That's your target, Prowl," Kit said in the raid chat.

"Roger that," Prowl drawled. "I'll tell the fire dancers. And the pirates."

Sinistre flicked his tail then, with a pump of his wings, soared off.

Someone pounded on the door as Prowl—visible to Kit's superior elf eyes—strode across the ship's upper deck, shouting and pointing in the direction of the selected longboat.

As Kit watched, the pirate ship bobbed in the river and slowly changed directions, making for the longboat.

The fire dancers assembled on the forecastle deck—the slightly raised deck located at the very front of the ship—and arranged themselves into orderly lines.

Behind Kit, the death knight grunted as someone rammed the door.

"I'm down," Long Claw growled in the raid chat. "Reynard is still skulking around the shadows, but it's not gonna be long 'til they break through."

Kit briefly turned around, but Solus had already moved to

join the death knight, and Riko and Waffle were casting spells in preparation.

Go, go, go! Kit bit her lip to keep from screaming as the pirate ship maneuvered closer to the opposite bank, drawing closer to the longboat.

Prowl ran back and forth between the front and back decks, shouting instructions to the dancers and pirates. When the ship abruptly swung—moving so the fire dancers had a clear view of the target—he had to cling to the railing to keep from tumbling over the side.

"Nature's Bindings," Riko shouted just as Waffle's griffon screeched. Somewhere behind them, someone yelped.

Kit licked her dry lips as the fire dancers moved in fast, synchronized patterns. They tumbled, flipped, spun, and leaped into the air as the silken cloth of their clothes twined around them.

One of the goblins in the selected longboat noticed the huge pirate ship. He punched one of his cohorts, then pointed to the ship. A bobokin also turned to see what they were jabbering at as it picked earwax from its giant, pig-like ears.

Kit risked a glance over her shoulder and cringed. Solus fended off a blow from a sentinel, then rammed him, shoving him back through the door and straight onto a slender swashbuckler. The death knight struggled against a fighter and a blademaster as Alistair jabbed her spear at a black werewolf.

"*What?*" Diablio gasped.

Kit whirled around in time to watch the selected longboat be completely engulfed in flames. The goblins shrieked and hopped up and down before the dancers' fire spread to them as well.

"That can't be," ViolentAlice nearly dropped the spyglass in his surprise. "NPCs don't fight with players. This must be some kind of—"

"It's not limited to the fire dancers and pirates," Kit said, daring to interrupt as the fight behind them grew louder. *I might have their attention right now, but if we don't settle this soon, we're all going to be killed, and I won't get another chance!* "The White Veil Nunnery, the village of Kamoi, the elves of Lèas, and the White Needles Dwarves have all pledged to join us as well."

Diablio rested his arms on a crenel. "But *how?*"

"Retha is not what it used to be," Kit said. "It's changed. There aren't just new quests and raids; there are new opportunities and new systems. You are right: before Lord Valdis returned, no NPC group would have fought with a player outside of quest-required combat. But that's not the case anymore."

ViolentAlice slightly shook his head as he stared at the longboat—which sank below the surface of the water, its occupants slain.

"It's real," Diablio breathed. "The game really is designed to pit us against Valdis."

"Yes," Kit said, remembering Noir's words. "We have entered a new age of Retha, which is a blessing. Though we are stranded, and EC doesn't know how to free us, we can save ourselves."

"By killing Lord Valdis?" ViolentAlice asked.

Kit nodded.

"It's crazy," Diablio declared. "Even though this performance is...it was..." he gestured wildly, seemingly unable to find the words to express himself. "We can't really defeat Valdis...can we?"

YES! They're weakening!

"We have to try," Kit said. "And if we stand united—not just as players but with NPCs as well—I think we can succeed." *Hopefully.*

Kit shivered as she felt a breeze brush her back when a weapon swung dangerously close to her body. "So will you stop the fight and help us fight off the goblins in the harbor?"

"The goblins?" ViolentAlice blinked. "Why the goblins?"

"I believe if we manage to run them off, the Imperial Empress will pledge herself to our cause—that's been the pattern so far, anyway," Kit explained.

Diablio and ViolentAlice stared at each other.

Kit tried to swallow, but her mouth was too dry and her breathing shallow while she waited for their answer.

She heard the whistle of an incoming sword and started to duck when ViolentAlice reached out and caught the blade with gauntleted hands.

"Steadfast," he shouted, his voice echoing loudly even though it came from the slender and slight body of his character. "Stand down!"

"Midnight Watch," Diablio shouted. "Stop attacking!"

The two guildmasters exchanged looks of disdainful approval, then shouted together, "We have a new target!"

20

BATTLE FOR ELBA

"I STILL CAN'T BELIEVE that crazy, half-cooked idea of yours actually worked," Noir said thoughtfully as he shooed a seagull away. "I guess that's why people are willing to believe you might manage to kill Valdis—because you come up with all these nearly impossible ideas and have the confidence to carry them out."

Kit, her eyes slightly bugged as she tried to keep herself from going cross-eyed, made a few finishing touches to the various parties that now filled her raid. "I actually didn't think it was very likely we would pull this off," she said as she shifted a few more players around.

The divine oracle straightened with a frown. "Seriously?"

"Yep." Kit rolled her shoulders back and glanced at the mass of players before her.

After taking most of the afternoon to stop the fighting city-wide, assemble, and organize, Kit's now massive raid—which included all of Steadfast, Midnight Watch, and those who had been fighting with them, as well as some of the bystanders who had been swept up in the fight—had crept into the harbor and watched the oblivious goblins and bobokins as they waited for the signal to strike. Currently, every party and player was hiding behind the elaborate maze of crates that kept the goblins from seeing them, but based on Kit's calculations, nearly everyone was in place; in just a few minutes, they would be able to attack.

"You are unbelievable," Noir grumbled as he picked up Trash Panda and took some sort of sparkly trinket from him. "You must be a card shark in real life."

"I've only ever played solitaire, so...no." Kit studied the raid again. She stood with Noir at the southernmost edge of the harbor—giving her the most complete view of the fight while still affording her a chance to dance for the Elba Tourists.

I have Steadfast and Midnight Watch separated with the Observational Fiends party and the Elba Clean Up party between them, so that should keep them from having any "accidents," but should I push another party in there as well? With the raid tag, they won't be able to harm each other, but someone might drop out just to get a cheapshot in.

She tapped her finger on her fan, then shook her head. *No, I have to believe they are invested enough that they won't resort to something like that.*

"Hey Teara, any word from Saint George or the Brave Heart Company?" Kit asked over the raid chat.

She had tried to PM the guildmaster earlier to let him know what was going on, but he had refused her message. Teara explained the situation herself, but Saint George had never replied to her after she confirmed all the player fights had been snuffed out.

"Nothing," Teara said, her voice flat.

"Saint George is an idiot," Noir announced—thankfully not on the chat, but to the Elba Tourists who were standing nearby. "And we don't need idiots here. We already have more than our quota."

"I find his apparent cowardice troubling," Reynard growled as he toggled the blades in his gauntlets. "And it makes me wonder why his guild is rated so highly if he skips out on actual battles."

Long Claw grunted, then nodded. "Chief says he's an emotional pansy—all bark and no bite."

Kit cast one glance over the intricate raid-party list, then gazed at the actual players themselves. As she had asked, all range players were located at the back of the party, ready to target boats and goblins that were in the middle of the river. Meanwhile, the close-combat players would take out the first line of boats—which helpfully floated at the end of the long piers that stretched out of the harbor.

"Elba Freedom Fighters, reporting in," the leader of the last party—a mixed bag of guilds and players—said over the raid chat. "We're in place."

She nodded in satisfaction. "Party leaders, perform the final ready check," she said before switching out of raid chat. She clenched her hand in a fist and pumped it in glee before turning to her party. "Okay, I think we're almost ready!"

"Why, Lady Kit, you sound positively delighted." Alistair smiled as she patted her horse's neck.

"Yes, because this is going to be a piece of cake," Kit said.

"Will it really be that easy?" Riko asked doubtfully. "I mean, we have superior numbers, but this fight will have boat and river combat, and if we don't go fast enough, we'll be fighting in the dark." She nodded at the horizon. The skyline was still a mixture of blue and gold as the sun sank west, disappearing behind the city of Elba.

"Yes," Kit said eagerly. "But it's *only* combat! We don't have any emotional messes to sort out; no one needs to convince the goblins to surrender; we don't have to be concerned about bystanders. This will be a simple, uncomplicated battle."

Nyx—glowing with her spirit-weaver magic—adjusted her silver glasses. "You really are doing this—trying to lead the efforts against Valdis, I mean—out of a deep-seeded belief in and concern for the game and its players, aren't you?"

Kit blinked. "What do you mean?"

Nyx shrugged. "When you, Riko, and Prowl all returned, I assumed you must enjoy being in a position of leadership, or else one of them—being more familiar with the current players —would have led. But I think I understand, now, that you lead because there is no other option."

"Right on the dot, Nyx," Riko said with a benevolent smile. "You have no idea how much tough-love it took Prowl to get Kit to settle into being our party leader. The only reason she's leading us is because it's undeniable that her brilliance in combat makes her the best choice. Wouldn't you agree, Reynard, Long Claw?" Riko purposely swiveled to face the reticent players, putting them in the spotlight as the rest of the party members also looked to them.

Long Claw ignored the question and swung his saber around in a couple of practice moves.

That's an obvious no, Kit thought.

Reynard, however, thoughtfully narrowed his eyes. "You're not what we expected," he said finally. "And I think...you do view fights differently than current players."

Kit stared out at the swarm of players. "Not really," she said. "It's just the scale. In a fight this big, you need to make sure you use every player to the right advantage, or you'll get over-confident in your numbers and lose."

Waffle chuckled and shook his head. "There is a great deal more to it than that. You don't give yourself enough credit."

Kit slouched a bit, the topic making her embarrassed. "Maybe, but I doubt it. Everyone, this is your last chance to check over your gear and stats. I'm gonna go check on Pax." She trotted away from the piers, aiming for her pet—who glittered in the setting sun like a diamond.

"Pax, hey. Hi." She stopped awkwardly next to him and shifted, scuffing her booted foot on the rough wood of the docks.

Pax paid her no mind and instead gazed peacefully at the sunset.

"I wanted to say thanks for saving me during the battle in Elba's town square." Kit cleared her throat. *I never thought I would be apologizing—legit apologizing—to my pet.* She pivoted so she could join the winged warrior in watching the sunset. "I wouldn't have survived that—no player would have survived that—without you."

Kit peeked to see if her words got any sort of reaction out of Pax, but he still stared at the colorful horizon.

"You're stronger than I imagined," she confessed. "I didn't think anything in Retha could stop an echo of arcane's magic. Really, there *isn't* anything that can stop one...except for you. So, I'm sorry for underestimating you. And thank you."

Pax finally stirred. "Do not mistake my act of benevolence as a sign I am growing to like you, elf," he said, his voice pitched in his familiar scoff—which made Kit relax and grin.

"I know, I know, you hate my guts," she said.

"No, it is merely that you are not yet worthy of my respect," he sniffed.

"But Solus Miles is?" Kit guessed. "Because you don't sneer at his back very often."

"Solus Miles has proven himself to be a capable and competent hero," Pax said.

"It really is just a matter of levels then," Kit sighed. "Maybe Miles is right. Maybe I should try to get to level cap by the time we face Valdis." She sucked her neck into her shoulders and glanced around, half-afraid the royal knight would pop out and drag her off to level right then and there.

"It's embarrassing to have a master that is not yet a legendary hero," Pax muttered. "Particularly given what will be available to you."

Kit straightened up and blinked owlishly at her pet, but before she could question him, he unfurled his wings.

"I am going to rise above the muck and filth your little fight is sure to bring, and fly. Do not count on my help in this fight," he warned her.

"Wouldn't dream of it," Kit said.

Pax eyed her—probably trying to guess if she really was respecting his boundaries or was judging him as childish. He snapped his lower wings, nodded, then flew off, gliding above like a dazzling beacon.

Kit watched him for a moment, then rubbed her eyes and sighed. *When this is all over, if we ever get off.* She didn't let herself finish the thought and instead slapped her cheeks.

"Kit," Solus said, interrupting her thoughts. "Elba Tourists are ready." He stood at the edge of the party, closest to her, though everyone else was lined up and facing the harbor.

Kit smiled at her pledged and glided up to him. "Thanks, Solus, for your help."

Solus shrugged. "Of course." He slightly narrowed his eyes as he studied her. "Are you...okay?"

"Yep!" Kit chirped. "The hardest part is behind us—though I'm not particularly looking forward to talking to the bratty Empress after this and trying to convince her to join our alliance, even if we save her skin by driving off the siege."

"All you'll need to do is tell her the elves and dwarves have agreed to help. Her surprisingly strong superiority complex won't let her stay out of the alliance then." Solus said.

"Oohhh, how appropriately devious! Good plan, Miles." Kit said as they passed Hide_N_Seek, Waffle, Lumina Myst, and Glowrious.

"I have had more experience handling her than I would like," Solus said dryly. "Be careful in the battle," he said. "I'll be with the front line, so I won't be able to guard you."

Kit stopped when she reached the center of their party. "Noir is sticking with me; I'll be fine."

Solus nodded and took a step to join Long Claw and Reynard at the front, but Kit impulsively reached out and grasped his hand. She regretted it almost instantly but made herself continue as it would have been *really* awkward to back away now. "You be careful, too," she said.

Solus raised an eyebrow. "It would be embarrassing if a pack of goblins managed to kill me when traveling with you—a magnet for disaster—has not yet been my end."

"Just wait," Kit promised. "Give it time, and it will be unavoidable."

Solus slightly shook his head, squeezed her hand, and glided away.

Kit turned around, intending to retreat a few steps, but she almost rammed into Riko, who was holding a hand to her mouth that did nothing to disguise her ridiculously big grin. "Aww, Kit," she cooed. "You're all grown up and having flirtatious interactions with your pledged!" Her voice echoed oddly as she spoke in the guild chat for Heroes of Retha.

Kit rolled her eyes. "You're being ridiculous."

"Am I?" Riko asked as she tapped her lower lip. "Or has puberty finally come for Solus?"

"Is there a reason you're being so bold in your declarations about him today?" Kit asked. "Usually you would at least try to hide your cackles."

"Relax, Kit," Riko laughed. "Both of you are just so much fun to tease. Now, lead on—general ma'am!"

Kit slightly shook her head as she flipped back to raid chat. "All party leaders report."

"Elba Freedom Fighters, ready."

"Observational Fiends, ready."

"Midnight Watch, ready,"

"Elba Harbor Naturalists, ready,"

"Steadfast, ready."

"Elba Clean Up, ready."

"And Elba Tourists, ready," Kit said. "I'll make one final announcement, and then we'll begin."

"Don't take too long," Diablio said. "The sun is setting."

"I know," Kit said.

"You're a night elf. Fighting in the dark should give you the advantage," ViolentAlice pointed out.

"It might help *me,* but it won't help the likes of *you,*" Diablio sneered.

"Gentlemen," Egelthas said with a smooth chuckle. "Please, save it for the goblins."

"Yeah," Teara added. "Because if we don't manage to drive them off, I'm fairly certain all who participated in your little brawl are going to lose major reputation points with the Imperials."

Kit fiddled with her controls as the raid leader, adjusting the volume of her voice so all players—not just the ones listening for her—would hear her over the squeals of the goblins and the chatter of their friends.

"Attention, players—" she cut herself off when her voice boomed so loudly over the chat, she felt it in her bones. *That was a little loud.*

Immediately everyone swiveled so they faced south, towards her. "Um," she said, trying not to wilt under the gazes.

Suddenly, a little trumpet sounded, and a new popup screen appeared.

Congratulations! You have learned the life skill: Center of Attention!
Your obvious and frequent bids to be the center of attention have given you the ability to reach great distances—though who knows who will notice you?
Effect: Greatly increases skill range at the cost of higher aggro

Kit stared, open mouthed, at the new skill. *What? But I— what?* She pressed her lips together as she tried to flick the screen away. *How insulting can EC get? I mean, as far as skills go, Center of Attention sounded like it at least had the potential to be useful. But...was it really necessary to say I make obvious and frequent bids for attention?*

"Sorry," Kit muttered into the raid chat. "One second." She almost growled in frustration when the glowing popup screen refused to move.

Eventually, the screen faded, and Kit shook her head to try and clear her thoughts. "I apologize; as I was about to say, we will soon be going into battle against the goblins. As a reminder, all range fighters, please destroy ships and fire on goblins that are *past* the front lines. The fire dancers and pirate ship will block the goblins from sailing south, but we need to watch their movements, as some of the longboats might try to flee upriver.

"Listen to your party leaders," she continued. "If you have an observation or concern, please bring it to them. If it is serious, they will point the issue out to me." She paused and curled her hands into fists as she tried to fight her nerves while the *entire* raid party stared her down.

"Thank you for fighting with us," she finally said. "Thank you for showing how we players really can be heroes. I am glad you are here, and I am honored to have you fight with me. Stay safe, and work with your party."

Kit waited until she saw the majority of the players nodded, then finished. "If you have a spell that has a load time, begin casting it now. Party leaders—on my mark."

Kit adjusted her volume in the raid chat so her voice was no longer at a booming strength, then took a great breath and rolled her shoulders back. *This is going to be fine,* Kit told the butterflies—or maybe birds—of nervousness that fluttered in her stomach. *Right now, I don't have to worry about how we're going to defeat Valdis; I don't have to worry about server morale; we just have to wipe out these goblins. It's just a raid—and raids are fun!* Feeling a little better, she smiled slightly as she glanced at Riko and Waffle, trying to gauge how far they were in their spells.

"You know," Noir scratched his cheek. "This might be one of the biggest raids formed on this server in the past year."

Kit glanced at the divine oracle. "That can't be true."

He shrugged. "Believe what you want, Kit. It just proves how differently you think from everyone out there...and how much we need you."

Kit frowned slightly at Noir, then turned around. "Are you ready, Riko? Waffle?"

"Ready when you are, cutie pie," Riko called as Waffle nodded.

Okay. Here we go. "Heroes of Retha," Kit called over the raid chat. She swallowed, her mouth dry from some worry, but mostly anticipation. "*Attack!*"

"Siren's Storm!"

"Song of the Ages!"

"Path of Flames!"

The distinct names of the rest of the shouted spells were lost in the roar as the close-combat fighters burst through the maze of crates and surged down the wooden piers, shouting battle cries and leaping into enemy longboats and ships.

The goblins shrieked in surprise as the raid descended upon them, grappling for the weapons they had carelessly laid down.

Kit waited until the front line was firmly established before she shouted, "Range fighters—move up! Stop at the piers. Support players—stay between the front lines and the range fighters," she said as she jogged down a pier.

Being a support character was a careful balance of trying to choose what players were most important to buff/heal. Kit was attempting to make that choice easier by letting the support crew straddle the area between the front line and the range fighters, making it easier to keep tabs on both of them.

Kit was about to launch herself into Serenade of Magic when she recalled her new life skill. "Oh, what the heck—why not give it a try?" she muttered. When she toggled the skill, her character moved to stretch one hand dramatically out in front of her and reached for the sky with the other. She stood on one leg —with the other slightly folded behind her—making her a rather theatrical sight. "Center of Attention!"

"Wow, they did not do anything to make that skill less of an embarrassment to use than its name already implies," Kit grumbled as the buff settled onto her. She immediately threw herself into Serenade of Magic, although the slow and purposeful dance was a rather odd foil to the furious pace of the battle.

The goblins and bobokins were finally starting to fight back. They armed themselves with pikes, clubs, and brutish swords so when the players reached them it wasn't quite so one-sided.

Most dangerous were the goblins armed with crossbows— which hit hard. There was at least one per ship, and in addition to inflicting the most harm, they also were the greatest threat, as the goblin wielding the crossbow could pick off players before they even got to the ship.

Kit eyed the harbor as the slow twists of Serenade of Magic moved at a pace that made it easier to observe the entire raid.

The Observational Fiends party—which also contained the eight players from Fellowship of the Bling—was doing the best. The close-combat fighters stayed together in pairs or trios as they hopped from ship to ship, while the bard stayed on the pier playing buffs, and their ranged players quickly and efficiently picked off one ship at a time.

Kit wasn't surprised by their teamwork or excellent skills in combat—she knew Observational Fiends had to be considered an elite guild for a good reason—but she did find it ironic that Teara, who took such great pains to remind everyone she was a first officer, had only to shout an order once, and her guildmates would respond immediately.

I don't think she's aware of how much they look to her, Kit thought as Teara marked a ship with her golden eagle, and the ranged fighters of Observational Fiends and Fellowship of the Bling took it down.

Unfortunately, the rest of the parties weren't fairing quite as well.

As she watched, a crusader and a swordsman from Steadfast jumped into a goblin canoe together, making it rock violently. They lost their balance and fell headfirst into the water, narrowly avoiding getting speared like a fish by some of the goblins.

They weren't the only ones to make sloppy mistakes.

Two days of non-stop fighting had taken its toll on the players. Everywhere she looked, players slipped up.

Some of the ranged combat fighters started to inch down the piers to get better shots at their targets, and they were taken out by goblins with crossbows.

Close-combat fighters would use powerful attacks that

capsized the boats they attacked—leaving *themselves* stranded in the water along with the goblins they meant to slay.

Unfortunately, even the magic players were messing up. Another druid released Siren's Storm *directly* over a ship already boarded by other players. The lightning strikes would have taken the players out if the raid tag didn't cut off friendly fire. Instead, it just destroyed the boat, leaving the close-combat fighters to scramble into a neighboring longship and get a bobokin axe in the shoulder for their troubles.

But even with the mistakes and mess-ups, Kit could see the real heart of the game shine through.

ViolentAlice ran up and down the piers, infusing his power in every weapon and blade he could get his hands on, regardless of whether or not they were in his party.

Diablio threw himself on a little mage from the Elba Harbor Naturalists party, yanking her down just in time to avoid getting speared through by a goblin who had swum up to the docks.

Alistair laughed as she fought back-to-back with Reynard. Together they protected a lower-level thief who had followed the front line out to the ships.

This is what Retha is supposed to be about—heroes working together to accomplish more than they could as a single person.

Pain cut through her thoughts when a crossbow bolt thumped her in the shoulder. Kit staggered for a few steps before—through sheer will—she forced herself to continue with Serenade of Magic.

"I've got you," Noir said. "Heaven's Hand!"

Kit breathed easier when the heal spread through her chest, driving out the pain as the bolt—sticking out of her shoulder like a flag—faded away. She gazed out at the water as she hurriedly flipped on the raid chat. "Party Leaders—tell your ranged fighters to take out all goblins or bobokins armed with crossbows."

"Okay!"

"Will do."

"Understood."

"Right-o."

"Yeah, yeah."

Kit nodded in satisfaction, then screamed when another crossbow bolt hit her—this one imbedding in her other shoulder.

"What the fudge-covered nuts?!" Kit growled through clenched teeth. The pain was a shock to her system that nearly made her choke on her own spit when she swallowed.

"Sanctified Mend," Noir shouted.

Kit still made herself keep dancing despite the pain, though as her wound faded, she suspiciously eyed the waterfront. *There!* A wet goblin that had a pool of river water at its feet stood at the very edge of a pier, loading another bolt into its crossbow.

"Hide_N_Seek—take out that goblin at the end of our pier!" Kit said hurriedly as the goblin raised its crossbow again.

"On it!" the scout said pleasantly.

Kit gritted her teeth and braced for more pain as her Serenade of Magic dance routine called for a pause—which would make her into a sitting duck.

But Hide_N_Seek was faster, firing an arrow at the goblin's head. It was dead before it could topple backwards and hit the water.

"Thank you!" Kit shouted as she kicked her leg up so high behind her, she almost touched her own head.

"There's a longboat making a break for it, traveling south," Teara shouted over the raid chat.

"Hear that, Prowl? Time to bring out the cavalry!" Kit shouted.

"We're on our way," Prowl said.

Kit slightly adjusted the direction she danced in so she could spot the ship Teara had pointed out.

It was one of the biggest ships in the siege—a galley, a ship mostly propelled by the goblins and bobokins rowing together. It probably held at least a hundred of them, if not more.

A wizard tried to throw a firebolt at the galley, but, spurred on by fear, the goblins and bobokins rowed their way out of range.

As the galley had to sail out of the slight cove the harbor formed to go south, the goblins and bobokins didn't notice the pirate ship until their single sail lit on fire.

Kit cracked a slight smile as a goblin squinted up at the smoldering sail, then elbowed its neighbor and pointed at the flames.

Together they peered at the sail, then shrieked when one of the shields fastened to the side of the galley burst into flames as well.

Goblins yelled and bobokins panicked as the fire spread down the ship's mast.

Then the pirate ship finally rounded the corner of the cove, making straight for the galley. It dwarfed the enemy ship, and in the fading light, the black skulls on the white sails seemed especially menacing.

"Fire!" the pirate captain shouted.

Three of the pirate-mages stood on the forecastle deck and made identical gestures. Runes glowed around them as, using magic, they punched small holes in the galley's deck. Water bubbled from the holes like a fountain.

Just beyond the pirates, the fire dancers completed a synchronized set of backflips on the forecastle deck and set the bow of the galley on fire.

Bobokins folded the tips of their giant ears over their eyes, and goblins screamed...until they realized the pirate ship was coming straight towards them and wasn't slowing.

The goblins and bobokins threw themselves overboard as the pirate ship plowed into the galley. The galley cracked like an egg, crumpling under the sheer size of the pirate vessel. Wood crunched, and pieces of the goblin boat were flung into the air like shrapnel, but the pirate ship sailed on, cutting a direct path towards the rest of the goblin fleet.

"Stand and face us, you survey seadogs!" the captain shouted.

"You cowardly Powerpoint!" a pirate added in with a bellow.

Kit snorted in laughter, but her mirth dropped immediately when a rock cracked her in the head with enough force to fling her to the pier deck.

"Ouch." She sat up—Noir already working a heal on her— and scowled at a bobokin that held a slingshot and a pouch of rocks.

The bobokin popped another rock in its slingshot and began to swing it, giggling in a piggish snort as it peered at her.

When she got to her feet, Kit switched to Battlefield March just so she could move faster. She managed to dodge the first rock. "Clean up on aisle nine? OUCH. And watch out for the rocks!"

One of Waffle's summons—a narwhal—burst out of the water, grabbed the bobokin by the grubby flap of its disgusting skirt/kilt, and dragged it off the pier and into the river. The bobokin shrieked and kicked but disappeared over the side all the same.

Kit rubbed her smarting skull and shook her head as she danced. "Support classes aren't nearly as satisfying as damage-dealer classes: if you're beaned, someone else gets to avenge you."

"Are you really complaining about your class in the middle of a massive battle?" Noir asked.

"No." While she twirled, Kit tried to get a good look at the piers and the actual harbor docks. *But if I'm getting hit, does that mean the goblins are attacking our ranged combat players?*

She gazed up and down the harbor, but besides a handful of goblins and bobokins that made it to the docks—and were usually fried, shot by an arrow, or kicked in the face when they finally got out of the water—the battle was wonderfully contained to the river, with the mages, wizards, and magic classes incinerating the ships farther out, while the close-combat fighters stormed longships and sunk canoes.

Then why am I such a target? I'm not even near the edge of the pier—Noir is far closer!

"You know, Lady Kit," Alistair called pleasantly as she slammed the glowing tip of her spear into a goblin canoe, creating a hole that began squirting water. "Those few levels we got while traveling to Elba have made quite the difference on your skills. Your range is fantastic—I'm still getting your buff all the way out here!"

Kit paused her dance just long enough to plot her distance to Alistair. Given that Kit was only about halfway down the pier, and Alistair was in a canoe two layers deep into the flotilla, her buff shouldn't have reached the cavalry knight. "That is—oh! My new skill."

Kit glanced up at the buff icon—the darkened shape of a person standing in a spotlight. "It gives me added range for a bit more aggro. I wouldn't have thought it would make such a huge difference."

She grinned in appreciation when a shower of white musical notes twirled around her while Rainbow-Colored likes surrounded her. Big, beveled, golden letters formed over her head, reading: "LEVEL UP."

That's level 64—Solus will be so pleased. Though it's not surprising given the sheer quantity of enemies our raid is taking down.

Noir snorted, jarring Kit from her thoughts. "You are experiencing more than 'a bit' of extra aggro."

As if stirred by his words, a cackling goblin that managed to climb his way up a support beam leaped onto the pier. It swung its weapon of choice—a nail-studded club—above its head, then scuttled for Kit.

"I think you are right, Noir," Nyx said.

Kit scurried to the opposite side of the pier. "Okay, we may need to have a party discussion, Elba Tourists."

"About what?" Waffle asked.

"The tradeoff of having a long-range dancer versus a soon-to-be-dead raid leader." Kit yelped as the goblin took a swing at her. It missed—barely—but passed so close, it brushed the tail of her coat.

"You are not about to die," Noir scoffed. "I can heal faster than the goblin can hurt you."

"What about my mental pain?" Kit yipped as the goblin tried to grab her.

"Not important," Noir said.

"Could someone take care of this goblin, please?" Kit asked. When Battlefield March called for a leap forward, Kit swung around so when she jumped, she kicked the goblin in the gut.

"Nature's Bindings!"

"Thanks, Riko," Kit called.

Riko winked as Kit hopped past her. "No problem. Hey Solus—did you hear that? I saved your pledged for you while you were busy."

"Do you have no shame, woman?" Prowl demanded.

"I'm not the one who was elected to stay on the pirate ship because they brought so little to the fight," Riko said dryly.

"You old hag!" Prowl snarled.

"Mouthy brat!"

Kit ignored their familiar banter and took another survey of the battle.

Though the Elba Freedom Fighters party was made up mostly of players who had been bystanders in the fight and were volunteers who had joined on a whim—the card-playing fae and dark elf from the cathedral among their ranks—they seemed to be doing the best.

The ranged classes were careful to concentrate on a single ship and essentially dismantle it before moving on to the next target. Meanwhile, a few of the close-combat classes from the party had slain some goblins and bobokins and swiped their canoe for themselves. They were able to maneuver around the battle much more quickly and easily than the other parties— though part of that might have been that they had a pirate class directing them.

Elba Clean Up, unfortunately, had spread themselves too thin. The close-combat classes were spread out in the river, and none of them were near the piers or docks. This left the support and ranged classes open to more damage.

To make it worse, the dock and pier where Elba Clean Up had made their stand jutted out farther into the river, making them a prime target for the bobokins and goblins who managed to flee their burning/capsized/wrecked ships. As Kit watched, two goblins shimmied up a ladder and launched themselves at a cleric.

A scholar and singer teamed up and took the goblins down before they got the cleric to half health, but it was still a near thing. *Their close combat classes are too far out in the river to recall in a timely manner, I'll have to send reinforcements.*

"Steadfast," Kit called over the raid chat. "Send a few close-combaters to help Elba Clean Up, please. They're struggling."

"That would be a real help, thanks!" the party leader of Elba Clean Up was quick to add.

ViolentAlice grunted. "Got it. Strongarm brothers—Kellivar, Greg, and Nick—you heard the raid leader. Move it!"

When Kit spotted three Steadfast guildmembers—a battlemage, a fencer, and a swashbuckler—trot up the docks, making their way towards Elba Clean Up, she nodded in satisfaction.

She performed a couple twirls and twists of Battlefield March, then turned her attention to Steadfast and the Elba Harbor Naturalists.

Steadfast did well in moving together and not overreaching themselves, but Kit could see the battle was tripping up the already-exhausted players.

Elba Harbor Naturalists moved mostly in tandem with Steadfast—not surprising, as most of the party was comprised of Steadfast's allies from the fight. Unfortunately, it meant Violent-Alice was bearing the brunt of the leadership and had to watch out for two parties.

Do I say something? It's too late to switch out party leaders, and though it might cause ViolentAlice a little more stress, I don't think it will hurt the raid.

The rhythm of Battlefield March pushed Kit into doing a brief handstand. When she popped upright, she had to adjust her coat and hat.

"Noir, Kit, look out!" Nyx shouted.

Kit swung around just in time to see a goblin shipmaster—one of a tougher breed of goblins, each of which were placed in charge of a ship—barreling in her direction. It ran like a silverback gorilla, swinging its overly long arms out in front of it and planting its hands on the ground while boosting itself forward with its legs.

Unlike the rest of the goblins, it had a headpiece consisting of a yellowed skull and red and green plant leaves, and a leather chestplate that was spattered with blood.

As a goblin shipmaster was an elite monster, he would be harder to kill...and harder to survive.

"Flip and fire," Kit cursed.

Before she could move or respond, the goblin shipmaster crashed into her, sending her flying. She hit the pier, skidding a foot and getting a few slivers in her hands and thighs in the process.

"Elba Tourists," Kit started, but she broke into a cough when the goblin shipmaster pounced on her, grabbing her by the throat and shaking her.

It threw her again, but this time Kit was ready, and her elven grace and athleticism kicked in.

She planted a hand on the pier as she flew backwards and managed to twist herself so she flung her legs behind her and landed in a runner's starting position. The attacks had taken approximately fifteen percent of her health—nothing too bad. Yet.

The goblin shipmaster snatched up a spear from one of its fallen brethren. It hefted the rudimentary spear over its shoulder, then once again charged her.

Ah. I can't survive that *quite so easily.*

Kit coughed as she flicked her fans open. "Need help," she finally spat out.

She didn't hear a response, and no one seemed to react as the shipmaster bore down on her. Fear made it hard to breathe as the shipmaster gnashed its teeth. *What do I do? What can I do?* "Elba Tourists!" Kit shouted.

Still, no one responded.

Kit braced herself for a painful impact as the shipmaster threw the spear at her.

Noir snarled like an angry cat. "Selfless Sacrifice!" he shouted.

White light encased Kit, and a golden cross glowed under her feet.

When the spear hit her, the light flared, and Noir shouted and doubled over in pain as the skill diverted the damage to him.

"Noir!" Kit shouted, her heart going frantic as his health bar took a nosedive.

The goblin shipmaster backed up a step, bared his teeth, then raised his spear again.

Kit glanced wildly to the sky—hoping Pax might see fit to intervene—but she didn't see the winged warrior anywhere.

The shipmaster leaned farther back as Kit took a swipe at him with her fans. "Violent Outburst!"

Though she opened a cut on the goblin's bicep, it barely dented his health bar.

Somewhere behind her, Noir—his health hanging on by a sliver—groaned. "Heaven's Hand," he said, making his health surge—though he wouldn't be back to full health in time for the next attack.

Kit's throat clogged with spit, and she clenched her eyes shut as the shipmaster lashed out.

"Holy Shield," a man shouted.

Kit cautiously opened one eye before straightening in surprise.

A crusader from Steadfast stood in front of her, braced against his shield.

The shipmaster tried hammering on the shield with his spear, but all he managed to do was shatter the rudimentary spearhead.

In the darkness of the setting sun, a shadow detached from a toppled crate. Kit heard the familiar *shing* of a blade being drawn, and in a moment, the goblin shipmaster stumbled forward—nearly impaling itself on the crusader's shield. A silver dagger stuck out of its back until a night stalker flicked off her cloaking skill and ruthlessly retrieved her weapon, yanking it out.

The goblin shipmaster roared and turned around. "Cry of Challenge!" the crusader shouted, dragging the goblin's focus back to him.

Kit hurriedly threw herself into Battlefield March—again—then snapped over the chat channel. "Riko, Waffle—someone back there, we need support *now*."

A samurai from Elba Freedom Fighters jumped from an empty canoe and landed on the pier with a roll. He sprinted down the pier, arriving just in time to attack the goblin shipmaster with the night stalker.

"Silence of the Night," the night stalker hissed as she flicked a dagger at the goblin's throat.

"Technique of the Sword," the samurai shouted before attacking the goblin with his katana.

"Nature's Bindings!" Riko yelled behind Kit. Within moments, green vines lashed around the goblin, binding his arms to his sides.

He toppled over with a tremendous thud and was gifted with an arrow in the shoulder from Hide_N_Seek before the night stalker, samurai, and crusader struck him.

The goblin shrieked in pain before the samurai shaved off the last bit of its health with a ruthless stab. The goblin faded, and before Kit could blink a popup filled her vision.

Notification: Rare drops pending in the que.

She flicked the notification away as she stopped dancing long enough to wipe the sweat from her forehead.

"Kit, are you okay?" Solus asked, his voice soft but audible via the raid chat.

"Yeah, back-up arrived in time from other parties." Kit turned around so she could peer back at the Elba Tourist party members who were *supposed* to be fighting with her.

"Sorry," Riko winced. "I panicked and tried to use Earthen Pit, but I forgot it doesn't work over water."

"No worries!" Kit returned her attention to the motley crew of her saviors and nodded. "But seriously, thanks for jumping in."

The samurai nodded before he went tearing back out to his abandoned canoe.

"Our pleasure." The crusader winked at Kit and saluted her with two fingers, then trotted back down the pier, rejoining the crowd on the docks.

The night stalker left without saying a word.

"You okay, Noir?" Kit asked when she felt the warmth of a healing spell invade her. She glanced up at her growing health points as she turned to offer Noir a hand up.

"That was awful," Noir complained. "And also really bad. I only have that one shielding skill, and it has a cooldown of forever."

"We'll be okay," Kit said as she glanced out at the river. "We've almost won."

Though the battle was not proceeding as smoothly as she would have preferred, they *were* winning.

Almost all of the smaller boats—like the canoes—had been sunk or taken over by players. Some medium-sized ships remained, but with their superior numbers, it wouldn't be long before the battle was over.

That's really what matters: winning. It's not like we're getting points for style. And what the server needs is a morale booster—which is exactly what this is. Or will be. I hope.

She sighed and rubbed the back of her neck. Elf or not, the muscles of her legs were twinging with exhaustion, and it seemed like work to breathe. *I regret not resting more in Kamoi like everyone else. I don't know how Alistair and Solus are managing this.*

"Kit, we have a problem," Teara said, her voice tight. "The two biggest ships that are left—galleys, both of them—are heading upriver. They're nearly even with the northmost pier right now, but it won't be long before they'll be out of range."

Kit forced herself to concentrate as she swung around to peer north.

As Teara had warned, two galleys—their wooden sides lined with crude shields—sailed upriver.

Teara had moved Observational Fiends upriver, so they shared the northmost pier with Midnight Watch. A few of Observational Fiends players had conscripted three canoes and were paddling after the galleys, but with the ships being as large as they were, it would take more time than they had to effectively stop the enemy boats.

Do we risk it and let them get away, hoping that it will still count as a "win"? Kit gazed out at the murky waters of the Nignay river, observing the heavy way players moved. They still attacked and still fought, but they had lost at least twenty percent of their fighting force, and those who remained were fighting exhaustion.

Nope. Not an option; we need a clean win. But how can we catch them?

"Prowl, can the pirate ship catch them?" Kit asked. She bit her lip as she shifted her gaze to the strangely menacing but beautiful pirate ship, which had pulled closer to the harbor than it should have in an effort to ram into two goblin boats.

There was a moment of silence as Prowl relayed her question to the pirates.

"Captain says we can try," he said finally, "but we'll have to finish these longships first to get to clear water."

There has to be another way. THINK!

"We magic classes can run north," Waffle offered. "We might catch them."

"Or you'll get stuck in the crowd," Kit said grimly. She narrowed her eyes as she studied the smaller ships some of the players had seized from goblin control. *Could we follow with our own little flotilla?* Her eyes landed on Solus Miles—who single handedly took out a goblin shipmaster with a skill that made his sword shine.

His cloak flared around him, vaguely reminding Kit of the way Sinistre looked when he furled his black wings. *Wait —Sinistre!*

"Miles!" Kit called to the royal knight over the raid chat. "Does Sinistre have any aerial attacks?"

Solus yelled a skill name, and a giant sword shot out of the deck of the boat, killing four goblins in one go. "Yes. Though I need to be riding him to use them, and he has fairly long cooldowns."

"Then can you call him and stop the two galleys sailing upriver?" Kit asked.

With her elf eyes, Kit could see Solus turn north and speculatively squint after the ships. "Yes."

"Then do it—please!" Kit said.

Solus nodded then jumped off the goblin longship he was cleaning up, landing in an empty canoe. Even Kit was impressed when the canoe didn't tilt wildly with his sudden weight.

He grabbed a paddle and directed the canoe to an empty patch on the river. "Sinistre!"

The dragon roared as it flew overhead, turning sharply before it tucked its wings and dove.

Barely more than a black shadow in the sky—which was now purple with the hint of night—Sinistre plummeted to the ground. When he finally unfolded his wings and pulled up, he was so close to the water, his tail lashed across the Nignay's surface.

Sinistre snatched Solus up with his front left paw and started climbing in altitude again, seemingly unconcerned as Solus climbed up his forepaw.

Kit had to work to keep her expression calm as she looked from Solus—half-hanging off his dragon pet—to the galleys, which were now nearly at the mouth of the river.

Is he going to make it? She held her breath as Solus finally slipped into his spot at the base of Sinistre's neck, and the dragon banked steeply.

The first ship made it out of the cove of the harbor and into the river—nearly disappearing from sight.

Solus directed his dragon so it pulled up just behind the ship then reared back, using its tail to counterbalance as he momentarily hovered vertically.

Sinistre cried—an eerie combination of an elk's call and a hawk's cry—and tilted his head back as blinding blue and white flames started to build at the back of his mouth.

The goblins and bobokins on the galleys shrieked and tried to shoot their crossbows and throw rocks at the pet, but everything except for one arrow fell short, and the arrow harmlessly pinged off the sturdy plate of his scales on his front paw.

Kit didn't realize how dark it had gotten until Sinistre dove forward and spat out a river of blue and white flames.

The goblins and bobokins on the ship farthest into the river tried to row double-time, but they were too late. Sinistre's attack hit them and set the majority of the ship on fire.

The flames were so blinding and dazzling that Kit could barely watch in the dimness of dusk.

The ship groaned as it crackled and fell apart. The hull cracked as it ran aground into a large boulder formation, and the mast cracked like a toothpick and toppled.

Sinistre blinked his massive copper eyes and turned his gaze to the second galley.

The bobokins were rowing blindly in their fear, and the goblin shipmaster that was leading the boat shrieked and slammed its spear on the deck as it tried—unsuccessfully—to restore order.

Instead, the bobokins kept rowing and rammed the back end of the first galley, which collapsed on impact and sent ash and sparks flying.

Within moments, the first galley and all of the bobokins and goblins that had tried to flee on it were gone.

Sinistre tilted his head and—to all appearances—listened to a command Solus gave him. The dragon cried again, then lurched forward, launching himself back into a moving flight pattern. He skirted the remaining goblin galley, his belly nearly scraping on the mast.

Just when it appeared he would harmlessly pass them, Sinistre slammed his tail across the width of the ship, nearly splitting the galley into two. The ship groaned as water frothed around it, eagerly seeping into the split and dragging the broken galley into the depths of the river.

When Sinistre had regained some of his altitude, he turned in a sharp circle and shot off two flaming balls of blue and white flames.

The flames spattered on impact, incinerating the ship in two strikes.

With that, the galleys were taken care of.

Kit cheered as she was again surrounded by a downpour of white musical notes and rainbow-colored lights with the level up notification that clocked her in at level 65.

"Oh, my gosh! That was amazing!" Riko stared, slack-jawed, as Sinistre roared and shot a stream of orange flames off over his head in his exuberance.

"He just decimated two *ships*." Waffle shook his head, then glanced at Kit. "It makes me wonder what Pax will be capable of when you two have a good rapport."

Kit shook her head as the prow of the second galley disappeared under the river's flow. "I doubt he'll be able to do that given that he's a different species and class. That was..." she paused.

"Incredible?" Nyx asked.

"Well, yes, but I was just thinking more that it was disappointing of me. I should have thought to use him sooner—especially since one of my old Milk Crown guildies always liked to complain that the eagles could solve almost everything in Lord of the Rings if used correctly, and that dragons were overpowered," Kit said.

Several members of the Elba Tourists swiveled, looking from the remnants of Sinistre's flames to Kit.

Kit blinked under their scrutiny. "What?" She asked, then was promptly distracted when she looked past them and caught sight of the few remaining goblin ships.

Looks like there're less than a dozen—that's just a fraction of them compared to what we first faced. And given how pumped everyone is about Sinistre, I think it's time to make the last sweep.

Kit toggled her raid leader panel and again adjusted the volume so she boomed above all other noises. "Great work, everyone. There are less than twelve ships left. But we need to consolidate our forces and finish this. Parties, rush the remaining boats, now!"

Her words were nearly drowned out by the roar of the encouraged players.

Within moments, wizards, mages, scholars, and sages had one of the remaining longships swallowed by water. A few moments later, meteors streaked from the sky and smashed another into kindling.

Meanwhile, the close-combat classes swarmed a longship, paddling up to it in stolen canoes. They made quick work of the goblins and bobokins there before moving onto the next.

A particularly cheeky saboteur—whom Kit dearly hoped Prowl would not copy in the future—set up several packs of fireworks on one of the decimated ships, lit them, then hurried off after the rest of his party.

The fireworks went off in an explosion of color and crackles, making the small boat snap in half and burn.

Everywhere Kit looked, players surged, taking the last ship just as the moon rose in the sky and cast a silver reflection on the river.

When the last goblin was slayed, torches flared to life in the harbor, and all the city gates swung open.

The siege was over. Elba was saved...as were the players who had been held captive in its walls.

We did it, Kit thought, barely able to process the idea in her exhaustion. *We stopped the fight. Maybe things can get better on the server. Maybe players will stop picking on each other!*

"You did it!" Riko shrieked as she threw her arms around Kit's waist in a fierce hug. All around them, other players laughed, hugged, and some even cried.

"You did what everyone said was impossible!" Riko laughed. "That will teach those shifty jerks back in Luminos to doubt *you*!"

Kit smiled and hugged Riko back. "It wasn't just me," she reminded her.

Riko rolled her eyes. "Can't you revel in the praise for even just one minute? Come on, let's go find Prowl!"

Smiling widely despite her fatigue, Kit let Riko tug her down the shoreline in the direction of the pirate ship.

They'd won, against all odds.

Now the question was: could she pull off an even bigger miracle and kill Valdis? In the deepest parts of her heart, Kit wasn't so sure she could.

EPILOGUE

IT WASN'T until dawn that things finally calmed down around Elba. Some players had loudly celebrated, while others collapsed, occupying every available inn room in the city.

Kit hadn't really had a chance to do either.

Instead, she spent the night talking. First, she had to sift through the raid drops and give the game the orders to distribute everything equally—which required a few snatched conversations with the party leaders.

Next, she had to inform Shashanna and her guild of the fight—which took longer than estimated since the RPers wanted detailed descriptions and were unsatisfied with the summary of "we rushed them and won with the help of the pirates and Solus' dragon." (Instead, they had to know how Sinistre *looked* as he shot off fire, and whether the sails of the ships rippled in the breeze.)

Once she finished with them, Gared and White Lady started PMing her.

Gared was perhaps the only guildmaster who was happy Kit had decided to forge on alone. Based on White Lady's evasive language, the other guildmasters were impressed Kit managed to pull off a win but would have a few words of reproach for her when she returned to Luminos.

I'll have to make sure I bring Solus with me for that meeting, or Half-Fang just might kill me, Kit thought as she sat on an uncomfortable stone bench in the harbor.

Though the sun hadn't yet risen, the eastern horizon was a promising gold color. Kit stared at the sky for a moment longer, then returned her attention to the raid panel.

Do you want to disband your raid?

Kit selected "yes." Her shoulders slumped with relief when the spread of health bars and party information that had been clogging up her sight cleared.

It's over. We won. Back to the slog, I guess. We'll have to rest for a few days in Luminos before we hit up our next NPC group, though. I think most of us are pretty close to passing out.

Kit glanced around the quiet harbor.

NPCs were returning to the area with the defeat of the goblin flotilla. NPC fishermen kicked seagulls away as they headed out in little rowboats for early morning fishing. Guards returned to their posts, and dockworkers reorganized the stacks of crates players had knocked over in the fight.

Besides the NPCs, the only players in the area were Teara's Observational Fiends and most of Kit's original NPC-ally-seeking party.

Speaking of Teara, the falconer strode across the dock—a little owl riding on her shoulder. When she reached Kit, she offered her a tired but happy smile. "Do you mind if I join you?"

Kit shook her head. "Nope."

Teara lowered herself to the bench with a slight groan. "I'm so glad it's over. I can't quite believe it."

"Me, either," Kit admitted. "It's so surreal." She shifted on her bench and sighed. "This morning, my party and I will have to call on the Empress and see if she's willing to ally herself with us since we got rid of the goblins."

"I'm surprised she didn't call for you last night once the city opened up," Teara said.

Kit shrugged. "The Imperial Empress is a little kid. She was probably asleep."

Teara laughed. "Probably."

"I don't mind." Kit stifled a yawn. "The other guildmasters have said they want me to return to Luminos immediately for a meeting. The Empress gave me the chance to say no—which is nice, as my party really needs the downtime."

Kit nodded meaningfully at Alistair. The charming cavalry knight was sleeping on a stone bench, snoring slightly. (Pax happened to be standing near her, shedding feathers on her as he leaned against a marble statue of a fish and studied his pretty sword.) Alistair had celebrated loudly and happily for an hour or so before nearly passing out on her feet.

I'm not falling quite yet because I'm an elf, but besides Alistair, Solus was the only other party member who didn't get a chance to really rest in Kamoi. I hope he's not passed out somewhere in a gutter. Kit glanced up at her mini-map and was happy to see the knight was apparently still on the docks.

Teara laughed. "I hope you told the other guildmasters to buzz off? They've no right to lecture you when you've already done so much." She paused to pet the puffy little owl on her shoulder. It shut its eyes and snuggled into her fingers. "Thank you for everything."

Kit leaned back and groaned with the stretch. "Thanks for taking a risk with us."

Teara shook her head. "No, I don't think you understand just how much you've done for me—for Observational Fiends."

Kit took her flashy pirate hat off and smoothed its feathers. "What do you mean?"

Teara stared at her hands. "We were struggling. Not just because of the siege in Elba and the fight—though that did make things a whole lot worse. I guess you could say we were so preoccupied with keeping the peace and trying to figure out what was going on that we forgot how much we love to play together."

Teara raised her gaze to the river—which was a pretty and playful blue, a stark difference from the murkiness it sported the previous night. "We only had fear and anxiety to bind us to each other. Nothing to laugh about or even team up for. Last night was the first time I've seen some of my guildmates smile in a long time."

Kit thoughtfully studied the first officer. "You're a good leader, you know. And your guildmates respect you a lot."

Teara shrugged. "We do okay."

"No," Kit said firmly. "The Observational Fiends party was the best one out there last night. You guys were more aware of what was going on and worked together the best."

"I can't take credit," Teara said. "It's just that my guild has some amazing players. I'm only a first officer."

Kit tilted her head as she considered the falconer's words. *I think she reminds me a bit of myself...only it's worse because she has an entire guild that believes in her.* "You might be a first officer, Teara, but you're the one your guild is looking to. Observational Fiends followed you into a wild goose chase when I asked you to join us in kidnapping ViolentAlice and Diablio. That took a lot of trust on their end, and it wasn't because they thought I could pull it off—it was because they trusted your judgement."

"The Observational Fiends' Guildmistress—"

"Isn't here," Kit ruthlessly interrupted her. "*You* were the one who led your guildmates out of this safely. I don't know if you're worried that some may think you're trying to replace your guildmistress or whatever, but, Teara, this is an emergency situation. Your guild is more important than preserving past roles. They have clearly chosen to follow you. But as long as you second-guess yourself, Observational Fiends is going to be unstable because it means *you* don't believe in *them*."

Teara inhaled deeply and hunched her shoulders a little, making her fluffy owl retreat down her arm to stand on her falconer's glove. "I hadn't really thought about it that way," she admitted.

"Sometimes I think half the reason why I have been able to do all these weird things so far is *because* I've been gone." Kit said. "I'm free of most expectations, and as I don't have a rapport with anyone, there aren't any social constructs holding me back —besides my awful character, anyway."

Kit twined a lock of her pinky-gold hair around her pointer finger.

"You could change your hair color," Teara pointed out.

"I considered it when I got my tattoo removed, but I decided not to," Kit said.

"Why not?"

"Well, I'm kinda starting to like it. But also...I think it helps." Kit tapped one of her fans on her knee. "Because if I—with my pink-haired elf dancer—can beat Malignus, I think it makes other players believe they might be capable of greater things, too."

Teara nodded, and together they stared at the river, watching the sky brighten as the sun peeked over the horizon.

"Woe, woe befall us," Noir said as he ambled through a maze of crates, making his way toward them while carrying Trash Panda. (It was a display of strength, as the portly raccoon's fat rolls spilled over his arms.)

"What's wrong?" Kit called.

"The most derpy and egotistical man alive has arrived. Hark, here comes *The Saint*." Noir rolled his eyes and sneered. He eyed Kit and Teara before shamelessly plopping down between them, squeezing into a space that was too small for him, forcing them to scoot apart to give him enough room.

Kit twisted slightly on the bench to watch Saint George—trailed by approximately twenty-five of his guildmates—stride through the harbor as if he owned it. When he reached their bench, he nodded to Teara and Noir but ignored Kit.

Saint George thrust his chin in the direction of the river. "I see you won."

Noir set Trash Panda down. "I imagine that was obvious based on the players drinking and partying—and, you know, not *killing* each other," he said.

Saint George shrugged and rested the tip of his massive sword in the ground. He squinted at the rising sun as he leaned into his weapon. "It didn't make much of a difference. The siege would have let up soon."

"We stopped the infighting," Teara said. "That's a *huge* difference. That's what the real problem was—not being locked inside."

Kit leaned back and watched the guildmasters, happy to observe. *Saint George made it perfectly clear how he feels about me, and at this point, I don't think it will change easily—though it would be nice to have another big guild helping out.*

"I guess," Saint George said. "I would have helped you with defeating the goblins."

Teara pressed her lips together. "I tried to message you. Multiple times."

Saint George shrugged again. "I didn't see them. As a guild-master, I was getting so many messages from guildmates and other guildmasters I guess I missed it in all the activity of Elba."

"Then please, illuminate me," Noir said as Trash Panda

wandered away. "What did you and your oh-so-busy guild do in a city that was absolutely empty as everyone else was here fighting with us?"

Kit elbowed the divine oracle. "Noir."

Saint George frowned slightly. "Why are *you* here, Noir?"

"I travel with Kit as her personal healer," Noir said, his upper lip curling in a slight sneer.

"You heal *her*?" Saint George pointed a finger at Kit. "You've got to be kidding me. She's a low-level dancer crippled by her character design."

Noir made a show of flicking a lock of his purple hair from his eyes. "She irritates me less than everyone else here—you included."

Kit watched Trash Panda linger around Saint George's boots with great interest. *He can't steal actual armor pieces, can he? I would think those boots would be bound to Saint George.*

Saint George used his giant broadsword to shoo Trash Panda away. "You still have an invite to Brave Heart Company —even though you are an ass."

"How many times do I have to say 'not interested' before you understand me?" Noir asked. "Or do I need to get a sign or something to hang around my neck?"

"Don't come crying to me when she gets you killed with her illogical, outdated plans," Saint George.

"Yeah, like her crazy plan to stop the fighting in Elba and end the siege—oh, wait..." Noir made a show of scratching his chin as if in deep thought.

Saint George shifted his gaze to Teara. "I spoke with White Lady and Phizzy. They are giving us two days off before we need to be back in Luminos. The Company and I are going to our guildzone. You can join us."

Teara shook her head. "Thanks for the invite, but I need to meet up with the rest of my guild."

"Fine. Report in to me, though, before Phizzy and the rest call you in," Saint George said.

Kit whipped her attention away from Trash Panda—who was wiping his paws on Saint George's cape. *What?! What a bossy ape—he's not her guildmaster!*

"Why?" Teara asked.

"I'll help you figure out what to say," Saint George said.

"There is nothing to 'figure out.'" Teara sat up straight and frowned. "I'm assuming they'll want a report of the fight, which I'll give them."

"Jeez, sorry, I didn't mean to offend you. I thought I would offer since you're just a first officer and haven't had to talk to other guildmasters much before."

"I'll manage," Teara said flatly.

"Whatever. Just leave my guild out of your report—I'll be making my own."

Teara nodded mutely.

A breeze ruffled Saint George's hair as he glanced at the river again. "Good work in Elba," he said. "And see you in Luminos." He strode off, his guild following him.

A male dwarf—whom Kit assumed was the first officer based on how he strode behind Saint George—glanced down at Trash Panda, then raised his gaze to Kit, Teara, and Noir and smiled brightly at them. "You guys were awesome," he said as he thumped past.

The Trio watched the Brave Heart Company wind their way around crates and barrels as they once again made for the city.

"At least that first officer seems nice," Kit said.

"Edmund Ironside?" Teara asked. "Yeah, he's the only reason Brave Heart Company stays together."

"How much would you like to bet that the-oh-so-helpful-saint tried to *order* you to report to him first so he can try to brainwash you into making it sound like he did way more than he really did," Noir asked. He picked up Trash Panda, who offered him a pouch of gold coins. "Thank you." Noir patted his pet on the head as he took the coins.

"He did help when we first arrived," Teara said. "It was only when it became clear we wouldn't be able to quell the fight that he left abruptly."

"That's still pretty horrible. You were supposed to work together," Kit said.

Teara picked up the puffball that was her owl and stuck him back on her shoulder. "That's just how it goes. Even the top guilds are pretty competitive."

"Well, yeah, but if you work together, you can do bigger raids," Kit pointed out.

"I guess that's just one of the reasons why raids aren't done very often anymore," Teara said. "The group sizes have shrunk, but it's just harder to work together."

"Personally, I embrace our combative attitude," Noir said. "I mean, why wish a person 'good day' when you can tell them to 'get lost?' I'd get rid of almost all players if I could, but since I can't, I may as well be as rude and abrasive as possible." He sighed. "I'm off my game—usually I can make *The Saint* turn red with fury. And yet he *still* asks me to join his guild—as if he could afford me," Noir scoffed and tickled Trash Panda under his chin.

"If it bothers you so much, why not join a different guild?" Teara asked.

Noir sniffed. "No one is good enough for me. Besides, why should I conform to the preconceived notion of other players that, as an experienced divine oracle, I must belong to a large, active guild?"

"I thought that's what you would want?" Kit said. "Because those are the kinds of guilds that 'can afford you.'"

"Yes, and then I'll be their pet heal slave, and that will make me snap, which will make some delicate dewdrop cry, and then the fussy and/or overly-moral guildmaster will get involved—blech. Too many politics," Noir said. "But you two might be on to something..."

Kit raised a pink eyebrow at Noir, then directed her attention back to Teara. Offering the first officer a slight smile, she said, "Why do you think Saint George offered to let you go back to the Brave Heart Company guildzone?"

Teara absentmindedly petted her little owl. "It's because Observational Fiends doesn't have a guildzone."

Kit blinked. "You don't?"

"Nope." Teara sighed. "Though I regret that now. We never bothered to get one because our guildmistress has an amazing place in Yuuyo's Bamboo Forest. We always just met up there."

"And you can't right now because...?" Kit trailed off.

"Because the guildmistress is off." Teara's shoulders slumped again. "She worked from home and also had a rental home unit from EC. She was our most active player and was on almost all the time, so it was easier to just set the permissions to let anyone enter whenever she was on than to constantly adjust it for all of us. Since she's off, we're locked out."

Kit paused, waiting for Noir to add something to the conversation, but the jaded healer was still absorbed in his own wonderings as he narrowed his eyes and stared at Trash Panda.

"I'm sorry to hear that," Kit said.

Teara shrugged. "It's fine. Most of us have houses, and not even a majority of us are on right now, so we can all fit in an inn. It's just not quite as nice."

"I bet," Kit said.

"I've got it!" Noir shouted.

Kit eyed him suspiciously as he put on a wide, beaming grin. "What?"

"You offend everyone," he said.

"I do not!"

"You do, too—your very existence is an insult. Invite me to your guild," Noir said.

"What? No! It's not even a real guild," Kit argued. "I didn't even want it—EC just gave it to me for show."

"Exactly. That will be irritation squared! Not only am I in a horribly named, tiny guild, but it is *your* horrible, miniscule guild! *The Saint* just might choke on his own arrogance when I strut past." Noir eagerly rubbed his hands together as he warmed to the idea. "Yes, that's it. I'll join right now—quick, send me an invite. If I'm fast enough, I can zip ahead and 'happen' to stroll past *The Saint* as he and his thugs reach the teleport gate."

"I'm not giving you an invite," Kit said.

"Why not?"

"Friends don't let friends join bad guilds," Kit said.

"You let Prowl and Riko join."

"These are Prowl's and Riko's secondary characters."

"So? Fine, then give me an invite because I'm acting as your personal healer, and you owe me big time," Noir said.

Kit narrowed her eyes at Noir, who mulishly jutted his chin out.

"I'd just do it, Kit," Teara said as she made a point of sliding *away* from Trash Panda when he patted her with his sneaky paws. "He's not going to let this go."

"Correct," Noir said. "Or I'll just go behind your back and get an invite from Prowl."

"Fine," Kit groaned. "But just for now!" She reluctantly opened her guild panel and sent him the invite.

"Thanks!" Noir accepted the invite, hopped to his feet, and set Trash Panda down. "If you'll excuse me, I have *The Saint* to annoy. Oh, Georgie!" He called out in a sing song voice as he trotted away, an unholy glee adding a spring to his step. He nearly ran into Solus Miles as the royal knight slowly approached them.

"I'm not sure if I'm surrounded by strange people because *I'm* strange, or if that's just how we gamers are," Kit grumbled.

Teara laughed. "Hello, Sir Solus Miles," she said when the royal knight joined them.

Solus nodded. "Teara." He shifted his gaze to Kit. "Noir belongs to Heroes of Retha," he said.

How could he notice that so quickly? He saw Noir for, like, five seconds! "Yeah, he wants to use the guild as a way to annoy Saint George."

"You'll let Noir join, but you won't let me join," Solus said.

Kit waggled her hat at him. "We're not having this conversation again! I already told you, you're too cool for my guild." Kit expected a snort of laughter from Teara, but when she didn't hear any, she glanced at the falconer.

"Sorry, I'm getting a PM from a guild member. I need to answer it—but I won't be long." Teara smiled briefly, then rose from the bench and hurried off, her little owl hopping off her shoulder and fluttering behind her.

Kit glanced up at Solus, who cocked his head as he studied her with eyes narrowed under a furrowed brow. She patted the bench next to her. "Want to sit?"

Solus unbuckled his sword and leaned it on the side of the bench so he could sit next to Kit. Once seated, he stared out at the river and released a slight sigh.

"I'm impressed you're still awake. Alistair passed out about two hours ago." Kit nodded to the still snoozing cavalry knight. (Pax was resolutely ignoring Alistair, even though she sneezed in her sleep when one of his fallen feathers landed on her nose.)

"I wanted to make certain the fighting didn't erupt again,"

Solus said. "But it seems my concern was unnecessary. They're doing much better."

"Mmhmm," Kit hummed in agreement. "You were right. They needed hope." She twisted her arms together and stretched them out in front of her. "And I'm hoping this will ease some of the tension on the server. The grim atmosphere was starting to be...troubling."

Solus nodded.

"You should be proud—I reached level 65 during the raid. Oh, and thanks for taking out those galleys with Sinistre," Kit added. "I don't know that we would have won without you."

Solus shrugged. "You organized everyone—that's really what made it possible."

Kit rolled her eyes. "You don't have to deflect a compliment —I'm just acknowledging your role."

Solus shifted uncomfortably. "I don't want public recognition," he said.

"I bet. It would only make people ogle you more than they do already," Kit said. "But I wasn't giving you public recognition. I was saying that—as me, Kit—I can't tell you how grateful I am to have you with me."

Solus' steely gray eyes shifted from the Nignay River to Kit.

Kit cleared her throat, slightly embarrassed by his scrutiny. "And...uh...I," she stammered, feeling unexpectedly tongue-tied.

Solus draped an arm over Kit's shoulders and tugged her towards him.

She reluctantly complied.

"We did well," Solus stated.

"'We' as in the raid?" Kit asked.

"Don't you and I count as a 'we'?" Solus asked.

Kit slightly hunched her shoulders, making her neck disappear. *That sounds like a loaded question I could easily—and embarrassingly—misinterpret.*

Solus chuckled—a dazzling, throaty noise. "You overthink things."

"It's not my fault you're the mysterious brooding type." Kit gave in and let herself scoot closer so she could lean into his shoulder. "And if this is going to become a thing, you should ditch the metal pauldrons for something *softer*. Might I suggest fur?"

Solus quirked a black eyebrow. "Fur shoulder pads?"

"The dwarves have them," Kit said.

"My armor is not dwarf-made," Solus pointed out. "It's supposed to be remnant pieces, forged when the Imperial Empire was at its strongest."

"I wasn't really trying to suggest something that would be fashionably acceptable or match your outfit," Kit said, leaning farther into him.

"Fine. Then for your comfort, I'll purchase fur-covered pauldrons," Solus said, a slight drawl to his voice.

Kit smiled as her eyes drifted shut. *I think, this is what I like most about Solus. When I'm with him, I don't have to worry or be in control. I know he'll shield me.*

Her smile grew when Solus rested his chin on top of her head.

"Kitten Lovemuch!"

In less than a second, Kit was at the far end of the bench, blinking rapidly as her heart thumped in her chest. *Whew, that was close. Wait, why am I embarrassed? He's supposed to be my pledged, for crepes' sake!*

Solus raised his eyebrow at her again, but Kit ignored it and made a show of standing and smoothing her jacket as an irate Diablio stalked up to her, ViolentAlice ambling somewhere behind him.

"Hello, you two. What's up?" she asked.

"Why did you disband the raid?" Diablio asked.

Kit blinked. "Because the fight is over?"

"So?" Diablio asked. "We were still talking in there!"

"Yeah, but you could have easily used your guild chat for that," Kit pointed out.

"But I wasn't only talking to members of my guild," Diablio said.

"By disbanding the raid, you also made it harder to plan our joint return to Luminos," ViolentAlice added.

Kit flopped her hat back on her head. "Our *what*?"

"Our return to Luminos," Diablio said, overenunciating the words.

"We're all going back together as a group," ViolentAlice said.

Kit flicked her eyes between the two guild leaders. "...Why?"

Diablio scowled and folded his arms across his chest. "I see how it is. You fight with someone and think it forges a sacred bond of companionship, but no. In the end it means nothing."

ViolentAlice tossed his character's thick braid of hair over her shoulder. "What he means is he thought we would return as a united group. It might drum up some support for our fight for Lord Valdis."

Kit felt a bit like a parrot as she repeated, "Our fight?"

"Yes, *our* fight," Diablio said. "After all of this," he asked, gesturing stiffly at the river, "you didn't think we would join you?"

"To be honest, no. I mostly just wanted to stop the infighting," Kit said.

Diablio looked like he wanted to strangle someone until Kit offered the pair a smile. "But if you're willing to join me, I would be honored to have you in the raid. Thanks in advance—I look forward to fighting with you again."

ViolentAlice nodded in agreement. "You'll want to leave after you speak with the Imperial Empress, I assume?"

"Yes."

"Okay. We'll resume organizing the exit," ViolentAlice spun on his heels and trotted away.

Diablio grinned and briefly posed with one hand on his waist. "Our entrance will be magnificent," he said.

"With your theatrics, yes," ViolentAlice called over his shoulder.

Teara emerged from behind a stack of crates. "I'm just confirming Observational Fiends will be ready to leave then, as well," she said. "I'll make certain I touch base with ViolentAlice, Diablio, and the players who were in Elba Clean Up, Elba Harbor Naturalists, and Elba Freedom Fighters."

"See," Diablio muttered as he finally turned to follow ViolentAlice. "This is why we should have kept the raid."

Teara raised her arm to let a red-tailed hawk settle on her wrist—her fluffy owl was nowhere to be seen. "I'm making arrangements for the rest of my guild to meet us at Luminos, but once I'm finished, I'd like to go with you when you meet with the Imperial Empress, if that's okay."

"Of course," Kit said. "We'd be glad to have you. Especially if you have high reputation with the Imperials."

Teara nodded. "I also wanted to say that I plan to be present at the next meeting you hold with the other elite guilds about Lord Valdis. Observational Fiends will support you from now on."

"It won't be too much for you?" Kit asked.

Teara shook her head. "You came for us when no one else could—or would. And you're trying to hold this game together. We'll manage."

"Thanks, Teara. I appreciate your support." Kit hesitated.

"And if your guild really is struggling to find a place to meet up...I think I can help you with that—temporarily, at least."

"How?" Teara asked.

"You can use Milk Crown's guildzone as guests," Kit said. "I'll set the guild's NPCs so they will let you in and out whenever you like."

"Won't Fame and Fortune get upset?" Solus asked.

Kit shook her head. "Not if there are people staying in the guildzone. Plus, it's convenient, as Milk Crown's place is in the Luminos Guildhall."

"Thanks for your offer," Teara said. "I'll ask the rest of my guild about it."

"Sure," Kit said.

"Great! If you'll give me thirty minutes, I should have things under control enough that I can come with you," Teara said.

"We'll be here," Solus said.

Teara waved as she also left, her mouth already moving as she connected with someone over a private message.

Kit ventured closer to Solus as she studied Teara's back. "That was...surprising."

Solus shrugged. "Not really. Given the level of expertise you showed, I would have been surprised if they *hadn't* decided to follow you."

Kit swallowed. *I guess this really means I'll have to start strategizing against Valdis...but where do we even begin?*

"Kit!"

Grateful for the distraction, Kit grinned. "Hello, Prowl. I was wondering when you were going to find me."

Prowl stalked in her direction, Fame and Fortune trotting behind him—pointing at some of the other players and murmuring to each other, likely as they dissected the players' armor. "I followed your orders like a good soldier and stayed with the pirates during the fight to pass along your orders, but enough is enough."

Kit planted a hand on a cheek and did her best to look innocent. "Why, I don't know what you're talking about."

"Milk Crown's NPCs! They're parasites!" Prowl said.

"Fame and Fortune are very helpful," Kit said.

"Maybe, except you didn't tell them to zip it before you left, so they spent the whole battle dissecting the different armor sets they saw." Prowl ran his hands through his spikey hair and yanked on some of the strands in his frustration. "Fortune spent a good two hours lecturing—in mind-numbing detail—about why Pax was able to reflect the echo of arcane's attack in the city square."

"What do you mean, why?" Pax sniffed, speaking for the first time since his pre-battle warning. "I reflected it because I'm incredibly powerful."

Fortune—who had caught up with Prowl—gave the winged warrior a scornful sniff. "It was also because that echo had positively horrific armor. Her damage is pitiful for an echo of arcane because her armor set is mostly comprised of agility boosts. A poor choice."

"There are cave wyverns in a cave system nearby," Fame said. "She would do well to go there and kill a number of them, as the wyverns have a .05% chance to drop mage gear."

"And even *mage* gear would be an improvement over what she has," Fortune sighed.

Pax narrowed his eyes. "I could have reflected her attack no matter how strong she was. A paltry *hero* cannot defeat me."

Fortune eyed him. "That is not apparent judging by your stat-less armor."

"Do you see this?" Prowl gestured at the NPC siblings who were studying Pax with pity. "I had to live with *this* for *hours*.

Solus, buddy, back me up here—I've defended you from Riko's money-grabbing clutches. Do me a solid and help!"

Solus picked up his sword from its leaning position on the bench. "It sounds trying," he said.

"Yeah," Kit agreed.

Prowl grabbed her by the lapels of her brocade pirate jacket. "Then tell them to stop following me, or shut them up."

"Okay, I will. I never said I wouldn't." Kit patted Prowl's hands, then peered around him. "Fame, Fortune, you're with me again."

"Yes, Kitten," they chirped.

Pax grumbled under his breath.

"Why don't you take a break, Prowl?" Kit asked. "I think we're going to try to meet up with the Empress in half an hour, but you're free until then. The rest of the party is somewhere around here."

Prowl rubbed his face. "I need a stiff drink. Wanna come with me, Solus?"

Solus shook his head. "Thank you, but no."

The saboteur shrugged. "Suit yourself." He strode off—giving Fame and Fortune a wide berth.

"Prowl," Kit called after him.

He stopped to turn around and suspiciously eye her, mashing his lips together in preconceived irritation.

"Thanks for staying on the ship," Kit said. "We couldn't have won without you."

Prowl relaxed and even awkwardly scratched the back of his head. "Yeah...you're welcome." He waved, then shuffled off, looking much calmer.

Kit smiled fondly, first at Prowl's back and then at Fame, Fortune, and Pax. *I never in a million years would have pictured a fight like this one when I played as Azarel...but this is just as satisfying as a Milk Crown win.*

"What are you planning?" Solus asked, interrupting her thoughts.

"I was wondering, if I hurried, if Fortune and I could catch up to Diablio," Kit said.

"Why do you want to catch up to Diablio?" Solus asked.

"So I can talk to him about his echo of arcane," Kit said. "Fortune is right; his guildmate should have been *much* stronger. In fact, I haven't ever seen damage that low for an echo at that level. She must have something screwy with her armor, and that *must* be fixed."

"In preparation for Lord Valdis?" Solus asked.

Kit furrowed her brow in confusion. "What? No! Because she's an *echo* and, as a fellow echo, I can't just stand by and watch her waste her potential."

Fortune nodded in agreement, though Pax rustled his wings and looked irritated.

"I think we could give her some quick tips in less than half an hour. Do you want to come with me?" Kit asked.

Solus shook his head. "I'll stay with the party. Have fun." He smiled at her—but it wasn't a smile of amusement or joy, but something more...*affectionate*, maybe? Or maybe that was just her hopeful interpretation of it.

Kit forced herself to keep smiling so she wouldn't gulp awkwardly. "Yep, we will! Come on, Fame, Fortune—and you too, Pax."

Kit set off at a jog, her boots making pleasant thumping noises on the wooden docks. Her mind was so tired, she could feel it spitting out thoughts with the frantic speed of a hamster running on a wheel.

What was she going to do about Valdis? The elite guilds couldn't *really* be upset with her for acting alone in Elba, could they? Would the fighting on the server finally stop? And what did Solus' smile mean?

Enough, Kit firmly told herself. *I just need to focus on one thing at a time. What's of greatest importance right now is to speak with the Empress. After that...well...I guess I'll figure it out when we get back to Luminos.*

With a plan settled, Kit's forced smile relaxed into the real thing as she caught sight of Diablio's back. "Hey, Diablio!" she called out to him.

When he spun around—his eyebrows arching up—she added. "I need to talk with you for a moment—it's about your echo of arcane."

———

Solus Miles watched Kit stride purposefully across the harbor, marching for Midnight Watch.

How many people would be offended because a skill that should have killed them didn't deal as much damage as it could have?

He shook his head. He was long past trying to puzzle through Kit's idiosyncrasies. It was better just to accept that she operated *differently.*

He turned to look back at the bright Nignay river. The sunken ships had already disappeared from the waters—removed by the game. Solus rested his hand on the hilt of his sword and tried to reach past the memory of Kit snuggling into him.

When she had first returned, he was relieved on two levels: coming back meant she had a new way out, and this time Solus intended to follow her straight into the worst parts of the game if necessary to get out, but also because it meant someone he knew —even moderately knew—was there. He wasn't alone.

She was a friend, of sorts, Solus mused. *But now...maybe she's more than that.*

Somewhere between grossly exaggerating their relationship for the sake of manipulating the council of hyenas and vultures that ruled the top guilds and marching on a city thrown into chaos, Kit had become important to him.

He was used to her bubbly presence bouncing at his side, used to fighting with a lot more defensive maneuvering than he previously did so he could keep her clear, used to her insane and crazy ideas. But perhaps what made her special to Solus is that she brought him into her fold.

He *liked* Riko and Noir. Watching Fame and Fortune dog Prowl about his old gear and acquiring new pieces had made him laugh more than he had in months. And he was able to sit with them and not be *the* Solus Miles—or at least not all the time—and instead laugh with them as a party member.

And it was all because of Kit.

When he realized he was getting a lot of stares and whispers, Solus set off, striding for the pirate ship Prowl had gleefully abandoned. (None of the players would dare venture onto the ship even if the pirates were openly allied with Kit—too many bad memories, probably.)

He walked stiffly through the harbor, his face expressionless as he strode at a pace he knew was a conversation deterrent. *Kit probably doesn't have a clue what she represents to me. But she has bigger worries to concentrate on. Like Lord Valdis.*

Valdis was a greater burden on her mind than most guessed. He could see it in the flickers of despair that crossed her elven face—particularly when she thought no one was watching.

Sooner or later, she would have to focus on Valdis. And judging by her conduct, she probably didn't think she could come up with a winning strategy.

I believe otherwise, of course, but I don't think that's something I can help her with. She gunned for Malignus because of her cousin's confidence in her, but even if I told her I knew she could do it, I doubt she'd believe me. Though, in the spirit of fairness, Valdis is on a different level from Malignus.

Solus trotted up the gangplank and nodded when a few of the pirates leaning against the railings called out to him.

"If it isn't the famous Sir Solus! Welcome back," one of the pirates shouted.

"That was some battle, wasn't it?" another pirate sighed dreamily.

"That sort of fight was the reason I wanted to be a pirate!" the captain declared.

Solus paused to see if the pirates expected a reply, but when they got busy toasting each other—with goblets of wine, which were likely forcibly donated by Riko at Kit's prompting—he took the moment to make his escape to the far end of the ship, taking himself as far out of the public eye as he could while remaining in Elba.

He leaned against the railing of the ship and watched the birds gliding through the sky.

I might not be able to help Kit with Valdis, but I can at least stop anything that threatens her and lend her the fame of my name. I wish I could do more but...frankly I don't think I mean enough to her for that.

Again the memory of Kit collapsing against him in her relief assailed him, and a tiny spark of curiosity, or maybe hope, flickered in his mind.

Maybe, hopefully, he meant more to her than he thought.

———

"So that's what we've done," Luther finished summarizing. He moved his water glass around as he waited—almost cringing—for Bryce's response on the phone.

I hope this wasn't a mistake, he thought as Kit's cousin was slow to respond. The late morning sunlight filtered through the windows of his house, and Luther drummed his fingers on the table. He had taken the day off from work—a rarity, though he supposed life-and-death situations were probably an understandable excuse.

Luther shifted in his creaking chair and watched his two-year-old sing to her dolls.

"That's really smart—and creative," Bryce finally said.

"Do you think it could help?"

"It certainly won't hurt," Bryce said. "And you've hit on an important point—no one outside Retha knows what she's doing. And if more people see it and understand, that will put pressure on EC so they *can't* just sweep Kit's, Prowl's, and Riko's involvement under a rug when they do get out."

"Axel is hoping it will go viral, but I would be happy if it just floated around the Retha community." Luther adjusted his hold on his smartphone. "Which is why I wanted to talk to you."

"We can't post this in the Retha community section," Bryce said. "EC will be all over it in a minute. You guys haven't done anything illegal with this, but when you sign up for the community tab, it's explicitly stated in the terms and conditions that they have the power to delete any posts they want—or even ban your account."

"Yes, I suspected something like that would happen. That's why I was going to ask if I sent you the video link, would you forward it on to Milk Crown?"

Bryce whistled lowly. "You guys are really playing hardball, huh?"

"Prowl, Kit, and Riko are heroes," Luther said. "And nobody knows it. It's not fair."

"You're right," Bryce said. "But it's a little too risky for me to blatantly forward them the video—particularly as I'd be using the company internet connection. So here's what we'll do: I'll text you the email address of three Milk Crown players, then text them so they know your message is coming."

Luther found himself nodding, even though Bryce couldn't see it. "That would work—what three?"

"Juliet—she now works for the government as a gameplay inspector or tester—and the brother/sister duo who were Milk Crown's Guildmasters."

"Okay. I'll get the hyperlink for the video and send it to them. Thanks for your help, Bryce."

"I haven't done anything. In fact, I'm the one that needs to be thanking you—for remembering them when you're already out," Bryce said. "And also for traveling with my cousin and helping her."

"I didn't help her," Luther said. "And she saved my life—even though I was an ungrateful jerk most of the time I traveled with her."

"Maybe, but Kit finds it hard to stand alone. You might not think you helped her, but I promise you did," Bryce said.

Luther shook his head. "I can help her now, which is the important thing. Thanks for those emails."

"Yeah. I'll get those to you ASAP. Let me know if there's anything more I can do to help."

"Will do. Good luck."

"Thanks; EC needs it," Bryce said, his voice lined with exhaustion, before he ended the call.

Luther leaned back in his chair so he could snatch up his tablet. The bigger screen would be easier to work with, plus he had the video bookmarked there.

His cellphone binged with a text from Bryce.

"Perfect," Luther muttered. "I'll just bring the video up..." He trailed off when the video loaded, and he saw how many views it already had. "400,000 views already? It's only been up for a few hours!"

Maybe Axel has a larger audience than I thought? A glance at the description revealed that Axel had asked his viewers to like and share the video to get the word out. Perhaps that was part of its popularity?

Luther shook his head as he opened up his text files to copy the email addresses Bryce had sent him. "I hope this helps them. I don't know how it can when they're stuck there, but maybe it will make things easier for them when they get out."

Because Luther had to believe they could get out. He had to believe Kit could pull off what no one in the world had and end Valdis. Otherwise this video wouldn't be a gameplay compilation, but a memorial.

THE END

THE RETURN TO LUMINOS

Kit dodged a werewolf player and marched forward as quickly as possible while retaining her elf grace. When she zipped around a corner of the road, the giant hedge that acted as a wall ended, revealing the sprawling and magnificent Guildhall.

"Is there a reason why we are practically *running*?" Noir complained. He breathed heavily, but he was right on her heels. "When I elected to join you and skip the 'fun' and 'celebratory parade' with everyone else from Elba I *didn't* know we would be trying to break a Retha sprinting record."

Kit course corrected so they made a beeline for the Guildhall. "I want to catch the guildmasters of all the big guilds before they find out we're back and keep them *inside* so we don't have a public...altercation."

"Still think they're going to yell at you, huh?" Noir asked.

"I'm *positive*," Kit said grimly. "They were not pleased that the Empress kept us in Elba for an extra day."

"Kitten," Fortune said, sounding scandalized as he and his NPC sister, Fame, trotted behind them. "That man is only wearing a loincloth for armor."

"Don't look, Fortune," Kit instructed. "I'm sure he's doing it for the...er...image."

"He doesn't even have *shoes*!" Fortune gestured.

"Stop pointing at him," Kit said in exasperation. (It was a good thing Pax had agreed to return to his egg/pearl before entering Luminos as he would have greatly exacerbated the problem.)

"His loincloth is a fairly common goblin drop," Fame reported.

Noir whipped around long enough to gape at the NPC. "Do you mean to tell me he is wearing a *used* goblin loincloth?"

Fame shrugged and repeated, "His loincloth is a fairly common goblin drop."

"Gross, I think I just threw up in my mouth," Noir grumbled.

"Focus, Noir," Kit said as they left the broad road and started up the much smaller walkway that sliced between two mazes of hedges and led straight into the Guildhall. "We need to drop Fame and Fortune off in Milk Crown's guildzone before we—" Kit cut herself off and skid to a stop.

"Before we what? Run into those idiot guildmasters—oof." Noir wasn't watching Kit—he was still gawking at the loincloth-wearing player—and as a result smacked into her back.

"Ahem," Phizzy—guildmaster of Corporate Force coughed. Behind him Ryunosuke of Tainted and Half Fang of the Killing Squad glared.

"Oh," Noir said. "Woops."

Kit gratefully let her elven race traits take over, allowing herself to adapt an elegant pose. "Hello."

"Kit!" Gared—the guildmaster of KOS—slipped between Ryunosuke and Half Fang, and offered her a smile and his hand. "Alistair gave me a brief report of the fight. You did an amazing job!"

Kit shook his hand and returned the smile. "Thank you. I couldn't have done it without her."

"Actually, you could have," Gared grunted. "But I'm glad she could help you anyway. If she ever shirks her responsibilities and spends her time waltzing around fraternizing, let me know."

"Alistair has always been willing to help," Kit said. "I don't believe I'll ever have a problem with her."

Gared raised his eyebrows. "We'll see. Noir—how are you holding up?"

Noir sniffed and flicked a lock of his purple hair from his forehead. "Well enough, I suppose."

"If you will excuse the interruption," White Lady, the guild-mistress of Silver Army, started, "But I believe we have more pressing topics to discuss..."

"Like Elba," Phizzy said bluntly.

"And how you went behind our backs," Half Fang growled.

Shuck a bag of corn! I came running here because this is exactly what I wanted to avoid—a public confrontation. Only this is even worse because I don't have Solus Miles backing me up. "I didn't try to hide my actions," Kit said. "All your first officers knew what I intended to do."

"And yet mysteriously none of them informed us of their actions," Ryunosuke growled. "You're not just satisfied with doing whatever you want, you're trying to turn our people against us!"

"That's not entirely true," Gared said. "Alistair told me. I simply chose not to inform the rest of you." He sighed and slapped his hands on his thighs, making his chainmail jingle.

"I don't know why your first officers didn't tell you what was going on," Kit said. "I certainly didn't forbid them from talking about it. That's a conversation you're going to have to have with them." She cast a nervous glance over her shoulder.

Even this far north in the city, Kit could hear the trumpets and drums from the celebration, led by ViolentAlice and Diablio. (Nearly everyone who had taken part in the goblin siege had coordinated with the two guild leaders for a joint return to Luminos that involved a parade and a general spectacle. Kit had known it would attract attention, which is why she moved in front of it, hoping to get the guildleaders before they left the guildhall. That effort had obviously failed.)

"In this matter I do agree with Kit," Phizzy said. "I, for one, trust Nyx to make an informed decision in my absence. But I still do not like it that you led her to Elba when we decided we wouldn't take any action."

"That just shows this is truly all your fault," Noir said with scorn crusting his words. "You all assumed Kit would be as helpless and dim-witted as you. She's the girl who beat Malignus—did you think she couldn't muster up a fighting force of her own?"

Kit wedged an elbow into the divine oracle's side. "You're really *not helping*, Noir," she whispered.

"Well it's not *my* fault they are both pig-headed *and* short-sighted—"

"Noir!" Kit hissed as she wondered if she could risk glancing over her shoulder. *The parade music is getting louder...*

"Kitten," Fortune started. "That werewolf has *terrible*—"

"Not now, Fortune!" Kit said, her voice going up an octave. (The *last* thing she needed was Fortune bashing all of the guildmasters' armor sets.)

"Your actions don't do much to convince us that we can trust you, Kit," Phizzy continued.

"If you really felt that strongly, we could have continued the discussion," White Lady said.

"Really? Because I got the feeling that since everyone besides Gared thought nothing could be done, you were through discussing it," Kit said.

White Lady's smile didn't falter, but even Ryunosuke nodded a little and shrugged.

"Perhaps..." White Lady said. "But from what I heard, it seems you had friends in Elba. If we had known, we might have changed our stance."

Kit glanced over her shoulder—the procession was *quite* loud by this point. *How did they get north so fast? I thought they would take forever to get up here...unless Solus is leading them. Then he's probably got them all jogging.* "That's a fair point," Kit said, somewhat distracted. "Why don't we talk about it more *inside?*"

"What, you're afraid of embarrassing yourself more than your terrible character already does?" Ryunosuke snorted.

"No..." Kit said slowly.

Half Fang shook a furry finger at her. "You won't distract us. You're going to get taken down."

"I'm not trying to distract you. I just think we should choose a better spot," Kit said.

"No, I think a public display might be necessary," Phizzy said.

"Umm," Kit looked down at her feet and listened to the trumpets that were loud enough they made her innards buzz. "I wouldn't be so sure about that..."

"You all are taking this far too personally," Gared said. "She went and she won. Really, it's up to her to do whatever she wants with her party."

"Except her party contains *our* first officers!" Ryunosuke scoffed.

Phizzy twirled his mustache and glanced over at the ninja. "If that upsets you so much, Ryunosuke, you ought to discuss this with Reynard."

"Enough talking!" Half Fang shouted, his voice almost animalistic.

"Yes," Kit agreed as she strained her ears, still trying to judge if the music was blasting just past the hedge walls or if it was—as she hoped—still a block or two down. "Let's go inside."

"No, I'm afraid your set-down must happen here, Kitten Lovemuch," Phizzy sighed.

"I'm not taking part in this," Gared said flatly. "I stand with Kit."

Half Fang scoffed. "Weakling."

White Lady hesitated, then timidly added. "There is something to be said for her victory."

"Regardless of whether she won or not," Phizzy said patiently. "She acted against our wishes. She should have shared all available information at the very least, and ought to have told us of her actions *before* she left. Quite frankly, it has me doubting our decision to follow you, Kit, as it makes you appear impulsive and unprofessional."

Kit had to bite her tongue from delivering her own snarky line about unprofessionalism and abandoning players. *Focus! I've got to get them out of here.* "Um," she said, searching for the right words.

Far down the path, Kit heard a distinct squawk, *"You suck!"*

Kit froze. *Oh, no. Please, no.*

Evidently, all the guildmasters heard it as well, for they looked past Kit.

"For once I am inclined to agree with you."

Kit slowly turned around, grimacing when she saw Diablio and ViolentAlice strolling up the path.

Teara and her Observational Fiends guildmates who had gone to Elba followed behind them, stony expressions settling on their faces.

Chocolate Chip me! While I'm not going to take the guild-masters' scolding sitting down, it's going to be a morale night-

mare if enough people see us arguing outside and word gets out about it!

"Diablio, ViolentAlice, have you finished with your parade so soon?" Kit asked as she planted herself in the middle of the path. "That didn't sound nearly as long and epic as you planned!"

Diablio glared at the guildmasters behind Kit. "We cut it short after we reconnected with friends here."

"Imagine our shock to learn that the top guilds *knew* that NPCs were joining you, and that the whole game is designed to pit us against Valdis." ViolentAlice's deep male voice was rather at odds with his female character, but he still managed to look scary in his anger.

"It made us wonder why we hadn't heard this before," Diablio said.

Gared grunted. "It was our failing," he acknowledged before he nodded to Teara. "Welcome back, Teara."

"Thank you." Teara offered the KOS Guildmaster a brief smile before shifting her gaze to everyone else.

"I'm glad to see you are in one piece." Phizzy smiled.

"Yes, thanks to Kit." Teara propped a hand on her hip. "Which is why Observational Fiends pledges an alliance with her."

Behind her, Metronome, Konk, and Shooty D'Arrow—a bard, rogue, and hunter who had fought with Kit in Elba— nodded in support.

Phizzy blinked in surprise. "Oh."

"You're won over just like that?" Ryunosuke scoffed.

"Yes." Teara stated in an even voice. "Because *that* was something none of you even tried to do."

White Lady's forehead wrinkled with concern. "Yes..."

"Hey, hey." Diablio snapped his fingers. "Don't forget about us. I'm ticked! How dare you all try to boss us around claiming you know what's best when you don't even tell us it's possible to beat the game!"

"You are either bottling up information on purpose, or you're just *terrible* at leading," Violent Alice added.

"Butt out, noobs," Half Fang grunted. "When you have the record my guild does, then I'll listen to you. But if you don't want to respawn in a few moments, buzz off."

ViolentAlice merely raised an eyebrow and Diablio scowled. "Oh, sure," Diablio said. "That's an impressive way to prove you are superior and better than us—threaten violence. A surefire way to inspire people to follow you—if they are mindless thugs, that is."

"*What* did you say?" Half Fang growled.

"Kit," Phizzy said, barely audible over Diablio and Half Fang's exchange. "Was it really necessary to have this playout here?"

"*You* were the one who insisted on staying here!" Kit said, keeping her voice light and airy—which made her words that much more annoying, she knew. "I tried to get you inside, I insisted on it even, but—as you might recall—you said a *public* display would do me some good."

"It was my error in forgetting what a strategist you are," Phizzy said.

There was a gust of wind, and Kit felt an arm wrap around her waist. "That was a *compliment*, wasn't it?" Solus Miles said in a voice that allowed for no disagreement.

"Solus Miles...you're still with *her*?" Ryunosuke asked.

Rather than answer the ninja, Solus leaned his head against Kit's. "They weren't picking on you, were they?" he asked in a throaty voice that almost sounded like a purr.

"No, not at all," Kit said, fighting a blush.

"She's lying," Noir said. "They were all prepped to yell at Pinkie out here."

"In armor that is rather *terribly* modified," Fortune muttered.

"Now they won't," Solus stated.

"Yeah," Teara nodded. "Observational Fiends won't stand for it."

Behind Teara, her guildmates nodded.

Phizzy removed his gold spectacles so he could rub his eyes. "This has become a mess," he muttered.

White Lady curiously gazed past Kit and the others. "Is that a parade?" she asked.

"We're celebrating our win in Elba," ViolentAlice said.

"Kit was *supposed* to ride in the front," Diablio complained. "With her celestial being out on display!"

Gared squinted, taking in the small part of the procession that was visible and crowding up the courtyard. "What the heck?" he growled as he spotted his first officer riding on top of a war elephant. "Alistair!" he bellowed as he stalked down the path, making for the procession.

"Gared! Hello!" Alistair waved from the top of the elephant and shook her head, making her black ponytail flare behind her. "Isn't this a marvelous pet? I think we should get one for the guild."

"Get down from there! If you fall off and break your neck you'll dent your armor!" He shouted.

Alistair ignored him and instead patted the elephant. "Though it is a pet, it can carry up to six people. Oh—if we got one for you it could fetch things from tall places for you—that's impressive *and* practical!"

In his rage Gared appeared to speak a new language.

"Reynard," Ryuonsuke snapped when he saw his first officer in the parade, poking bunches of colored fire that the fire dancers had created. Ryunosuke shouldered his way through Observational Fiends, making a beeline for Reynard.

When Diablio waved to some of his guildmates, they struck up the trumpet blasting and drum playing with renewed vigor. "Let's go for another lap!" he declared.

"Glory hog," ViolentAlice said.

"Oh, so Steadfast will bow out of the procession, then?"

"No."

"That's what I thought!"

"Oi, we're not done here," Half Fang sniffed.

Solus Miles rested his free hand on the hilt of his giant sword. "Yes, we are."

The werewolf flattened his triangular ears and narrowed his golden eyes, but eventually nodded his wolf head and looked away.

Kit—still held secure by Solus—shifted in his grasp so she could address Phizzy, who was ruefully studying the chaos around him. "Would you like to discuss Elba at a later hour?"

"No, I suppose not. At least not in the way we planned, for it seems we judged wrong, and you were right to return to there," the gnome sighed. "Though I do hope next time you'll *tell* us your plans, and that you'll still explain what happened in Elba?"

"That's reasonable," Kit agreed.

Phizzy nodded. "Well played, Kit."

"I didn't really mean to," Kit said.

"Perhaps you didn't," Phizzy agreed. "But you are obviously seeing the returns of your earlier investments, and that is more what I was referring to."

"Thanks...I guess," Kit said. "Though I didn't do it for personal gain, but the players."

Phizzy looked thoughtful as he nodded. "I see. If you'll excuse me, I think I will follow Ryunosuke's example and search out Nyx. Care to come with me, White Lady, and find Waffle?"

"Yes." The elven lady paused then slightly bowed her head to Kit. "I apologize, Kit, for…"

Kit waved her off. "I'll tell everyone the whole story after we get settled. Then we can prepare for the next NPC target."

White Lady smiled, then followed Phizzy down the pathway, heading for the procession.

"Who do you plan to target next?" Solus asked Kit as he released her and stepped back, giving her room.

"I was thinking the Fae Kings," Kit said. "I'm hoping they'll be an easy win."

Solus Miles shrugged, then glanced at Fame and Fortune. "You're taking them back to your guildzone, still?"

"Yes. Do you want to come?"

Solus nodded, and together they made for the Guildhall doors, leaving the exuberant laughter and music behind them.

THE END

OTHER BOOKS BY A.M. SOHMA

Second Age of Retha

The Luckless

The Desperate Quest

The Revived

OTHER BOOKS WRITTEN UNDER PEN NAME K.M.SHEA

The Snow Queen:

Heart of Ice

Sacrifice

Snowflakes: A Snow Queen Short Story Collection

Timeless Fairy Tales:

Beauty and the Beast

The Wild Swans

Cinderella and the Colonel

Rumpelstiltskin

The Little Selkie

Puss in Boots

Swan Lake

ABOUT THE AUTHOR

Author by day, but a hunter (or very frazzled priestess) by night, A. M. Sohma is a lover of books, video games, and sweet armor sets. She aims to write entertaining stories with relatable characters, and spends her days lurking in libraries or wasting time on the internet.

Made in the USA
Coppell, TX
22 December 2019

13683976R00247